PEACE STATE

ALSO BY AMBER BIRD
Peace Fire
Peace Maker

PEACE STATE

PEACEFORGERS: BOOK THREE

AMBER BIRD

BARYCENTRE
PRESS

This is a work of fiction. Names, characters, places, and incidents are either the product of the author's imagination or are used fictitiously. Any resemblance to actual persons, living or dead, business establishments, events, or locales is entirely coincidental.

Copyright © 2021 by Amber Bird

All rights reserved. This book or any portion thereof may not be reproduced or used in any manner whatsoever without the express written permission of the publisher except for the use of brief quotations in a book review.

Worldwide Rights
Printed in the United States of America

First Edition

Cover Design by George C. Cotronis | www.cotronis.com

ISBN: 978-1-945636-20-2

www.AmberBird.com

For my Simon.
For my chosen family.
For my true homes.

PEACE STATE

CHAPTER 1

On the other side of shock, my system flooded with adrenaline. My mind was drowning in images of our boys, of Bryan and Jonny, bullet-riddled and prone. Of their bodies shoved into black SUVs and taken from us. Of the puddles of blood they'd left behind.

My ears were pounded by waves of remembered sounds. Of the biting thunder of the shots fired by Shay's people that took the boys down. Of Zane admitting they had betrayed us, had always been loyal to the Peaceforgers. Of my own sobs echoing in the fueling station lot once we were alone. Of the golden promise from a holographic Kitty, sure she would be our literal deus ex machina now that she knew she was in an alien ship. And then of the shame-filled apologies that poured out of her as she realized she couldn't actually *do* anything.

My head and flesh buzzed, crackled with dread and desperation and "drive fast! escape! run run run!" to the point that I was sure I would fly apart, like the shattered pixels of an 8-bit vidgame space invader, at any moment.

It hadn't even been 30 minutes since it had all gone down, but it still seemed too unreal to have been more recent than a lifetime ago. And I was trying to somehow process that near past, help Riles sort our future, and not fuck up our present. It was...a lot.

Fortunately, Riles had sent Kitty away as soon as she panicked, leaving one less voice in my ears. Giving zir space to do zir own sobbing whilst I'd pointed our vehicle back towards Seattle, speeding until we hit the thick of downtown traffic. Surely, in this more populated area, the Peaceforgers wouldn't attack, not under any guise. (Did they have faces other than Secure World Systems, Divine Community Church, and the anonymous black-masked thugs who'd shown up multiple times in the last few weeks to attack us? Not knowing scared the piss out of me.)

So I led what, for the moment, appeared to be a one-vehicle car chase. As much as it could be a car chase in the trapped and crawling pace of permanent rush hour. But pursuit *was* surely impending. And there was little doubt an alien cleanup crew was en route to disappear the puddles of blood (*Bryan's* blood, *Jonny's* blood...dammit) and this very vehicle, this getaway car that was doing a bad job of getting us away enough. And there was no doubt that we were chased by dozens, probably actually hundreds and maybe even thousands, of camera eyes as I tried to drive casual. Tried to run without looking like we were running. Tried to somehow not look like the bullet-marred vehicle we were. Mostly, I was counting on the magic of psychically willing nobody to notice us, a plan in which I had very little confidence.

I was stuck in the driver's seat, wishing that Bryan were here (or alive at all) to do the meat stuff. Painfully aware that my brain being in its "we just saw an action movie so we have to go fast now!" state wasn't helping. (Though, in fairness to my brain, some actual action movie shit *had* just gone down right in front of my eyes. In the meat, not just on a screen. Guns, betrayal, and the slaughter of our friends weren't exactly rom-com fuel.)

I squinted into the rearview. We were at a stoplight, and I was determined to notice anyone following us. I hoped they'd help by holding up a sign that indicated they were tailing us. Something like "We're chasing you, human hacker scum!" would do. Though the right kind of non-descript black SUV was also starting to become a good clue that bad things were about to happen to us.

"Katja?" Riley's voice sounded like maybe zie had already said my name more than once.

I shook my head. Right. Sorting the future with Riles. "Uh. Okay. Uh..." I struggled to keep enough attention on the road as I ran through the mental checklist of things done and in progress.

We'd grabbed, cleaned, and sent to law enforcement and media, as appropriate, the camera footage of the boys being massacred. (Because fuck you, Shay. Hope you enjoy jail and your fake church enjoys being investigated for involvement with you shooting our boys, you fucker.)

Riley had planned the tricky shell game to help us get away without really getting away. A game in which we were the peas, and the shells were a fleet of other mini-SUVs just like ours and an equal number of random hotel rooms. (Shout out to online hotel booking and online car buying and delivery making it a little easier for us to disappear right where we were.)

We'd turned up the game by planting misdirections and calling decoys into action. (Thanks to Lex and her random street drek allies, mobilized to drive the extra vehicles and/or crash in the extra rooms.)

Which left... "New hideout?" And, having suggested that, I could now concentrate on not crashing and let Riles take care of the rest.

My brain turned our next hour (ugh, Seattle traffic) into quick snaps until the adrenaline flipped off: ditch vehicle at posh hotel, load into new vehicle, move into new not-posh hotel (long-stay executive suites, really, the kind just cheap enough to have internal rooms without windows), obtain supplies, sort escape contingencies, fake physical security (because, come on, we were not the ones for that, were we?). Snap! Snap! Snap!

And when the adrenaline finally, suddenly, stopped driving me, I felt like I was coming to from some kind of bodysnatcher situation where I'd watched someone else move me, decide for me. Then there was a rush of something that came in behind to fill the void the adrenaline left, something like...hope or delusion or denial? Something that was just as driving, that scrabbled like an animal in my chest, tiny claws digging at the base of my throat. On some level I knew it was irrational, but I gave into it. I let it convince me that I didn't know what I knew, that I had made a mistake.

I almost dropped the container of Thai food I was inhaling as I dove for my computer. "What the hell is wrong with us? You never believe someone is dead until you check their pulse...Whether it's the monster or your friends." I could hear more than feel the sticky mix of panic and frustration in my voice. Maybe I wasn't fully in the driver seat of my body and brain yet after all.

I looked up and saw that Rye was blinking quickly, as if zie still needed to clear zir head of zir own mix of bodysnatching or danger juice (adrenaline? fear? anguish? some secret and intense Riley-only emotion for fucked up times like these?). But then I saw it spark in zir eyes. Zie knew what I meant; zie bought into the denial.

Zir breath hitched with worry and shame. "The boys!" Rather than scramble for zir own machine, zie made sure mine was hooked to the big screen the suite had come with.

The voice in my head whose job it was to try to protect me from feeling shitty about my mistakes assured me, with an infuriating tone, a smooth mix of too-calm logic and soothing, that the boys were surely dead (there had been *so much* blood) and getting ourselves safe had been the smartest, most rational move. *Shut the hell up*, I thought at the voice, opting to side with the hopeful denial. My fingers sped over my keys, pulling up my camera tracking and editing program. Telling it to find any footage of the boys, to trace the route the Peaceforger cars had taken. If they were more than bodies, we had to find them. And something in me needed to find them even if they were just bodies...

Riles and I stood close to the screen to watch what my program found. I had a flash of how we must look. No windows to let sunlight into our suite, and behind us the dim, yellow light from the bulb over the small dining table. The cool light of the screen in front of us, outlining us, two dirty and frantic hacker kids. The glow picking out the dust on our black hoodies and hinting at the grime on our black jeans, because life was too stressful to buck certain stereotypes. The cold of loss and of sleeping in an underground squat still clinging to us. I almost laughed sadly as I realized that we two shabby losers, and maybe an AI who wasn't as powerful as she'd momentarily assumed, were all that stood between Earth and subjugation or annihilation. I *almost* laughed sadly...but then reminded myself that, especially once we rested, our brains and our hacking skills were anything but shabby. Making the fate of the world anything but sealed. So, rather than laugh, I leaned in closer to the screen, balancing my computer on my hip.

Initially, my program easily tracked the vehicle that held the boys, Zane the Betrayer, and their sister Shay. Showed us the drive from a variety of cameras along the way, as they and the others in that Convoy of Death sped from the fueling station parking lot on the outskirts of Seattle, back towards denser parts of the city (kind of like we had), and then fucking disappeared into the same area without cameras in the International District that they'd used before. Used the night they'd ambushed us at the church's plant and grabbed Quinn. Well shit. The dramatic voice in my head wanted to wail something like "that area eats all our boys," but I kept my mouth shut and kept looking for helpful cameras.

We couldn't find footage of them leaving the area, which didn't mean they were still there. They could have a blind path out or underground tunnels, lest we forget their bloody underwater door that proved they were willing to be ridiculously super villain-y in their ways. They could have stayed in the area, or they could have switched vehicles like we'd done ourselves not an hour ago. Too many fucking options, and no way for us to know which was reality.

Riley swore under zir breath, then zir fingers scrambled on zir keys. "I'm trying to see if maybe I can grab that NOAA satellite we used before and turn it toward the area."

I shook my head. "You can try. But if it wasn't pointed there at that time and recording whatever happened..." I shrugged a little despondently. "I think we're unlikely to get anything useful from that satellite. Just more fish footage or a look at streets too many minutes late."

Zie sagged. "Dammit. You're right. Obviously."

"We can ask Kitty," I said, "whether they're on land or on the ship...She has to be able to see through cameras or read logs or *something*, right? Getting two of the people who probably blew SWS HQ seems like something the big wigs I'm assuming are on the ship would get messages about."

"Yeah. Okay, yeah. Gimme a sec." Riles opened zir messaging app to the Kitty conversation, and I watched over zir shoulder.

Riley: Hey. Can you do something for us?
Kitty: 3D me now?

So, once I shifted away from the camera's field of vision (and double-checked that we'd tucked away all the hotel-branded shit, just in case), Riles turned on the 3D on zir mobile, and Holo-Kitty showed up in all her wee, idealized glory.

"What do you guys need?" Holo-Kitty swiveled her head through a 180-degree arc, like she could see all around and was talking to everyone, not constrained by the field of vision of the mobile's camera. Like she wasn't just looking at Riles and she knew who "everyone" included. Instinctively, I moved away from her "glance" for a moment anyway.

Riles looked at me, like zie was asking permission to share at least what zie needed to ask for help. When I grudgingly nodded, zie said, "We need you to...If you can look through ship cameras or logs or something...Bryan and Jonny got shot and taken, and we don't know where they are or if they're...alive." Zir voice had hitched just slightly, and zie paused a moment to push through the emotion (whereas I had the luxury of just starting to quietly cry, 'cause I wasn't the one talking). "We're hoping you can see something or find something to help us figure it out."

Kitty's eyes got big. "Oh. Damn. You guys. I'm so sorry!" She thought a moment. She was a great rendering, so I had to assume Kitty had an amazingly solid sense of self to hold on to the idea of her physical form so well, with so much nuance and detail. "So that means it's you and Katja. You're down...well, I don't know what Jonny's skills were, but Bryan was your muscle. Your real-world sensibility." She suddenly looked very concerned and peered around. "You guys aren't staying somewhere stupid, are you? I mean, you two aren't *devoid* of real-world know-how, right?"

"Baby, we're playing it safe, and we're using all our skills. It's okay," Riles assured her.

Kitty didn't look like she believed zir, but she just nodded, and said, "Okay. Don't get caught or killed. I'm going to go try to figure out what's up with the boys." And then she disappeared.

Riles shrugged at me. "I guess we keep working and we hope. Unless you've found some cameras we missed that would catch those streets in the I.D.?"

"Not yet. Help?"

And then we spent half an hour failing to find any sort of camera we'd missed. Not even a good angle from cameras outside the area that might have been pointed just right to catch the vehicles as they headed into the blackout zone. So we left a program crawling through social media feeds, looking for pictures from the previous hours that were geotagged as being close to the area. Maybe sometime in the next couple days we'd get lucky and some tourist posting about the dim sum they'd grabbed this morning had caught our target vehicles in the background of a selfie.

After admitting failure, I sighed, a little guilt seeping in where that breath had been. "I know I should get right to figuring out our next move or something but…"

"But sometimes it's hard to think when you feel shitty and dirty," Riles finished the thought for me, briefly holding zir shirt away from zir chest with nose wrinkled in minor disgust.

I nodded, and something like hysteria tried to sneak out of my mouth on the back of a laugh. I swallowed it. "The irony of Team Run the Fuck Away being the ones left here to do this…"

"Yeah…"

I took a deep breath, a hopefully calming breath. "Right. So. I could use a shower and clean clothes. And it would be nice if that came before I do…more. Whatever's next."

"Well, your big choice is this: Do you want first shower or," and zie pointed to the meager welcome basket in the kitchenette, "the sole muffin?"

"If it's all the same to you…" I might be filthy, but I wasn't the sort of savage who didn't give their fellow filthy friend a chance to state preferences.

"It is. I might shiv someone for either at this point."

With no trace of hysteria, I laughed. I had no idea why a muffin might be so enticing to zir. "Fair enough. Then, I'll go shower. And you enjoy your carbs."

Win some, lose some, and why not both at once? (What was I missing about the muffin and its allure?)

In the shower, I collapsed against the wall, sobbing as quietly as I could. Pretending the sound of the water would cover the sound of my heart breaking and all my hope threatening to pour out. (Thanks for the generic and overwrought but painfully spot on imagery, dramatic observer in my head.) Good times.

What would I do if Bryan, who had been a part of my life and my soul since I was so wee I could barely recall, were gone?

And, surprised at the intensity of my grief over him, what would happen if Jonny were gone? I hadn't been conscious of how every bit of me just assumed he was a permanent addition to my future.

And had any of our actions the last few weeks actually mattered? (When the logical voice in my head started to tell me they had, I shifted to asking if they had mattered *enough*, and logic shut right the hell up. It didn't think it was wrong, but it knew I was too deep in my bitterness to listen.)

Had we even appreciably slowed down the bloody Peaceforgers? Had we convinced a single person in power that SWS were villains? That Divine Community Church were predators? That there were fucking aliens trying to ease us into a dystopia in utopia's clothing before we could realize it and stop it?

Well.

I stood and mechanically washed my hair, cutting off my tears abruptly and trying to take a calming breath.

Well, it didn't really matter. Or didn't do any good to despair either way. Did it?

I would have to suck it up. If not me, and hopefully Riles, then who?

I would see this through. Whatever that meant. And I thought about what that might mean as I rinsed my hair.

If our boys were alive, they wouldn't stay prisoners of the Peaceforgers—physically or digitally—if I could do anything about it. We'd chosen each other as family, and family—good family—should mean fighting for each other until you couldn't anymore. Until you were *sure* they were gone.

Kitty should be saved as well, shouldn't she? After what she'd given for the fight, didn't she deserve that? I nodded to myself; no question about it. We could postpone arguments about whether she was conscious enough or human enough a being still to merit efforts and basic respect until we'd at least made sure she was safe enough.

And, as for the bigger picture…If this bloody planet went up in flames, in the aliens' so-called peace fires, it wasn't going to happen due to a lack of effort on my part. Dammit. I felt my jaw getting as hard as I wished I were. I nodded to myself again, grimly resolute this time. As had happened often over the last week, the words of Rabbi Tarfon came to mind. I might not be able to fix the world, but I couldn't stop trying.

The real question was going to be just what I was justified in doing to try to fix it.

That made me pause a moment, literally stand still for a breath. I'd already been an active part in crossing lines I'd never have dreamt. I'd helped a bomber evade the law and made sure the only repercussion for his actions was deep guilt…and then I'd slept with him and fallen for him, so…I'd been part of physically breaking into and stealing from one building, which felt much more serious than all the digital break-ins and thefts I'd been part of, even if what we'd stolen was still just data from the bad guys. I'd helped blow up another building after throwing in with that aforementioned bomber. I'd been part of mistakes that had gotten innocents killed, including my beloved Gran…As well as both Bryan's and Riley's girls (and maybe also turned into something like an AI, at least in Kitty's case). Part of efforts that got people fighting for the cause—Huw and Quinn and now probably Bryan and Jonny—killed. Part of efforts specifically intended, and successful in that intent, to kill people…a whole room full of Peaceforgers. I was just lucky that said room full of Peaceforgers had killed the room full of their human collaborators moments before we did, sparing me *that* guilt. Oh, and couldn't forget that all those things had likely moved up the timeline of the secret alien dystopia.

I was still mostly sure most of the time that I'd done the right thing, that I'd done the best thing at least, given what I knew and what resources I'd had. But that didn't leave my soul feeling clean, and the soap I resumed vigorously applying to my skin wasn't going to fix that.

After all of this, the best I could hope for, the only salvation I saw, was to press on. To be willing to give all I had left in an effort to actually, finally save people from the whole Peaceforger threat.

At least I (probably) had Riley still to do it with. Though Riles and I didn't just have to try to save our boys. We also had to pretend to be the heroes they so wanted to be. Somebody had to be the Jonny. Somebody had to be the Bryan. And, at the moment, there were only two people who could do it. Even if it meant more than just gently nudging powerful people who were already in the know (useless bastards). Even if it meant more stains on my soul.

I knew it was a dramatic metaphor, but I felt entitled to a little drama at this point.

I supposed every soldier stains their soul in the name of the greater good for which they fight and kill. And I flattered myself by daring to presume that we were soldiers somehow, that we were pursuing the greater good.

So we'd keep doing what we were doing. We'd be heroic, or as close to that as we could manage. We'd take on whatever soul staining was necessary to spare the rest of humanity.

I snorted at myself as I kept piling on the overblown thoughts. I felt like I was trying to build myself up into some kind of cinematic hero, when I was probably just some jerk with her head up her arse.

I tried to think how I might give Riles a pep talk, one that would also be aimed at me. One that wouldn't just be thinly veiled despair and hysteria. Hopefully one where I didn't mention stains on souls quite so much. But zie interrupted.

Zir voice floated in from the other side of the bathroom door. "Hey. I just want you to know...I think we should make a pact to fight until it's over, one way or another." Zie laughed and added, "Or until we somehow have Bryan and Jonny back to be the heroic ones."

I exhaled in relief. The pep talk I couldn't think of wasn't needed. I called out, "Aye, poppet. I totally agree. Fight until there's no need or no way." I felt a trickle of even more relief as my voice didn't sound like a crying person who'd been thinking a lot about their stained soul.

I could practically hear zir nodding as zie said, "Courage isn't lack of fear; it's acting the way we know we should in spite of it. That's what Gran always told us, right?"

I smiled a little. "Yeah...And those are the people we want to be, the courageous ones. That's the only way for us to be in the right this time."

"Cool. Okay. Um...I'm going to go ask Kitty what the hell the delay is."

Go Team Run the Fuck Away (After We Rescue Our Boys) (And Also Hopefully Kitty) (Oh and After We Make Sure Somebody Takes Care of the Aliens). We needed to reconsider; that name wasn't going to fit nicely on shirts.

CHAPTER 2

When I came out after my shower, Riles presented me with half the muffin with a flourish. "Badass heroes like us need our nutrients."

I chuckled and accepted the gift. Around a bite (a very mediocre bite, which didn't solve the mystery of why Riley had valued it as highly as a shower; had zie been seduced by the promise of carbs and wee chocolate chips?), I asked, "Anything from Kitty?"

It clearly pained zir to report, "Naw. Nothing useful. Uh, I think she might have been overly optimistic before. I think she's...doing her best. But maybe isn't exactly kicking ass over there yet. She's...uh...she's looking through every individual camera, or trying to, and trying to figure out how to look through more than one at a time. And, it sounds like, trying to figure out how to not just end up with a random camera, one she might already have checked. I don't think she's even started figuring out how to find logs."

"Ouch." I winced. "Well, okay, anything she can do for us is appreciated and is more than we can do for ourselves at the moment. And...I guess just trying to do our best and be graceful about it applies to Kitty too."

Riles grabbed zir waiting stack of clean clothes and headed towards the shower. "If you touch my mobile screen right now, it's set up to accept your print and give you access rights. So you can talk to Kitty if she shows up."

I gave zir a thumbs up, then pressed that thumb to zir mobile screen. I didn't snoop through zir mobile...because I have integrity and respect zir privacy...and not just because my phone rang. It was Lex.

She was staying at the decoy suite at the posh hotel where we'd ditched our previous vehicle. Even knowing she and Marleina might get a visit from investigating Peaceforgers who thought they'd find Rye and me there, I was still more than a little jealous. At least it was a voice call, so I wouldn't have to see her lush surroundings.

"Hey! You guys settled in?" I asked by way of greeting.

"Dude." She sounded furtive. "Are you totally sure us staying here is okay? Feels sketch us staying here in the lux instead of you."

I laughed, trying to pretend all was light and my own dwelling wasn't a comparative let-down. "You're good to stay at least a month for now. Use the room service and stuff. And, really, since our car's ditched there, you've got the greatest risk of anyone."

Still sounding unsure of her right to be there, she said, "Okay...But, uh, speaking of everyone else."

"Yeah?"

"Figured best just one call to you from me, not everyone call you to report. So, this call's to say all those decoy cars and hotels and shit are taken care of and occupied and etc." She laughed a little. "And, given this is the nicest favor ever asked of any of us, this be more like you earning favors. So, keep that in mind, yeah?"

Ah. We hadn't really thought about that sweet side effect. Nice! I grinned. "Excellent. Though we'll see how people feel once the assholes looking for us start sweeping through everybody's rooms."

With a nasty giggle, Lex assured me, "Think some drek are looking forward to the excuse to shoot those assholes."

I let out a little laugh. "Okay, just make sure they know these blokes usually wear body armor. Treat them like zombies."

"Aim for the head!" she crowed. Then, "So, room service is here..."

"You go eat. And thanks. We really appreciate you helping cover our arses."

"Girl? After all you people done already? And not just 'cause this be a stupid plush suite? Pleasure be mine and Mina's."

It was good someone was getting some pleasure out of this.

Rye walked out, toweling zir hair and clearly contemplative. "I think we should email blast the info about contaminated cures. People should know they've got Peacemakers in them."

"Huh." I thought about it as I pulled up some news channels on the big TV, sticking with those that had either resolved their hacker issues or stayed in the grasp of *benevolent* hacker babysitters. "I mean, I guess the Peaceforgers know we know now, don't they?"

"Thanks, Senator Hansen, you motherfucker," Riley snarled at the air. "With all I've seen that asshole do in the past, with all the times he's given me reason to hack his privileged, old, white ass in the past..." Zie gave a frustrated sigh. "I should have known. I just honestly thought that his xenophobia and 'keep America pure' bullshit would work in our favor."

"So, we'll obliterate that dickhole later. And maybe, in our blast, we'll mention that we tried to get this same info to law and government, but one of them tipped off the church. Maybe name him..." I considered the repercussions.

Rye considered fuck all. "Yes! Yes. I'm writing the email now, and I'm totally calling him out. And then we blast this to everyone. Literally."

I sat at my computer, typing as I talked. "I'll make sure our remote comrades are up for helping. It might still be irresponsible to tell everyone about aliens, given the potential for panic backed up by existential crises and shit, but this tainted cure thing..."

Because it was just midday in Seattle (which seemed impossible; it felt like midnight or even days later), all our people still seemed to be up, including those on the other side of the world. And none of them doubted the veracity of our claims. Which meant, as soon as Riles had the email ready, we really went to town. We let the remote folks do things their way, but we made sure ours went to any email addresses we had, which now included plenty of politicians and media, doctors and engineers, and all sorts of hackers, and we set it up with the same helpful virus (I thought of it more as a non-killed vaccine) as we'd used on the one wide-release demo day email. Basically, once it hit an inbox, it would find any email addresses that account had on hand or that came in after the email hit—in the address book, the sent mail, or other messages in the inbox—and resend itself to those. Then the copy it sent would do the same when *it* hit an inbox, and repeat like that forever. And, yes, we put a timer on the code so it wouldn't do it until the end of the world (so, not *literally* forever). Because we were *responsible* criminals.

We included both the 3D printer plans for the Peacemaker detector Doc and Engie had designed and info about assorted locations that we knew should have a stack of them already printed. You know, on account of us having hacked and made many 3D printers mass print them previously in the name of making sure there'd be enough for everyone. *Responsible* criminals.

We decided not to tell everyone that Divine Community Church had actually created the disease, not just the cure. Not yet. It just felt a bit too far, like too much at once. We figured we'd let people get angry and have their Peacemakers removed, prove our info had been true. Then, when we dropped the info about the source of beat down flu, they'd all be more open to believing us and more ready to act against the church immediately, whilst their emotions were hot, instead of needing to act to save themselves.

Also, we put in the info about what strainer mesh size could screen out the Peacemaker vIIs from the cure. Didn't want to ruin the one source of healing people had. Though I wondered if anyone would read that far.

And, just to make sure there'd be evidence, I called Dr. Scott as soon as we sent the email.

"I'm assuming this is about the emails I just got and appear to have sent about the beat down flu cures?" She didn't waste a hello on me.

I cleared my throat. "Uh, yeah. Sorry. Desperate times..."

Scott sighed. "You're not wrong. This is a mess, huh?"

"You have no idea." I gave a weak laugh. "But I won't burden you with the other pieces yet. I...I was hoping for a favor. If you're able."

"Go ahead and ask. I'm too experienced and you're too perpetually involved in big things for me to preemptively agree," she said.

"Fair. Okay, so, do you have any cures on hand?"

"Yeah, a few doses. I was going to destroy them now, obviously. And then figure out how to balance my guilt at being part of the delivery system for that shit with my need to financially survive. Fighting the urge to just spend all day for weeks doing free brain surgery on those I helped infect, you know?" Scott sounded grim. I didn't envy her conundrum.

"Well, don't destroy them. And not just because, if you read the whole email, there's info further down the page about strainer mesh size to get the little bastards out of the doses. Instead, let me offer you a chance to help and take the edge off your guilt," I suggested.

"I'm listening."

It took a bit, a little back and forth, because she was clearly trying to stay off the law's radar, but I convinced her to reach out to her other doctor friends so they could all get some cure doses to appropriate law enforcement agencies around the world. Basically, just in case the Peaceforgers had managed to destroy all on-hand evidence, I figured I'd use the respectability of doctors to put evidence right into the hands of the law. I also suggested they let the media know they were doing it.

"But refuse to do it on the record. Tell them you're afraid for your safety given the power that SWS and the church have held. You want to save lives without getting harassed or worse for it. Plus, we'll keep an eye on their systems, just in case they put your name in the record anyway." I paused, done with my spiel and requests, but still trying to come up with arguments in case she objected.

After what seemed a moment spent considering, Scott replied, "Okay. Got it. If you message me all the law and media people I should contact, I'll get the doctors together."

"You're brilliant! Thank you, doctor." I felt some real hope growing in me as I hung up. And then I had a similar messaging session with Doc, Jonny's doctor friend in New Mexico who'd been our team's doctor for all the Peacemaker shit so far. He was faster to buy in. No surprise there.

With our lists of people to send to already on hand from past mailings, I quickly got Dr. Scott and Doc info on law enforcement and media to include when they reached out to share their evidence. Riley set up a little program to watch all those law enforcement and media sources, to make sure their names didn't end up on anything.

I hoped many other medical folks were doing this unprompted, but I knew damned well that hope wasn't an action plan.

Whilst Riles worked on some more physical security shit and on making the room look less occupied-by-us in case housekeeping or somebody ignored our "go away" door hanger and came in, I pulled up our list of people who'd been sent the latest secret email. You know, now that sending info to the doctors had secret mailing lists at the forefront of my mind. This was the one that had been meant to help powerful people learn that aliens were real, that SWS and Divine Community Church were alien plots, that the disease that had been burning through multiple countries—as well as the cure the church was giving out freely—was also a plot...We knew that was a stack of heavy and fantastical-sounding allegations, but we'd spent so much time trying to pick the right people and trying to build a compelling email stuffed with proof. We'd even gotten them some alien DNA. So. Since we hadn't looked in a few hours...Since the betrayal by Senator Hansen had let me know that, in spite of the initial positive actions we'd seen, not everyone was acting as we'd hoped...

It was time to start working through the list, one by one, and see where we'd gone wrong. Or at least get a sense of what more we might add to the case for those who didn't seem to be leaning the right way. After all, we couldn't exactly run off an alien invasion all on our own.

I got basically nowhere before Riles interrupted me with a shriek and turned up the TV. I looked up to see footage of Shay, the Peaceforger bitch who'd been in charge of the goons that shot our boys, pushed into a police car. Looked like they were in front of the main Divine Community offices.

As I listened to the anchor, I got my camera program running a new trace, trying to see when Shay had arrived at the offices and where she'd come from. Maybe we could trace her back to the boys. (She hadn't arrived on foot, so it was going to take a little work to figure out.)

"Shocking allegations this afternoon about Shay Brice, the new Divine Community Church Seattle Cure Outreach Lead. Like most of us, many of you have likely just received an email suggesting that the beat down flu cure doses provided by Divine Community include a Peacemaker vII in them. But our station, and apparently the Seattle PD, were also tipped off about something else. Before we play you the footage we received, we want to warn sensitive viewers that the following contains brutal violence."

I looked away, locked eyes with Rye, as they began to play the footage we'd sent them and SPD. The footage of the boys being gunned down. Even knowing the version the news had would contain blurs over Bryan's and Jonny's faces so I couldn't see their reactions and could pretend it wasn't them, it just wasn't something I could handle. Before I could get choked up, Riley's eyes got "oh shit" big. Zie opened zir mouth to tell me what zie'd just realized, but the anchor started to talk again.

"We had our experts examine the footage, and they concur that what appears to be Shay Brice directing this assault is authentic. *That* part of the footage was not tampered with. As far as they can tell, only the blurred faces of the two men gunned down by the people Ms. Brice is leading have been altered." There was a pause, the sort that implied a change of scene, and the anchor went on.

I looked up to see that her pinched face had indeed replaced the footage of our friends being shot.

"We reached out to Shepherd Michaelson about both the allegations of tainted cures and this attack, but we were told he was busy overseeing the dousing of the flames that ravaged the building where the cure was being manufactured." She didn't say it, she couldn't say it, but the slightest lift of an eyebrow suggested that the timing of this was mighty suspicious.

I agreed. I didn't recall setting those fires. So, unless someone else had known where the plant was and done it, this was definitely some classic evidence destruction shit from the church.

"We also reached out to Seattle PD, but they're declining to make a statement at the moment. So, we'll be back with more on both the contaminated cures and the brutal shooting that appears to have been directed by Ms. Brice as soon as we have anything new. For now," and she got jovial suddenly, "let's see what Ted has for us on an adorable new trend for your pets!"

Riles muted the TV and grabbed my hand, making sure zie had my full attention.

I drew my eyebrows into a confused V.

"Kot. That video. The one that everyone now has access to. That just played on the news."

"Yeah?"

Riles leaned in, deadly serious. "It's not clear if you just watch it as the news plays it, and even if you slow it down the angle isn't really clear. But *I didn't fuzz out Zane's tongue.*"

Oh. Damn. Right. They had shot out their definitely-not-human tongue to take out Bryan at the end. I offered a weak, "Well, maybe this is us subliminally prepping humanity for the truth?" When zir look told me that wasn't soothing, I just shrugged. "Hey, the tongue thing was how *we* found out."

If it was good enough for us, it was good enough for the rest of the humans.

I'd only made it through looking at a small fraction of the people who'd gotten our "here there be aliens...and manufactured diseases and tainted cures" email before I sighed and stopped for a break an hour later. It's not like I could send them a poll or something.

Do you believe in aliens now? Y/N

I had to go through their messages and calls after they'd read our email. I had to see what they'd looked at online and on their computers, how long they'd looked, where they'd gone (web sites, internal info on the topic, requests for more info from other places, shit like that), who they'd talked to (if there was any way to tell) or messaged after, what their admins and underlings had started researching after, and so forth. I wasn't going to get a whole story this way, and none of them had written blog posts detailing their responses and the reasons for them, the unhelpful bastards. But they might mention in a message to a trusted colleague that they'd just read something unlikely and disturbing. They might ask one of their employees to get them some info on SWS or the church. Or they might, as soon as they saw the word "alien," just stop reading. (Email open in an in-focus window for less than a minute and not returned to? Probably not a good sign.) In those cases, they might not even get to the video or DNA stuff we'd gone to such pains to get for them. Fortunately, that last group was the smallest, and currently contained only some of the more conservative politicians in our list, people we didn't have much respect for anyway.

"Why are you scowling?" Rye asked as zie hung a laundry line across our room ('cause it wasn't like we were going to go sit in a laundromat just now).

"Oh." I carefully relaxed my face, banishing the unintentional scowl. "Sorry, just concentrating. Looking through reactions of people who got our big email this morning. Trying to figure out what we achieved. I know I've only looked at a small group of them in-depth so far, but it seems from the quick skimming like most haven't dismissed us entirely I'm just scowling at the ones who have and the lack of action overall."

Riles stopped and pursed zir lips unhappily. "So, *why* aren't we seeing any action?" Zie caught zirself leaving out a detail. "I did some looking for signs of secret action too, while you were in the shower," zie noted.

"Ah. Okay. Well, I couldn't say." I pushed away my natural inclination to despair; I tried to put on my hero mindset. It fit about as well as a fighter pilot helmet on a toddler, but it was what I had. "I've only looked in-depth at a fraction of the recipients. And we haven't done a super thorough search for secret actions, not really." I nodded, trying to encourage myself as much as Riley. "And, really, that was all just this morning, right? I mean, it was a Saturday morning—which was a bad call on our parts—and a lot to process and come to terms with. Even if they think they believe it, it's huge and unreal-sounding and...and they haven't lived with it for weeks like we have."

Riles seemed eager to buy into the optimism. "Okay. Yeah. That totally makes sense. Good points, Kot!" Zie stood up straighter. "Plus," and zie pointed at the TV with its muted news channels playing.

There was some satisfying action at last. I didn't turn on sound, but read the scrolls and closed captions, not hating this news. News of a very angry public who felt betrayed, for the second time in only about two weeks, by a trusted institution. News where some anchors had gotten their hands on the contaminated cure, had gotten doctors (most of them hiding their identity, but still...) to confirm what they too were finding in the cures. News of crowds gathering in protest outside Divine Community buildings, and even some vandalism. The current anchor said they were trying to verify reports of Divine Community free clinics literally being burnt down in some remote locales.

So far, the only thing anyone had from SWS on the topic of cures tainted with their Peacemakers was a sentence, posted on their site and repeated verbatim if anyone got an interview. "Secure World Systems has no knowledge about any aspect of the preposterous allegations made against Divine Community Church." After a certain number of repetitions, it felt like the corporate version of being dumped by Valmont.

Unnecessarily, Rye summarized, "It kind of seems like at least we've dealt a serious blow to this particular Peaceforger plan."

I nodded. "Not done in the most ideal way, but done."

"So...does that mean we can focus on the boys? Maybe we're done doing the heavy lifting with aliens now? While they take a sec to get their heads around it?"

I almost said we could, and then a thing that had been nagging at me quietly finally formed in a clear way in my head. "Actually, we have to sort out one more thing."

"Old school hacking takedown of the church? 'Cause I'm ready!" Zie seemed not just ready but also eager. Of course zie did.

"Mate, stop making me disappoint you." I laughed. "I mean, sure we can do that soon enough. But I was actually thinking that Kitty needs to explain how she knew to warn us."

Rye's mouth made an "oh" shape, and I saw in zir eyes that zie'd also forgotten but, now that I'd brought it up...Zie picked up zir mobile to tap out a message. Kitty replied immediately, and was soon displaying in 3D from Riley's screen.

"Hey, guys. What's up? I'm afraid I don't have any useful info for you yet."

It was the first calm moment of talking to her like this. Even earlier, when we were safe in this room, I'd been too deep in my feelings over our missing boys to really notice how her voice sounded like old time phone connections, distant and with an edge of a hiss. Like her voice knew better than her image that all she really was right here was air.

"Actually, baby..." Riles tried to make it sound casual, but Kitty could tell as surely as I could that it wasn't. "We were kind of hoping you could explain how you, uh, how you knew to warn us. At the fueling station. How you knew they were coming for us."

She scrunched her tiny face up, thinking as she explained. "It was like...I've been trying to remember things, and I've been thinking a lot about what happened that day at SWS HQ. So...Maybe that was doing, um, like a computer search? Which, sadly, isn't working yet to find out about the boys. Anyway, it was like I heard someone whisper, but in that language they speak here, about having a location for the people who were behind HQ going down and going to get them." Her face smoothed and she shrugged. "You nerds could probably make a better guess about what really happened."

Riley and I exchanged a "we should talk privately" look, and zie said, "Okay, thanks, baby. Sorry to interrupt you."

She grinned cheerily. "Any time! Now, we should all get back to work. I'll be damned if I'm not going to figure out how to at least see through cameras well really soon." And she blipped out.

After zie made sure zir phone mic was definitely fully and mechanically muted, Riles suggested, "Maybe she *was* subconsciously running a search and intercepted something like an email or messenger communication?"

There was no way to know, and that bugged me. So I just chewed the inside of my cheek some more and nodded.

"So, now what?" zie asked.

"Now..." I had to think. I felt like there were too many threads to hold in my head. "Now, for my ragged brain to have a chance, I think I need to make lists of shit to handle. Also, I have no ideas for action beyond that, so..."

"So lists!" Zie was entirely too pumped at the thought.

CHAPTER 3

I typed the lists as our ideas came, driven by a (possibly vain) hope that we could break into brainstorm mode and magically uncover our next steps. It wasn't as productive an effort as we'd wanted, and we considered the lists we now had displaying side by side on the TV.

Objectives
* Find out if boys are alive
* If yes, save our boys
* Save Kitty (download??)
* Support takedown of PFs (probably)

Things we can/should do
* Backtrack Shay
* Get some actual sleep
* Backtrack Zane
* Check PD records on Shay arrest
* Check on families
* Not just cry and sleep
* Hope Kitty works
* Hope we stumble on info RE our boys

Riley took my portable and started another list.

Days
* Demo Day
* Raid Night
* Carbonite Day

I stopped zir. "Uh, what?"

Patiently, as if it were the most obvious thing, zie explained, "Well, we keep calling the day we demolished SWS HQ 'demo day,' so I thought it should be formalized. And then I thought it would be easier to talk about shit that's gone down if we have names instead of descriptions." Then zie got a wicked little smile. "Plus, it makes us sound cooler and makes it easier to start the legends about our exploits." Rye put on zir thinking face and stared at the screen.

"Wait, before you think of more (which, side note, might be overkill), I'm guessing Raid Night was the night we raided their factory?" I waited for zir to nod confirmation. "But what's Carbonite Day?" I quickly added, "I get the allusion, but..."

Very matter-of-fact, zie said, "This morning, our boys got betrayed by someone one of them trusted, taken out of action, and carted off by the enemy. And, if the allusion holds, one of us ends up in a bikini, killing the gross alien and freeing our boys. Who, if the Universe lets the allusion work well, would still be alive somehow."

"Can we skip the bikini? Wrong season." Yes, that was the most important thing for me to point out.

With unwarranted seriousness, zie replied, "Huh. Good point. Okay, we can just kill aliens and rescue the boys, no wardrobe requirements. Close enough."

"Cool." I had to allow us a quick grin. We were ridiculous. "Now, I vote no more day names. At least not right now. Not until we do the rest of our list. Or not until we need one for the day we rescue the boys and maybe one for the day the Peaceforgers fuck off." With exaggerated gentleness, I noted, "More named days at this point would be reaching. And you're better than that."

Zie shook zir head and dramatically rolled zir eyes. "You just don't love fun and joy."

"I am, indeed, the worst," I confirmed. "So, uh, what order do we jump on this stuff?"

"I swear it's not just because I'm a social butterfly," Rye said, "but we can't do this alone. And, you know, at least this time we don't have to vet anyone. Just send our alien email to people we already trust."

"We do eventually have to get the word out," I agreed, even though none of this was on our action list.

"And...I actually think we should be liberal with this. Obviously, make sure Kitty knows all the details that are relevant that she might not know already. Plus the remote team, Doc and Engie, Lex and Marleina..."

"Oddly, I agree. And Dr. Scott for sure. Engalls, if we didn't Bcc him on the morning emails..." I started flipping through my sent messages, trying to figure out if Engalls already knew.

"But, also, I think we don't tell them to keep it secret. They should share with people they think should know." Riles thoughtfully chewed a nail.

I considered that. I didn't think we should put it on blast, but maybe the truth should start leaking and seeping out. Maybe, whilst it had been right in the afternoon not to tell the world, the world was now in a state of useful anger and distrust. Plus, it couldn't be long until someone found Zane's tongue in the assault video, footage already declared authentic by the news.

We built a new email, and it was a lot like the old email, or at least the parts about aliens existing. Mainly, we didn't have to totally hide who we were (no more than normal hacker-level hiding) and we were gearing it less for "you have power; please use it sneakily" and more for "don't know what we can do; please brainstorm...and share carefully." Plus, we pointed out the footage anyone could get now of Zane's tongue crossing inhuman distances to hit Bryan. Riles and I gave each other "hope we aren't fucking up" looks and sent that bad boy.

"While we're in a sending mood..."

I looked at Riles. "Yeah?"

"What about, just with our remote crew, sharing the drone info? Or is that too far?"

That was a good question. I chewed the inside of my cheek and considered. Bryan hadn't shared any plans for the info he'd gotten on hacking our country's military drone controls. "I think...My main concern is that this is military tech that could be turned back on our country once this is all done." I held up a hand. "Not that I'm a patriot. But fucking around with military secrets and which lines we can cross is more Bryan's thing. And the kind of thing that could end up in the sort of wars that humans love to wage."

"Ugh. Okay. That needs more research and thought. 'Cause us trusting them on the 'Net is different. You're right."

Carefully, I said, "Since we're talking trust…"

Zie raised an eyebrow, as if to invite me to go on. But zie must have had an inkling, 'cause zie checked zir mobile, making sure that all cameras and mics were still off.

"So, uh, Kitty…Same old question we've been asking for weeks, plus some new considerations. Are we sure it's her? Her without any Peaceforger bullshit? Her and…capable of running around in the computer without tripping up anything?" I tried not to sound like I probably would have sounded back when I just saw Kitty as Riley's useless girlfriend.

To my surprise, Riles didn't bristle. There was no defensiveness in zir voice when zie said, "Those are good questions. She's a potential blind spot for me, and anything we trust her with is a weak point for us. Potentially." Zie sighed sadly. "I can't really know. I *think* it's her. I *think* it's just her, and that means she'd be on our side. Uh…" Zie shoved zir mobile under some cushions, as if to make it even more deafened and blinded. "As to your third question…I love her, you know."

I nodded. I did know.

"And, you know, it's okay for people to have different strengths and interests."

"I hear you, poppet. Whatever you're about to say, you're not talking shit on your girl."

Zie let out a relieved breath. "Cool. So, yeah, anyone, even us, would probably struggle in her situation. New paradigm, alien language, all that. But…not really sure about her being capable in a digital context. She's still learning. We've seen that today, but, you know…Even if it's as easy as thinking and things happen, she probably wouldn't know enough to effectively watch out for booby traps or leaving digital footprints."

Well, at least zie still had perspective.

"But I guess the question you didn't ask about Kitty is whether we have a choice." Riley sounded like zie hated that it came down to that.

Zie was right, though. For the moment, we didn't have any other way into the Peaceforger computers. "Okay. True. Can we…I think it makes sense for her to be able to contact me and vice versa. But I don't want her on my mobile like she's on yours. So...Can we set up a group chat, so she can ping me through that, and only through that? My screen is for Hello Kitty, not Holo-Kitty."

My joke was stupid, but Riles laughed. It was lovely.

Before we could start working through our list of actions in whatever order felt right in the moment, we got hit with a flurry of responses from the people we'd emailed. It was now just barely not-too-late on the other side of the world for people to still be awake and/or obsessively checking every ping, if one took into account stereotypical hacker bedtimes and the paranoia of having been involved in recent epic events. Which also applied, for instance, to Engie in Wales, who wasn't some nocturnal digital warrior but who was undeniably involved. So, as near as we could tell, of the ten people we'd emailed, eight had already opened the email.

The first responses were basically "haven't gone through it all, but if you say it's this, I'm with you to fight it." Then came responses with clarifying questions or even just "no fucking way! really?" replies. But, to my great pleasure, they all seemed to believe us. Already showing more intelligence and responsibility than those in power. Go fuckin' figure.

I took a quick break to send another email to the bastards who'd gotten our morning email, a quick throat clearing sort of thing to direct their attention to the Zane's Tongue video. Though I did leave off Senator "Fuck Humanity" Hansen. Because, no, fuck *you*, Senator.

Then, back to the replies. Where even Engalls was in.

If it were anyone else, I'd call bullshit; but, from you? Okay.

So maybe not all cops were stupid.

It would have been nice if presidents and generals had all been so reasonable. But I guess we were just lucky that none of them had gone to full-on war as soon as they got the email. Not, of course, that it would matter now if they did. Because our most recent and less exclusive email had humanity in general on the warpath over the vIIs in their cures.

One of the things that can come with being Autistic is difficulty making choices in the moment. (Just one part of the suite of fun called "executive function issues."). So, that was my excuse. No idea what Rye's was, but I was ready to honor it. Why was it so hard to just grab our list of things to do and get working? There was too much silence happening given we were supposed to be action heroes.

I stood and started pacing, pretty sure I'd read that physical activity could get your brain working or something. And maybe it wasn't bullshit, because I at least thought to say, "Okay, so, first thing on our list of objectives is to find out if the boys are alive. Which means we need to find them or signs of them..." You know, completely ignoring the list of *actions* we'd also made.

"What if I set up a tracker to watch all hospitals and morgues," Riles took a quick breath as zie stumbled over the word and what it implied, "Both a text tracker and also one for images entered for new patients, in case they get listed under wrong names or as John Does?" Zie didn't even wait to see me nod, but got to work.

"Yeah. Good. And I'll...Oh! I know we don't have the processing power to keep eyes on everything, but..." I sat and pulled my portable onto my lap. "You know that bullshit PerpTrack system the law's been using to try to hijack footage from all cameras they can access to keep an eye out for wanted people? The one that doesn't need a specific starting point like my wee program does? Well..." I paused to execute a bit of tricky code, worming my way into the PerpTrack system. "I'm going to set up Bry and Jonny as searches, but do it in a super secret mode that only shows the search and its results to whoever set it up. Have it ping just us if it has a hit."

"Might as well do it for Zane too," zie noted, then bitterly added, "but feel free not to have that search on the super secret mode."

We both worked then, a more acceptable kind of silence, with Riles finishing first and using the time to go through the Seattle PD stuff on the Shay arrest. As I worked, zie gave me the highlights. Shay was in custody but the bail hearing wasn't set to happen until Monday. From the unofficial conversations recorded by the station's cameras, they were delaying because there was no way the PD was going to let it happen sooner given they all knew or were people who'd gotten the beat down flu cure. And, also unofficially, they figured it was cut and dry, thanks to the fast actions of the person who got them that anonymous tip before anyone could get at the security cam servers.

When I was finally done and sure I wasn't accidentally fucking our boys over, not actually making them criminals and police targets in the system, I stretched. My back was not appreciating the tension of the day we'd had. I moved on to circling my shoulders carefully and squinted at our list of objectives and actions. "Okay. So...I think tracking back to see where Shay came from before she was arrested this afternoon is all we have left that we can do in terms of getting the boys. I can do that. Uh...Any thoughts on the next thing? On getting Kitty downloaded?"

All the joy Riles was experiencing, as zie read about SPD taking actions we liked without us having to do much to make things happen, evaporated. "I think...We don't know how much memory she'll need or even if our tech has the capacity to handle...whatever she is. And we don't know how to connect to their computer, so we can't even be sure she could get here. Though, if we could figure out the first bit, she could just...try? Like, will herself here or something?"

I nodded and reached over to give zir hand a squeeze. This was almost something within our skill set, but not quite. And we'd failed for weeks to figure out how to connect to the Peaceforger computer. We hadn't even been able to sense Kitty with any equipment we'd gotten that should detect all kinds of wavelengths of transmissions and such.

Zie noted, "If I can just figure out...figure out how to get her to do some kind of diagnostic? Maybe we could at least sort out *size*. But I think I need to do some serious research into AI, 'cause that's our closest baseline, to see what sort of hardware and shit we *might* need."

Weakly, I said, "We always did want to try our hand at real AI. So, yay?" Dramatically, I put my hands over the mics on Jonny and Bry's computers, which we'd joined so they could run Ada, my pseudo-AI, and whispered, "Just remember not to make Ada feel like she isn't a real artificial intelligence. We don't need a machine uprising in addition to this other shit."

Rye laughed a little, then said, "Okay. So, I'll *sneakily* research AI instead of just doing an informational interview with Ada, and you..." Zie considered our lists, then shook zir head. "You already said you were going to follow Shay back."

I hadn't just said it; I was already on it.

It was slightly tricky to follow Shay, at least initially. As a leader there, she had a parking spot in the very small underground parking area at the main Divine Community building. And there'd been a lot of cars in and out even just in the first half the day. Plus, I had to find cameras at angles that let me see makes and models—not just colors—of cars. Even so, I had a bit of a sneer twisting my mouth as I poked at Department of Licensing records, hoping to narrow down what car she might have been in, whilst the computer continued to run traces on the routes of any car that came in during the small window of time during which she had to have come in. I bet getting caught being murder-y on camera was the sort of thing that lost one sweet titles and sweeter parking spots when one was part of a secret organization. Yeah, I *was* going to eat up any petty victory when it came to these arseholes. And I wasn't going to feel bad about it. Not that parking spots are a petty thing in Seattle.

In less petty victories, it looked like Shay had arrived at the Divine Community building in her own car. Once I found the right car in the footage, it was easy to follow it back. And the parking at her point of origin was just uncovered enough that I could confirm it was sure as hell her.

I had traced her back to Gas Works Park, so named because it contained the cool-looking remnants of the sole remaining coal gasification plant in the United States. It was right on the water, and this kind of solved the mystery of who'd bought the park (because protected public lands hadn't actually been protected for decades) and turned large chunks of it into a closed-off site of unclear industry. It felt safe to assume that, like SWS HQ, it had an underwater door. But assuming was all I could do at the moment.

Shay's car had been there since at least the night before. The only vehicle to have arrived there today, which I easily traced back to the camera dead zone in the ID, had been big enough to have held at least half a dozen people comfortably. So, clearly, it could have held Shay, Zane, and the two boys and still have had room for a couple of the big blokes with guns. Watching things in forward motion, the vehicle pulled in through large doors, which were immediately closed behind it, and that was it. So, yeah, *maybe* our boys were being held there. But, given we'd attacked them more than once on land, it seemed more likely they'd been loaded onto some kind of shuttle thing and taken out to the Peaceforger's ship. That's what I would have done, you know, if I had a spaceship parked underwater.

I felt kind of shitty for the pang of jealousy the sci-fi kid in me experienced. Setting aside the great pile of everything else, if they were alive, our boys were probably on a motherfucking alien spaceship. And we weren't.

I showed the relevant footage to Riles.

Zie must have had the same dire assumptions and realizations about how impossible that made rescue, because neither of us said anything, just did some synchronized swearing and throwing non-breakable things. Fuck.

Glumly, I noted, "Guess that means getting them back relies on Kitty. Or on us breaking into the gas works and maybe their ship."

The infinitesimal odds of success if we tried to do that were enough to overwhelm any excitement at the thought, the very small possibility, of maybe being on an actual alien ship before this was all over.

Since I was already on camera stuff, and since any moment of pause might result in me doing more crying than was on our action list, I pulled up footage from a camera that captured Zane's parking spot at home. Time to see where they'd gone after we'd left them this morning, before they'd led their fucking sister in to massacre us.

I saw us talk to them, I swore nastily as Bry kissed Zane the Betrayer goodbye, and then I watched us part ways. Our vehicle took off for the fueling station and Zane...Well, that was the question, wasn't it?

I kept an eye on the time stamp. I didn't have cameras in their place. Or I did, kind of, but all their webcam could tell me was that, right now, nobody seemed to be home. It couldn't tell me what had happened earlier. I set a wee program running to let me know if there was motion or a dramatic light change in their flat (so, not the slow change of sunset). If they came back, they might say or do something that gave us other useful clues, and we'd be able to trace them back to wherever they'd just come from.

"Why the hell weren't we constantly monitoring Zane's webcam before?" I asked, cranky and not necessarily expecting an answer.

"Because we're idiots," Riles flatly replied, then sighed. "I'm hiring a criminal intern to just watch a wall of screens with the webcams of everyone I have to even slightly trust other than you guys from now on."

"Aw, we've got a little NSA junior here!" I teased, but secretly started pondering whether I should be spying on Lex and Marleina and...everyone. Anyone we were trusting. That just felt...shitty. No two ways about it. It felt shitty, even if my paranoia was telling me it was smart.

I sighed. Okay. Back to the task at hand. I'd decide about being a privacy-invading asshole after.

I did a quick search of logs, looking to see if Zane had called or messaged anyone whilst they were inside. I kept an eye on the time stamp, opening another window on my screen to show footage of their front door, just in case they'd left that way. At least in terms of human devices, human tech like their computer or phone, they hadn't sent any messages or made any calls that I could tell. I set an automation going to copy their computer contents, just in case there was something useful and they wiped it before we had a chance to look. We could sift through that later.

After a few minutes, the cameras showed that they'd exited via their building's front door. My brain sparked, caught on an image that had seemed too normal to notice when I'd watched the footage of them at our car. "Oh, shit! I forgot; we've got Zane's bag." I paused the program's playback.

Riles and I exchanged a terrified look, grabbed our bug-detecting watches, as well as the one nicer detector we had, and dove for the stack of other people's bags. It was a small stack, so it was mere seconds before we were hustling it into the bathroom—in case something exploded when we opened it—and away from all our gear. Even with the threat of explosion in mind, we just dumped it into the tub, upended that bitch and poured it into a heap.

It looked like an innocent heap of (mostly) clothes and toiletries, but we still used a fork from our kitchenette to poke through it. I don't think either of us breathed until we were sure our bug detectors weren't going to go off. I mean, they hadn't gone off when we'd done the sweep of the suite on arrival, and the bag had been there, but my paranoid brain needed to be sure.

I sagged against the tub in relief. "Holy fuck, mate. We got lucky."

Riles let out a breathy laugh. "How damned basic are we? If they'd put anything in there..."

"Seriously."

Zie seemed to bounce back as zie said, "Well, now that we know it's not deadly or dangerous, let's look at every item and talk shit about their taste. Even if we have to pretend it's worse than it is."

And then we did just that. Though we also made a stack of things that we might wear if it were laundry day. The rest got shoved back into the bag.

In the middle of it all, there was a book, a big, thick blank book style thing, like you might use for a journal or to write your poems in or whatever if you were very prolific. But not like the usual cheap, narrow ones. I did a quick 'Net search and found that it was as expensive as it looked, so like some rich person might write their stuff in. And it was full of...well, fuck if I knew, because the writing in it wasn't just cramped but was also entirely in the Peaceforger script.

With a mix of awe and disappointment, Riles said, "Can you imagine how fun this would be to translate if this were just a game?"

Yeah. Seriously. I nodded, then said, "Well, I guess this means we at least never need to worry about being bored now." I stood. "I think it's safe to get back to it."

Back to our portables we went.

I used my camera program to track Zane as they headed over to a building a mile or so south of their own that was filled with live/work artist lofts. Not cheap. Fortunately, it was enough not-cheap that it had a camera-rich security system. I could see who that fucker buzzed and track them right to the door of one of the lofts. I got a quick glimpse of someone as they let Zane in, but I was failing to find any cameras in the unit. Whoever lived there was carefully keeping out all cams and mics, including mobiles, as far as I could tell.

That wasn't perfect, but I wasn't dead-ended yet. It didn't take a hacker to use an address and unit number to find the name of the owner because, oh lucky day, these lofts were condos. They were *owned*, not just rented. Which meant I could easily look at public records to find...well, owner of record. Didn't mean it was the occupant, but one step at a time.

Public records showed the owner was Isa Green. No hacking needed. A quick 'Net search showed that Isa Green was a Seattle-based abstract painter of increasing renown who tended to create pieces she hoped would invite "contemplation and peace of spirit." No hacking needed. I checked out the paintings, which did not suck and which I might even have liked if the colors she tended towards were more like those I liked. No hacking needed. Isa, who looked like the person of whom I had gotten that quick glimpse, was pretty and pale as any

Peaceforger we knew of and made no secret of the fact that her ubiquitous brightly colored and ever-changing hair was wigs. No hacking needed.

Of course, then I did have to hack to use the camera in her building corridor to confirm that it did look like Isa was the sole occupant (or the only one who'd gone in and out that door in the last week with timing that suggested she slept there and spent most her days there as well). I also made sure to grab the best face pics I could of anyone else who visited during the week, along with time stamps so I could follow them later. Clearly, this job I was doing was a non-stop party.

I rubbed my eyes. I was tired as hell.

Riles caught me yawning and asked, "Tired?"

"Beyond tired. But afraid to take a nap and delay...whatever it is we're doing." I interrupted myself with another yawn.

Leaning over to see why my screen had spots of interesting color, zie asked, "What are you working on now?"

I turned my portable to make it easier for zir to see. "This is who Zane visited between us picking up our car at theirs and them joining us at the fueling station. When they said they were going to go see the leader of their rebel group."

Zie gave a little whistle of appreciation. "Hot alien with...well, if it's actually her doing it, talents." Then Riles considered my face and asked, "But what are you working on that's time-sensitive?"

"Well, what if I can follow Isa or one of her visitors and find the connection to the rest of them? Maybe find a building we don't know about that the boys might be in—like that sketchy one they took 'Randa to—or see whether she's working directly with SWS or the church?"

Riles took my portable from me, setting it aside. "That's a lot of maybe and searching. Not quite random, but mostly." Kindly then zie said, "We've both got alarms set on our searches, and everything else we're doing is just in hopes we'll run across something. And we're wrecked, so we'd probably fuck up anything important or tricky."

"Bed time?" I asked.

"Bed time," zie confirmed. "At least for a nap. We're no good to anyone if our minds, the one real asset we have, aren't working."

I knew it was true. How often had I been the one to say as much?

So I didn't argue. Instead, I willingly curled up with Riles, with Jonny's and Bry's mobiles right by us like talismans for their return, and got to sleep on an actual bed for the first time in weeks. I felt guilty for how much a part of me wanted nothing more.

The call from Lex wasn't really a surprise, and it came just before I was fully asleep. "Hey! Just thought you guys should know the assholes just visited us."

It took my brain a second to register what she must mean: Peaceforger goons checking in on the places we might be staying, just like we had known would happen. "Everyone okay?"

Riles turned on the bedside lamp and gave me a look, ready to be concerned about whatever news I was getting. I smiled at zir and shook my head gently. No worries, mate. Zie nodded and slipped out of bed and into the loo.

Lex laughed, and I could hear Marleina in the background talking shit (to the air?). "We're good. 'Cause we're in a rich place, they were really quiet about breaking in. But we weren't quiet about freaking out and telling 'em to fuck off." She paused a beat, making it easier to hear Marleina's threats. "Mina is still reliving the fun."

I let out a wee laugh of my own. "You badasses."

"It doesn't hurt we knew they'd eventually show, so we already knew some of the shit we wanted to talk. We just followed them as they tossed our stuff and made sure it was really just us here." She snorted. "They left right before the seriously out-gunned hotel security showed up."

"Was it the big blokes with black balaclavas?"

"Yes! Just like in..." she caught herself, reined in the glee, cleared her throat. "Uh, like the fuckers in the fueling station vid."

That made me feel like I was falling into a black hole in my gut for a moment. I managed, "Well, I'm glad you're safe."

The awkwardness wasn't going to go away, and she caught that. "Anyway, that's it. Thought you should know. Uh, have a good night, girl."

I tried to make my tone extra kind, 'cause I didn't want to leave things weird. "Thanks, Lex. You and Marleina too."

"Oh, yeah, by the way, she figures you guys are okay to call her 'Mina' now, after everything that's gone down."

And I let that be my happy bedtime story. The gorgeous Marleina had decided to allow us the intimacy of using her diminutive. Weren't we just the luckiest survivors...

Lying in the dark, in a bed that was okay (definitely better than a mattress on the floor or just plain sleeping on a dirt floor), I tried not to eavesdrop. I could hear Riles and Kitty failing to be quiet in the bathroom. I couldn't imagine how Riley must feel, to have been sure Kitty was dead and then discover that maybe she wasn't.

They were giggling and talking a mile a minute. And I didn't have to hear the words to know that this was the most genuinely happy Riles had been in weeks.

I sent out...a wish. Let's call it a wish, because a prayer holds a lot more baggage. So, yeah, I sent out a wish. Not like "please, please let me get the presents I want" or even "please, please make that pretty person look at me and fall in love." This was from somewhere so deep in me that I didn't know whether to call it my heart or my gut or even my soul...But, oh, I would burn this world down to have our Bryan and Jonny alive and back.

I made sure to cry into the pillow, to not disturb the happy, holographic reunion in the bathroom. *Let me have a reunion too*, I thought, over and over, until I fell asleep.

CHAPTER 4

I woke because...because I woke. I'd had wretched nightmares, and I could feel that my cheeks were uncomfortably coated with dried tears, but I'd been so tired that my body had refused to wake up from the terrors, had just pushed through into the next sleep cycle. And my brain...Holy shit. On the other side of the nightmares? My brain hadn't felt this clear and capable in ages. Full of guilt for sleeping whilst our boys were...well, we didn't know what they were...so, full of guilt, but clearer.

I didn't have new ideas or plans, but I could feel the clarity and brightness and...And any failure to come up with next steps was going to be entirely due to ignorance, not due to a brain fucked up by lack of sleep. So, hey, that was something.

Beside me, I felt Riles stretch as zie sleepily asked, "Bitch, did we just sleep through the night?"

I checked the clock and sighed, a mix of bliss and disappointment. "Yeah. So, we're rested, but that means none of our searches found anything." I tapped on the bedside lamp, squinting briefly against its yellow light.

"And nothing from Holo-Kitty," zie said, checking zir mobile, just in case we'd slept through pings from her.

I pushed up to sitting. "I was hoping sleep would help me figure out the Perfect Path to take next. Instead, I just have a list of things we could work on in addition to your AI research."

"Cool." Zie snuggled up against me a little. "At least we won't have nothing to do, even if we accomplish nothing." Zie yawned and pushed zirself up to sitting. "You had an alert set on Zane's webcam too, right? Which means they didn't come home last night?"

I nodded. "Yeah. But, once they do come home, we can trace their path back and see if that helps us confirm whether the boys are on land or at sea." I pulled my computer from the bedside table to my lap, hoping to jot down all my ideas about actions we could take before I forgot.

Rye grabbed the remote and turned on the TV. "Let's check in on what sort of Sunday service bullshit our favorite supposedly religious bastard is peddling." Zie gave a nasty little laugh. "This is going to be some breathtaking scrambling to cover his ass I bet."

As zie got the TV set up with a split screen of news and the channel that would broadcast Divine Community services, I slid out of bed to dress and get our coffeemaker going.

Whilst we waited for the Divine Community Sunday morning shit show to start, we watched the news and checked our feeds and accounts. Without digging any deeper, it appeared the state of things in the world we'd woken up to was something like this:

SWS had stopped trying to rebuild their computer network. At least they didn't seem to be connecting any machines to the internet except...Maybe they were just getting on to send and receive email? We felt pretty sure we weren't missing much. Not now.

There was a new, quiet little forum that was invite-only where one of our remote comrades had started trying to get those of us who were clearly anti-SWS working together. Even though they couldn't have known who the others involved in the previous efforts had been, they'd managed to invite all our surviving remote comrades. As well as those of us in Seattle. Not me-as-MindKiller "us," obviously, but me-as-D3AD_L1NX and (thanks to our work creating a fake past for my new 'nym) me-as-SecantSight "us."

And it wasn't just that limited set of "us" there. I think the slowly spreading revelation that SWS were aliens and were still getting their Peacemakers into the world had led to a lot of people increasing efforts to knock their shit out. Some of those "a lot" had been invited.

Anyway, bugHunt (the forum, a wee play on what programmers do to find errors and a term from an old movie about killing dangerous aliens) was where the info about the SWS network came from. I wondered how long before those who knew posted the alien angle there openly and everyone could join Riles and me in wondering if SWS were just opting to exclusively use Peaceforger tech to connect now.

But also. Also, in spite of signs that they'd been beaten into the dirt, SWS had pushed ahead with their Peacemaker PR campaign, rolled it out whilst we'd been watching our boys get gunned down. The one I felt like we'd discovered years—not weeks—ago and that we'd assumed would get shelved after we exposed them. They'd tweaked it very slightly, since the damage we did to them on Demo Day (thanks for the caps, Riles) meant they had to work hard to repair their rep if they still wanted to get in on that sweet Black Friday sales action. They'd doubled down on the points and approaches meant to give them a particularly rosy glow, of course. The most fucked up part was that their sales hadn't hit zero, not on any of their products. There were still people out there buying every kind of thing they sold, still people who were chatting about the potential use of Peacemakers on parenting forums or forums for those taking care of their older parents. It made me sick to my stomach.

It only slightly took the edge off the sick to see that there were a lot of other people who were agitated.

Those sales though, especially the Peacemaker ones...Those meant that everyone who'd been working to blow up any SWS facility they could find was definitely missing a warehouse, a manufacturing plant, shit like that.

In selfish news, I noted with relief that SWS had finally stopped talking about me. They were totally focused on their positive PR angle.

In potentially more hopeful news that wasn't just about me, someone on the forum reported that Johnson and Smith, the surviving SWS execs from Demo Day, might not be getting away with everything. It had been done carefully and quietly, but the post we saw claimed that the Seattle PD had brought them in ASAP for questioning. Records, as reported by this someone on the forum (and quietly verified by Riles and me once we read it), showed they'd been questioned in regards to the deaths in Conference Room Beta and something about hiring people to kidnap, torture, and sometimes kill people.

"One was even a friend of that Katja chick SWS kept trying to pin everything on, so I totally believe it," reported the forum someone.

I had to pause a moment to feel sad and shitty over 'Randa when I read that. She wasn't even actually my friend, and she'd still paid for knowing me.

And, whilst they weren't in jail or whatever, the execs had been put under a sort of modified house arrest, restricted to their homes (luxury units on the same floor of the same building), the current SWS main office, and a specific travel route between those places.

I paused again, this time to go switch some work orders on the Department of Public Works schedules. That particular travel route was about to be filled with construction-related traffic delays. Suck it, assholes.

Of course, I could hack their tracking anklets, so I didn't doubt they could do the same, or that they could at least employ or order someone to do the same. But the anklets might still make it easier to see what shit they got up to. I added some SWS exec following to my to-do list. Or, rather, I set up yet another task for my computer, an order to ping me if their anklets went off route.

And their friends at Divine Community? On one lovely hand, an angry populace had continued to strike at them all through the night. Vandalism! Fires! Lawsuits! Mean social media posts! There were plenty of people who were more than a little upset with the combined news of tainted cures and one of their leadership gunning down innocents.

On a less lovely hand...Sunday services were continuing as scheduled, and the law didn't have enough of anything on Shepherd Michaelson to do more than question him. (Records showed he'd spent Saturday claiming ignorance and that he had an appointment to talk to detectives again on Monday.)

Also, all through the day Saturday, not only had Michaelson found time to heal people with his alleged miracle hands, but a couple of the next tier of leadership had started manifesting those same "miraculous" abilities. So, of course, their congregation numbers were swelling. With the hope of magic bullets to fix their troubles, not everyone was managing to keep their proven crimes in mind.

Oh, and their fucking flu was continuing to spread at the pace laid out in their fucking documents. How the hell were those in power, those who'd seen the documents in question thanks to us, not getting this? I could have stabbed myself in the face.

But I'd save that until after the morning sermon. I didn't want face wounds distracting me from the glee of watching Michaelson squirm.

The service started with choirs and congregational hymns that the music director conducted with gusto. And the folks in charge of cameras did a great job of showing the perfect balance of faces: the hopeful faces in the front row of the audience (who were likely there because they'd been selected for healing), the glowing faces of choir members, and the intense faces of engaged audience members who didn't appear to just be there for the spectacle. After about 15 minutes of music, Michaelson strode confidently and calmly onto the stage.

He didn't speak for a moment, just took in the congregation with a small, beatific smile on his face. When he finally spoke, it was a good thing he had a mic on. He kept it warm and low, like they were having a cozy, private chat.

"Friends, I stand before you with a heart full of conflict. And, before I can get to the wondrous Divine, I need to address the horrible things. I need to address things we all learned yesterday."

I leaned forward hungrily. I didn't know what I expected him to do. I wouldn't have believed any contrition he showed, but I might have enjoyed watching him cry. Even if it were mostly fake, I'd have known there was enough fear of getting found out in it to make it not *entirely* fake. And he did look super contrite and burdened. So, maybe...

I hadn't noticed Riles was also leaning forward until zie whispered, "Cry, you fucker. *Beg.*"

Michaelson didn't cry. He didn't beg. But he did sound Very Concerned Indeed. "Like all of you, yesterday I learned that someone had been contaminating the cures we were sending out into the world to save people from beat down flu." He began to pace, but it looked controlled; he wasn't a man driven by emotion. "And, like all of you, I learned that one of our own, one we had trusted and had recently even given a position of authority had been involved in the unforgivable act of murder."

He paused. He let his head hang a moment, and then he looked up at his audience, and something had shifted. I could see he had an answer that he was confident in. He picked up his pace, he looked at the audience more, he got a little louder.

"Friends, I spent yesterday wondering who would burn down the plant where we manufactured cures, but where also—I've since learned—someone was contaminating those same cures. I spent the day looking for some kind of information to help the police determine who was behind the contamination. And, finally, I spent the last part of the day wondering how we could have been so wrong about Shay Brice."

He stood still as he repeated, "Shay Brice."

Fuck. I saw where this was going.

And then he was on the move again, working the crowd with a little more energy, with a touch of passion. "Now, I think we can all agree that we hope, when we gather together as a church, as a community, that we can trust each other. We hope that each person we meet with here has a heart as full of true intent as our own. We serve together and worship together. And we who lead understandably treat things more like, well, a church instead of a business. Even the parts that are about the business of keeping our buildings and our works running. And for that, I must apologize." He didn't sound very apologetic.

"You see, if I'd treated parts of this like a business, we would have done a thorough background check into those we put into...I don't want to say 'important' positions, because that belies the fact that we're all doing important things here when we work to spread the Light. But positions where broken trust can do more harm." He paused a moment to let people feel their own importance and to understand the importance of trust.

"I would have discovered that Shay Brice had a troubled childhood. That she has connections that, well, I'll leave it to the police to untangle all those ties. I can't tell you all about them, because I don't understand them. But!" He got almost jovial. "But what I do understand is that all of yesterday's troubles lead back to Shay. That, now that she is in police custody, we can return to our good work, to our worship, and to our philanthropic efforts without worry. Just with a little more wisdom."

He smiled broadly. "We can return to creating cures that are safe. We can work knowing that, now, our leaders and others in positions of trust with Divine Community Church have been carefully looked into, vetted as if the business of spreading the Light were as important as any worldly business out there. Because we know it is." He held his arms open and slightly down, like he was finishing a dance routine with a bit of a ta-da move, but kept his face up and beaming. "We can move forward again," he proclaimed.

And all those people, hungry for the miracles he brought, exhaled in relief. This story was believable enough. They were free to accept those miracles without conflict.

As if sensing that it was the miracles they wanted, he added, "And surely we can at least feel confident in the righteousness of those who've been manifesting the power to heal lately, can't we?"

The audience agreed. Some murmured and some shouted, but none of them were going to turn that down.

"Now." He was clearly transitioning from the topic of guilt, and he'd not really groveled at all. Dammit.

Riley snorted with disgust. Then sighed and noted, "I see that SPD are on their way to get info from this asshole as soon as he gets off the stage."

Well, that was something. Not that it was something truly useful, but...Yay for SPD trying?

Michaelson's voice was softer again, but free of conflict or concern. "Now that we've addressed the horrible things. Let's talk about the Divine." He paused with a soft smile, eyes closed and face slightly upturned for a moment, as if the Divine were there, honoring him with its presence.

When he spoke again, he did so with the hushed tones of a man describing the sacred, his voice a low rumble that welcomed us all in. "My dear friends, I come to you with...something amazing. And I suppose we shouldn't be surprised. After all, we've seen how some of us have been blessed with the power to heal, to do great miracles on behalf of the Divine." He paused, his own healing hands slightly lifted, and gave everyone a satisfied smile as the congregation murmured again. Confirmed, just in case anyone listening was stupid, that, oh, they certainly knew about those miracles.

"So, I trust that you'll believe me when I tell you about the..." He choked up. Apparently. "The very special experience I had last night. A gift from the Divine, a comfort beyond hope, at the end of a challenging day that left me wondering about my ability to do the work correctly." He paused again, eyes shining, taking in the congregation, who hung wide- and hungry-eyed on his every word.

In our lair, we were hanging too, but I suspect our eyes were much narrower than those of his followers.

"Last night, as I sat meditating on the Divine, wondering what I might say to keep inspiring you all on your path in spite of the horrible news, I was visited." The man took one of his beloved pauses, and you could hear the whispers of the congregation. His voice got stronger. "Visited by pale-skinned, white-clothed messengers from the heavens, sent by the Divine to direct me. To tell me that the most important thing for us to focus on was peace."

Riles and I looked at each other, eyes wide and worried. Zie was shaking zir head slowly. What the actual fuck...

We sat through a pretty typical sermon on peace, or I assumed it was typical because it didn't hinge on aliens. Which was my main criteria these days for things being normal-people kind of typical. And I almost stopped paying attention, but he got back to the good stuff (aka the worrying as hell stuff) as he wrapped up.

"And all of this I've said about peace? I want to take just a few seconds to point out...Well, I hate to call anyone an enemy, but I want you to consider what you've seen over the last few weeks. I want you to think of the chaos, the selfishness, the crimes committed by the so-called 'heroic hackers' out there." He actually used his fingers to make scare quotes. "I want you to ask yourself whether all that is in line with the peace we've talked about today and often in the past, or with the righteousness we talk about all the time. Can these really be heroes, any of them, if they're bringing this sort of chaos?"

He paused a short beat, as if giving them time to ask themselves right away, before delivering his closing thought. "Now, you know I hate to end on dark thoughts, and that's part of why I've saved this for the end. Those heavenly messengers? They are coming. The miracles you've seen me do are nothing compared to what we'll see when they come. And what I want you to ask yourselves, once you see the light—or, rather, the darkness—about those hackers, as we wait for the day of the blessed arrival, is this: When they come, if those who aren't part of our community refuse to open their arms to these saviors, what will you do? If they threaten, whether by their hateful attitudes and pride or by violence, to drive away these helps sent from the heavens, what will you do? How far will you go to move forward the cause of the Divine, the cause of peace?" He looked into the crowd as if he were looking for the answers in their eyes.

I mumbled, "How are those not dark thoughts?"

And then he sounded full-on revival tent preacher, just like in movies, his volume and energy escalating with every word. "I want you to examine in your hearts how you've reacted to attempts at peace, how you've stood up for what's right in the past. And I want you to find the light in you that lets you do *whatever* is necessary to make sure that this whole world is engulfed in the cleansing fires of peace and truth!"

The congregation lost their shit and, after some arms wide and prayer hands gestures, Michaelson exited stage right.

I realized my mouth was hanging open in shock. He'd practically admitted he was part of the Peaceforgers thing with his "fires of peace" bit. Oh, and also...

I closed my mouth and cleared my throat. "So, uh, I'm not being paranoid. He's preparing them to accept invasion, isn't he?"

"Because I'm known for my clear head and complete lack of paranoia," Riley pointed out.

Dammit. We really needed Bryan...

But we also really needed to make sure more people saw this. It kind of seemed like this should help make our case, or at least be one more thing to point to when we said "told you so"...if the

Peacemakers they would put in our heads still let us do things like that.

We blasted email out to everyone who'd gotten previous "aliens!" emails. And, because we'd noticed some people on the secret forum setting the groundwork for telling everyone about the aliens, we messaged those people. We pretended we were also just random hackers in on the secret who thought they might want to have this new, fun tidbit of info.

Whee.

As we ate another of our non-stop "just add boiling water" meals, we took a moment away from our computers. But there were no moments away from the problems.

"So," I stared into my Styrofoam container of hot noodle food, trying to see if I had an answer as I asked, "what do you think their timeline is?" I looked up to see Rye's face scrunched up in thought.

"You want a guess?" zie asked. "Because, darling, I hate to disappoint, but I'm not actually privy to all things extraterrestrial." Zie sighed dramatically and murmured, "Such a disappointment."

I laughed a little at the dramatics, then said, "Yeah. It's a safe bet you have a better read on human behavior than I do."

Zie grinned and winked, "Ah, but these are aliens. Aren't you the one who's said being Autistic in this world makes you feel like an alien? So maybe you're the one who ought to guess at this question."

Airily I deflected, "Totally different species of alien." And then I had to tease zir a little. "They're more the aloof super villain type of alien. So, again, more your speed."

"Hm. Yes," zie nodded like it was serious truth I was laying down. "I see what you mean. Okay then!" And then zie took a moment to consider before opining. "I think the intelligent student of human nature—which I'm going to suggest they should be after decades of trying to pretend to be us—would take a few months."

"A few months?"

"Yeah. Because you want to make sure the church kids are so used to the idea of you showing up that they don't freak at the not-quite-human alien invasion." Riles paused a breath, then said, "That also gives some time to make sure the press—and the general public—get wind of the whole thing. It gets seeping into non-follower minds too, right? Maybe everyone freaks a little less when they show up." Zie shrugged. "Maybe the church even gets new converts when it turns out this wasn't just another overblown promise from a religious leader."

We both paused then. I assumed I wasn't the only one whose brain was playing a montage of similar historic and recent promises or actions from religions or cults. Mass suicides, some massacres of non-believers, and plenty of "what I really meant" sermons after specified dates came and went without the promised noteworthy events. I thought of souls attached to comets and wondered if they'd come back with the spaceships.

I shook my head to clear the daydreaming. "That makes sense. Let's go with that. Keep it in mind whilst we try to figure out how to stop them or at least get ourselves safe over the next few months."

Riles just nodded, looking a bit dazed. Guess I wasn't the only one with no clear idea how to do any of that stuff. Awesome...

Quick call from Lex. "They hit someone else this morning. They busted in a little louder there, but they also got guns in their faces. So, maybe they'll be more cautious next time?"

Riles and I took some time to make sure we knew our plans if they came to check out our suite. We set Ada up to keep an eye on some cameras that might give us warning if the goons were about to hit our building. We even did a couple drills to make sure we hadn't missed anything. I liked to think Bry would have been proud. Amused at our toddler-like level of capability, but proud.

CHAPTER 5

My disgust was shifting from others to myself. I couldn't think of anything real to do to get the boys back. My brain wasn't trained or wired or whatever for this. But, if I didn't think of something...If neither Riles nor I could think of something, who would save them? *Or their bodies*, said the shitty voice of reality in my head. *Maybe there are better things to take fruitless actions on*, it suggested. I did my best to ignore it, which I guessed meant I was still firmly in the denial phase of the grief cycle. Peaceforger bastards better watch out for when I moved into the anger phase...

I don't know if it was desperation for something meaningful to do or caring about Jonny (probably both), but I figured I could at least make sure Jonny's family were still safe. Fortunately, I already had practice hacking Jonny, so it was easy enough (relatively speaking) to get into his files and figure out who his contact was for keeping an eye on his family.

I used his mobile to send a message:

Everybody still ok? Need anything?

Figured no good would be served by mentioning that I wasn't Jonny, that Jonny was at least captured and possibly dead. Unless his family asked for pics of him or something, I could easily enough keep sending money or whatever. Make sure there was still a chance for a happy family reunion. (*Or keep them okay in memory of him*, piped up shitty reality voice.)

Jonny's person, who was just listed as EP in his contacts, replied quickly:

All good dude. $ you sent gonna last. Will msg if change.

Right. That was good. A bit less involved and action-y feeling than I'd hoped, but good. Even if I was disappointed at how easily that particular so-called action item had gone. Even if I was back to trying to figure out what to do a little too quickly, dammit.

Riles cut off my impending moping. "We have so much food, including many little bags of chips." Zie tore into a massive box and tossed something cheese flavored at me. "Which means it's time for us to settle in and hack some shit. Or follow some bitches on cameras. Or...whatever."

"What about yours and Bryan's families?"

Zie narrowed zir eyes. "What about those assholes?"

"Well, I just thought maybe, like Jonny's family, they might need some safekeeping?"

Zie snorted. "Yeah, we tried that."

"You what?" I hadn't heard about this.

"In spite of what they think, we're not actually pure evil. So we tried to send them quick messages about avoiding shots or whatever." Zir voice was as sour as zir relationship with zir family. "The replies were dismissive and shaming. And neither of us are welcome to contact them again, so."

"So." I sighed. "I'm sorry, poppet. That's shitty."

With a mix of righteous smugness and aloof dismissiveness, zie arched zir eyebrows and confirmed, "It is. And that's why their fates are in their own hands now. I have better family to protect."

I lightly punched zir shoulder. "Damned straight you do!" And then I deflated a little. "So. Next up?" If I'd had a hard time keeping straight all we needed to do when there were twice as many of us, I was totally overwhelmed now.

Riles must have made a list of zir own to supplement that one we'd made together, because zir eyes scanned zir screen in a list-reading way, and zie said, "Unless you've got some kind of new idea..." Zie sighed, then added, "Which would be an amazing development. Waiting for PerpTrack to find the boys or even that alien traitor isn't giving me the sort of fast service I expect in our modern age."

I echoed zir sigh. "I wish, poppet. I fucking wish." I pulled my packet of snacks open and crunched sullenly. Stupid technology. Stupid Katja brain.

"In that case, next on my list is figuring out what's up with Isa." Zie waggled zir eyebrows. "Want to stalk a pale hottie with me?"

Isa. Supposed heretic. Maybe. If Zane the Betrayer could be trusted when they'd said they were going to go see their heretic leader right before they met us at the fueling station...

The action item there was to check on both her and people who visited her. We didn't really know what we were looking for, but something had to help us figure out if Isa was really a heretic, right? We figured, if she wasn't a heretic, she might be the person helping Zane get the word out about how to get us. If she *was* a heretic, at the very least, she might want to know that Zane actually wasn't. At the most? Maybe there was a secret heretic army that would help us kick Peaceforger arse. Dream big, Katja!

We did rock-paper-scissors to decide who got to follow Isa's movements, hack her files, and look into her phone records. With the fact that she might be the one who'd helped Zane sell us out, we were both hungry for her blood. You know, if she *was* that one. We were both also just hungry for some "normal" hacking. Something we could pretend was just like...well, just like a month or so ago. No, exactly a month ago.

I paused, my hand in the air, no shape thrown, as I realized that. A month ago today, my building had been blown up. Just a month. Not the years it seemed. Fuck. I sighed, got over myself, mumbled an apology. Threw paper whilst Riles threw scissors.

When Riley won, zie chomped at the air like zie was biting Isa and let out a victorious whoop. "I'm going to eat her alive." Zie paused, then said more reasonably, "If she's guilty, of course. No wanton devouring, of course."

"Of course," I agreed with a little less than full sincerity. "Never anything wanton about you," I said with a wink.

Until we could get Zane, and we'd get to that, Isa might have to do. You know, if she was guilty.

Anyway, that left me to find and follow Isa's visitors. Though it quickly became clear Rye was going to have to help on that one when zie was done with Isa. She was a popular woman. Even just looking at the footage from Saturday (yesterday? just yesterday? really?) and so far today, she'd had at least a dozen people in and out. And it kind of seemed like every visitor she'd had, starting from about the time we'd been attacked at the fueling station, looked on edge...even before the cops had grabbed Shay or Michaelson had promised his congregants an invasion.

"Riles, you think this looks like a lot of people worried that they've been betrayed?" I turned my portable's screen towards zir and stepped through flagged positions in the footage from the camera outside Isa's door, shots of people coming and going.

Zie leaned in, studied the footage, moved it around a bit zirself, then nodded slowly. "It's possible. I wouldn't make a call based on that, but, sure. Maybe." Zie sounded the slightest bit disappointed at the possibility.

I jostled zir shoulder. "Cheer up, poppet. If she's innocent, we still have Zane to destroy, plus maybe a mess of heretics ready to help us. Yay!" I forced extra jolliness into my voice.

With a snorted laugh, Riles admitted, "It's okay. You aren't the one who ruined my dream. So far, I can't find any sign of her interacting with SWS or Divine Community. No messages that sound like her being nefarious. Or even sneaky." Zie leaned back. "In bad news, that might also mean she's not part of a secret group. We might be entirely on the wrong track."

I paused my effort of grabbing face shots of Isa's visitors to use for IDing them and considered the current apparent dead end. "Does she live with someone?"

Riles shook zir head. "Not that I can tell."

"Did you hack her webcam yet?" I chewed the inside of my cheek. "If they're worried about being exposed, maybe we can catch them talking about it?" I hoped she'd uncovered it since the night before.

"Um..." Rye's fingers clattered over the keys. "And, okay, webcam acquired. I'll just keep this in a window and eavesdrop while I work." Zie threw the window up onto the big screen and leaned closer to zir computer. "Though it seems like we finally found someone smart enough to cover their cam and even muffle their mic." Zie made a grumpy sound, then said, "Well, I still need to actually see places she's been before today. I'm not dead ended yet, bitches!"

I nodded. "Yeah, she hasn't left since Zane's visit." I stretched, took a deep breath, and got back to my own digital identifying and tracking.

And there were no good shortcuts when trying to figure out which of Isa's visitors might be on the side of evil. I knew I couldn't discount someone just because they worked for a known asshole. It had sounded to me, from shit Zane had said (though everything they'd said had to be suspect now), that Peaceforgers could just get assigned jobs once they said they were committed to the cause. Logically, to not get caught, even the heretics would have to pretend to commit. And, just as logically, they could end up working for SWS or Divine Community whether they wanted to or not.

So, with that in mind, I was going to need to dig a bit into each of them, going to need to follow them. But, again, unless I saw them cackling over the bodies of children with beat down flu or gleefully ramming Peacemakers into old people, I wasn't sure what I could see that would tip me off. And I couldn't farm this out to my remote comrades, because they could end up following a similar set of people and land back at Zane, then Bryan, then the rest of us.

So, I looked anyway, because who knew? Because maybe there *was* damning enough footage, and who else would find it? And I was still looking when Riley admitted zie couldn't figure out Isa and started picking up some of her visitors. And still looking when Holo-Kitty popped up (which was when I first realized we hadn't heard from her in a number of hours).

"You guys, don't hate me. I...I still haven't found anything useful." Her little 3D avatar drooped. "I'm really sorry." And then she stood up straight and set her jaw, determined. "But I'll keep looking. I just didn't want you to think I'd been erased or whatever."

I said, "Thanks, Kitty."

And Riles said, "Thanks, baby. I know you can do this!"

And then she blinked out. And I noticed we'd been at this for hours. With no successes. And no new snacks. I moaned and flopped backwards.

"I have chocolate and protein coming for you," Riles assured. "And maybe we can switch tracks for a while."

"Okay. Yeah. Good call." I grinned. "Thanks for being the reasonable and responsible one. I'll do it next time." I laughed softly at myself. "Maybe we just need to have a constant stream of chocolate coming this way until we win." I got serious, took a deep breath, rubbed at my forehead. "Is there anything useful at all?"

"I was thinking we should look for patterns. So, it seems reasonable to assume Isa is important, right? She was the one person Zane went to see right before we left, and she gets a lot of visitors."

I nodded.

"It also seems reasonable to assume that not all visitors would necessarily be important. Maybe none of them. Right?"

Again, I nodded. "How do we work with that?"

"Well..." Zie clearly hadn't gotten that far yet. But zie got there before I jumped in. "What if we map their messages and movements, try to see places they intersect or mundane messages that more than one of them gets. That sort of thing." Zie typed as zie talked. "I'm going to have Ada scan the stuff we have and look for that shit. I like my brain, but I know that I don't have the processing power your fake AI has."

I made a shocked face, mouthed the word "fake," and put my hands over the mics on the machines joined together to be Ada. As if the mics weren't disabled. As if they were her ears and she had feelings to hurt. Because I'm very mature. But, more reasonably, I said, "Yeah. Fair point. I mean, if *we* were sneaking around, we'd be too clever for meat brains to figure out." I gestured around at where we were. Clearly, we were kicking ass at sneaking around.

After we paused for food, Rye fell into a fabulous rabbit hole of AI research. I was a bit jealous, even knowing the stakes (saving the virtual girlfriend) and the complications (who was, at the very least, a *conscious* AI and was currently living on an alien computer, so who even knew if she'd translate to our stuff?).

Because, me? I was back to the same task at which I'd been failing for...it had to have been at least a week now.

Yes, I was back to trying to hack the satellites. And I knew I wasn't going to have any good luck when I suddenly couldn't even get into the NOAA satellite we'd been using for a while now. It was frustrating and embarrassing. Though, I noted with some shame, less embarrassing with just Riles to find out; at least I wasn't going to drive off the boy I liked with this proof that my brain might be too stupid to admire.

I considered going back to tracking Isa's many visitors, but my stubbornness rose up. I continued to beat my head against the fucking satellite issue.

When Riley took a break from zir research, I was more than happy to take a break as well. In the name of preparing for the scenario where we actually had to take some fight-related action against the impending Peaceforger "arrival," we decided the best way to do that whilst also doing something that might not suck was to practice with the drones and other remote-controlled fighting machines. Boo-ya! Or something like that. After all, we were just starting, which meant the training simulations. You know, vidgames. Excellent!

Except that it turned out that the training simulations were just what you'd reasonably expect: first person point of view as you drove or flew things. And I kind of don't love that part of vidgames. In fact, I fucking hate flight simulators...and driving games. *HATE*. So, yeah, all the unmanned vehicle training made me want to stab myself in the face. Did I mention *HATE*? The only way it could have sucked more would have been if the interface were a fucking slider puzzle.

I should also probably mention that I *sucked* at flight simulators and driving games. Which may or may not have anything to do with why I hated them. So, might-not-suck action option turned out to suck. At least for me. Turned out Riles was secretly kick-ass, which would have been good news if zie weren't entirely not graceful about being better than me. Bastard.

Whilst I grimly, clumsily put myself through the paces with the drones, I tried to make my brain manifest other ways to be useful. Half of my mumbled "come on; just work, asshole" moments were aimed at the drones, and half were aimed at my brain.

Before I'd managed to shame my brain into bloody bits, an alert pinged on my machine. When I glanced to see which of my dozens of automated tasks had turned something up, I couldn't believe our luck. "Oh. Hell yes!"

Riles gave me a confused look, which was fair, because I'd just had yet another seriously disappointing drone run. I had to blink a moment and remind myself that, for better and worse, even zie couldn't actually read my mind.

"Sorry. Right." I gave zir my full attention. "You won't believe which of my keyword trackers just got hits on an FBI messenger conversation." I grinned, hoping zie wouldn't make too many guesses before I could cut to the chase.

Bless zir heart, zie tried to puzzle it out. "FBI. So, that means something massive or across state lines, right? Then obviously, something to do with Demo Day, the tainted cures, or the alien email we sent. Which means..." Zie rolled zir eyes. "Which means way too many keywords I could guess. Which would delay my pleasure." Zie threw zir arms in the air like some mad deity. "Pleasure me now, woman!"

After we paused to giggle, I slowly, clearly said, "Under. Water. Door."

Zir mouth hung open. Zie recovered and whispered, "Seriously?!"

I nodded and we both laughed. At last! This was just the sort of weird shit we needed the powers that be to find and confirm from the allegations we'd sent them.

I pulled up the message thread and re-enacted it, using two voices.

Voice One was kind of meaty sounding. "Uh, sir, you got a sec?"

I turned, as if Voice Two had been there physically, facing Voice One. Voice Two was gruff and impatient. "It's Sunday. Better be good."

I turned back. "I think maybe you should just see this, sir." I showed Riles my screen, pictures of the underwater door from the inside (a view we'd never seen) with rubble to both sides of it, and one from the outside that was clearer than Rye's robot fishes had gotten us.

I paused so we could exchange quiet, excited scream faces. I also saved those images locally to a folder that was basically like my digital scrapbook of this whole thing we'd been doing.

Voice Two was still gruff, but less impatient. "Confirm what I'm looking at?"

Voice One was nervous about sounding like a crackpot, but he knew at least he had photos on his side. "Sir, it appears to be an underwater door. Opens from a secret basement level under the SWS HQ into Puget Sound."

Voice Two had never quite seen anything like this. "Well, I'll be damned." He recovered his boss-like demeanor to ask, "And was there a craft or scuba gear nearby?"

Voice One was relieved to be taken seriously, so he could get back to sounding like a confident, if slightly meaty, agent. "No, sir. Not that we've found yet."

I nodded on behalf of Voice Two and ordered, "Okay. Keep me apprised, agent."

I stopped. End of scene. The Oscar, obviously, goes to me! That was really it anyway. Except now I could see the word of the door rippling out through all those involved in the investigation who had clearance. I hadn't turned off my tracker, and it let me know that the agent was telling his peers and that the boss was telling his peers and superiors.

We squealed happily, viciously. This must surely help our argument, must surely prove that SWS were something more than just ambitious suits.

Rye pivoted to zir computer. "We have to see if this is changing the actions of the people who got the alien email."

"Yeah..." There was something like sanity trying to worm its way into my work process, slowing me down. My gaze drifted to the two webcam windows on our big screen. Zane's still showed an empty flat, and Isa's was still covered. So, you know, super useful. But I still stared at them a while. I eventually realized Riles was doing the same.

Zie sighed, and, as if zie'd already forgotten the underwater door victory, furrowed zir brow with confusion. "What I still don't get is...Why the hell didn't Zane rat us out at the fueling station? And why didn't they hang on to the boys' mobiles? There's no way they didn't know there could be useful info on the mobiles."

I stared at Zane's tiny place, walls plastered with a collage of pictures. It looked like they were all amazingly beautiful nature scenes, the kind of thing that pollution and greed had pretty much made into memories these days except in a few places. I felt a moment of deep disgust with humanity, and I wondered if maybe Zane's treachery was rooted in the same sort of feeling. I chewed my lip and suggested, "Maybe they're just too cowardly to stick with a side?"

"Yeeeaaah..." Riles shook zir head, as if trying to let the topic go.

I sighed, and my brain let me in on the sane approach it had been trying to sort out. "Anyway, I think our remote comrades can still be trusted, and I think it's time to ask them for help. Ask them to help look into what people who got our alien email have done about it. That's as safe as any of the SWS stuff, right?"

Zie was still staring at the useless webcam windows on the big screen, but then zie blinked and turned back to me. "Yep!" Zie grinned. "I keep meaning to do something about the fact that it's way ridiculouser—shut up, grammar cop—for the two of us to do work that would feel like a lot even if...if we had everyone. So, yeah. Let's figure out how to share the load so we don't risk humanity."

I nodded, thinking. I was pretty sure knowing who'd gotten the email, or even being able to trace the email back to some kind of sender, wouldn't let them put any of us in danger of being found. Just 'cause I trusted them to fight the right bad guys didn't mean I wanted them to know who I was in the meat. "I'll write the email."

So, Rye got back to kicking ass with the drones (since we were sure Bryan would agree we shouldn't share that particular task given how utterly shit I was at it), and I wrote an email for each of our four living remote comrades. I gave them all the full list of recipients, but in four totally different orders, asking them each to start at the top of their list. I hoped they'd find loads of tiny, secret moves being made.

But, like I kept reminding myself, hope wasn't a strategy (or an action plan or whatever...I see you working on a new motto, brain), so I begged my brain to try to figure out how we few, we hacky few, we band of coders, might somehow beat the technologically advanced aliens whose computers we couldn't access at all yet. Argh!

I idly skimmed bugHunt whilst I thought...And discovered there was a thread devoted to talking about that Katja person (aka me) whom SWS had been accusing of all the bombs and leaks, trying to figure out why the hell SWS had it in for her (aka me). And given the most active people in that conversation— which was already surfacing some basic hacks of the info I considered public and/or had put out there to be found if I *did* get hacked—were our remote comrades? I figured we'd better hurry and find as much as possible for all those people to do. I wasn't so cocky as to assume my cover stories and defenses were impenetrable. Especially since Jonny had cracked it all...

I felt myself hold my breath a moment at the thought of Jonny. I willed myself not to cry. I distracted myself by saying, "Hey, poppet, did you see the whole Katja thread on the forum?"

Zie froze and turned zir head slowly, eyes wide. Zie understood the danger. "Oh shit, girl. Seriously?" Zie regained momentum, rushed across the keys to pull up the thread in question. "Well...at least it calmed down in the minutes since you sent out your email to the troops?" Zie cringed, then did weak jazz hands. "Yay?"

I snorted out a laugh and shook my hands in the air too as I flatly replied, "Yay." Then I shook my head. "I guess now I can also spend some time making sure there's nothing to find and trying to derail them." Suddenly, my heart was in my throat and I was blinking back tears. "I just want to get to the end of this shit and be able to be myself. Even if that doesn't include my old 'Net self."

Riles shifted towards me, probably intent on offering comfort, but I felt myself unexpectedly bolting to my feet. It was like something in me thought it could outrun all this shit. "I, uh, I think I just need to take a walk." My feet moved, a quick pace, carrying me through the pseudo-rooms in the suite. Even if I counted the laughable space of the bathroom, it wasn't anywhere near as much square footage as the warehouse or even my flat, but it was enough. It had to be.

My brain was a useless jumble, like some kind of rapid flicker of disjointed images. Memories and bits of problems, flashes of incomplete plans and anxiety anxiety anxiety. Fuck. My head felt like it had a thick vise closing in from the outside and a core of whirring lightness. The thickness was trying to crawl down through my body in tensing muscles. And some primal instinct desperately pushed me to find a small, dark space. Fuck. It had been a long time since I'd had a full-on meltdown.

Back when things had been normal, back when there weren't mind control plots and aliens and all that bullshit...back when a whole fucking world wasn't hanging on the things I did, when it had been just a side effect of living in a world that didn't care to make space for people who weren't entirely typical, who didn't fit the so-called default...I'd just go with the meltdown, let it release the tension or whatever had led to it. But now...

Fuck. This flipping out over how I couldn't risk a meltdown was just adding to the tension. I tried to breathe carefully, tried to focus on how lucky I'd been that this hadn't happened the last month.

I startled, realized I was in the living room again, when Riles softly said, "Baby, I can duck out to check on escape plans. You do what you need to do."

"But I can't." I managed a choked whisper. "Not until this is all done."

Lovingly, zie said, "Bullshit. Take care of you." And zie took zir laptop and ducked out of the suite.

I didn't know that most other kids didn't have meltdowns until the first time I did it in front of Bryan and Riles. And, because they were little kids, they weren't mean, but they also didn't pretend not to see it or pretend it was typical. It might look like a typical tantrum to an adult when it's a kid doing it, but the difference was obvious to discerning kids (at least for kid Bry and kid Rye). And, because I was a little kid, when they asked me questions about it, I answered frankly. So, as much as someone who wasn't on the spectrum could get it, my people did.

However.

I'd lived in this world long enough that I'd developed a sense of shame around anyone else seeing or hearing my meltdowns. But Riles had been right that letting the meltdown happen was the good choice. And I could keep it quiet enough that the sound was unlikely to be noteworthy to anyone outside the suite.

So, I took a blanket and pillow to help muffle and pad things, turned off lights, and pushed a bedside table out a bit so I could have a pocket of space surrounded by two walls and some furniture. And I just...let it happen.

And, a while later, on the other side of the meltdown, I felt both exhausted and lighter. Relieved.

I sat, leaned against a wall, and just enjoyed the silence. It was both inside and outside my head. Magic...

When I felt like I could be around another human, I messaged Riley.

Zie returned quickly and gave me a little smile. "I have some takeout on the way with an assortment of foods I know you love best." Zie tilted zir head, considering me. "You feeling better?

I just nodded. I was still a little fuzzy, but I felt pretty sure food and a little time would help that. And, in my head, the manic flashing images had rolled back to a normal speed...or what I considered normal. I might not have any new ideas, but I felt pretty sure that I was now in a far better state to follow through if I did get some.

After massive cartons of fries and an equally massive slice of chocolate cake, I was only picking at the pizza as I worked. I wasn't making any exciting headway, and I hadn't come up with any new plans, but I felt like I was settling into a familiar space. And we hadn't even been in our new lair for two days, but it also felt like we were building a routine somehow. Which meant we were as close to my happy place as we could be, you know, all things considered.

To be fair, Riley had a triumph that was also a win for me in the whole "for fuck's sake please end this thread about Katja" effort. Basically, after a little bit of humoring and not openly opposing things, Riles posted:

Soooo, no offense to anyone, including Katja the Boring AF, but aren't there actual villains? And we're wasting our time on someone who's already been harassed by SWS and had their hackers up in her shit?

It didn't take long for everyone else to buy into apHellion's view point. The talk shifted to trying to figure out if maybe SWS was scrambling to use her (aka me) as a scapegoat because they already knew there was a whistleblower in their midst who might have been behind the bombing. (How fucking great would it be if they assumed that vicious bitch CFO Williams somehow deserved the blame for all that as well?) It might even have been a real shift 'cause nobody rose to the bait when I messaged them privately (using Jonny's account, not my new one...or my old one, obviously) to ask if we were definitely off the Katja thing, or if they thought we should keep quietly digging.

Hurrah!

I didn't let down my guard, but you better believe I slept better knowing that.

Slept, again, to the sounds of Rye and Kitty whispering in the loo. Catching up at the end of another day, almost like life was normal. Bully for them.

CHAPTER 6

We didn't get to sleep uninterrupted. Ada woke us with an alert that was clearly set up by Riley. Because I'd never programmed Ada to say, "Results, bitches!"

I woke slightly, looked around, and whispered, "Did something happen?"

"Did wha?" zie mumbled.

I was closing my eyes to get back to sleep, because I'd probably just heard something in a dream, when Ada said it again.

"Results, bitches!"

I sat up. "Right. That was definitely a thing."

Riles giggled quietly. "And that's why I set the alarm to go off again if not acknowledged within a few minutes."

As I rolled towards a computer to dismiss the alert, zie reached out to hold me back. "Nooooo! One more. Please?"

Who was I to deny zir some joy? So I froze a moment, arm reached out, until we got one last "Results, bitches!"

With a blanket to wrap around us both, Rye scooted over by me to see what Ada had found.

In short (because who the hell needs the long?), there was, indeed, a potentially meaningful pattern in the messages and movements of Isa and the worried visitors she'd had on Carbonite Day. Just as we'd hoped. It hadn't been easy to find because it was just a word or two, and it varied based on the first letter of the recipient's first name *and* the day of the week *and* the weather in Seattle. Yeah, seriously, the weather.

"Well, it doesn't say whether it's a heretics meeting or a book club...but it's definitely something." I chewed a nail, trying to see if there was more there.

"Of course, it also doesn't say whether it's just them or a bigger Peaceforger meeting." Rye sighed. "Time to figure out who some other Peaceforgers are and see if they were there too."

"Whereas my smart next move is to look at cameras pointed at doors where they're meeting and see if they all skulk in cautiously...all trench-coated and shit..." I was totally crossing my fingers for trench coats.

I opened my camera tracking program, grabbed the data from Ada about the who and the where of these possible clandestine meetings, and got to work.

There were no trench coats or obviously furtive glances. The Universe is a horrible and disappointing place. In fact, there was nothing obvious in any sort of helpful way. Yeah, we're still not friends, Universe.

All on my own, no help from the Universe, I hunted down mobile numbers of the Peaceforgers who were meeting. And then I checked to see if they actually stayed in the bookstore they were theoretically hanging out in. Which, per the cellular points and Wi-Fi hotspots they pinged, they didn't. But they did leave from the store, when they finally left, with books in hand. So...okay, that was promising. Promising-ish.

If I'd had to guess, I'd say they'd gone out through the employee back corridors that linked the bookstore with other shops in the complex. I overlaid a map of the complex on the results of the route their mobiles said they took. Looked like they'd ended up in a shop that sold bondage gear.

A quick search showed me the shop had a basement that was available for events and advertised as having complete privacy and discreet staff. Perfect for play without shame *or* for secret heretic meetings, right?

I nudged Riles. "Hey, start here and work backwards to figure out who might be aliens and maybe even heretics." Because the Universe wouldn't even give me aliens who wore lazy disguises and painted H's on their heads to indicate they were heretics instead of just members of a secret BDSM club. Ugh.

Another quick report from Lex. One more of our decoy lairs had been hit. No one hurt on what you might call our team, but one of the goons got a knife in the leg. I clearly couldn't claim to be a pacifist when I definitely felt vicious glee at that report.

"There's something going on," Riles replied, eyes narrow with suspicion when I told zir the latest.

"Huh?" was my smart response.

"Why the hell aren't they rushing through all our places? We turned off location services on all the vehicles, but there's no way it's taking them a full day to find potential lairs." Zie started typing. "Here, I'll tell you how long it takes me to find our people knowing only what the Peaceforgers would know."

I didn't bother typing as I countered, "Yeah, but they'd get a lot of hits for new people checking in Saturday. Or within a day or two before as well, if they're trying to be clever like us."

Riley sat back. "Shit. I wonder how many innocents have had the goons bust in." Zie sighed. "And they'd also have to wonder if we were moving every day. I retract my suspicions. At least a little. But we'd do better," zie smugly assured me.

I nodded, then added, "Plus, they'll also need to have more people actively protecting the SWS execs, Michaelson and other Divine Community big wigs, and probably other important properties and players we don't know about."

"So we probably spend the next few months, or however long until we get rid of them, waiting for them to hit us?"

I just gave zir a bit of a resigned shrug, and I got the same in reply.

Dammit. I really hated uncertainty.

Our remote comrades were also reporting in, letting us know as they looked into each person who'd gotten our "aliens are real!" email. As we'd hoped, events of the last couple days had helped our case. Had made the recipients a little more willing to consider the possibility that our message wasn't just paranoid fiction.

Cures proven tainted? Yes. So, more people were making it through reading the email.

Divine Community employee arrested for ordering the gunning down of a couple guys right after our email went out?

Guys who were arguably trying to get out of town? Caught on video where it sure looked like one of the people on Team Guns had a crazy tongue? Yes. So, more people were doing a little more quietly looking at the church and the DNA.

The leader of Divine Community talking about something that might be interpreted as aliens whilst doing some healing that, honestly, it was more comfortable to frame as advanced tech than as mystical? Yes. So, more people were having hush-hush, strictly theoretical conversations with scientists who specialized in topics that might have something to do with extraterrestrial stuff. And also having less-theoretical conversations with other sets of scientists about what sort of tech could heal like that.

And underwater door? Yes. Well. Now there were people we could continue to feel good about, at least in terms of them being less likely to tattle on us and more likely to act, people who were having secret meetings with military and law enforcement agencies.

But there were other people who had subtly but completely shifted to looking at how they could make a buck or get some power if this was true. People trying to get hands on Peacemakers and pieces of the door, trying to quietly build secret teams full of brainy people. Sadly, they also had the specs for Peacemakers and instructions for removal that we'd provided—because we were decent and wanted to save people— to help them move ahead as they tried to figure out how to have influence over those same people. Cool...Except the opposite of cool. Traitorous assholes.

I used each report on a person to update our mailing list. I desperately hoped we'd never have to send another sneaky email again. But, if we did, we'd now have more data to help make our choices. Maybe we'd do better at guessing the people who definitely shouldn't be trusted vs. the ones who might not entirely suck.

"Do we step in?" I asked Rye.

"And do what? The information's out; we can't force anyone's hand. Until we have more info we can send to the ones who aren't traitors, we just..." Zie made a frustrated noise, partway between a sigh and a grunt. "We're going to work on what *we* can do. Drones, satellites, maybe a heretic army." Zie sat up straight, smoothed zir hair. "Honestly, darling, we just do our best to make up for what those bitches lack."

I grinned. "Just like we always end up doing."

"That's right, baby. Just like that."

I noticed neither of us was mentioning that we still had no real idea how to make up for the lack of our boys.

In the interest of making up for what we knew or feared the powers that be lacked, or doing the best we could to that end...In the interest of staying sufficiently busy whilst we waited for Kitty to bring word about the boys (our only current hope)...I settled back into the methodical task of tracking the people who'd met with Isa, trying to find clues in the mystery of "are they heretics or just aliens who dig BDSM?".

Riles, without making me feel like a failure, took a turn at trying to get into the satellites.

My efforts weren't just boring as hell, they were also fruitless. They felt like wasted hours. Wasted hours regularly interrupted by messages from Zane.

Yes, after almost two days of leaving us alone, they were back on their bullshit. It was both sad and annoying, the barrage of pleading. The same sort of claims they'd sent right after we'd literally just watched them help take out our boys.

Like somehow repetition would make us believe they'd been misunderstood, would convince us to give them a chance to explain. Peppered, as the hours progressed, with claims that they had to tell us something. Thinking back on the things they'd felt it important to tell us in weeks past, I snorted as I wondered aloud, "Do you suppose they want to give us the very important and relevant details of where their people land in terms of Coke vs. Pepsi?"

"Or Blur vs. Oasis?" Rye smirked.

Anger inclined me to get on a roll. "Or tea vs. coffee."

Feeling the spirit of it, zie kept it going. "Or cats vs. dogs."

"Spice Girls 1994 vs New Spice Girls."

We went on like that for a while, and I almost replied to Zane with our guesses about topics. But they didn't deserve our hilarity.

When we'd trailed off into giggles, I finally cleared my throat and tried to get back on track. "So, uh, satellites. Tell me you've procured an army of them and I am just too big a noob."

Riles huffed and grumbled a bit before saying, "No joy. I *swear* I got in before—"

I cut zir off, reassuring zir, "I know you got in, poppet. I saw it."

Zie nodded, accepting my words for what they were. "But I don't know if you're a noob, because I can't get in either. Not even to the NOAA satellite we were just using last week."

"Ugh." I sighed. "Fucking Mondays."

"Fucking Mondays," zie agreed. Then zie asked, "So, I guess this means you haven't found shit either?"

I shook my head. "Not a thing."

"Okay. Then you're going to shift to helping me."

"Uh." I squinted my eyes, confused. "Because my failures the last week have shown that I'm going to be very helpful?"

"Because, you useless noob, we're going to divide up seeing if the people who own the satellites just got smarter than us..." Zie paused as we both snorted derisively at the absurdity of that prospect, then suggested the alternative. "Or if maybe some of them are having troubles too." Once the words were out of zir mouth, the same idea seemed to hit us both.

My worried eyes met zirs. "Oh damn. Because, at best, that would mean some other hackers got hold of them. And at worst..."

"And, at worst, maybe it means the space people got control of our space stuff. And...Oh." Zie bit zir lip and started typing. "I want to make sure Mars and the Moon seem okay. Have we checked on either at all this last month?" When I shook my head to indicate we hadn't, zie said, "Because, if it's the Peaceforgers fucking with the satellites, who knows what they've done to the rest of our non-terrestrial holdings?"

"Or if they already took over our smaller civilizations and then made sure Earth didn't hear about it," I worried.

Zie nodded and got to work looking into the state of those colonies. Whilst Riles did that, I made a list for us to work through of the governments and corporations that *should* be in control of the satellites we'd been trying. And I started digging into those.

Good news: The assorted Mars and Moon colonies looked fine! It wasn't like any of them were booming civilizations just yet. They were small enough still, struggling enough still, that working together was how they rolled. They were peaceful enough that maybe the Peaceforgers would think they were actually doing just fine. Good job, space humans.

Bad news: Everybody was having access issues. Everybody. Governments and corporations alike were trying to hide that they had added "figure out what the hell is wrong with our satellites" to their to-do list in the last couple days. Which was going to slow down their insufficient, quiet anti-alien efforts, I'd bet.

But we'd also peeked in on assorted 'Net forums, super sneaky secret ones, where people generally talked about hacking into satellites. Except, now, they were talking about failing to do that. It had started Saturday night, with people posting in ways they hoped would save face if they were the only ones having an issue. By hours that could be considered Sunday morning, if you wanted to be technical about which hours belonged to which day, they were starting to talk openly. They were trying to figure out how all the satellite owners had managed to suddenly block them out. And then they were starting to report back—so I should have just looked there first—exactly the same info we'd found about the owners being locked out too.

Which, we reckoned, left only one option...one pasty, alien option. Ugh. I had really hoped, if I ever met aliens, that they'd be more "space adventure mates" and less "all your planet are belong to us."

I put my head in my hands and said, "I'm just going to change our name to Team Ugh. That will fit better on the team shirts."

Team Ugh checked in with their (our) remote team. We didn't want to give too much away about what we'd done or might do, but it seemed like we should warn those of our people not already on the sneaky satellite forums that something was up.

Then, whilst some of them talked paranoid (but now seemingly sensible) plans for hiding out if the Peaceforgers took over, some of us got back to looking for allies and enemies.

We dug into communications involving those who'd gotten our alien email, those we'd hoped would be allies. We sifted through communications that involved SWS and Divine Community, including shit on blackmail forums collected by eavesdropping on phone calls. And I wasn't sure if we'd just not looked correctly before or if it had just started, but things were continuing to be very "fucking Mondays" out there.

We found way too much proof that both SWS and Divine Community had slews of people and businesses courting them still. Trying to make deals. Trying to get tech. Trying to put themselves in position to get whatever power or money might trickle down to them from those alien-run conspiracies. I was angry, but also wanted to vomit a bit from fear and disgust. If shit went down, the powers that be would only fight for their own power, not their people. I don't know why I'd thought that would be any different now than in the past.

Someone—we didn't find who—had even brokered a deal that had CEO Johnson and COO Smith out of house arrest. They hadn't had charges dropped, but that couldn't be far behind. And what did charges matter at this point? The trackers had been removed, which meant those assholes could now just run if they wanted. Run to a space ship. And we wouldn't even have satellites to track said space ship. Fuck.

At least, somewhere in all that time spent digging, Zane had finally shut up. We were really winning...

Right after I noticed Zane had stopped, Kitty popped up. Her hologram had always been crisp, but now she looked glitchy. When her audio was extra tinny and crackly too, I started to worry. What if, just like she'd come to be, she was un-coming?

It was hard to read her tone. Was she excited? Stressed? We couldn't tell, and her words weren't helping. We were pretty sure she'd started by exclaiming, "You guys!" And then...maaaaybe she had tried to say she'd just found something?

And then she was gone. Just blinked out. And there was no question what Riley's tone was.

Mindful of our status as people on the run, zie managed to keep zir volume at whisper-shouting, but my mind read it for the scream it was. "Kitty? Kitty??" Zie looked at me, wild-eyed. "What happened? Where'd she go?"

Obviously, I didn't know. I just made a worried face, shook my head, and put an arm around zir. I weakly suggested, "Maybe it's to do with the satellites?"

Zie looked skeptical but didn't stop me, so I went on.

"Maybe, even if we can't figure out their frequencies or whatever, maybe they've been using our satellites to amplify their communications?"

Slowly, zie nodded. I didn't know whether zie actually believed my idea or just wanted to believe, but zie said, "Yeah. Okay."

"Okay." I was relieved zie'd gone for that. I didn't have anything else, and I couldn't lose zir to grief. Couldn't have it be down to just me, not when I was shoving my own feelings into little boxes to be dealt with later.

We wouldn't be changing our name to Team Functional any time soon.

We settled back into the unglamorous task of researching. But, to be fair, I didn't mind the task. I minded the results, of course, but I wouldn't have made much of a hacker if I didn't like research.

So, we built up our list of who not to trust and who to trust, theorizing about what tools or opposition that might put in our way. Because we didn't really know what the hell we were talking about, it was more a useless distraction than anything else.

And then.

My phone pinged in a way that let me know the call was being sent to the contact info I'd been giving to people like Dr. Scott and Zane. And I almost ignored it, assuming it must be Zane again. I took my time getting to it, yawning as I reached for it.

And then I froze mid-yawn. Pulled my hand and the phone it held slowly towards my face. Staring at the number. Oh shit. "Riles?"

Without looking up, zie said, "Yeah?"

When I didn't reply or answer the phone, zie looked up and stopped typing. It must have been clear the phone was the source of my worry, because zie just reached over carefully to take it from me.

"Oh, fuck. Kot, this is Isa's number." Zie looked the same mix of worried and surprised that I felt.

Because it *was* Isa's number. Mutely, I nodded. And the phone stopped pinging. I held my breath as we both stared at the phone. Would there be a ping to signal voicemail?

There wasn't. And Riles handed me the phone.

I opened my mouth to ask a number of obvious questions, but then my phone let me know I had a message (text, not voice). I didn't even pre-read, just read it aloud. "Is Zane with you? They said they were trying to reach you, then they stopped replying to me."

I looked up at a confused Riley.

Zie asked, "She thinks they're with *us*?"

"Apparently." I bit the inside of my cheek. "Or it's a ruse to get us to reply."

Before we could consider the possibility, I got another message from Isa. As I read it aloud, Rye shifted around to stand behind me. "If they didn't get through to you, and if they aren't with you, we could have a problem. There are things you should know."

Riles rested zir chin on my shoulder, probably reading the message zirself, then scooted back over to zir own space. "I'm going to see if I can confirm these are from her phone."

We glanced up to the windows on our TV where we hadn't seen Isa leave her flat that day (at least not via her front door) and hadn't seen her open her webcam cover. Where we hadn't seen her get any visitors. Where we had no visual confirmation that she was the one sending these messages or that she was doing so unprompted.

So we dug into her phone and message logs. We hadn't seen her messaging with Zane, so we had obviously missed something. At best, we could say that the last two messages did, indeed, seem to come from her phone.

I pulled up the window that might show us the view from her phone's camera. Like the webcam window, she'd continued to keep it covered. Same with her phone's mic.

"They could have been communicating in some way like how Kitty was contacting us?" suggested Riley, staring at the same useless windows.

"Maybe she has a burner?" But then I shook my head, rejecting my own suggestion. "Not a burner for these last two messages at least." I started doing a broader search, looking for signals from Zane's phone to anyone else, especially near Isa's location.

Using a wee custom program to troll through all communications in Isa's area, I finally had some luck. "Hey! Burner for receiving Zane messages confirmed." Though my excitement waned when I saw the content. "Oh. Nothing useful. Just that Zane is trying to reach us, and our generic contact info so Isa could try too. But long enough ago that I guess that's why she assumed they might be with us."

"Then why did she use her real phone, not her burner to message us?" Riles leaned into the screen, as if zie could glare some truth out of the dark windows.

I shrugged, guessing. "Maybe she thinks we'll answer if it's from a person, not a burner? Maybe she thinks that makes it less suspicious?"

Or maybe she assumed we'd have dug into things and would know who she was. That possibility was the one that worried me most.

"Well, I just cannot even with that right now. I need a moment to contemplate, you know?" Rye looked about at zir limit, scowling and unsure.

"Gran always told us to remember the phones were our tools, not our masters, and we didn't have to reply to most anything immediately." I was feeling pretty at my limit as well.

Nodding at the wisdom, Riley said, "Then, in honor of Gran, I'm just gonna take a minute."

Who was I not to join in with something to honor the best woman I'd known? I put my phone aside to take a breath before switching over to handling (aka failing to find solid info to guide our choices as regards) the one more thing that had just been added to our list of confusion.

The bastard Universe had one last thing to throw at me, to make my brain too noisy to sleep. This one came via someone on bugHunt, on the theoretically dead thread digging into that Katja person that SWS had it out for.

Riley notified me by sighing unhappily at zir screen, "Why won't you just leave her alone?"

"Her who?"

Zie looked at me sadly. "Her you. Not that it's not intriguing, but...There's new stuff about you on bugHunt. Well, new stuff about Gran actually."

Ah. There was the magic word that, even with her gone now, raised my protective instincts. Made me want to fight. So I dove into the forum, like a bomber en route, ready to blow up whoever had had the bad taste to invoke Gran.

One of our comrades had, they claimed, not been purposefully searching, but had neglected to shut down an automated search. And they hadn't planned to share whatever the program had found when it buzzed at them, but this was too interesting. Not, as they noted, relevant to anything, but too good not to share.

"This" was a police report, filed by Gran. Huh.

It turned out that, Halloween 1999, Gran had filed a missing person report in Woodinville, a town about 30 minutes away. The person who was missing? Nicholas Simon Brennan.

"Isn't that your grandfather's name?" Rye asked.

"Yeah..."

"The one she always made up ridiculous excuses for why he wasn't around?"

"Yeah." I only half-paid attention to Riles. I was trying to find clues or a way of connecting myself more to Gran or...something—anything—in the police report that somehow seemed helpful. She was gone and this was the closest to a new memory I'd get from her.

In the report, she'd said she'd gone to a party with her husband the night before, somewhere out in a field next to woods, to hear some band play. And then a light, surely a helicopter, had come down from the sky in a clearing somewhere in the woods. A light that her husband had gone to investigate. From which he hadn't returned. And that was it. According to the report, she hadn't had any other information to add. Except that she had been sober because she was pregnant, so she was sure she hadn't imagined it.

In the end, after some pressure from my grandad's rich parents and a random call to one cop's buddy in the FBI, the official "finding" had been that my grandad had run away from the pressures of a baby. They said he'd done so via a helicopter rented by his friends, because his friends—and maybe also my grandad—were hackers and therefore inclined towards just such dramatic and irresponsible acts. Riiiiiiight...

Obviously, we'd known Gran's replies to "what happened to your husband" were fake. She generally said something like, "He told me the all-women *Ghostbusters* ruined his childhood, so I 'got rid of him,' if you know what I mean." And she almost always referenced something that had come out or happened after he was definitely gone. I'd always just assumed it had been a garden variety divorce.

"Did you know this?" Riley sounded almost accusatory, as if I'd kept some tasty secret from zir.

"I didn't. She told me the same stories she told everyone and," I shrugged, "it seemed rude to dig into Gran. You know?"

"Same," said Riles. "But, maybe now..."

"Maybe now," I confirmed. I wondered what I'd find in her files, on her computer.

Before I could hypothesize what might be in the places where I'd respected Gran's privacy, Riles pressed, "So, you don't know anything more about this?" Gran was an alluring mystery suddenly.

I scooted over to zir, pulling up a photo on my phone as I talked. "What I know...That he existed, that he hasn't been around since my mum was very young." I let out a short laugh, thinking of what I'd just learned. "Very, very young apparently. And that he and Gran were both pretty when they were young." I showed zir a photo from some time in the 1990s when they had both been around my age.

"Aha!" Rye jabbed at the picture. "Now I see why you don't burn as easily in the sun as I'd expect."

"Yeah," I laughed a little. "That's due to his mum's side." I used my fingers to zoom in on my grandfather's face. "Literally all I know about his parents is that...Well, one, a few generations before her, his mum's people came from Spain and, a few generations before that, his dad's came from Ireland. And, two, in spite of how they liked to talk a lot about their heritages, they both actually identified as 'affluent asshole,' culturally speaking."

Riley snickered, then pointed out, "You have his eyes."

"I have his eyes." I grinned, no longer so displeased about having things in common with him now that I knew maybe he wasn't the basic bastard I'd assumed.

"Good thing he was pretty." Riles went a little dreamy. "I bet Gran felt pierced to her very core by those dark eyes the instant they met."

Before we could get too caught up in the mystery, and even though there were pages left to skim in the case file, I summoned all my willpower and said, "But. We have other stuff we have to concentrate on. Plus, sleep. So, I'm tabling this until tomorrow, when we need a break from all the alien shit." I glared at zir in mock accusation. "And no sneaking around to look now. This is mine, bastard."

Zie stuck out zir tongue cheekily, but followed that up with a nod.

I almost believed zir.

We tried to get back to figuring out what to do about Isa, to figuring out her motivations, but we found no new information. And we ended up trapped in the same circular discussion every time we tried to talk our way through and choose our next steps. It was always something like:

Riley would say, "What if she knows what happened to Kitty? We should just answer."

And I'd counter with, "Sure, but what if she knows because she did it? What if this is a trap?"

And Rye would frustratedly demand, "Isn't Kitty worth the risk?" And zie would maybe throw in accusations about my opinion of Kitty based on shitty (recent) past behaviors.

Then I'd remind myself that I'd probably be saying the same things if it were Jonny, so I'd reply, "She's worth risks, but she's also worth us not getting caught so that there's still somebody left to save her."

In the end, which came too late at night to reply to Isa even if I'd thought it was a good idea, we compromised on a (probably stupid) longshot plan. If there was no Kitty by morning, we'd buy an assortment of bugs online. Not insects, though the idea of spider-bombing her had its appeal in the wee and irrational hours, but the electronic kind. We figured we'd have them rush couriered to her, get ones we could control by bouncing some signals through her mobile, and...Well, the theory was we'd turn them all on and get a glimpse and maybe even some sound when she opened the package. Maybe we'd get lucky and find some that could move, kind of like the ones Jonny had used, so we could have them dash into shadows and hide in her flat or something.

Yeah. We were really bad at the meat space thing. And generally frustrated in all our pursuits, it seemed. We weren't finding new leads or information to help us move forward with old stuff. We weren't even coming up with new ideas about things to poke into, but felt trapped just watching other people not do what they could do.

I laid in bed, when we'd finally given up on the day, swearing to myself that I was going to do something—even if it was something stupid—in the morning. I wasn't going to end another night with nothing but angry tears crawling down my face. Tears that got heavier when I heard Riles crying in the loo at night instead of chatting with Kitty. Because there was still no Kitty.

CHAPTER 7

I hadn't forgotten my pledge to myself the night before or our plan to kind of bug Isa's place. But, with climate control (bye bye, cold!), no windows, and a reasonable bed, I wasn't waking up early. At least not as early as I had been. So it was 9 a.m. by the time I was sucking down my first coffee and trying to sort out best options for thwarting aliens and for bugging Isa. I was staring at our big TV with its many windows, willing something useful to happen in the ones that came from cameras in Zane's and Isa's places.

Trying to find a new avenue of attack, I mused, "So, we've caught the Peaceforgers trying business and religion...And Zane said they'd ruled out running for office. Where do you reckon those bastards will show up next?"

Clearly lending me only half zir attention as zie tapped to scroll through things on zir computer, Riles said, "I'm betting entertainment. Adulation and influence, right?" A little dreamy-eyed, zie looked up and asked, "Who doesn't want *that*?"

"Yeah. That's a good one. Or..." I tried to come up with an idea of my own, eyes pointed at but not quite focused on the TV. On the windows where we still weren't seeing any action from Isa's or Zane's cameras. On the windows showing the results of various programs we had running. On the windows with news. Idly, I suggested, "Education. Shaping minds, but not physically."

"They could have Divine Community open a school; there's plenty of precedent. Or do one under some other guise, bring in non-religious types too." Riles nodded. "That totally makes sense."

And then the scene in the news windows changed abruptly. To my credit, when I saw it, I didn't drop my coffee cup; I managed to carefully set it on the table. And, through a throat closed with sudden fear, I managed to whisper, "Or maybe they just show up."

"Huh?" And I don't know if zie looked at me first or straight at the TV, but zie gasped, "Oh shit!"

Because there on the screen, as shown in a breaking newsflash, was a motherfucking space ship. Pale and sleek with vivid blue lights so that it matched the Peaceforgers' skin.

I realized I was standing, as if I might spring into action. But I didn't. I just crept up to the TV where, probably thanks to Riles pushing buttons, the window with the ship was now taking most the screen. The other windows all formed a row along the bottom, a visible representation of what was actually top priority just now.

Everyone else must be seeing it too, because my computer and my phone were lighting up, bombarded by messages. But they could wait. This was as close to a cinematic alien moment as I was going to get in this whole mess. I imagined, in fact, that the world was now living the typical "aliens arrive and people stop to stare" montage, all the world staring at screens or staring up at the sky. Alarms going off in government facilities. An assortment of scientists and science-fiction enthusiasts hitting record on their devices so they could watch it all back later, searching for details.

And only a few of us knowing that, in fact, they'd been here a long while. The chyron on the news window let me know that, to most the world, they had been here only a couple minutes.

Whispering through my fear, I asked, "Is this another one? Do we have two fucking ships of them now?"

Riles must have un-muted, because there was suddenly sound, a newscaster's voice over the image of the ship that now floated over (not under) Puget Sound. "...just hanging silently so far."

I jumped, startled by the sound. Then laughed nervously, feeling silly. Before I could settle, the image was replaced by something from the Peaceforgers. Which somehow startled me into a more useful state.

I sat back down, looking to see what was happening in the rest of the world. And it seemed they were all seeing what I was seeing: a clean, bright ship interior with curved walls; a semi-circle of five Peaceforgers, not hiding their true appearance (the poreless pale skin, the head ridges, the milky grey eyes, and no ears or noses...the main traits they'd hidden to try to blend with humans) and looking serene; and one Peaceforger front and center, smiling kindly out at us. I didn't know enough about Peaceforger genders to even guess what sort of Earth gender to loosely map to them. That must be driving some of the humans watching totally batty. I had to smile at that.

They paused a moment, as if to give us a chance to take in the sight and get used to it. Probably also to give more people a chance to tune in. During the pause, I confirmed via the 'Net that there was just the one ship, at least in the air. I went ahead and called that good news.

They spoke, and their voice was smooth and warm. "Friends, we have come as messengers of the Divine, in hopes of helping you usher in an age of peace and prosperity."

A quick check told me they were providing subtitles in other countries and regions. For some reason, it made me feel better that they weren't somehow simulcasting a spoken version in all those languages.

"It is, for us, always a blessed day when we can bring our gifts to a new people. And we will stay for as long as you'll have us, healing and sharing. Hopefully bringing peace and prosperity. Doing what good we can, what good you'll allow us to do."

They slowly turned their head, as if scanning the whole crowd of humanity on the other side of the screen. Stated intentions backed up by that ever-present smile.

"We understand that, at present, your species is divided into many different groups. We want to assure you that our intentions are peace for all, not just those over whose waters we now hover. We hope, as we reach out, that your governments and ruling bodies will reply, will accept what we offer."

As if anticipating the objections of the common human, they continued, "We also want to assure you that we are not just here for those in positions of power or privilege. Our mission of peace is intended for *every* member of your species. We will work to ensure that what we bring is as easily available to the poorest and least powerful of you as it is to those who have more."

Their smile broadened. "Thank you for allowing us to be part of your planet's story. And now, with apologies for taking control without asking, we relinquish your airwaves. Peace to all." And with that, and a genial nod, we were back to a news station that wasn't ready for its viewers.

The camera they were broadcasting from was still pointed at the ship, but the sound was a newsroom rushing to get itself back together and not yet aware we could hear them. A babble of voices. One voice louder than the others demanding, "Just figure out how we get an interview, dammit!" An abrupt moment of silence. And then the cheery voice of the newscaster.

"What you just saw appears to have been live from our own city, and we'll do what we can to get our new visitors back on again soon. Now, let's talk about what we saw!"

The volume slid down and the windows on the screen redistributed. I turned to Rye, the master of the remote. Zie appeared to be very focused on the serious job of controlling the TV, so I waited until zie was ready to turn zir mind to another task or conversation.

Once zie sat and put down the remote, I said, "Well. That happened." I could hear that my voice was flat. It matched the strange, numb feeling in my chest.

"At least now we've been proven right? Go us?" Zie started to give me a tentative jazz hands.

But zie dropped zir hands and, instead, we did some synchronized swearing. What the fuck were we going to do now?

To buy my brain time to figure out what the fuck, I did a quick check of my many messages. Most were just versions of "welp, guess you were right." Even those on our team seemed shocked. It's one thing to hear about something fantastic and a whole other, potentially terrifying thing to have that something actually show up on your planet.

Beside me at the table, any terror Riley might have been processing was cut short by the return, crisp and clear, of zir

Kitty. She came shrieking back in, and my message answering was slowed by half-listening to their conversation.

Somehow breathless, Holo-Kitty's first words were, "Are you guys okay? Did I disappear before you heard there was something happening?"

Kitty hadn't been clear on what exactly was happening, just that something big was coming. But she was clever enough to have known that anything big for the Peaceforgers would probably leave us fucked. Especially when she realized that she couldn't get through to us. She and Riles were all high-pitched exclamations as they told each other their sides of what had happened.

Based on what info Kitty had managed to collect since she'd disappeared on us, this was the same ship that had been in Puget Sound. "I think we submarined out to the middle of nowhere then, like, threw up deflector shields or something and slipped out into space at night," she said.

I scrambled to do some quick searches and found reports of some radar irregularities from some vessels out in the middle of the Pacific Ocean the night before. It looked like some other monitoring equipment that might have caught their exit had been, like the satellites, out since the day before. If we hadn't been so focused on the satellite part of things, we might have noticed the panic extended farther. It also looked like people were still failing to find the ship on their radar. So, okay, maybe we just had the one to deal with.

Before I could let Rye know the good news, such as it was, messages from Zane started hitting my phone again. Their first message was kind of an "I told you so," an honestly earned one. I wasn't answering, but was now reading a wee bit less dismissively. And I wasn't taking it as unwarranted attitude the many times they noted that they'd told us so regarding needing to tell us something big.

Isa messaged again too, asking to meet and "discuss mutual interests." I had to think about if and how I'd reply, especially since she and her sneaky secret group hadn't slipped up in any way we could find; I didn't know if she was actually a heretic. I waited until Riles and Kitty were caught up and each back to their own work before I said anything.

"So, uh, Isa wants to meet." Then I pursed my lips, frustrated at myself again. "And the ship thing totally delayed us in sending her bugs."

Rye stopped doing whatever it was zie was doing on zir computer to give me a considering look. "Are you going to? Meet, that is. I feel like...the bugs idea seems even less bright now that I've slept. And, uh, now that Kitty's back."

I did a shrug and grimace combo that I hoped said, "I don't know and am not qualified to decide what to do."

"Because Zane has seen your face, so they—and this time I mean 'they, the Peaceforgers'—definitely know that Katja Brennan isn't as innocent as everyone else now thinks." Zie stood, giving zir room to pace a little and gesticulate a little more dramatically. "So, on the one hand, maybe this is when you hook us up with the alien resistance and we have a satisfying guerrilla warfare montage before the final, victorious battle. Or!" And zie spun dramatically, jabbing a finger in my direction. "This is a trap, and they have a special and painful end planned for you, no matter what happens with the rest of the human species." Eyes bright, zie seemed to conclude as zie exclaimed grandly, "This is all very adventure-y, and I just want to eat sweets and stay in bed." And then zie flopped back into zir chair, yielding the floor for my response.

Which was an extended, frustrated sigh. Then, "And if I just play it safe and don't talk to her, even if her group aren't badass saviors of humanity, I'm still wasting a resource." My brain struggled to come up with what resources we'd want besides badass fighters. "She could probably...uh...Oh! Get us tech to get on Peaceforger frequencies. Act as a less hapless inside person for us. At least paint us some better art than the generic shit currently hanging on these walls." I side-eyed said generic shit, then gave Rye a "right?" look.

With restrained intensity, Riles nodded, then noted, "Being able to interact with their frequencies gets us a step closer to saving Kitty." Zie shifted thoughtfully. "But maybe she could also get us tech specs. So many tech specs I want..."

"So, do we apply everything we learned in movies—"

"Which are obviously very realistic and educational," zie interjected.

I nodded gravely, well aware of how wrong we were and how poorly that particular educational system had served Jonny when he tried to hook up with us. "Yes, very reliable guides for our lives. So, we use all our cinematic education to set up a meet?" I paused, held my faux confident pose a moment...and then let my head drop back. "We are so not making it out of this alive, are we? I fucking hate having to figure out meat space stuff."

"Please." I could *hear* Riley arching zir eyebrow. "We are too fabulous and smart to die."

I didn't exactly believe that, but I never could resist joining zir in pretending I was too diva to do wrong or to die. I sat up straight and shared some smug looks. Then I sat back a little and asked, "What about Zane?"

"One alien at a time, bitch."

Our planning might have gone more quickly, but the local news was abuzz. As you'd expect. Most of it was recapping the same things over and over, but our usual station had sent out Brad, their regular on-site reporter, to have a chat with Shepherd Michaelson.

Understandably, Michaelson was aglow with his own rightness. (Though a very few of us knew it wasn't just about being right.) After all, he'd told us they were coming.

Brad went straight for that, of course. "Shepherd Michaelson, just a couple days ago you made what seemed like pretty wild claims in your Sunday service."

Good-naturedly, Michaelson chuckled. "Now, most my congregation would say that claims like that don't seem so wild coming from a man who can heal." He winked, as if to assure Brad they were still pals. "But, yes, I was told they were coming. And here they are. I can't wait to meet them!"

"So, you're saying these are definitely the," Brad read from his tablet, quoting Michaelson, "'pale-skinned, white-clothed messengers' you saw and said were coming?"

With endless good humor and patience, Michaelson said, "Unless there's another group just like them out there." He smiled, a touch of awe in his face and his voice. "And what an amazing day for humanity. The 'peace on earth' so many have prayed for is about to be helped into being."

Before Brad could go in for his next question, one of Michaelson's people handed the shepherd a note from off camera. He quickly read it and tucked it into a pocket. Apologetically, he said, "Unfortunately, the responsibilities associated with leading my flock and being the one our new friends contacted first have increased a bit since this morning."

I bet. The 'Net and some digging of our own told us that Michaelson was getting plenty of calls from people in power, as well as an influx of new potential church members. A larger influx than the influx he'd already been getting since he started doing his "miracle" healings. Not ideal...

We were nailing down the last details of our ill-advised plan to meet with Isa when we were interrupted by one more thing on the news we couldn't ignore. Having a gold star day, our favorite local news channel already had an interview with the "newly" arrived aliens. Intrepid studio reporter Rachel had somehow beat out live-on-site reporter Brad, and you could tell it was the best day of her life.

In a posh executive office somewhere, Rachel sat in a chair across from three Peaceforgers I didn't know. Except that one had been the speaker in their little arrival video, and the other two had stood behind them. I wondered how much threat they'd sprinkle into their message of peace.

The barest professionalism stood between Rachel and total fangirling as she spoke. "I'm Rachel Villa, and I'm in an office—generously provided by Shepherd Michaelson and Divine Community Church—with three people who are new to this planet, but whose faces you probably already know."

She paused as the shot switched to just showing the three calm faces of the Peaceforgers, then she continued her introduction when the shot switched to the camera pointed at just her face. "Normally, before an interview, I'd make sure I could easily say the names of those generously meeting with me.

However, as they kindly pointed out, the human body isn't capable of making all the sounds necessary to say their names. Therefore, they've chosen some common names in English."

The shot switched back to the Peaceforgers. In her best "formal introductions" voice, Rachel said, "It's my pleasure to introduce you to Morgan," the one who was, as in the invasion video, front and center nodded, "Jayden, and Emery." The other two each nodded when their name was said.

I probably should have noted things about the two backup singers, but I assumed the one of them on lead was the important one. I could always watch the interview again later. (Also, if I'm ever an alien invader, please remind me that that's the exact right time to embrace a truly interesting and colorful name. Especially if my appearance is going to counteract any efforts I make to try to play the "I'm just like you" card with the natives.)

"They'll teach us more, we hope, about their culture and biology later, but I've already learned that they have different enough biology and social structure that we ought to always use 'they' and 'them' as their pronouns." The shot switched back to a view that took in all parties involved in the interview, and Rachel beamed at us. "And, now that we've all met, we're grateful for the opportunity to ask Morgan and their companions a few questions. Though we'll warn you now that, as you might guess, they're very busy, so we'll only have a few minutes with them this time."

She turned to face them fully, and the shot they broadcast the next few minutes switched between the view of everyone and the view that was just the Peaceforgers.

Rachel started easy and basic. "First, what should we call your people?"

"Friends." Morgan smiled, clearly aware they weren't giving quite the answer she wanted, but not trying to be an asshole about it.

"Of course," Rachel grinned. "But we often identify groups by their place of origin."

Morgan nodded and said something that was definitely in their language, paused a beat, then said, "And that's why you probably can't call us something related to where we're from.

Not until we've had a chance to learn whether you've seen even our home galaxy so we can tell you what name you already use." They and their friends were oozing kindness, so it didn't come off condescending like it could have.

I growled at the TV, "Or you could just tell her the name we already know, you prick."

Clearly daydreaming the scenario, Riles asked, "Can you imagine what would happen if they tripped up and *did* say they were Peaceforgers?" Zie sighed happily at the thought. "That would be beyond incredible."

Ignoring our input, almost like they couldn't hear us, Rachel conceded with a nod, but suggested, "Well, if you'll be around long, friends, we'd be happy to help spread the word if you choose another thing to call yourselves." She looked at her list of questions. "Now, you said that you're here to help bring us 'peace and prosperity.' Could you say a little about how you'll do that?"

"Answering broadly, so that you'll have time left to ask another question or two...We have advanced technology, including medical technology that supplements the gift of healing the Divine has blessed us with, and we hope to at least open healing centers. It's amazing how much peace can come from not fearing for one's health or life."

Rachel nodded, then asked, "Perhaps you can stop the beat down flu epidemic spreading through our world?"

"We hope so!" Morgan enthused. "And it's not just the health of individuals we hope to help with. We can help heal the environment with some of our technology. We can help with improved emergency response technology that might heal communities faster. Many things like that. But it's not just technology we're bringing." They got very sober. "We also bring many ages of practice at living peacefully, a whole planet without wars and other planets visited and helped. We hope you'll allow us to offer guidance and mediation so that Earth too can have that."

I saw something shift in Rachel's face. The thing is, whilst it can sometimes seem impossible as an Autistic person to navigate human expressions, I've also spent my whole life *trying*. I've studied human faces like they're an alien species, trying to learn the clues. Which means that, sometimes, I see things that others don't. In this case, Riles gave me a confused look as I leaned towards the TV and hissed, "Get those bastards, Rachel."

And, clearly urged on by my encouragement from the other side of the screen, Rachel said, quickly (like she didn't want to lose her nerve and/or get cut off), "You're not actually the first group to come to humanity recently with technology for peace or promises of a cure for beat down flu. Are you aware of the Peacemaker scandal involving Secure World Systems or of the tainted cures and killing perpetrated by someone in a position of responsibility here at Divine Community Church? And, if so, where do you stand on their actions and why should we trust that you won't do more of the same?"

She looked relieved but electric when she got it all out. For the briefest moment, it looked like she regretted it or couldn't believe she'd done it, but she never dropped her eyes from Morgan.

Whether they were ready for it or just distressingly unflappable, or maybe just because their culture had different body language (naturally) so I couldn't tell they were nervous, Morgan didn't look worried. They started looking very serious, then worked their way to earnest as they delivered their almost-practiced reply. "We have tried to make ourselves aware of current events, because we can't help you if we don't know your context. And the events you've mentioned are all distressing. As you imply, the best intentions don't necessarily mean the best path to a solution will be taken. And, unfortunately, our dwindling time with you in this interview won't allow for a nuanced reply. But I can assure you that we have no plans for secret implants or murder. When we heal people, we won't even need to touch them, so that ought to at least allow you to trust our cures. Including our cure for your, uh, beat down flu." They almost sounded like they thought it was adorable of us to call it something so accessible. For a moment, it seemed like they might cross the line and be a little too obvious about thinking we were a lesser species.

They paused a breath, then got serious again. "For us, one of the things we've discussed and focused on around the events you mentioned is the people responsible. We wonder how true their intentions were and just how they found themselves on such objectionable paths. And, to help those people while also helping make sure we're as educated as we can be about how your people think and work, we're already negotiating to have the people involved in those scandals entrusted to us. We hope to learn from and then to better them."

Rachel didn't have a response for that. And, unfortunately, she couldn't hear Riley's and my responses to it. I wondered what sort of ass-kissing shits from our planet were profiting from letting the Peaceforgers have their people back. I wondered if it would say bad things about me if I wildly hoped the right humans died in the fight to get these pasty bastards off our planet. I wondered how much more of this bullshit Riles and I could take.

CHAPTER 8

Time to meet Isa. Time to hope we didn't have to see how good our escape plans were. Just in case, I'd insisted that Rye not come along; I needed to make sure one of us was still fine on the other side of this. But zie was riding along in an earbud and in a tiny camera I'd put on a hair clip ('cause spy-style glasses with secret video cameras in them weren't exactly a thing we had on hand).

Right before I left, we reserved a variety of rooms all over the city. Then we took advantage of the wonderfully hackable nature of self-driving taxis to send a number of those to different pickup points, set to go to drop-off points near but not at any of those rooms. We grabbed the cam footage from previous taxis' trips, all prepped and poised to be replaced in over the footage of the actual drives that night for all the taxis.

I put on my g/ap mask and a non-distinctive hoodie, hat, and scarf, and then I made sure to exit through the parking garage and into some shadows. I always appreciated the early sunsets of autumn and winter, but I was feeling a little extra love now that I was trying to dodge all eyes. Especially when the shadows got me to my taxi pickup point without having to act like I was being sneaky.

After a bit of a circuitous trip with multiple stops, the taxi pulled into the parking garage of the building where we'd decided to do the meeting. I ducked into the lift and headed up to my floor. The lift didn't stop to pick up other riders; Riles was now owning the hotel's computer and anything controlled by computers in the hotel. And no hotel camera footage of me was being saved to any sort of storage drive, because Riley. And I was guided through halls when they were empty by, yes, our Riles. Then to the room that Riles had booked, not once having seen or—we hoped—been seen by another person.

Zie hadn't said anything about it, so I wasn't aware I was walking into a quite nice suite. *Quite* nice. Whilst I prepared for

Isa, I made sure to grab everything in it that could fit in my bag. I was disappointed that the plush bathrobe was, in fact, too plush for that. And I reckoned I couldn't stay sneaky on the trip back if I added a fluffy white robe to my ensemble...Though maybe I'd try...

Once Rye was sure zie had sufficient computer control and had all cameras in the hotel and around it set up with programs that might let us know if we had incoming trouble, I messaged Isa. I told her where to go (not where I was) and how long she had to get there (exactly the amount of time it should take her, plus 5 minutes, because we're not complete bastards). And she agreed.

With my mobile, I piggybacked as Rye followed her via cameras and tried to check out things we, in our totally-not-good-at-meat-stuff brains, thought might bode ill for us. And, when it seemed fine and she made it on time, I messaged her again and we did it again. Three more times.

"I think we're good, Kot. Yes?" Riles didn't sound sure.

I didn't feel sure either, so we were at least agreed on that. "Yeah. Sure." I exhaled, a resigned puff of air. "Let's get her here."

We watched Isa via the camera pointed at the back seat of the self-driving taxi we'd sent for her. The footage would never hit the company servers, but we commented as we watched the live feed.

"She's actually pretty, not just photo-manipulated pretty," Rye noted.

"Very. And really calm." I paused a breath, chewing the inside of my cheek. "What do you think it means that she's so calm?"

"Darling, do you really want to spin up anxieties by exploring all the good and bad reasons she might be calm?"

"Mm." Zie had a point. I let it drop.

"Okay, hang on. I'm going to hack the taxi and the garage, like I did for you, so Isa doesn't get out on the street. Minimize the number of cameras I'll have to clean."

Whilst zie worked, I did one last check of the room. I made sure I could easily get out the window and take an escape ladder down. I made sure all curtains were closed and anti-surveillance equipment was on. I made sure my gun was loaded and in easy reach. When I looked at my phone again, the view had switched to cameras in the hotel that followed Isa's path.

"So, she only seems to have one thing on her that's transmitting, at least at frequencies we can detect. It's her phone, and she'll need that for the room number. Once we send that, I'll deactivate her phone for the duration." Rye was driving now, in charge of everything zie could influence on and around Isa, who might be coming to chat...or might be coming to kill me.

Isa hesitated a second when the lift stopped on my floor and Rye messaged her the room number. As soon as she nodded and stepped out, pocketing her phone, I stood and faced the door.

"And phone deactivated."

"Thanks," I mumbled. I checked my posture, glad I was sufficiently healed to stand up straight and firm. I put my phone in my pocket as I saw Isa lift her hand to knock.

She'd barely rapped once when I opened the door. I was gratified to see that she was slightly startled by that. Cool.

She was slightly taller than me, but I didn't feel small as I stood a moment looking her over, appreciating the vibrant blue wig she'd chosen and the way it matched her lipstick. Then, I nodded and took a couple steps back so she could duck in.

I closed and locked the door behind her. She waited, as if she was as eager to keep me in her sight as I was to keep her in mine. I gestured towards the suite's living room area.

It wasn't until she stood in front of the couch that she extended her hand to me. "I'm Isa."

I wasn't trying to be a bitch when I paused a moment before I took it, shook it, tried not to be judgmental about what a gentle grip she had. "Katja. But you know that, because your people have been making sure to put my face all over the place for weeks."

She sighed and sat gracefully. "We are nothing if not a persistent people. I'm sorry for that."

I sat on the chair that faced the couch, too aware that I was still likely in reach of her tongue. If she paralyzed me, would Riley be able to save me from afar?

That wasn't the only question I had, but I'd decided not to ask her anything until she started the conversation. After all, she'd asked for this meeting.

She didn't leave me waiting for long. "Zane seems to believe you're capable and trustworthy."

I couldn't resist arching a brow and coldly noting, "Too bad we can't say the same for them."

She shook her head. "They didn't betray you, not unless they're also betraying me. They just did what they had to when things went wrong. But," and she put up a hand to stop the protest clearly about to come out of my mouth, "that's not what I wanted to talk about." She scooted forwards and leaned towards me. "What did Zane tell you about me?"

Riles had been quiet, but suddenly whispered, "Don't give a real answer. Ask her what you should know."

I hoped I'd looked like I was considering what to say, not like I'd been listening to an earbud. I mirrored her, leaning forward, and asked, "What do you *think* I should know?"

With a strange smile, she sat up and quietly said, "I wish I didn't think you needed to know anything." Then she sighed and, at a regular volume, said, "I think you should know that some of us are opposed to any plan that involves depriving you of the right to decide your own future. Our people would call us heretics. Um..." She considered. "We aren't soldiers, though. That's not really a thing *any* of our species are anymore. And...we're only a small fraction of our people. So we haven't been good for much more than keeping an eye on things."

"You're saying you're only good for information gathering?"

She nodded, looking a little ashamed. "We were hoping you might manage some action with our information. Once we have anything that seems...actionable."

In my ear, Rye snorted, "Holy shit. They have nothing, including clues, and they want us to do their damned job for them."

"Which means," I sat back in my seat, trying not to let any sneering or weariness into my voice, "that you don't think that you have anything solid to offer. That you *want* to help, but saving my species from yours is on me.”

Isa’s guilty look was answer enough.

“Fucking figures,” Riley mumbled. Zie sighed, then said, “Okay, you might as well start asking her for shit. Give her a chance to be useful.”

“Right. Then I’m going to give you a chance to be useful.” I was trying to sound steady, scary calm.

“Word thief.” Riles snickered.

Warily, but not unwilling, Isa nodded at me, inviting (or that’s how I was going to read it) my demands.

“Boys, but carefully,” Riles prompted.

“First, the men your people shot...” I was going to credit her with being smart enough to know how that ended.

She winced. “I was afraid you’d ask that. Whatever happened with them, nobody in my group has heard. I’m sorry.” And she sounded like she meant it.

I swallowed my bitter disappointment, tried to play it cool. “Okay. Consider us interested if anyone *does* hear anything.” I paused a moment to give Rye a chance to chime in, then went on when zie didn’t. “So, can you get us tech? Or specs for tech?”

Her eyes moved up and to the right, her head slightly bobbing as if she was moving down a remembered list. Then she nodded. “I think so. I think I’ve got contacts for a wide variety of things. It might depend on what specific tech, but...Go ahead and tell me what you’d like.”

Honestly, we’d mostly thought about how to save Kitty or hack the ship, but I figured it was probably not wise to just say that (I mean, I’m not a *complete* strategy moron). So I tried to list a few things I thought might help our goals without saying what our goals were. “Ideally, I’d like the actual tech, but specs would be a start. So...gear for detecting and/or connecting to the frequencies your lot’s stuff works on. Like when you’re transmitting and receiving messages, including Peacemaker signals. Any Peacemaker specs, especially those that wouldn’t have been on SWS servers, because I know you’re all still making those. Gear that would let me interface with your computers, even if that means we need to learn your language and get one of your computers.” I managed to neither salivate at the possibility nor let on to how ridiculously unlikely I knew that was. "If you lot use some communication device to talk just to each other, especially if it could be used to listen in, that would be handy. Healing tech. Specs and documentation about your ship and shuttles. And I'll take anything else you can get your hands on, anything to help get me on level with your people." That exhausted my list of ideas.

"Greedy bitch." Riles in my ear was sure being helpful...

Isa was very gracious, not laughing in my face. Instead, she nodded, mumbling under her breath like she was repeating the list to herself. Then she said, "I can do some of that. Probably. I'll message you specs as soon as I get any, though I'll also see if I can follow up with a translated copy of any spec. Unless you think you'll be working with Zane again, because they could obviously translate."

She didn't say it like a question, but she still managed to hang it in the air like one. And I just let it stay there, unanswered.

"If I do get you actual gear, you'll want to think about where we can make the exchange. I trust you'll want to choose somewhere that feels safe to you."

"I've already got some ideas," I told her. "You just get me the gear. And, if possible, either some kind of documentation for using it or a few minutes to demonstrate it to me." I thought a moment. "Oh, and a personal one, because it's a hobby of mine...and because I'm guessing you can't just get me the library of all knowledge your people have?" I quirked a hopeful eyebrow and paused a moment.

She seemed to consider that, and I hoped she'd figure it out, but I pressed on with my request before she made any kind of response. Because it wasn't actually a casual hobby I wanted info for. Obviously.

"I don't know if your people do AI, but if so...if you can get me anything on their work with that or that sort of thing, I'd consider it some super intriguing bedtime reading." I tried to sound like I dreamt of electric sheep.

"Thanks." Riles was a whisper in my ear. "Risky, but thanks."

I smiled. "Okay, I think that's it."

At zir normal volume, Riley reported, "Ready to get her back home. Just have to push the button."

Isa returned the smile and stood. I stood as well and, this time, accepted her extended hand without hesitation.

"Thank you for taking the chance and meeting me," she said. "I've wished for years we could find someone who could take action. I hate feeling impotent and watching a whole planet at risk." She looked at the door. "Do I just..."

"Go," said Riles.

I nodded at Isa. "Yeah, just head back the way you came. There will be a taxi waiting where the last one dropped you off."

She gave me a small wave as she left, cementing my quiet instinct that she was actually just a nice, awkward person in a shitty situation. Once she closed the door behind her, I locked it. I wanted to collapse with relief for just a second over the fact that I wasn't dead or captured, but I also wanted to get back to our lair. As I pulled the escape ladder in from the window and wiped any surface I'd touched and not yet wiped, Riles gave me status updates of Isa's trip back home and of zir surveillance of the hotel.

"I think she was legit, Kot. I'm still going to bounce you through some stops on the way home, but I don't think she was followed."

"Well, make them quick stops, poppet. I just want to eat crisps and plan the rebellion with you." Really, I just wanted to eat crisps and watch cat videos, but we were pretending Team Ugh were heroes now, so.

Back in the lesser comfort of our suite, I presented Riley with the superior offerings of the nicer suite's mini bar. "Just to say 'thanks' for making the meeting somewhere lovely."

Zie kindly split a chocolate bar with me and handed me a packet of my favorite crisps. "I figured, if she was actually just setting you up for murder, you might as well die in comfort."

I settled in at the table, my computer in front of me. "Are there any better friends in the world?"

"Nope, baby. You got lucky." Riles grinned and put a blank document on the big screen. "Okay. Rebellion ideas. Go!"

And then we spent a couple hours failing to make satisfying plans. Watching as people dug into their courses of action, with greedy traitors now also trying to suck up to aliens and/or trying to figure out how SWS execs being taken in by the aliens would ruin deals they'd been working on. The good guys had moved from cautiously looking into "what if aliens" to cautiously planning how they might deal with the aliens that did, indeed, exist.

We also watched coverage of a supposedly last-minute meeting held by Divine Community. They'd packed all their meeting houses (and any building that it might be reasonable to have the public in) and broadcasted the program to them. Nothing noteworthy in the message Michaelson delivered, just more of the same. But, holy hell, there was definitely something noteworthy about how many people had attended. And it sounded like, after the broadcast, high level Divine Community leaders had all displayed mystical healing powers. I wondered, once humans saw how the Peaceforgers worked in their healing centers, what Michaelson would say to explain away the strong similarity to his own supposedly miraculous powers.

Of course, even if I could have come up with ideas, I'm sure the bloody Peaceforgers would have been ahead of me. I was just hoping Isa could get me enough tech to let me even the playing field. Or at least enough to stave off the mind control or fire for long enough to let the people with actual power and weapons figure a way out of this.

It was surprisingly delightful to hear Riles and Kitty resume their bedtime chat tradition. I smiled into the darkness, feeling hopeful. I wanted to believe in signs so that I'd feel less silly about low-key believing this was a sign that we were now headed towards everything being okay.

CHAPTER 9

When we got up Wednesday, we learned that the Peaceforgers were no longer taking things at all slowly. I couldn't figure how they were getting so much done unless they'd woken up more people. Then Isa messaged:

Anyone who didn't have a high enough profile situation on Earth has been directed to pretend they're moving, allowing them to leave their human lives without raising suspicion, to live and work visibly as aliens. (Lots of surgeries to remove the prosthetic ears and noses, repair head ridges, etc.) That will make it harder for some people to get things to me, but easier for others to get access to things. I'll still be me, though, so I'll get in touch as soon as I have things for you.

Ah. Okay then. And what had all these people been up to whilst we slept? Well, thanks to time zones and refocused efforts of their people (could we count them pulling most everyone off SWS as us finally winning that particular battle?), they'd done some...let's call it pop-up healing sessions in the countries that weren't sleeping, focused on the biggest cities. They'd been sure to stop in and meet with the governments of all the awake countries too. They'd made some time for short, strategic interviews. And then, because we were on the North American west coast, they'd already started working their way across the Americas as reasonable waking hours rolled in for the other time zones whilst we slept. There were so many photos of a benignly smiling Morgan...

From what we could tell, they hadn't done a tremendous amount of healing or had any long meetings, but they'd done enough. Unless you were deep in some jungle without access to news of the world, you'd heard of them. And over 75% of the coverage was at least cautiously optimistic and accepting.

Looking at a variety of social media sites, it seemed like the average person was only slightly less open than the news was to the possibility that the aliens really did come in peace. And those who were openly suspicious ranged from firmly but politely questioning to gibbering spigots of hate and paranoia. Even though the reality we knew kind of made the paranoia of the latter group seem *slightly* reasonable for once, I just couldn't feel okay weaponizing their bigotry and/or mental illness.

After taking this all in, Riles pushed back from the table with a huff of frustration. "Some of the politicians smiling with them got our alien email. They should know better." Zie folded zir arms in what I'd call a sulk if the situation were less serious.

I tried to lift the mood, even if I wasn't sure the mood was inappropriate to the circumstance. "At least nobody's agreed to let them build healing centers yet. So maybe some of them are just playing it cool?"

Zie narrowed zir eyes but conceded, "Maybe." Then zie sighed. "I'm just fucking tired of all the shit we have to guess about instead of being able to logically draw conclusions or find proof."

"I hear you, poppet." I stood up and got some ramen meals microwaving. "But we can get some solid clues from all the monitoring we're doing. And we can check in with the team about new info on our message recipients. And maybe we'll have gear from Isa to let us monitor the Peaceforgers soon. You know, at least get more data to back up our guesses. And that's almost like proof and logic." I almost believed the cheery view I was peddling.

"In response, Morgan and their people said they were waiting to share directions for building their technologies because, quote, 'these are powerful instruments, and we need to make sure that we only share with species who have shown they can be trusted to use the information responsibly.' But they didn't clarify how we could show them humanity is trustworthy." The news anchor barely hid her smirk, and I wasn't sure if she was smirking at the Peaceforgers or at the fact that humanity definitely couldn't be trusted and shouldn't hold their collective breaths as regarding getting the tech.

And that, Hillary, is why Rachel got the in-person interview with Morgan and you didn't, I thought at Hillary the anchor.

But then her face perked up and she got her professional demeanor back. "And we'll return to that topic later. Right now, we have word of a devastating earthquake in Bolivia. At an estimated 6.9 magnitude, it even shook buildings in Sao Paolo, Brazil."

The news window filled with an image from a camera on the scene, presumably operated by an affiliated station. The chyron at the bottom said it was an image of Santa Cruz de la Sierra, Bolivia. Some curious and quick searching showed me that it was a city with tall buildings. Or it had been. Now, it was a city with a lot of rubble. Fuck.

As we watched, trying to ignore the estimates of lives lost that Hillary was delivering in pained tones, the camera view got even more newsworthy. Suddenly, three bright, aerodynamic Peaceforger shuttles swept in gracefully and lightly settled on an area that wasn't a pile of former buildings.

Hillary stumbled verbally. "Oh. Uh. So, we're going to switch you to the audio from our affiliate, and we'll provide the translation." She looked to the side, a little uncertain as a man who definitely hadn't anticipated being on air took a seat beside her. She explained to us, with a knowing smile, "And we'll do this the old-fashioned way so none of our hacker friends get tempted to hijack subtitles."

The man cleared his throat, and he slightly furrowed his brow as he stared at the table. Then he nodded, like he'd picked up the thread of something, and he started to talk. Started, I assumed, conveying the words from Bolivia as the audio he was translating played softly in the background. "Let's see if we can get the aliens to tell us why they're here. Excuse me! Excuse me! Can you tell us what you're doing?"

The camera view now included a short woman, looking surprisingly pulled together in the middle of the rubble. Most the Peaceforgers just kept working, opening doors on the shuttles and pointing small hoses attached to levitating tanks into the air, aimed at the rubble.

The one Peaceforger who turned to acknowledge the woman smiled and simply said, "We're here to help. Please give us one moment." But they said it in Spanish and our local guy translated for us.

"What do you think they're doing?" asked Riles. Zie was keeping one eye on the news and another on zir computer. "I don't see anything in what we know about them that gives me any clue."

Wearily distrustful, I quipped, "Harvesting all the freshly killed humans to replenish their food supply?"

We snorted in something like laughter, but I wasn't sure I meant it as a laugh. What dangerous rabbit would they pull out of their pasty alien hats now?

The reporter followed along with the Peaceforgers as they did...whatever it was they were doing. She told us the numbers and information she was getting, the estimates of people who were dead and who were surely trapped and about to be dead. It was gruesome. And then something slipped into the building they were standing in front of.

I pulled up another window with a duplicate live news feed so I could scroll back in the original window's buffer for a better look at the something. I moved to frame-by-frame playback...and it looked like the something was shining metal, long and narrow, and it slid into the rubble like it was nothing. I exchanged a look with Rye. Neither of us had any clue what we were looking at. But the damned Peaceforgers sure looked pleased. Especially when another of the narrow things slipped past them.

And then something was emerging from the rubble. Something human sized, bright metal now dusted with dirt. Something that set down gently in front of the Peaceforgers and the reporter...and unfolded to reveal a person.

The reporter motioned her camera in, so we all got to see the Peaceforgers bust out their healing hands as the woman exclaimed, "It looks like he's alive!"

A Peaceforger looked up at her briefly, smiling and nodding to confirm. And, before our eyes, they healed the man. (I wondered how many other people noticed it looked a lot like how Shepherd Michaelson healed people.) He had started as a bruised and bloodied body with limbs twisted ways they shouldn't be and a skull that looked slightly caved in. But, after a few minutes, he was pushing himself up to sitting just in time for more capsules to land with more people.

The reporter took a break from being excited about the rescued survivors to ask the least busy looking Peaceforger, "Can you tell me how you're saving these people?"

They beamed. "I'd be very happy to." They pointed at the hoses a couple of the Peaceforgers were still aiming at rubble. "We're sending out..." They paused, trying in English to see if it landed. "Nanomachines?"

It was the Bolivian reporter's turn to pause, a finger to her ear suggesting someone was remotely making sure she understood. She nodded.

The Peaceforger continued, "The nanomachines seek out life signs and attach themselves to those who are alive. As long as someone is alive, the nanomachines send out a signal that the retrievers can follow. The retrievers, uh, I can't reveal too many details of the technology, but they move in, collect the survivors, and find their way back to us."

"And is it safe? Won't the rubble be further destabilized, making it more dangerous for everyone?" The reporter cleared her throat. "We're grateful, of course, but..."

The Peaceforger assured here, "We are no strangers to rubble, and we've used these for many years." They smiled again. "But, yes, the way it operates includes stabilizing the rubble it moves through to ensure we don't do more harm than good."

The reporter was satisfied, and nothing new came from her reporting efforts. Not even in the following hours, once the news moved on but kept checking in on the situation in Bolivia and the number of survivors the Peaceforgers saved.

When they reached Morgan for a statement, Morgan simply said, "We're very sorry that the people of Bolivia have experienced this tragedy. And it's our privilege to help minimize the losses, to show by our actions that we truly are here for all people."

I wanted to punch them in the face. And I wondered if they'd somehow caused the earthquake so they'd have a chance to swoop in and help. Maybe they'd caused *all* the assorted emergencies they'd spent the day swooping in to help with around the world. Maybe they'd *made* all the chances they were quickly taking advantage of to prove they were the good guys.

"Oh, shit!" Riley sat up straight and stopped talking. Zie looked at me, excited.

"Good 'oh shit'?"

"More like 'lightbulb going off.' A mystery solved maybe." Zie was bouncing, so I just let zir go. "You know that earthquake survivor rescue stuff? The nanomachines and retrievers?"

I nodded, even though it was probably rhetorical.

"That's how they got Kitty, right?" Zie grimaced a little at the topic, but was too excited by this possible answer to switch off zir bounce. "And probably the execs. But now we have a viable possible answer to that question." And then the hope hit zir eyes. "Which means maybe there's not just an AI to retrieve. Maybe there's, like, a whole Kitty to rescue."

Oh. Wow. Maybe zie was right. "Riles, that's awesome! Let's definitely see if…if we can get her to locate her body?"

"I mean, that would be so much better, right? If she's just jacked into their computer? She just needs to get back in her body and…" Zie looked a little less hopeful. "Okay, maybe sneaking her off the ship will be harder than getting her downloaded." And then zie grinned. "But totally worth the work."

"Totally," I agreed, already irrationally jealous that Kitty, who didn't care about science fiction, had been on the ship and I hadn't. I didn't know why her being not-an-AI had changed it for me. I'd be sure to include this when I got to talk to a therapist about all this someday.

Zane messaged again. This one got our attention.

Your friends are alive.

I read it to Rye, and zie spit out, "Bullshit!" but with a touch of hope and awe. Then asked, "You think they're telling the truth?"

"Why didn't they tell us sooner? I mean, I want to believe, but..." I sighed. Fuck. Maybe this was a ploy to get us to reply.

"And do you think they mean Kitty too?"

I didn't want to encourage too much hope. "I don't think they'd know for sure that Kitty is ours. Not unless somebody told Zane they had her and where they'd gotten her from." I tried to soften it with a gentle hand on Riley's shoulder.

Zie took a breath, let it out slowly, clearly trying to get centered. "Good point." Zie nodded, clinging to what rationality zie could have in the face of Kitty things. "Good point. Okay. So...Do we reply?"

I typed a moment, pulling up the cameras (front and back) on Zane's phone. As had been the case all along, the cameras were covered. Which was a smart security move, and I wished they were dumber. Same story for the microphone. Damn.

"I really hate when they do something right," grumbled Riles. Then zie suggested, "Can we ping a location?"

I got typing as I mumbled, "Here's hoping the satellites are working, even if we can't control them. 'Cause I feel like the cell towers aren't exactly going to cover this."

The satellites continued not to work, but the cell towers did their best, getting us as close as verifying that the signal was coming from around the Puget Sound. So, they could be sitting on the waterfront somewhere...Except that, using some wi-fi connection points on some ships out in the water to try to get better triangulation on the phone...well, now we could say they were either drowning in the sound or...on the ship. Probably on the ship.

I double-checked that their messages weren't actually originating somewhere else and just being bounced through their phone. They weren't. Guess we knew where they'd been instead of their home.

"So, now we know it's *definitely* a trap or the truth, nothing in-between," Riles said.

"Maybe if we complain long enough we'll suddenly, magically be good at this meat space shit..." I sighed. "Okay, I literally have no idea how to decide."

Riley chewed a nail thoughtfully. "Do you trust Isa? Is the fact she seems to trust Zane enough to help?"

"I mean...I don't *not* trust her. But I'm also very sure that my desperate hope for proof of the boys is kiiiind of impacting my objectivity." I stared at my phone a bit. "Okay, can we use Kitty?"

Looking a bit guilty to admit it, zie said, "Can we come up with a plan that only needs her to ping Zane's phone? Because I'm not sure she can do much else reliably."

"I'm going to message her. Let's see if she has ideas." I tried to ignore that we were having to trust a lot of people we couldn't be sure were on our side. I was too paranoid by nature for this shit.

Fortunately, before I could spend too much time thinking about that, we had Kitty in 3D. Or the thing we hoped was Kitty. And, probably thinking of my tendency to do a poor job of being careful in potentially difficult conversations, Riles immediately started talking.

"Baby, we have a lot of things we think are happening on the ship, and we don't want to neglect including you in figuring them out. We know you've been working hard to try to learn to navigate your situation."

Sweetly, she said, "Oh, baby..." then turned her little holo-face towards me, straight-forward. "So, you guys need me to do better and actually be useful? And something has made it so you don't feel like you can wait on my slow ass anymore?"

I gave a little shrug and nod. "I mean, if you want to say it more like I'd say it..." I grinned. "But I swear I'm working hard to remember that you're in a totally, if you'll excuse the pun, alien situation. And it's not like I think you have work ethic problems."

Kitty laughed. "I hope you'll take this the right way when I say I wish it had been one of you nerds, not me, who ended up stuck in the computer." She nodded resolutely. "But if wishes were horses and all that. So, let's figure out what I can do or what I can try to do."

Rye said, "We've been told that our friends are alive. But we don't necessarily trust the source, and we don't know which of you they mean."

"Oh! That's great news! If it's true." Kitty smiled broadly. "It must be the boys, right?"

We both nodded, but Rye added, "Probably. But we also don't want to rule out that maybe you're actually just hooked up to a computer, that maybe your body is still around."

Her eyes got big with surprise, and her voice was barely more than a squeak when she asked, "Really?" After she took in Riley's eager nod, she looked at me, a little more skeptical. "Really?"

I didn't want to piss off Riles by disappointing zir girl, but I wasn't going to lie. Trying to sound very even, I said, "We know the Peaceforgers can both extricate *and* heal people who've been trapped under rubble, so it's *possible*."

"Okay." All business, she said, "I'll add myself to the list of things to look for on cameras. Now..." She made a noise like clearing her throat and looked a bit frustrated. "I seem to have gotten better at choosing cameras to look through, but I'm not 100% and these assholes have, like, ludicrous numbers of cameras. *Lu.di.crous.*"

"What if we could help you narrow down where on the ship to look? At least for the boys?" Riley definitely had an idea.

Kitty nodded. "I think that puts it more within my capabilities. And it at least gives me a narrower focus to work on if I'm not there yet."

"What are you thinking?" I asked Riles.

"Well, as you know, I am a student of all things to do with love and attraction."

I coughed, "Sex."

Very obviously ignoring me, zie went on, "And it's my academic opinion, the very thesis of my idea, that, if you discovered your lover was on the very space ship that you were on, you would find a way to see them. You would bicycle past their holding cell, over and over."

Pretty In Pink reference aside, I agreed with where I thought zie was going, but decided to let zir go there without me interrupting. Worst case scenario, if I was wrong, I had an idea to toss in.

Kitty encouraged, "Okay, Ducky, that sounds reasonable. Keep going."

"And I stand by my former belief that Zane is into our Bryan. So, if you can figure out how to use Zane's phone to find them, you can follow Zane. Eventually, they'll lead you to Bryan."

Exactly where I'd thought zie was going, so I quickly agreed, though I noted, "Of course, unless she's not mentioned it, Kitty hasn't yet figured out how to track people's location by their phones."

"Yeah, but, I can look through their phone cameras and see where in the ship they are."

Riles shook zir head. "Their cams are covered."

"Dammit. Okay." Kitty's face was thoughtful. "Well, give me their phone number, and I'll see if I can do anything with that."

I was distracted by the ping of a message on my phone. And I almost gasped when I opened it. But I swallowed the sound and instead said, "Right. I think we need a new question. Because the one about whether or not the boys are alive might have an answer." I held up my phone and turned it, making sure both Riles and Kitty had a chance to see the photo Zane had sent.

We'd have to check for manipulation, but the photo appeared to be a quick snap of Bryan and Jonny. They looked horrible; clearly, the Peaceforgers hadn't given them the full healing tech treatment. But they looked alive. (Because we were sure as hell going to count barely alive as alive enough to be rescued and to make hopeful birds flutter in my chest.)

"Show me again." Kitty leaned towards me, as if her hologram could actually see.

I held the picture up and moved it slowly towards the camera on Rye's phone that was, basically, Kitty's eyes.

"Stop! Okay, hold it there." Kitty studied the image. "I think, on the right, there's a mark that's like a room number. So, that should narrow cameras I need to look through." She thought a moment. "And can you show me a pic of the alien I'm trying to follow?"

After Riles flashed her a paused shot from a video of Zane, she gave us a little salute. "Back quickly as I can manage." And she blinked out.

We didn't do anything for a moment, just looked at each other with a mix of uncertainty and hope. Then, after a quick bit of joyful squealing and without zir having to ask, I pushed a copy of the pic to Riley's phone and moved another to my computer, where it would be easier to work with. Time to see if it was the real thing.

"How am I supposed to be sure my analysis is good when we're dealing with aliens with superior tech?" Riley waved a hand at the TV, where news windows showed Peaceforgers healing people and slipping bodies out from rubble.

I rubbed my eyes. That same question had kept me staring at my screen too long as well. If the pic had come from a human, I'd say it was untouched. I'd be sure the boys were alive and on the damned alien ship. But it hadn't come from a human. I answered Riles with a sad little grunt of agreement.

That evening, Isa messaged that she had something for me already, with documentation attached to the message and translated documentation headed my way as soon as she could manage. I took a quick peek and had no idea what we were about to get. I forwarded the documentation to Engie, promising a translated version once I had it. I was hoping, since she'd seen Peacemaker schematics, she might be able to find enough similarities to get going.

I assumed she only woke up enough to check her messages because she knew we were all still in danger. She messaged back quickly.

I'm basically drooling! Will see what sense I can make. If you're getting tech, maybe see if they can get you tools to make/maintain the tech?

I rolled my eyes at myself for not thinking of that and added the request to the message I was drafting for Isa. I hoped I wasn't coming across as too greedy. Though, given her species was trying to enslave the minds of our species, I kind of felt like "too greedy" wasn't a judgment one could fairly apply to our requests for help to stop that.

We took a quick look at what shops she frequented that weren't walking distance from her loft, and we ordered her a self-driving taxi to take her there. Much as I hated the risk of leaving whatever she was sending unattended, Rye wouldn't budge on refusing to have the taxi pick me up first. Which was fine, because I also hated having to go out and deal with things in the meat. (I am a mass of glorious contradictions.)

Obviously, we watched her ride to the shop via the taxi cameras, and we provided a credit on her account so she wouldn't have to pay her fare back home. And then we faked the taxi's transmissions so that anyone looking at data or camera footage would think it took an old man from that shop to his home nowhere near us. When the taxi thought it was arriving at his home, it was actually pulled over at the curb to let me lean out of the shadows and grab a small bag from the back seat. The first real info from the taxi came 15 minutes later when it arrived somewhere that was 15 minutes from both the fake old man and from our place. (I wasn't sure if we were being super sneaky and fooling anyone watching, or if we were just so bad at this sort of thing that the only people we were fooling were ourselves...)

By then, we'd checked out what was in the bag.

It was a small device, a quite thin rectangular block, with small enough proportions that I might easily compare its size to a phone. But one of those smaller ones you can fit in your pockets, not the big ones that might as well be mini-tablets. Made from the same light-colored metal that the Peaceforgers seemed to favor, one side looked a little glassy (maybe a screen?), and one end of that side had a couple low-profile slider-like controls and a small inset keypad. Everything sleek and shiny.

The only other thing in the bag was a scrap of paper with looping and lovely handwriting. "Frequency detector" was all it said.

"Holy shit." I grinned as I messaged to let Engie know what we had. "This is *golden.*"

Rye didn't say anything, just started a list of the things we might be able to use the detector for. Kitty was top of the list, of course, but we might also find a way for us to get into the ship's computers. We should at least be able to tell if they were bugging us, maybe even listen in on communications (depending on the specifics of this particular little gizmo). You know, that sort of legitimately super useful and helpful thing. Nice!

Soon after she got home, Isa messaged.

Full instructions in attached doc. Last one was apparently just a quick start and technical specs. Not in English yet. Sorry.

After running a check on the file to make sure it was safe, I opened it to find a good-sized instruction manual for the frequency detector. As she'd warned, not a word of it was in English (or any other Earth language). But at least it was something.

Riles and I did our best to take useful photos of the device (though we couldn't open it to photograph its insides, so...). We sent pictures and instructions to Engie, with apologies for all the limitations on what we could send.

We also got a program running to see if we could parse anything usable by applying the word list Zane had helped us make to the text at hand. (We could not.)

Late enough in the day that I wondered if they'd hoped it wouldn't be seen by too many people, the U.N. released a message on behalf of its member nations by posting it on their site. It wasn't addressed to anyone, and I could see it being aimed at the Peaceforgers or at other humans.

We are always eager to find new solutions to improve quality of life for our citizens. However, we are mindful of the way that eagerness can override reasonable caution. In the interest of our citizens' safety, we cannot approve health facilities built around technology that hasn't been vetted by experts in relevant fields. Citizens are free to take advantage of opportunities to receive care, and we look forward to the opportunity to evaluate and understand new health solutions. The U.N. can provide experts to expedite approval across member nations when new technologies do arise.

A quick bit of hacking through their records showed that they'd spent the day bitterly fighting amongst themselves. So, I wasn't counting on all the nations to actually stick to the statement. And I didn't need to hack anything to know that some of the nations involved would almost certainly be trying to broker individual access to the tech already.

I hoped that would be enough to keep the Peaceforgers from going nuclear just a little longer.

I hated the bastard Peaceforgers even more for making me actually value human corruption a little. Though I made a note to keep an eye on who made deals. If we made it through this with the planet intact, some of us were going to have to make sure nobody dodgy had better tech than the rest of the world.

CHAPTER 10

Thursday felt like some kind of routine was actually gelling. Or at least like we mainly knew what to spend our time on. Like I didn't have to expose my executive function struggles by constantly having to try to choose what to do.

What we wanted to do was plan how to get the boys back, but we needed more info from Zane or Kitty. Or at least needed Kitty to confirm that the pic Zane had sent was legit.

What we wanted to do, though not as desperately as getting our boys, was play with the frequency detector, but we had no way to be sure it didn't also transmit. So it sat there, in its bag (out of sight wasn't actually out of mind, but it helped), on the table. Even with the bit of—in the loosest sense—a dictionary we'd compiled so far, even with Engie's big brain and experience, the language in the documentation was beyond what we could parse, at least this quickly. Which meant we were waiting to see whether Engie's brain or the translated documentation would get us working first.

So, instead of saving the boys or doing frequency stuff, we did the new usual.

We checked in on forums that were kind of dead. Oh, unless you wanted to argue about the aliens and see people's newest photos of Morgan and their best pals. In that case, there was plenty of "action."

We were delighted to see, though, that one of the things that was being suggested on some forums was that this kind of sounded like that whole Peaceforger thing with SWS, and didn't those old pics of the execs look like, I don't know, maybe they were alien/human hybrids or something? We crossed our fingers and hoped that would become more than a fringe idea.

We kept an eye out for results from searches we had running and for action on the Zane and Isa cameras. Booooooooring. And fruitless.

We kept digging into and watching the moves of people who got our "aliens!" email and others in power. But, honestly, even with our whole team on it, that was too much work for too few resources. We were just randomly choosing which of the way too many people to look at. We tried to set up some automated searches and notifications to help with that, but we were no longer living in a world where you could use "alien" as a trigger word for notifications and have it be meaningful.

We researched AI, just in case that was still relevant to saving Kitty.

We took some tries at the satellites again...and continued to fail. We hoped our days of needing to use the satellites were over.

We practiced with the drones. Ugh! I hated sucking at drones more than I hated failing at satellites since this meat-based shit was one of our very few remaining options. Especially if we couldn't get into the ship's computers to deploy our usual computer-based weapons. And given the Peaceforgers weren't likely to be shamed off the planet, the media manipulation we'd been getting a little better at probably wasn't going to be a strong weapon. So. Either the powers that be needed to be prepared to use the drones...or we did. Because sucking at a task is only made more delightful by the literal weight of the world hanging on one's not sucking.

We distracted ourselves from the weight by doing a lot of random bullshitting and speculating. Most of it was fluff or didn't lead to conversation. Most of it.

When Riles asked, "What if Kitty isn't the only one who was alive when the Peaceforgers found them? What if Quinn was alive, and now he's also wandering some kind of digital space?", we lost an hour to guilt and trying to figure out if we could find an answer. After all, Quinn had been a good friend for years, and he'd given us first a hideout and then his life (we thought) since this whole shitstorm had started. And we now wondered if maybe we didn't have strong proof that they'd actually killed him that night outside the Divine Community plant. If they'd realized he was connected to us...

We lamented that he'd be in even worse shape than Kitty, at least in terms of trying to figure things out, 'cause he'd never even used a computer thanks to his parents' religious beliefs. We really talked ourselves into a pit of worry and self-loathing. Until we realized that at least it would mean he was alive and we'd have a chance to find and rescue him. You know, if we could confirm he'd actually been loaded into the Matrix or whatever.

Whilst we were failing to figure out how to confirm that, I had another non-fluffy thought. But mine started as hope, since we were trying to angle our brains back that way in the moment.

Really, it started as desperation, triggered by talk of Quinn and Kitty. Triggered as my brain cycled once again through the continuous quiet litany of people who'd died in the last few weeks. We *knew* 'Randa was dead. We had plenty of evidence Huw was dead. We knew Gran was...As I choked on the thought, unable to finish it, my brain whispered, *But what if they uploaded her somehow? Because she's related to you.* My gaze, which had been unfocused, aimed at the middle of the table and came into focus. There was that bag with the frequency thing, the one we weren't using because we didn't know if it would transmit. Maybe that had also sparked the thought. My brain fell over itself to draw parallels and suggested, *We know that, to some extent, Peacemakers are also transmitters. What if they uploaded her that way?*

"Oh!" I sat up straighter. When Riley gave me a questioning look, I said, "Peacemakers aren't just receivers." I leaned forward, intent on making this work. "We *know* they transmit 'cause they definitely send location and emotion info and all that. So why couldn't they transmit more?"

I knew zie hadn't made the hopeful leap my brain had, because Riles looked a little sick when zie asked, "More?"

I nodded eagerly, hoping zie'd catch my enthusiasm. "What if they could upload people? Like...However they loaded Kitty in, but remotely? It might be slower, but they'd have the time, right?" I was practically vibrating as I delivered the cherry on top of this sundae. "And, because they're sure I'm the problem, they would *totally* have uploaded Gran. We could maybe get Gran back too!"

Zie paused a moment, face making the little twitches of a person trying to process a thought. "Okay. I see how that makes it seem good to you." Rye was talking very carefully. "And I would love, *love*, to end this bullshit 'adventure' with all of us getting all our people back. Definitely including Gran. But." Zie sighed. "Look, babe, if they can upload...Every person they upload...What if they can search them? Like data? What if they know everything about us Gran knows? What if it's not just Gran, but *all* the people with Peacemakers. Including people who have power or can influence those with power?"

I felt my chest tightening a little with fear. Shit. That would be bad. I signaled that I understood by adding to the worry. "They wouldn't even necessarily be uploading them as full people, like Kitty. Just pulling in all they know."

"The better to *change* their thoughts or get by whatever defenses are keeping those bastards from taking control of people. Or of our weapons." Riles sounded as grim as I felt.

Thinking of them controlling people, I suggested, "Like that girl they made kill the kids." It was my turn to feel a little sick as I remembered that.

Zie nodded, mouth pinched. "Like that girl."

I felt sorry my brain had ever speculated. New worries, and no way to confirm or deny. Nice job, brain...

With our new worries, we watched through eyes half-closed with suspicion (is it suspicion when you *know* they're up to no good?) as Divine Community announced that they would be letting "our new friends from heaven" use their clinics until they were approved to open healing centers of their own.

"After all," Michaelson said, "we have seen how they heal the same way we at Divine Community heal. Surely this is proof, this shared miracle, that they are also blessed and considered worthy by the Divine."

As they shook hands at the little press conference, both Michaelson and Morgan were grinning so widely that I was sure they were going to unhinge their jaws and start swallowing babies. People would still have to show up to the clinics, but we'd seen plenty of sources confirm that people had done just that. It was easy to talk about being wary of healing tech (or supposedly miraculous healing powers) and people you didn't understand when you were healthy, but plenty of people weren't healthy. Even without beat down flu, most countries had shitty health care systems, and some conditions didn't have cures. Or they hadn't had cures until now.

Who was I to judge the people who went to those centers? I mean, yeah, we should be cautious, but there were plenty of stories about human doctors who were fuckups, and I wouldn't tell anyone to avoid *all* doctors. So.

"At least now we know where to send the drones," Riley grumbled. "Easier to get them now that they're not hidden in the ocean or even all tucked away on the ship."

"Yeah," I grudgingly poked holes in zir positive spin, "but there are also non-complicit humans at the clinics, and shrapnel from a ship destroyed in the sky sounds more dangerous than if we blow it up under water."

"You are *not* invited to any more of my parties, bitch. Total killjoy," Rye snarked whilst also somehow sulking.

Kitty was pinging our messenger like crazy. We were both wrapping up other things, so it went on enough seconds that we were both laughing as we finished and turned to her.

I mimicked Kitty's voice as I reached for my phone and tried to stop laughing. "Guys! Guys! Guys!"

With a flourish, Riles finished up zir thing and scooted over to see my screen as I opened the messenger. Where, in fact, it did say:

Guys! Guys! Guys!

At least the first message was that. And the rest were variations. We had to pause a moment to stop laughing before we pushed the button to let Kitty pop up and be 3D in our faces.

And then she squealed, "Guys!"

I had to swallow really hard not to start laughing again.

Fortunately, Rye instinctively matched her enthusiasm, and zie had the personality to pull it off with authenticity. "Baby! Hey, what's going on?"

"What's going on, you nerds, is that I found the boys!"

For a moment, time froze. I thought that only happened with bad shit, but apparently unbelievably good shit also did it to me. I whispered, "What?" 'Cause there was no way I'd heard her correctly.

She nodded, excited. And then she spilled out words at an even faster rate than usual. "Okay. So. I was working on cameras, like I've been doing for aaaaages. But narrowed down because you guys had that picture. And I actually stumbled across Zane, and they totally did a Ducky, just like Riley said. So I could just go camera to camera to follow them. And they couldn't really pause long outside their room, but I could just sit there as long as I wanted. And the boys are definitely here and alive. I mean, really fucked up, but alive!"

Cautiously, Rye said, "Are you sure? Because..." Zie looked over at me quickly, like zie needed to confirm I would agree. "Because, if they're alive, that dictates what we need to do."

"Let me..." Kitty screwed up her face. "If I can transmit me, maybe I can transmit them, right?"

And then the image we were seeing in 3D changed.

When it was Kitty, it was crisp; it was a perfectly detailed little Holo-Kitty. No question. But now?

It looked like old-fashioned TV. Really old. Low resolution, grainy. And there seemed to be two people lying curled on a floor. Two people my brain really, really wanted to see as Bryan and Jonny. But I also knew my brain well enough to know I was too biased for a logical assessment.

I caught Riley's eye; zie was clearly as uncertain as I was.

And, in case zir face wasn't reply enough, zie said, "Maaaaaybe?"

I shrugged. Yeah, I didn't have a better read on it.

The image wavered and then became Kitty again. She quickly took in our faces and her smile dropped. "Was it not good?"

"It was a good first effort, baby. Just, uh, a little grainy." And then, with the sort of true encouragement that only Rye could manage in a situation like this, zie said, "But how cool that you found a new thing you can do? That's badass!"

Even bloodless, Holo-Kitty managed a pleased little blush. Then she assured us, "Well, contrary to some recent evidence,

I'm a fast learner. Sometimes. I'll get you full quality pictures in no time."

Whether or not I believed she'd manage that, and pushing aside a wee bit of lingering paranoia that she wasn't actually Kitty but was a Peaceforger-controlled lure, I found that I now kind of believed that the boys were probably alive. Which was amazing and daunting. Because we had to do something about that. Just in case Kitty's and my belief were right.

Once Kitty left to see if she could figure out a way to be helpful in rescuing the boys, Riley and I just contemplated the walls a moment. Zie eventually got up to pour boiling water into noodles and make us both yet another "fancy" on-the-run dinner.

I was uselessly just tumbling things over in my head, but I didn't try to vocalize any of it until I was holding a warm noodle cup in my hands. "I wish my excitement hadn't immediately been kneecapped by the feeling that we've now definitely got this...almost impossible thing to do."

With a tone of over-the-top optimism, Riles said, "Get onto the alien spaceship, find the cell without being caught, open the cell, get our very wounded boys out without making their medical situation worse, and then get back to Earth? Easy! Yeah..." Zie trailed off into a sigh. "Fuck."

"Right." I sat up and started making a list of the steps zie'd said. "Let's just...maybe we figure it out one thing at a time."

"At least, of those five things, we can probably get Kitty or Zane to lead us to the cell. So, that's 20% of the plan down." Zie didn't sound like zie was sold on my approach even as zie offered that bit of figuring out, but zie also didn't offer an alternative approach.

Instead of admitting I didn't have strong ideas for the other 80% or mentioning that we'd likely have to trust Peaceforgers who claimed to be on our side to make it happen, I noted, "We probably can't blow the ship whilst we're on it to rescue them, not until we have Kitty. But let's keep that in mind in case you solve the Kitty retrieval thing suddenly."

"Mm." Zie made an agreeing kind of noise, then added, "And we can't blow up the ship at all, even if we master the drones, until we have the boys off it."

I sighed, frustrated. "I guess I need to answer Zane, don't I?"

"Dammit," Riles confirmed.

I kept it short and didn't bother with context. I trusted Zane to catch on quickly.

Can you get them back to Earth?

For someone who'd been desperately trying to get us to reply to them for days, they sure didn't reply quickly. After about five minutes of staring at my phone, I gave up and made myself get back to work.

We might get our boys, but it sure seemed like those in charge were going to let the Peaceforgers get our planet. Which meant there was plenty of work to get back to.

When my phone pinged, it wasn't Zane. It was Isa.

Translation of user manual for freq detector.

In spite of my excitement, I still remembered to scan the file and make sure it was safe. And then, even before I read it, I sent a copy off to Engie and made sure Rye had zir own copy.

It was twice as formidable in size once translated, so it was good that I was a fan of reading. In case having the ability to use this tech wasn't exciting enough on its own to make my brain engage, I reminded myself that this was better than science fiction about fictional aliens; this was science *documentation* about something from *actual* aliens. And I was sure as hell going to try to at least enjoy that I personally knew aliens, didn't just know *of* them, something I'd always hoped would happen...Even if the end of the story was looking increasingly likely to be "and then humans let their own greed sabotage things, so they ended up dead or, basically, lobotomized."

Fucking Zane didn't reply. I fell asleep cranky and trying to work through the manual. No surprise that I had stress dreams about having to learn super abstract alien tech without assistance, and in the middle of a fire fight, to stop the impending exploding of the planet. Thanks, brain. And Zane. Going to let Zane take part of the blame for that shit.

CHAPTER 11

Fridays had been far less exciting to me since I'd been bombed out of having a day job. And, on the one hand, I *had* been constantly telling people I wanted less excitement. On the other hand...It wasn't really about Fridays, was it? It was about knowing that you were about to have a break from the thing you hated, the thing that dominated your life. And I could really have done with some of that right now.

But I tried not to sulk as I ate my cereal and scanned the news, read my messages, and so forth. I noted little signs of both humans accepting Peaceforgers and humans staying wary as hell of them. I further noted that the numbers weren't strongly enough skewed towards wary, not even among those in power who'd been warned (by us) that this bullshit was coming.

"Kot?"

I glanced up at a weary-looking Riles. Had zie been up all night talking to Kitty?

Zie said, with a voice so heavy I knew zie knew it was a massive task, "I think we need to plan how *we're* going to take care of the Peaceforgers. I just...Those bitches are doing a really good job of playing saviors, and I just...Have you seen the post in bugHunt about the gifts to leaders?"

I had not. I shook my head slightly and tried to do "I am curious; please continue" eyes.

Zie cleared zir throat and leaned in towards zir screen, as if zie were going to read that post. But then zie sighed, like maybe zie just couldn't subject zirself to it again, and looked up at me. "Basically, while they continue to hold back on big deal tech, the Peaceforgers are making time for any leader in any country who wants to meet. Because, obviously, they don't have to ask for an invite; everybody wants to at least get a close look. And, when they meet, they're giving gifts. Bullshit, mundane stuff for them, like one-sheet digital albums with pictures from other planets or a small rod that makes plants healthier. But it's making leaders sure they can ride the Peaceforger train out into space or magically fix any crop issues if they can make the plant thing larger. And it sure seems like Morgan—or whoever is in charge of a given delegation—is encouraging that, saying ambiguous shit about looking forward to working together or seeing what they can help the human species grow to become as we make choices that let them share more powerful gifts."

I saw where this was going. "Which means, in all likelihood, the leaders now want to at least pretend to trust and work with them long enough to get that."

"Yeah. Which means we probably have to come up with a plan where *we* save the world." Zie had rarely sounded more annoyed, but also somehow utterly despairing.

I had to close my eyes and give myself a pep talk. *We're going to try, because it's right. Because nobody else can and will. Because we have to be the Bryan and Jonny for now. Because, even if we can't fix the world and the situation it's in, we can't desist from trying.* Then I took a long, deep breath, and let it seep slowly out of me. I imagined I felt some hint of calm around the edges, but maybe it was just shock. I nodded. "Okay."

"Step one is obviously saving the boys and Kitty, so we don't have to worry about hurting them when we...attack. Or whatever we're going to do." Riley might not know how to do it, but zir tone made it clear zie had no doubt this was definitely the first thing we had to do.

"And we can't see how to do this, save the world or whatever, other than attacking?" I knew I couldn't see another way, but I hoped that Riles had ideas, especially since zie'd "whatever-ed."

Zie snorted. "It's not like we can reason with them."

"Can we...I don't know...Scare them into leaving?" Because it sounded silly when I said it out loud, I clarified. "You know, threaten them with the common cold or something that isn't going to hurt us but will take them out?"

"They've been surviving here, living with us, for decades..." Zie shrugged apologetically, probably just as disappointed as I was that the only answer we could come up with, once again, was "kill 'em all."

And then I realized, "Plus, even if they get in their ship and go, it's not like they can't bomb us as they run away."

Riles nodded. "Right. So, we have to take control of their ship and/or destroy it. And do whatever cleanup planet-side of those who aren't on the ship."

"If we could only get at the ship's computer..." I let the familiar lament trail off.

"Or if we could show Kitty how to do what we need..." Riles let that similarly familiar wish trail off too.

I shook my head firmly, trying to dislodge old worries, maybe spill out new thoughts. Chewing the inside of my cheek, wondering if starting from the end and working backwards might help our brains, I said, "So, ideally, we have their computers...what? Send an 'everybody come home' signal, and then have it blast them away, locked out of any dangerous weapons systems, once they're all on board?"

"Oh, and make their computer unable to navigate back here. Which, admittedly, doesn't save any other planet, but does save ours."

"Yes!" I liked talking ideals better than realities. "So, if we could do that or show Kitty how, then we'd be good, right?"

Zie looked guiltily at zir phone, like zie was looking at Kitty, and said, "In the...seemingly unlikely event we can get Kitty to do it...Yeah, we have her do that, then we...download her, if we conclude she's...she's not a body anymore." Rye looked super uncomfortable as zie said, "Though we should also keep a Plan B where we...we would have to use the drones to destroy the ship and take out any Peaceforgers on earth."

"We know drones can target individuals, so we can do it one at a time if need be. Maybe use their extra-controversial auto-targeting feature, since there are just the two of us." I felt dirty even talking about it, but maybe it was time these shitty weapons did some good.

"As long as they can't trip some kind of 'explode all Peacemakers' switch on their way out..." Zie gave a sad sort of laugh. "Which means we also need to sort satellites out somehow to be ready to block that. Like we did on Demo Day, but on a way bigger scale. And hope their ship can't broadcast worldwide without using satellites..."

"Poppet, just this once, I'm going to pretend the physics we understand are on our side. That they haven't found some science that lets them broadcast from where they hang in our sky and somehow have it go through the whole globe unassisted."

"I will buy into that viewpoint. Which means, if we can even just sort out temporarily disabling satellites, on purpose and not 'disabled' because the Peaceforgers have taken them...and somehow still use the drones?" Zie was looking at the ceiling thoughtfully.

"So, pieces of this. Get back boys, get Kitty—"

"Which probably needs to be preceded by figuring out what state she's in, whether there's a body or not," zie begrudgingly acknowledged.

I nodded. "Yes. And the only way I can think of, short of us kidnapping one of their leaders..." I paused for a moment of fake, desperate laughter. "Kitty is going to have to look for data about herself. So, we have to help her figure out how to become a search engine."

"I feel like, as long as we have voice contact with her, she can concentrate enough on that—'cause she talks to us now with no effort, and she found the Peaceforger-to-English dictionary— that I can talk her through it. Which," zie conceded, "we might want to consider for letting us try Plan A. Even if that sounds ridiculously difficult. Me talking her through it, that is."

"Maybe...I work with Zane to figure out getting boys back, though Kitty is very welcome to volunteer help, and you work with Kitty to figure out her situation. Then...one of us works to figure out getting her back here, whilst the other one works to get her doing our Plan A actions on the ship's computer." My brain hurt just thinking of how any of that would work, especially coaching Kitty.

Clearly thinking the same thing, Riles tossed out an apt metaphor. "That last one is going to be harder than super old school text-only adventure games. Serious 'this is an open field west of a white house' Zork shit. But harder and probably not at all fun."

"But still better than being the first one done with their second task, or the one who learns they can't do the task, and therefore has the job of programming the automated hunt-and-kill function on the drones." I'd said it flippantly, but my soul felt dirtier for even thinking it. I desperately hoped I wouldn't have to be that person. (*We're back to thinking about stains on our soul, aren't we?* asked the wildly tired voice in my head.)

With a similar tone of moral regret, zie noted, "We'll also have to program the lot that need to attack the ship. Plenty of shitty work to go around."

"Fuck. I just realized we don't know if, for instance, the ship has a force field or automated anti-missile weapons or other shit like that." I wanted to swallow my tongue. I wanted something to be straight-forward.

"One more thing for Kitty to figure out?"

Everyone had so much fun stuff on their to-do list. So much...

Before I could properly get to brainstorming (aka guessing wildly because I had no actual info to work with and Zane hadn't gotten back to me) how to get the boys, Riley's computer shrieked. It was just one sharp sound, not loud enough to be heard outside our suite. The sort of sound that I'd have assumed meant some video started to auto-play when Riles opened a site, emitting just a burst of obnoxious aural discord before zie hit mute.

But then Riles stood up so quickly zir chair threatened to fall over. "Shit! They're here." Zie started slapping computers closed.

I paused a moment, confused. "'They'?"

Zie urgently hissed, "Narnia time."

I leapt up too, a straight shot of adrenaline crackling through me like terrified lightning. "Fuck!"

If we were doing Narnia, it could only be one "they." "They" as in the Peaceforger thugs. The ones in black and masks, with guns and hammering fists. The ones who'd beat the shit out of Riley. The ones who'd shot Quinn...and then Jonny and Bryan.

They'd finally come to kick down our door. And we didn't have the safety that every other person behind every other door they'd kicked down had. We were actually the ones they wanted. We were already disappeared and, therefore, could be permanently disappeared without consequences. We wouldn't get off as easily as those in our decoy rooms had.

We rushed to clear everything that would tip off the thugs that this was, in fact, the room they'd hoped for every other time. That we were, in fact, the ones who'd killed their people and threatened their "benevolent" dystopian plans for us.

Before I felt sure we'd done all we needed, the cameras we were keeping half an eye on told us they were already in the corridor outside our door. We rushed to the big wardrobe against the back wall of our room, cramming in like rabbits diving for their warrens when the dogs come.

We held our collective breath, frozen and listening intently. If we had been rabbits, our ears would have quivered with the effort, if not with the fear. We had our bags with our most essential items on our backs, and we crouched like we thought we could actually run. (Holy shit; we really were freaked out bunnies...) Riley had tucked away zir phone, probably feeling more need for both hands free than for eyes on the cameras. It was fair to assume we knew where they were.

And then we were sure of their location as we heard the click of them opening our door. They must have hacked the lock, afraid of another run in with startled thugs with guns, so they could slip in quietly. But the tiny alarm we'd put on it was sounding in our earbuds. I quickly tapped my bud to turn down the high-pitched squeal of it in my ear.

I gave Riles a quick, questioning look, inclined my head towards the exit. Should we bolt for the door?

Zie shook zir head once, sharply.

With nobody in sight, the thugs stopped being silent. They closed the door to our suite behind them. There'd be no witnesses for what went down in our room.

One of them commanded, "Search everything. Find me proof of who's here. Or really impress me and find an actual person."

Everyone laughed a little at that, unaware for the moment that they *might* find a person.

A new voice jokingly called out, "Anyone quaking in the tub or stuffed under the bed?"

Meaty man voices all chuckled at that.

Fortunately, that wasn't followed by the noise of a room being tossed. Maybe they'd wandered into enough wrong suites by now that they were open to the idea that this was the wrong room and they might want to leave the occupant ignorant of their visit.

They were no longer silently gliding though; I could clearly hear the footsteps of some big meatsack crossing to the wardrobe. I cringed back then froze at the soft squeak, loud as the alarm in my ears had been, as Big Meatsack opened the wardrobe...

And found nothing. From the other side of the back wall—or, really, the back wall then the room wall then the back wall of the wardrobe in the room behind us where we stored our spare stuff and where we happened to be hiding—I heard Big Meatsack report, "Nothing in here."

I hoped he didn't look closely. I hoped our work, where we'd cut through and put hinges on this side of the back wall, was as well done as we thought. I hoped...and then I heard the doors shut firmly.

I looked at Rye, and we silently, joyfully screamed. Zir ridiculous, amazing escape idea had actually worked. (Look, if the villains could go over the top with underwater doors and shit, we could do the same.)

Riley silenced the door alarm, maybe not even noticing it until the fear had passed. Instead, we could now hear the muffled sounds of search through a few wee bugs we'd tucked around the room. And then zie pulled up the equally wee cameras so we could watch.

It was a satisfyingly boring thing, but also perfect, as the thugs each shook their heads at the person we presumed was Head Meatsack of this little force. I beamed with pride as one picked up the decoy family photo (my idea!) to show him, as if to add that to the mounting evidence that this was not our room.

Head Meatsack joked, "I'd call this a failure, but none of us got stabbed this time."

Everyonc laughed and headed out.

We waited a while, both to be sure and to scan as best we could from inside the wardrobe—with one of the bug scanners we'd collected the last few weeks—for any bugs in the room that weren't ours. We also took a moment to make sure this backup room was still okay, whatever that meant. For me, it meant wandering around its small confines, making sure no bags or gear looked "wrong." (Yeah, I had no idea what I meant by that either.)

After about 30 minutes, which was 25 minutes after building cameras showed the thugs exiting through the garage, we decided it was probably okay to go back to our room. Do a proper bug scan. Get back to work.

"Next time," I suggested, "let's go through the one that lets us drag Aslan into our fight. Adding one more cat to the team can only help."

Because Zane still hadn't gotten back to me, I thought I'd sit with Riles and see if I could help as zie tried to talk Kitty through searching for info on herself and on the ship's defenses. But then I got distracted by an argument that involved, I knew, our four remaining remote comrades. So I left Riles to do zir thing and I read the conversation.

> kiss-the-sky: Don't want us not asking the important question, so I'm asking. Are we totally sure that 100% opposing the aliens (Peaceforgers?) is the right move? World is pretty fucked up. Peace and healing are good...
> fischer_queen: u fuckin serious?
> kiss-the-sky: Just asking us to consider. Not running out to sell us out, asshole.
> 5x5: And what would we do if we decided we weren't opposing them anymore?
> cacheMoney: KTS just wants to get weird with one. Get a tasty of the pasty. Then push a button and blow the rest of us up.
> kiss-the-sky: For fuck's sake. Any of you saying the world *isn't* fucked?
> kiss-the-sky: Anyone?

kiss-the-sky: Ok. And any of you so fucked up yourself that
    you think peace and healing are *bad*?
cacheMoney: I mean, depends on who's being healed.
kiss-the-sky: Now it's my turn to ask if you're fucking serious.
    If you'd say "fuck healing everyone if it means a guy I
    hate is healed."
kiss-the-sky: ???
cacheMoney: j/k. My bad. Sorry. Wrong time for it.
fischer_queen: u rly think peace is worth the price tho?
kiss-the-sky: But the price is on us. Or could be. What if we
    could somehow use our powers to fix the price?
cacheMoney: You figured out how to hack for peace? Why
    didn't you say so??? I'm in!!! For real!!! Show me this
    magic!!!
kiss-the-sky: Fuck you. Just trying to be careful. It's not like
    we ever actually talked about whether we could do that.
    Just don't want us to make things worse or lose a chance
    at the good shit without thinking it through.
5x5: If people want to brainstorm ideas for how we could do
    that, I'm in. I don't have ideas yet, but I haven't thought
    about it honestly.

And that was it. Thread dead. Nobody had ideas, or at least
none they thought were promising enough to put in front of
their peers. Huh.

Rye's murmuring from the loo briefly distracted me. I leaned
back in my chair and saw zir using dry erase markers to map
something on the mirror as zie talked. Zie leaned against the
counter then, eyes closed, maybe visualizing what Kitty was
seeing and experiencing.

I turned back to my computer, opening a new window, so I
could take a deeper look into kiss-the-sky. Obviously, we'd
vetted everyone before bringing them into the team. But we'd
done that when we thought this was about a corrupt
corporation. We hadn't double-checked once we knew it
involved a church and aliens.

Nothing popped out at me as a red flag. Maybe they really
were just being cautious. We'd asked a lot of questions among
ourselves, just not this one. And it did seem to read more like

"explore all options" and less like "destroy all humans." Still, I set a little watchdog on all their known devices and communication options. If they did reach out to authorities or Peaceforgers, I wanted to know. I thought about doing that to everyone, but it seemed like overkill. This was a good group. Even kiss-the-sky was probably totally fine. I'd probably remove the watchdog in a few days.

Still, for now, no harm exercising a wee bit of extra caution, right?

Whilst I was reading more of the frequency detector manual (which was sounding like it was also maybe a little bit of a frequency transmitter and converter), Zane finally replied. Though their reply was about as helpfully verbose as the message *I'd* sent *them*.

Working on it. Will need help. Stay ready to act.

How the hell was I supposed to be ready in a useful way if I didn't know what sort of acting I might have to do? I rubbed my temples and tried to think of what might be needed. All I could figure was a ride (we had a car, so, sure?) and/or bodies to help in a fight or a distraction. It's not like we could be counted on to send a shuttle up or, as we were too painfully aware, hack the ship's computer.

To cover the possible need for bodies in meat space, I messaged Lex.

If we needed bodies for a fight or distraction, have we used up our favors? (I can't be more specific 'cause I don't know anything about this thing yet.)

I was in love with how quickly she always responded to me. Communication crush!

We can help. Plenty of readily available bodies. Especially while you're paying hotel bills. LOL

I figured that was as close to ready as I could get. I sent her a kiss-blowing emoji and got back to my scintillating manual.

...And then I figured that, if Zane could blow up our phones with messages when it was pretty clear we were ignoring them, I was totally good to ask for more info.

You thinking extraction, backup in a fight, distraction, ??? And when?

I pretended to read, but kept one very critical and impatient eye on my mobile. Fortunately, they didn't keep me waiting too long.

Probably distraction. Thinking at Gas Works. Tomorrow at sunset? Aiming for that.

Before I could send a thumbs up emoji, they added:

Remember, they can't run. Not sure even walk well. Definitely can't walk far.

Good thing it was November and the sun would set during normal business hours. Because it sounded like, if all went well, we had a surprise visit to Dr. Scott to look forward to, and I hated the prospect of ruining her work day far less than I'd hate ruining her personal time if it was later in the day.

Riley dragged back to the table and slumped into a chair. Zie didn't look great.

I put my hand on zirs. "What's up, poppet?"

Zie swallowed, near tears but not crying. "The good news is that we did some good work on figuring out how to be a search engine. The mediocre news is that, when not in motion, the ship's defenses aren't currently set to be automatic."

"That's mediocre?" I asked as gently as I could, because clearly there was bad news still to come.

"Mediocre because they do exist and I'm not sure how quickly someone could turn them on."

"Ah." I squeezed zir hand. "Got it."

"The bad news..." Zie sighed like zie could breathe out zir sadness. "Kitty doesn't have a body anymore. They barely got her loaded into their computer, not even sure it would work 'cause it's a new thing, just in time. Just before she, uh, she died."

It just felt so cruel that zie had to mourn this death afresh, especially now that we knew the partner I'd been mourning wasn't lost yet. I scooted over and put my arms around zir. Zie didn't cry, but zie breathed heavily into my shoulder for a while.

When Riles was breathing normally again and I'd put a cup of tea in zir hands, I updated zir about the question kiss-the-sky had raised and the message from Zane.

"And do you have a distraction plan?" zie asked, ignoring kiss-the-sky for the moment.

Disappointed, I admitted, "I don't. And my brain just...won't right now for some reason."

Sipping zir tea carefully, taking zir time, zie said, "Okay. So, that's as much as we can do on step one, other than goading our brains to hand us distraction plans. Step two...do you want to work on how we get Kitty, how we download her, or on working with her to program the ship's computer?"

Neither sounded quite as straight-forward as I'd have liked. "I'm not sure I have a preference. What do you think?"

"I think the world is cruel and life is bullshit," zie replied with false jovialness that dissolved into slumping sadly. "But you're probably farther into reading about the frequency detector than I am, which will probably be useful for figuring out downloading her. Or so it kind of seems. And, much as it hurts my brain, I do love my time with Kitty. And I've already done some computer crawling with her that way. So..."

"So, once I order us a bit of a nicer meal, because you deserve it both for helping you eat the bad news feelings and as a reward for coming up with the Narnia plan, I'll go back to reading my manual and seeing if anything in there helps me—or helps Engie help me—figure out how we might download from the ship."

"I'll make sure all the research on AI stuff is easy for you to find. And...Look, this is important. Tell me if I can help." Zie looked intense and frayed.

"Don't worry, poppet." I tried to put on my most reassuring smile. "We'll get her back. You might as well start shopping sexy robot bodies." I shifted to a grin. "Just be careful you don't make her titanium, just in case she starts the robot uprising. She's already impossible to beat."

Rye managed a tiny grin and said, "I'm more concerned about cleaning up the fingerprints if I have a *chrome-plated* girlfriend."

I returned the grin and silently renewed my commitment. I was going to get zir the chance to do just that. No matter what.

Out of the blue, Riles started laughing and mumbling, "Oh, damn, that is the best!"

I didn't even have to ask. As soon as zie saw I was looking at zir, zie spilled zir masterful plan for a distraction the next evening. *Masterful.* Or at least silly and potentially entertaining and probably even effective.

We didn't dare share details with Lex et al. just yet, but we got confirmation we'd have at least a dozen bodies where we needed them. We also made some orders, asked Lex to have the biggest person who'd confirmed they were coming memorize a thing, and posted a few announcements on Seattle forums just to add to the crowd.

And we were both still giggling over the plan as we tried to fall asleep, so we were going to have to make sure we had eyes and ears on it somehow. Even if nobody appreciated Rye's genius like I did, I'd definitely want to see it all clearly.

If nothing else, I always appreciated a night I laughed myself to sleep instead of crying.

CHAPTER 12

Saturday, we tried to pretend like we could be useful and productive. Like we could take in and process information and ideas. Like we weren't, basically, kids waiting for Santa. If Santa were a pasty alien and the presents he brought were beat up humans.

As much as I was nervous (there was plenty of potential for one of us to actually end up dead), I was also really fucking excited for this to go down. Fortunately for us, it was completely reasonable to head out as early as the late afternoon. When Riley barely started to hint it might not be too early to leave, I was on my feet. I pulled on my hoodie and bag, made sure my g/ap mask and hat were situated for maximum identity obscuring, and grabbed the frequency detector.

"You sure?" Riles asked.

I nodded, tucking it in my pocket. "I finished the manual. And I wouldn't use it for much yet, but I specifically figured out how to turn it on, not transmit anything, and detect whether there's any Peaceforger-made tracking shit on the boys."

"Cool. Also, I'll drive. You should make sure the doctor doesn't leave her office early." Zie grabbed the car keys, pulled up zir own mask, and led the way to the garage.

I had my camera program get to work covering our tracks, erasing us from stored camera footage in the hotel and on our wee adventure. Like sweeping our footprints behind us as we went. Then, once we were in the car, I called Dr. Scott.

I knew she had my burner number saved in her phone because she answered with, "Am I working late tonight?"

With a minimum of nervous laughter, I said, "We'd be wildly appreciative if you would."

She sighed, like she couldn't believe she let us push her around this way, but then said, "Obviously. You headed here now?"

"After sunset."

"Okay, then I'm taking a dinner break. Message me if you're going to be early, or you'll find a firmly locked alley door waiting."

"Thank you. I can't even explain how much that means. But you'll see."

Pretending (I like to think) like it was nothing but business, she said, "I'll make sure my bill reflects the importance of the work." And then she laughed, a short but not unpleasant bark. "Okay. See you soon."

Now to hope we saw everyone else we were counting on first.

Bless the ubiquity of black mini-SUVs in this city. Even before we found the cluster that, based on turned off license plates, were probably ours, we saw enough others to make this particular shell game feel extra shell-y. I was pleased to note the delivery vehicle was also a black mini-SUV, though it had branding on its side.

We didn't get out right away, but I messaged Lex to bring some of the delivered supplies with her and come to our car. It wasn't just that I was lazy or wanted a chance to say hi to Lex and Marleina without their friends spotting us. We also had some wee cameras and mics to put into play. Because, seriously, I was going to be very sad if I missed this. Plus, we could show the boys later and give them a chance to marvel at the genius.

"Busy here tonight, yeah?" Lex asked as I finished sticking the last camera on.

I grinned. "It might be we also told assorted other groups there were a variety of things happening here tonight."

"Like a fire spinning demonstration or a popup holiday market or some bullshit hipster sea shanties by the water at sunset." Riles cackled. "We figure things will go down before people realize their events aren't happening. We're hoping an audience might keep the aliens' thugs from being too liberal with force aimed at your guys."

And then we explained to them what they and their guys should do. They laughed, but it was hard to tell what kind of laughter it was.

"You're fucking crazy. I love it!" Marleina might actually have been laughing with us, not at us, at least a little bit.

Lex shook her head, but sounded amused. "It's a good thing you meant them to drink the booze you had delivered. It's gonna sell the show *and* make our people more likely to love your idea. Or at least totally likely to be a little foolish for you."

Marleina nodded. "Truth. And good job ordering a lot. I can promise none of it's gonna go to waste."

"Whatever it takes to help everyone know we're incredibly grateful," I said.

Then we said our goodbyes and good lucks and they went back to tell their people the plan. We checked out the scene, such as we could see, through the cameras and mics we'd handed off. Fortunately, the sound and vision they delivered was that Lex and Marleina's friends found the plan uproariously funny and were definitely into it.

Around sunset, our folks wandered into the park along with an assortment of other Seattle residents. Everyone was complaining about parking, but still appreciating that the drizzle had taken a break. (Hell yes. Thank you, Mother Nature! I rarely hoped for less rain, but times we needed people outside were times I considered hoping for it.)

Our people were just dispersed enough, and the crowd just varied enough, that I don't think anyone thought much of how they looked. Which was to say that nobody seemed to think it was weird that there were scruffy people in all black clothes and Guy Fawkes masks, with armloads of those instant fireplace logs and backpacks full of booze, headed for the park as well.

We lagged behind, knowing their destination wasn't ours, and watched from behind and from our phones, thanks to the cameras we'd tucked in some of those masks. We stayed in the trees that bordered the park, our own Guy Fawkes masks ready.

I took in the landscape. To our left were the actual gas works and related buildings, making up about half the park, which were now fenced off and restricted. There was a pier in front of us (just for looking at the water, not for mooring boats) and some big and mismatched art pieces (that were probably modern around 2010) to the right. Farther to the right was open space, dominated by a hill. At the top of the hill was a stone sundial, a flat one that was set into the earth. I'd spent my share of summer days as a kid walking a circle around that, telling fairy stories about the inlaid stones and bits of shiny things in the sundial. It had been years, though, since I'd seen it.

As people who weren't in our crowd saw the masked groups converging at and heading up the hill...that did get a little attention. People nudged and pointed. Our mics told us they were now wondering what was up, but mostly still focused on figuring out where their events were. It sounded like some of the fire spinning crowd were considering heading up the hill too, given the masked folks had wood to burn and the sundial would make a cool, safe-ish place for spinning.

Our people got louder as they went, pausing to set down their wood so they could lift the masks just enough to drink from containers tucked in their pockets and bags. And they weren't sipping. By the time they'd made it to the hilltop, they were properly boisterous. And I had real hope that the sudden and unexpected crowds had started pulling Peaceforger attention from their Gas Works buildings over to the human masses. I would have kicked somebody to be able to hack their system and confirm it...

We watched through the mask cameras, switching between views in search of the best one, as everyone started piling their fireplace logs in the middle of the sundial. One jovial but in-charge guy, a formidable mountain of wild black hair and studded leather, started directing the way the wood was piled. This dude had obviously seen bonfires before, even if they hadn't been made of this sort of log. (We'd tried and failed to find any other sort of wood we could get delivered when and how we wanted. We'd agreed not to sweat this particular aesthetic. Honestly, the fireplace logs might add something to it. Right?)

By the time they had a pile of logs—and it was quite a pile; our people numbered closer to two dozen, probably due to our reputation for being generous with the payoff—my binoculars showed me they did indeed have the Peaceforgers' attention. There was a growing crowd of their security just inside the gate of their fenced section of the park. They were clustered together, discussing and gesturing towards our impromptu bonfire party. Excellent.

I didn't even need Riles to tell me the fire had been lit; I knew it by the roar of wild joy from the crowd around it. As well as by the way all security heads jerked up and turned to the hilltop. I traded Riles the binoculars for zir mobile, and snickered, "Pretty damned sure we got their attention."

"They're heading over," zie said, then stepped to the other side of the trees and swung zir binoculars up towards the Peaceforger ship that floated over Puget Sound. "Zane must have been watching too somehow. Here comes a shuttle." Zie paused. "It just dove, so I'm going to assume it's in the water and submarine-ing its way to us."

We both leaned in to watch the impending show on zir mobile, and I tapped to make sure my earbud wasn't going to be too loud. From what we could see and hear, this is what went down:

Our allies for the night danced around the fire, singing unaccompanied renditions of anti-government and anti-corporate punk songs. They whooped and shrieked and seemed to genuinely enjoy the work. When security showed up, the mass of them having made the exodus from the facility to the hilltop, our folks had just decided to bring someone's phone into the festivities to have it play what was, presumably, a playlist of the very sorts of songs they'd been singing. It took security a while to get them to turn the music down and to find someone who'd talk to them. Fortunately, this spectacle had, as hoped, drawn plenty of people over from the other groups, so security meatsacks dared not—in spite of being in very generic uniforms with generic badges that wouldn't tie them to a particular company or group—get too aggressive.

Finally Head Meatsack (maybe actually the same head meatsack from the raid on our place, but I might have imagined the similarity in their voices) managed to get into something like a conversation with our very own Mountain in Charge (MiC).

Head Meatsack asked, "What's going on here?" Shouted it, because there was no way he was going to actually silence our crowd.

MiC, muffled by the mask but still loud enough to be heard, cheerfully but not-helpfully, replied, "Bonfire Night, man!"

Head Meatsack shook his head, obviously confused. "Bonfire Night?"

(A message from Zane flicked across our screen. The boys would be out in a few minutes. Fuck yeah!)

"You know," and then MiC recited the line we'd asked Lex to have someone remember (and thank whatever non-random deity might be out there that he was the person asked to do this, 'cause he was perfect), "'Remember, remember, the fire in November.' Yeah?" And, even with the mask obscuring his face and muffling his words, I could tell he just *knew* everyone knew what he meant.

As a delightful touch, his friends weren't too drunk to pay attention, because they were all chanting—though not quite in unison—the line. Or at least "fire in November." It sounded like the not-ours crowd were mostly laughing or even joining in the chant.

The thing is, nobody had been thrilled to lose half the park to some unknown corporation. Everybody over the age of 18 in that crowd had almost certainly hung out in the buildings that were now fenced away from us. These corpsec meatsacks were the closest they'd get to the face of the anonymous villain. They had no friends in the crowd.

Though someone in the crowd did unhelpfully shout out, "Well, actually, it's 'the fifth of November.'"

MiC turned his head towards the shout. "What?"

The person didn't emerge from the crowd, probably because someone else had already booed them for saying it, but they repeated, "Sorry, but it's 'the fifth of November.' In that poem. Not 'the fire in November.'" They had the decency to sound abashed at having ruined the fun.

But MiC wasn't going to lose so easily. "The fifth? Well, that was exactly a week ago. Happy Bonfire Night anniversary, man!" He roared, and his comrades roared with him.

It was a drunken and joyous sound, and someone soon got everyone chanting "Fire in November!" again. As the message on our screen flashed to let us know it was time, security was reduced to trying to figure out how to break up the now-reignited and expanded (thank you, citizens of Seattle) party.

We tried to stick to shadows as we darted for the front gate of the Peaceforger holdings. We saw a mass of shadow wobble and stumble from a door next to—but not lit like—the front door. We headed for that mass, our Guy Fawkes masks now on.

I hoped Rye couldn't hear me as I mumbled, "Don't cry. Don't cry. Be the badass." I mostly couldn't believe this was happening, but also mostly was scared as hell. If we got caught, we were completely fucked. My heart was beating its way rapidly out of my chest. Good thing careful breaths could slow that and hold back tears.

Fortunately, there were plenty of shadows for us almost all the way to the fence. We waited to enter the light until we saw the mass doing the same.

And, from the shadows, we saw Zane barely keeping them moving. But they *were* moving and it really was our boys. Holy shit. I almost cried then; I almost shrieked. But I remembered the carbonite reference Riles had used and told myself, *Princess Leia didn't cry when she got Han. Stop.* It worked. Just enough.

We dashed forward, quietly putting a Guy Fawkes mask on each of the three people now stumbling to the other side of the light. Then we took the weight of our boys off Zane. I'd ended up on the Bryan side and felt a quick twinge of disappointment it wasn't Jonny I had. But then I felt an immediate replying twinge of "bitch, this is your *Bryan*" that was joy and guilt mixed.

Zane didn't ask about the mask, but I saw them turn their face up towards the fire on the hill, probably hoping to collect enough clues to figure it out on their own.

We hustled into the trees, through the trees, and across the small parking lot. Before we could turn to go the remaining distance to our car, before I could even stop to consider what the hell to do about Zane ('cause I sure as hell didn't want them to come with us), a driverless taxi pulled up in front of us.

The display flashed, "Zane."

I whispered, "Thank you." And chose not to tell them how stupid it was to book a taxi in their own name.

They nodded, put a hand on Bryan's shoulder, and paused just long enough to whisper in my ear, "I deactivated their Peacemakers, but you'll want to get those out soon as you can." And then they were in the taxi and on their way.

"Right," I said. Then assured everyone, "The car is right over here. You're almost done walking."

Bryan grunted in response, and Jonny just sort of exhaled loudly. As quickly and carefully as we could, we got them to the car. And we paused a moment so I could pull out the frequency detector and do what I thought should let us know if the Peaceforgers had put trackers on them. Then used a human bug detector. No good running if they were bugged. (They weren't. Not that I could tell. The only signal I could find seemed to be...maybe a dormant Peacemaker in each of them, if I'd read things in the manual correctly. If Zane was telling the truth about turning them off.)

Whilst I scanned him, Jonny put a hand weakly on my arm. "Kot." It was barely a whisper. "Kot, is this real?" He sounded like he might cry.

I kept not-crying as I gently squeezed his hand. "Yeah, baby. It's real."

Bryan managed to croak, "Thank fuck," and Jonny just gripped my arm a little tighter.

Riley clicked the key fob to open the doors and said, "I'm driving. You should ride in the back with them."

I knew, tactically, that meant I was trapped if we needed to get out and fight or something. But I was willing to hope we wouldn't, willing to let hope be my plan just once, 'cause there was nothing I wanted to do more than sit and hold their hands.

Of course, as we drove, I didn't hold hands. I carefully took off Guy Fawkes masks. I carefully replaced them with scarves wrapped loose but high, so that faces were covered. I carefully settled loose-fitting stocking caps on their heads, wincing at the thought I might be hurting them. I couldn't be careful enough.

They just sat, eyes mostly closed, looking quietly beaten up and stoic. Because of course they did.

Then, just to be safe, I called Dr. Scott.

She was quick, clipped. "Yeah?"

"Incoming. Still good?"

"Yeah." And she hung up.

In her defense, Dr. Scott had had no idea what she'd be opening her alley doorway to. So, yeah, she went a little tight and worried for a moment, but she recovered quickly. All business. And she bossed Riley and me around, telling us where to put boys, what things to grab for her, all that stuff. We tried to be gentle, but the moans, sharp inhales, and muttered swears from the boys—until Scott had them sedated—made me feel we were failing at that.

"I'd offer to call in a second person I trust, but I've seen the news footage from last week often enough to guess we're strategically better if people don't know they're alive." She didn't even pause for my answer, just handed me some scissors and gestured for me to start cutting Jonny out of his shirt.

Once people were unclothed enough, with sterile sheets to cover them and the heating turned up enough to prevent a chill, she had Rye and I cover our hair and scrub our hands. Just in case.

I can't even pretend to know what all she did, but bullets were pulled out and open wounds were covered or stitched. There were some shots, one instance of me having to apply pressure on a pretty gruesome wound, and many scans made and notes jotted down. One time I was sure Bryan had stopped breathing and we were going to lose him, but she used a mask thing on him and he was fine—at least in terms of breathing— after a few moments (during which I don't think Riles and I breathed either). Oh, and there were two Peacemakers extracted and destroyed. Both apparently turned off. Just like we'd been told.

When they were both stable and sleeping off the anesthetic, Dr. Scott said, "Okay. Let's bring you up to speed, and then we can talk about payment and getting them dressed." Seeing the "get them dressed in what?" look Rye and I exchanged she said, "Don't worry. They aren't cool enough to wear in public, but I do keep functional spare clothes around. You might not be the only people who've showed up here right after taking a beating."

She pulled up her notes. "If I had to guess, I'd say they've been shot. With guns, I mean. Which, obviously, isn't a Sherlock-level deduction, but I'm making sure you keep that in mind. They've been shot. Multiple times each. That's not a small thing." She tapped the screen and moved her eyes in a way that suggested she was working down a list of things to tell us. "Your one friend..." she gestured at Bryan. "It looks like some kind of shot—like needles, not bullets this time—was administered to his neck. I didn't find anything in his blood, including not finding anything the computer couldn't identify. So, I *think* that's nothing to worry about. But, you know..."

I knew. Of course, I also knew what the puncture likely had been. Fucking Zane's tongue. So I volunteered, "I think it was a paralytic or even a toxin that, apparently, is only deadly in sufficient quantities."

Dr. Scott nodded. "Got it. Then I more strongly think we're okay there. But still just thinking, not guaranteeing." Another tap on the screen, and eyes shifted down a little again. "We got lucky, really, No broken bones this time." She paused and gave us a look, because we'd probably brought her more broken bones than was reasonable given none of us were brawlers. "Um...Really, it looks like someone has been beating them and torturing them—some of the cuts and some burn marks make me think that—to get them to talk, probably. Given what they know. They're dehydrated, malnourished, and likely were being kept alive via some kind of...I mean, like I said, nothing in their blood, but there had to have been tube feedings or stimulants or something."

"How do their brains look?" Riley asked.

She swiped her finger a few times, and brain scans came up on the big display beside us. For all the good that did us.

Before I had to venture my guess that no big, dark spots meant we were good, she went ahead and told us.

"The brains look okay. Physically. Now that we've got the damned bugs out of 'em. I'm actually more optimistic about their recovery, even if the healing might take a bit longer (because, as noted, bullets). And that goes for the chances of that one who's just had his second visit with me too." She inclined her head to indicate Jonny and sounded pretty pleased.

I was ecstatic. When we'd brought Jonny in the first time, she'd seemed uncertain he'd live or be okay if he did. So, this was kind of awesome and hopeful.

"I'm going to send you home with all kinds of instructions and some meds. Do they have beds where you are now?"

I looked at Riley. Good thing we had the Narnia room, 'cause it was about to get crowded. I nodded. "Yeah, reasonable beds. We'll keep it as clean and climate controlled as we can too. Just tell us all the guidelines, requirements, whatever. We'll follow them."

We left with lists and bags and with two broken but probably-going-to-make-it boys. And, as Riles drove, I did some ordering to make sure we could pick up or receive ASAP all the things we'd need to keep them okay. Because I'm awesome, I also made sure to order some convalescing clothes that they wouldn't entirely hate. (Listen, if old books could tell women to pretty up even when sick because it would help them feel better, I could sure as hell make sure the boys didn't have to look down at baggy grey sweatpants and white undershirts for however long it took them to be healed enough for clothes that would look cooler but be less comfy to live and sleep in all day.)

"Should we move?" I asked, leaned forward so I wasn't shouting to talk to Rye.

"Hm..." Zie considered. "Pros for moving are that we've been there a week—and people in movies are always staying on the move—and that we could go somewhere with enough bed space in one room."

I nodded. "But cons are that they've already raided and cleared our room and that we now have two more things to move if we have to go to Narnia. And they've surely discovered they're missing prisoners, so might be on high alert."

Both boys mumbled some form of confused, "Narnia?"

With a quick laugh, I promised, "We'll tell you all about the fun you've missed. Later."

Riley suggested, "Maybe see if the hotel has more traditionally adjoining rooms or even one with two queens?"

I snickered a little. "I like how you're implying that our Narnia plan somehow adjoins the rooms in a way that other people would agree would let us reasonably compare them to 'traditionally adjoining' rooms."

"Yeah, yeah. Fuck you, bitch," Riles laughed. "Just do a search and pretend to be nearly as useful as the genius who conceived both the Narnia plan and the Bonfire Night plan."

In a poor imitation of the Mountain in Charge, I exclaimed, "Happy Bonfire Night anniversary, man!"

Zie echoed me in a tone that told me this day—or at least this night—had probably now been named.

It turned out that, in fact, Second Home Suites had two floors that, rather than being aimed at working stiffs, were aimed at families. If we went up just one floor, we could get one of their family suites, which was the same as our current suite, but with room for one more bed and a sofa that pulled out. Perfect.

Obviously, I made sure we'd have two suites, back to back, so that we could do the Narnia thing again. Whilst I vetoed Riley's suggestion that we install a ladder and/or pole between our current room and our new one above it, I admitted to myself that I might eventually buy into the idea of a trap door. If we got stuck there long enough. Again, if the bad guys could have ridiculous shit, so could we. Dammit.

We picked up deliveries, got the boys into bed in one of our new suites, and then started the careful process of moving our stuff up without being seen.

Nobody knows how to party on a Saturday night like Team I Guess We're Stuck Here.

CHAPTER 13

Before we called it a night, Zane messaged.

I know it seems like not the best night for it, but we should probably talk. Also, I have things for you.

I turned my head to give Riles a weary and slightly annoyed look. Zie was already giving me the same thing. So, we sighed and did rock, paper, scissors. I lost. I considered playing the pity card ("but I just got my boy back") or even the Kitty card ("but I'm working on getting your bae back"), but settled for playing the "best two out of three" card. And immediately lost again.

Rye patted my head. "I'll set it up just like we did with Isa, but a different hotel. So, you can at least go somewhere swank for this." Zie started typing, putting the plan together. "I'll also take care of replying. You get cleaned up a little."

If I had to lose, at least I'd lost to someone who liked me and was suggesting something much nicer than I'd been planning. Left to my own devices, we'd be in a grungy alley like this was some kind of sketchy drug deal. So, I didn't argue.

I got tidied, I checked on our sleeping boys, and I headed out. Riley's voice in my ear guided me, and I knew zie was making sure to sweep camera footage in my wake. When I showed up, there was even a basket with nice chocolates, a bottle of champagne, and a chocolate cake (yeah, a whole one) waiting for me. Because I hadn't been sure what Zane was bringing me, and because I was damned well walking out with a plush robe this time ('cause all posh hotels have them, right?), I'd brought a larger bag and was figuring out how to use the plastic from the gift basket to wrap the cake and bring it back with me. (No shame. I hated food waste. Which was, obviously, my only motivation there.)

I got the rope escape ladder ready in the window, still not trusting Zane, and then pillaged the room. This time, I also took the pillowcases.

"What the hell are you doing?" asked Riles in my ear.

"Girl, we deserve nicer pillowcases for our pretty faces," I retorted.

Zie didn't argue. Instead, zie also had me duck into the corridor to pillage more nice bedding from the housekeeping closet on that floor. I liked how zie thought.

When Zane arrived, all I had left to do before leaving was gently settle my cake on top of whatever they had brought me.

Zane started to open their mouth as soon as I opened the door. I shook my head, pulled them in, and closed and locked the door behind them.

I pointed at a chair that would let me watch them and keep an eye on the room in general. "Sit."

They put down a bag by their chair (which I tried to pretend not to notice, in spite of Rye asking, "Oh! What's in the bag?" excitedly in my ear). They waited until I sat too, then tried again. "I'm so, so sorry."

I sighed. "Yeah, you've mentioned that before. But you can see where we'd think you're full of shit."

Earnestly, they nodded. "I can. But, if I hadn't paralyzed Bryan, he'd be dead. They weren't there to retrieve prisoners but to stop a threat. If I hadn't stepped out, Shay would have killed the guys, taken their phones, and have cracked them quickly."

"So, why didn't she kill them anyway?" I almost believed them. But I was still mad.

"I think she was surprised to see me. Given everyone knew I'd been caught on video saying stuff I wasn't supposed to..." They shrugged. "I just think I threw her off. Plus, I think it was harder for her to actually kill someone with another of her kind right there. Someone she'd grown up daydreaming of nonviolent missionary successes with." They looked at me like that was all the answer they had and hoped it was enough.

And it kind of was, but... "But now there's no way they won't know you took the boys. So whatever damage control you did with your people? They'll never trust you again."

They shrugged, almost looking believably casual. "I'd already assumed that was my future when I said you could use the videos and my DNA."

Fair point. I was still not happy with them and was sure there had been a better solution...but what was I going to do? I took a moment to narrow my eyes and consider them.

In my ear, Riles whispered, "Maybe not a fucking traitor. Plus, I don't think we gain anything by beating the shit out of them yet."

I nodded. "Okay."

"Okay?" They looked like they didn't believe it.

"I mean, I'm not asking you over to our new hideout. But I'm willing to consider that you might have had good intentions. And that you've done some dangerous things for us. For which we're grateful." I sat up straighter. "Right. So, you said we should talk."

Almost like they'd forgotten there was a reason other than a face-to-face apology for this meeting, they blinked rapidly a few times, then nodded. They picked up the bag I'd been pretending didn't exist (because I thought that sold me as "too cool to care") and held it out to me. "Tools to service or check out a lot of our gear. An interface device," they paused when I probably drooled on myself, "that's not connected to our, uh, network anymore. Like a mobile without access. Unless you *want* my people to be able to find you?"

"Maybe not today." I hid my disappointment at not being connected to their network behind feigned reasonability.

"Anyway, it's loaded with specs and documentation. But I'm supposed to tell you that, until someone finishes a...a translation program, basically...it's all in our language right now. Sorry." And they did actually look apologetic.

I looked, I hoped, much cooler and more nonchalant than I felt. Specs would probably have pictures or diagrams, so Engie would have clues to work with if I could get her this info.

"Um...I'm also supposed to tell you that we're working on either a, uh, send/receive unit or safely enabling this interface.

We just have to make sure we do it without our people being able to track and destroy you." They looked at the ceiling, lips moving like they were going through a list. "Oh. And a healing tool. There's one in there for you."

I definitely did not look cool as I failed to hold back a giddy grin, and Riles squealing in my ear did not sound cool. Fuck yes!

Wincing as they delivered the bad news, they cautioned, "It's too complicated for me to even tell you how to use it quickly. But we wanted you to have it so you could use it as soon as we can figure out how to teach you. Uh, none of us have heard of another species using it, so we just hope you can. We're pretty sure you can. Eventually." With a shame-thick voice, they said, "I wanted to make sure you could help save Bryan—and Jonny too, obviously—as soon as possible. And I told Isa that the healing tool is important, so she'll help get that figured out before she gets you translations for random specs or manuals. Unless you ask otherwise."

I took a deep breath to regain my cool, then said, "Thanks. Now, you said this was the good?"

They looked up at me, grim. "I know that I'm about to tell you something that isn't enough information. So, uh, first I want to tell you that we're all listening and will tell you more as soon as we can. Okay?"

I nodded and felt my eyes narrowing, wariness creeping up my face.

"The consensus is that," they took a deep breath, stalling, then finished reluctantly, "humanity is lost and we, the Peaceforgers, need to take action. Which, generally, means either something very heavy-handed or, uh, deadly." They practically whispered the last word.

Trying not to be angry at them for not knowing more, and ignoring Riles emoting in my ear, I asked, "So, do you know a timeline or plans they're considering or...anything?"

"Just...uh...I think I overheard...I mean, I *did* overhear the last part of a conversation. But I want to be clear that I'm only...75 or 80% sure I'm right about what I heard."

I attempted an encouraging nod. A "do go on; we're so desperate we'll suck up any info on this you have" nod.

Obviously motivated by my powerful nod, they said, "I'm pretty sure that all resources that wouldn't be noticed have been diverted to mass production of Peacemakers."

In my ear, Rye complained, "I am so sick to fucking death of motherfucking Peace-fucking-makers. Bastards!"

I tried to pretend I was taking the news okay. "Well, that's better than just nuking us from orbit or letting beat down flu take us. So, okay."

I just looked at them, not sure what else there was to say. And they just looked at me.

Until Riles cleared zir throat and prompted, "Was there anything else?"

Pretending it was my question, and delivering it more patiently, I asked, "Was there anything else?"

Zane thought a moment, then shook their head. "No, I think that's all. But I can message if I've forgotten anything."

"And you're safe? Isa is taking care of you?" I didn't have a reason other than curiosity, but I tried to make it sound like it was motivated by worry for their safety. You know, like it might have been before they poison-tongued one of my best mates.

"Yeah. We had safe houses and things in place just in case anyone ever needed them. So, I'm okay." They looked pleased I'd asked.

"Ask about deactivating Peacemakers," Rye suggested.

I pretended it had just occurred to me, all on my own, not come through a bud in my ear. "Oh, hey...You said you deactivated the boys' Peacemakers. How? That seems like handy information."

"You do it with a frequency detector like Isa already gave you." They started to reach for their pocket, realized I was suddenly tense and reaching for a gun, then went slow motion as they explained, "I'll show you. I've got it in my pocket."

What they pulled out was, indeed, not a gun. And it did look like the frequency detector Isa had gotten me. "So, will a frequency detector also transmit, or are your people just not big on making different devices easy to identify from across a room?" I laughed, trying to make it sound like this was a joking matter.

"No, this *is* a frequency detector. But that's not really an accurate translation of the item's name. I'd probably call it..." They shrugged. "Something less succinct. It doesn't have a lot of transmission capabilities. Or not that I know of. If you got the manual for one, the transmission would probably be downplayed. It's got to be within a few feet, sometimes closer, of your intended receiver, and it's really basic stuff. Most of us think of it as...kind of like you might think of the fob to open your car doors, but way less range. Plus some frequency...conversion or...translation? capabilities. Anyway, uh, because I didn't program mine myself—I just pushed the button—I don't know how you'd do it, uh, program it. Sorry."

I nodded. I thought it all made sense. I hoped maybe we could do some reverse engineering and make something that would broadcast farther than a few feet.

I stood, waited for them to stand, then headed for the door. "Thanks for the bag of stuff. And for getting the boys back to us. Uh, given the deactivation thing, another frequency detector would be awesome. If you can get it."

They just nodded, then said, "Again, I'm sorry. And...And I'll get you more information or things as soon as we can get them. Try to maybe get you steps for making the frequency detector turn off Peacemakers."

"Sounds good." I spared a smile, before I put a finger to my lips. "No more talking now." I unlocked and opened the door, trusting Riles to do the rest.

Once the door was closed and locked again, I quickly pulled in the rope ladder, arranged the new bag so that it had the flat interface device on the top, and then gently settled the cake (yeah, I was serious about the cake) on top.

Riles was paying enough attention to see that and cracked up in my ear. "You are the best, stupidest person I know. Let's see if we can get you home with that treasure intact."

And we did our best. Triumphantly, I pulled it out once back in the suite to reveal some smeared frosting but no other obvious damage.

"And that," explained Riley, "is why a dense chocolate cake with ganache for frosting is the best choice for hungry fugitives."

We ate a slice each, setting aside the rest of it and the champagne in hopes we'd get to celebrate the boys being well enough to stay awake very soon. And maybe some of the goodies in my Peaceforger gift bag would help us get there. Or at least help us win the battle so the boys could heal in actual peace, not the bastardized and oppressive thing the Peaceforgers called peace.

During their nighttime chat, I heard Riles ask Kitty if, whilst we slept, she could verify that all possible resources were working on manufacturing more Peacemakers. Zie didn't say where the tip had come from, but she must have guessed.

"Oh! I thought all the extra stuff going on was just because they'd lost a couple prisoners. Congrats, by the way!" She paused. "I'm still working to understand the language well enough to be useful, but let me see if I can get you more info. Confirm that at least part of the extra is about making more of those nasty mind control bugs."

If we could buy just enough more time, Kitty seemed to be getting the hang of things. Slowly but, given her determination and the fact she was actually quite clever, surely. She sounded more confident. And it somehow sounded like a more authentic and more warranted confidence than she'd expressed when she first popped up.

Maybe she actually *would* help us win. That hope was back in play. For a second night in a row, I fell asleep feeling hopeful. I could get used to that.

CHAPTER 14

"So, new plan," Riles said when I woke and sat up. Zie was already at the table, working. "Kitty says they're definitely increasing manufacturing. They might even *not* be looking for the boys, because they're going for another plan now or something. Anyway, maybe not new plan, but we have to figure out how to take out their Peacemaker control machine and/or the satellites before they do anything with it."

I yawned. "And a good morning to you too, bastard."

With an exaggeratedly large and obliging grin on zir face, zie brought over a cup of coffee for me.

I laughed and shook my head. "You're still a bastard." I looked over at the boys. They just looked like a couple guys in shitty clothing having a nap.

"I took care of morning medical stuff," Riles told me, "so we can get right to work. Because."

"Yeah. Because. I hear you." I pulled the covers back and turned to sit on the edge of the bed a moment before standing. I pretended for one breath that our to-do list was something less intimidating, like ruining a bank or stopping a corrupt human military from bombing noncombatants. Then I stood. "Right. Let's have a look at our plan, see where and how we fit in taking out their machine. Which, if you'll recall, Zane previously said was on the ship. So."

"So," Riles agreed, then handed me a bowl of cereal and sat back at zir computer. Zie looked intense, serious, but somehow noble. Like maybe saving the world was starting to agree with zir.

It didn't take us long to realize we couldn't make meaningful plans for the machine if we didn't know how to get at it. We could plan to use drones if it was planet-side, but if it was on the ship...well, our only plan at that point was that we'd have to speed up our timeline as much as possible to make sure we killed them before they got a chance to flip a switch.

Because, obviously, we'd been taking our sweet time figuring out how to help Kitty program the ship's computer and how to download her. Just lollygagging like it was nothing. Obviously. So, you know, just no more of that. No more relaxed pace. Pick it up! Easy peasy!

I mentally gave myself a gold star every time I didn't literally sob. And, for the record, my sticker chart was filling up. I expected my reward any day now. Any. Day. Now.

Isa got a second frequency detector to us. Now, if only we could use that to detect whether they'd built other machines on Earth or to make our brains do better at our Kitty tasks...

Holo-Kitty looked pinched. And she talked carefully, which made me wary.

"Okay, guys, I've been doing a lot of searches. Trying to find all the pieces, trying to figure out the machine and alien situation, trying to figure out what I am." She let that hang there a moment.

That was fair enough. If you didn't plan to be uploaded and become a purely digital being, I could see that being an existential crisis. Hell, I could see it being an existential crisis even if you planned it, like the way something big isn't real and you can't truly process it until you're in it.

Out of the corner of my eye, I could see Riles was in "cautious and watchful" mode. Since zie knew Kitty way better than I did, that made me kind of nervous.

"And while I was looking into what I am, obviously I looked at anything to do with..." She laughed, but it didn't sound real. "How ridiculous when someone who loves goth things can't just talk about death?" She paused a beat, then went on, very matter-of-fact. "Well, anyway. Anything to do with the day I died. There you go."

I saw Rye incline zir head, as if about to bring up a counterpoint. It must have been one zie'd brought up before, because Kitty brushed it off.

"Yes, I know, it might be more realistic to say I transitioned, as I am still clearly here in some form. But you know my objections." She didn't elaborate; apparently, it was enough that Riley knew them. She did think to say, "And I'm sure you're capable of telling Katja all about that disagreement later. Not the relevant point here."

Holo-Kitty started pacing thoughtfully, her wee hands clasped behind her back. "I think we can all agree that there's no reason the Peaceforgers would expect humans to see their ship logs, correct?" She looked at us in a way I couldn't quite read...But I suddenly felt like I was at the school principal's office, about to be caught and punished for something I'd thought I'd gotten away with.

Slowly, I nodded. I felt my eyes and mouth narrow a little with wariness.

"And, so, we should all be able to agree that, unless they're reporting back to a higher authority and trying to cover their asses, they'd keep their notes about their own actions during an investigation into," and she made air quotes as she used Rye's name for it, "'Demo Day' truthful. Yes?" That look again.

If possible, my nod this time was even slower. Too slow to give me a chance to note my one objection to her assertion before she continued with her planned speech. (You know, that people tend to keep records and write history in ways that build the narrative that serves their purpose, even when they're trying to be honest and factual.)

Then she went faux "intrigued" on us. Here was the accusation or the trap. "See, I totally think so too. Which is why I found it super interesting that, if I'm reading it right, they didn't have a whistleblower." She laughed a little, definitely fake. "I mean, we know they didn't, right? I was in there to let you fake that. So...so they are pretty sure they didn't have a whistleblower, and that nobody on their side pushed the self-destruct button."

Oh shit. (But also, why the hell, once we decided to treat her as real, hadn't Riley already had the conversation I thought was coming?)

She turned the "intrigued" up a bit, with a touch of a totally fake little smile. She waved her finger in the air, like some black and white era lecturer pointing out an interesting thing. "And then I remembered that, while I was in there, the people talking about being ready to blow were..." And she got icy, stopped pacing and gesturing, and looked at us dead on. "My team."

Peripheral vision told me I wasn't the only person carefully frozen. This was, in fact, where I'd thought this was going. Dammit. But, also, what the hell, Riley?

"So, listen, my friends. My beloved. My new friend with whom I thought I was sharing a growing mutual respect. I just kind of need to know. And I shouldn't have to ask."

I am the worst friend, because I thought, *Damned straight you shouldn't. Riley should have told you.* And then I sort of nodded in a way that I hoped said, "I am on your side. You are so, so right. Ugh. Riley. WTF, mate?"

Kitty said each word like it was a very pointed sentence. She took her time. We let her. "Did. You. Initiate. The. Self. Destruct?"

To zir credit, Rye said, "I have meant to tell you ever since we decided you were really you and not a trap. I'm so sorry, baby."

But Kitty's look cut zir short. She wasn't exactly feeling forgiving. And I couldn't really blame her, could I?

"And you knew, in advance, that you were going to do it?"

Mutely, we nodded.

And she nodded too, but in a tight way. "Okay, bitches. I'm out. I need a little time away from you assholes. A little me time. Because fuck you."

And then she blipped out.

I was annoyed enough that I knew I should take a breath before I asked Riles any of the questions I had in my head. I couldn't exactly go out for a walk, so I was relieved when I heard a voice whisper roughly, "Hey."

It had come from one of the boys. And that would have been relief enough in itself, but now it also meant I was going to have sufficient distraction from the Kitty situation too. Good job on the perfect timing, boy.

I walked quickly over to the bed, taking them both in. The sedative Dr. Scott had asked us to give them was wearing off. Jonny looked like he was dreaming, and Bryan's eyes were cracked open.

I smiled at Bryan and, without looking away, directed, "Riles, water." Then my better self cleared its throat in my head and I added, "Please." I sat carefully on Bry's side of the bed, took his hand. "Hey yourself," I replied.

He tried to smile. "So, we're out? We're safe?" His voice was tattered at the deep edges, probably from pain and remnants of dehydration.

Riley sat on the edge of our bed, facing Bryan and I, and handed me a mug with water. Zie leaned forward to tuck pillows in behind Bry as I helped him sit up a little.

Whilst I steadied the water for him to drink, I finally answered his questions. "You're out. And now you're in…I guess this is our fourth hideout since Jonny blew my building. Or fifth, technically, since we changed rooms last night to make sure you had a bed. And it's as safe as Riles and I could make it."

Bryan nodded like he understood, and turned his head to look at Jonny. "He going to wake up too?"

Riley let out a little laugh. "Girl, believe it or not, Dr. Scott says he's in less shitty shape than the last time we had him in there."

Bryan looked surprised. "Really?"

"Aye, and," I grinned, "this time she was even willing to say that we should *expect* you both to live. So, that's exciting and new."

He was still a bit groggy from, well, all the things, so I watched him process slowly. Finally, he asked, "What day is it?"

When Rye and I exchanged a glance, I wanted to pause the moment so I could point out the fundamental differences in us as demonstrated by the moment. My face, I hoped, was asking zir whether we should carefully tell them they'd lost a whole week on the ship. Rye on the other hand, was giving me a look that probably meant something more like, "I am going to claim it's been a much longer time; please play along, because it will be a laugh." And I might have gone along with it another time, but not today.

I turned back, answering quickly, before Riles could. "It's Sunday, the 13th. You were on the ship a week."

"Shit." Bryan sighed. "It felt so much longer. But I also hoped we hadn't been out of commission that long." He sighed again. "Okay, catch me up. Tell me everything."

I looked over at Jonny, expecting that he'd be awake as well soon, with all the same gaps to fill. "What if we make you a meal instead? That way, we only have to tell you both everything once."

"Can you at least point the TV this way, then? I've been missing my stories," he joked, slipping into an impression of an old lady voice at the end.

I almost jumped up to do it, but caught Riles staring me down. For once, I was pretty sure the psychic connection was real as I caught zir meaning. I obviously couldn't turn it to face him until we told him about the Peaceforgers "arriving." Didn't want to jump right to that and have him freaking out before Jonny woke.

Wryly, I said, "If by 'stories' you mean 'news,' no can do." I got up and got a computer set up so that I could stream him a movie there. "The doctor says rest or else, so I'm probably not even supposed to *tell* you all the stressful shit."

Riles hastened to add, "Not that it's all stressful, babe. Just some of it."

I moved on to fixing a meal of soup, bread, and pudding. I'd order out for something heartier later, but this seemed vaguely like a recuperation meal. Rather than sitting and watching movies with Bryan, Riles had started queuing up the files of assorted types zie reckoned we'd want to show them as we told them about the last week.

Fortunately, the hope that had me making two trays of my kick-ass recuperation meal wasn't in vain. I heard a quiet, "Oh, fuck..." from the bed and turned to see Jonny trying to push himself to sitting. Riles and I rushed over to repeat all the things we'd done for Bryan.

Bryan asked, "Do you feel less shitty than last time you woke up from being medically sedated?"

Jonny coughed, but it was also kind of a laugh. "Oddly, yes. And not just because I'm in a bed in a room actually made for living, not on a table in an abandoned break room." With surprising strength, he grabbed my hand and pulled me closer for a kiss. "Hi."

I didn't cry; I swallowed the surge of emotion that welled up in me. And I hoped this was the last time I'd have to feel the overwhelming relief that comes when the person I'm in love with wakes up on the other side of medical attention. "Hi. Welcome back." I opted, instead of crying, for grinning like a fool for a second.

"Okay." Bryan was eating his food as quickly as he could manage. "He's awake, so turn off this damned movie you're trying to distract me with and tell us what we missed."

And we did, with visual aids and pauses for reactions.

I'd asked Dr. Scott about their brains, and they were proving her right. Once they confirmed we'd updated them on all the things, not left out anything just to spare them stress, right up to the moment before they woke when Kitty had peaced out, they went into action mode.

"We need to get you on a video hookup with Engie to look at the frequency detector," Bryan said.

"And we need to get both Engie and Doc on the healing tech. Doing human trials with it ASAP. And I volunteer as tribute," Jonny quipped, then pointed at some of his bandages and stitches.

Both seemed to be trying to sit up straighter.

"And give us our computers," demanded Bryan.

"Look, I don't want to be the asshole here," I said, "but this doesn't seem like resting. And we're under doctor's orders to administer more sedatives if you don't rest."

They were like hero twins, all the differences in their appearances overcome by their matching folded arms and stubbornly set jaws. Determined to kill themselves trying to save the rest of us.

"Bitches, do not give me reason to play Nurse Ratched," Riles threatened.

"Listen, sweetie, much as I'd love you to play nurse with me," Jonny replied, his cheeky grin creeping out, "I feel like we should save that fun for when I'm healed up and the world isn't in peril."

"Can we compromise?" Bryan shifted to negotiation mode. "Can we define what 'rest' means, and you guys not knock us out without consent?"

Oof. He had to bring consent into it. Which was fair, but it was going to make it harder for me to strictly follow the doctor's actual orders. (She'd even given us multiple forms of the sedative, just in case we had to trick them into letting us get them to sleep.)

Riley came to stand by me, arms folded and eyes wary. "What terms are you hoping for?" zie asked.

"Plenty of people play on their computers while they're resting," noted Bryan, playing innocent.

Jonny nodded seriously, like this was a great piece of wisdom, and murmured, "Yes, very true. When I was home sick from school, my mom let me play on my computer."

I snorted. "Right. Because you two would just be playing solitaire or reading fanfic if we gave you your computers."

"I'm not asking for permission to get back to my morning jogs," Bryan pointed out. "I'm sure my brain can handle this."

Riley and I exchanged a side-eyed look.

Zie said, "I can call Dr. Scott, or even Doc, and confirm that stress and high-stakes computer work aren't actually restful. And give them a chance to lay out their own strict rules here."

"You're wasting us if you just make us sleep." Bryan was starting to sound annoyed.

"Or maybe we're saving you," I suggested. "Trust me. We've wished for you guys back plenty of times. And not just because we love you, but because we wished you could take care of some of the shit for us. With us."

It was quiet as we let the boys think about what to suggest next. They couldn't comfortably twist to face each other, but they turned their heads and leaned a little, cupping hands to help block the sound as they whispered.

I mirrored the position and suggested to Riles, "We should get trays ordered, something to rest meals and computers on."

Zie nodded and actually got working on finding and ordering trays whilst the boys conferred. Zie didn't look up when they finally turned back to us.

Looking slightly unhappy to admit it, Bryan said, "Jonny has pointed out that we *are* fucked up and that you two managed to handle things on your own for a week. Including meat space things. Even if it involved cutting a hole in a wall."

Riles didn't even look up as zie exclaimed, "Narnia is a magical place, you haters!"

Even Bryan had to laugh a little. He conceded, "Okay, yes, Narnia is magical and...if nothing else, the plan was so outside normal that it worked. Anyway..." He got back to serious. "We know you're just trying to do what's best. So..." He sighed. "We'd like showers and some of the less shitty comfy clothing you said you got for us. We're very grateful that you've been taking care of us. And that, we're guessing and hoping, you'll continue to?" He pretended that was a question.

Because we're assholes, Riley and I looked at each other like we were considering maybe not continuing to take care of them. We had a discussion with our faces, not our words. Should we? Maaaaaaybe? Then we shrugged and sighed, as if we were beyond begrudging when we nodded.

I held that posture a moment...then laughed and grinned at them lovingly. "Obviously, you beautiful idiots." The price of getting them to rest, or one of the prices, was going to be doing all we could to make sure they didn't need to get out of bed for anything but the loo. But what else could we do? We kind of loved them.

"We'd like to be able to share ideas we have, because it's not like we can stop our brains from coming up with them. But we also agree to let you make plans without us. So that you don't stress us out." He rolled his eyes. "Though how I'm supposed to not be permanently stressed with the current threat hanging over the planet..."

Overly innocently, I said, "I mean, we do have sedatives to help with that."

Bryan glared at me briefly, moving a bit too quickly in and out of the glare to be entirely serious. "But you know how cutting us off from our accounts and the news will just make us feel...not actually free. And a little too impotent."

He paused as we all waited for Rye to make a dick joke.

Zie looked up from zir phone, noticed all eyes on zir, and said, "Hey, I'm way too empathetic to that feeling to deliver a punchline right now."

It seemed both like years ago and like days ago that Riley had been the one doped up due to injury and denied zir computer.

Bryan nodded and went on. "So, we promise we won't go on the forums or even do any hacking. We'll just check our accounts, watch the news, that kind of thing."

"And we'll sleep if we feel drowsy," Jonny said, "since rest is such a big deal." He paused and admitted, "I know it's a big deal. I just haven't had a great week."

I wasn't sure I trusted them not to dig, but I nodded. Riley nodded. Decision made. The boys looked relieved.

"Speaking of not great weeks," I tried to make my voice softer, "You up for telling us about yours?"

There wasn't really much to tell. They'd been kept in that one room, tube fed, treated harshly. If they weren't just lying on the floor of the room trying not to die, they might be in that room or an adjacent one, being cajoled, bullied, and tortured by a Peaceforger they were able to point out in the row of them behind Morgan in the Peaceforgers' "Hello, world" video on the day they pretended to arrive. It was Jayden.

"Well, you're clearly important, because that's one of Morgan's two companions." I pretended to be impressed.

"Part of why they failed," Bryan diagnosed, "was that they had a lot of different questions they wanted us to answer and we were too fucked up to keep up."

Jonny agreed, nodding his head and saying, "My brain would still be trying to push enough through the pain to figure out how to tell them I wasn't going to reply, and they'd already be on to the next thing."

"They tried the 'good cop' thing once," Bryan said, "but it was too much like that asshole who murdered 'Randa. Same tone of voice and 'oh, wouldn't we all just love peace' shit. So, I was too busy reliving the trauma of watching them kill my girlfriend to fall for that."

That might be a top contender for shittiest silver lining ever.

CHAPTER 15

Once we had the boys set up with their computers and we'd turned the TV so everyone could see it, Riles and I sat at the table for our own quiet conference. As much as I wanted to add the boys' voices right back in, to get their insights, I didn't want to let them stop doing their version of rest too soon. Besides, girl and non-binary power! Or something like that.

"Just to get it out of the way, now that there's enough of a lull for me to demand answers..." I scooted my chair as much closer to Rye's as I could. I found I was definitely still kind of annoyed at zir as I whispered, "How the hell had you not told Kitty yet about us being the ones to set off the self-destruct?"

Apologetically and a little sadly, zie replied as quietly, "I kept meaning to. I swear I did. But...when do you think is a good time to tell your partner that you'd all, including you, their beloved, known that setting off the self-destruct was part of the plan? That you'd known it when you didn't do everything possible to stop them from going in, that you'd just thought it best not to mention? That you were all, then, guilty of their...I mean, I can argue that it's a transition all I want, but it was death. And she cared a lot about meat stuff, so it really matters to her that her body was destroyed. And..." Zie took a breath, then sounded kind of defensive as zie asked, "And why is it my job to tell her? You could have told her too."

I didn't have a reply I liked, even though it seemed inarguably obvious whose job it was to tell her, so I aimed the topic a different direction. "How long do you think she's gone for?"

Zie shook zir head sadly. "She's never been this mad at me. And she usually just cuts people off who betray her. So..."

"Fuck!" I was still whispering, but I looked over my shoulder anyway to make sure the boys hadn't heard. Fortunately, they appeared to be engrossed in their machines. "So, it's possible that we will have to talk her into letting us save her. And that she's not going to help with Plan A."

"Yeah." Riles sounded miserable. "And I'll feel okay messaging her over and over to try to get her to come back and let us save her, but it kind of feels super shitty to do that same thing to have her help us after what happened to her the last time she helped us."

I sighed but nodded. "Which means we need to keep at the AI angle, but also start programming the drones." Now that we were, in fact, going to be stuck using the drones, I felt the filth around my soul harden. Gran had had a lot of opinions, and she wasn't shy, so I'd grown up feeling sure that military drones were pure evil, used almost exclusively for base and cowardly work. And, whilst adult me knew non-gross reasons to use them, I still hated that we were using a tool that had, in fact, been used for so many corrupt and nasty things.

"I guess..." Zie sounded torn. "Obviously, I want to work on the Kitty-based issue, but you're ahead of me now, aren't you? With the time you've spent on the frequency detector?"

"If I say 'yes,' will you think it's just because I'm trying to avoid anything to do with the drones?" I didn't actually know how to honestly answer zir.

Fortunately, zie just put a compassionate arm around me, squeezed me, and said, "I will think it's also that. But, don't worry; part of why I'm so amazing is that I sold my soul forever ago. There's nothing here to stain."

I'd been wary of getting emotional, lest I feed into some bullshit gender stereotype thing or make the boys feel like they had to get out of bed to save Riles and me from ourselves. But then I kind of had a moment where I realized that that was stupid. Not only did the boys know we were capable humans, but it was pretty clear that shit could and had happened. That we could suddenly and unexpectedly lose one of us. We should emote when we could.

So, carefully, I perched on Jonny's side of the bed, leaned against him kind of. Close enough that he didn't have to reach far to take my hand, that he could do a little lean of his own and kiss me. It wasn't a long kiss, but it felt like he too had some emotion going on.

He rubbed his cheek against mine and whispered, voice rough with something that might have been tears held back, "I didn't think I'd live to see you again."

I held back my own tears and squeezed his hand. "We couldn't have just left you there. If you're alive, I'm getting you back. Always."

"Even if it means you have to take care of my busted ass yet again?" he asked, an edge of a smile on his words, though their centers were all guilt.

Maturely, I opted to let humor help me cover my emotions. "I said I was getting you back, mate. I'm just taking care of you 'cause I lost the coin toss over that with Riles." I let out a little laugh.

"It's your warmth and nurturing I admire most," he laughed back at me.

As I was trying to sort out how to work with Engie on the Peaceforger tech, I was interrupted by the boys laughing. And the laughter soon became mock-shouted choruses of "fire in November!" Noticing my curious stare, Bryan grinned and synched his computer with the TV.

It shouldn't have surprised me that the previous night's shenanigans had been caught by at least one person's phone and uploaded. It must have been someone who got there just ahead of the security thugs, because the initial shot was the burning stack of logs and the celebratory street drek in Guy Fawkes masks. I could hear the quiet laughter of the entertained person holding the phone.

A finger pointed and a man said, "Over there," and the person holding the phone turned it the direction indicated. The security guys were cresting the hill. And then we watched the same conversation go down that we'd seen less clearly from our own bugs.

Seeing it, not just hearing about it ('cause we hadn't had time to coherently piece together our footage or at least pick out the best continuous take from one camera), the boys were probably laughing hard enough that it wasn't restful. But it was also not like I was going to be an asshole. They say laughter is the best medicine, right?

Jonny asked Bryan, "May I?" And, when Bryan nodded, he took over the TV, showed us how far the video had spread. Not only did the footage we'd just watch have hundreds of thousands of hits, but there was already a blog (fuckyeahfireinnovember.com) hunting down and re-posting videos and memes people had made. I assumed there'd be fanfic soon.

I'd say we wasted time on the blog, but there's nothing wasteful about so delightful a pursuit. Plus, we figured the boys could probably handle cake, so we busted out what remained of my carefully transported treat. That way, it wasn't an accidental time waste but a cheerful celebration.

And now I knew that I'd finally added something pure to the world, even if I didn't dare admit it was part of my legacy. Not until the Peaceforgers were gone. No need to get them aimed back at me. (As if they had ever truly stopped being aimed at me...)

I caught Riles updating zir list of named days. "I was going to call it Bonfire Night Anniversary," zie noted, "but given it might be too easily confused with the original holiday, and given the unexpected popularity of it, I'm pretty sure I'm now morally obligated just to call it Fire in November."

I did not disagree.

I was having a hard time sorting out how we'd manage to take out the Peaceforgers and their facilities outside the U.S. without help. Not that there weren't American drones in other countries, but it seemed like us trying to cover meat space things all over the planet all alone wasn't the best strategy, especially when we had comrades other places.

"Riles, we have to find a way to get the remote comrades doing more than just research." I sighed. I didn't love anything to do with stuff in the meat, and asking others to really get involved with that seemed extra un-fun.

Zie looked up from zir work, nodding, then went back to typing as zie replied. "I think we need to message them directly, not just talk on the forum."

"Mm, yeah, that's too public," I agreed.

"We'll just tell them that we got a tip we trust, that the Peaceforgers are massively increasing Peacemaker production, and..."

"And we can't suggest drones, but we should point out that they'll probably need to look into answers that involve making sure the aliens can't just hang out and heal people. Because...Because the latest Peacemaker is so small that they'd barely have to touch someone, so their very presence is an active threat."

"And maybe we say we've heard from others that they might consider," zie shrugged, "a...short list of things. Things we mostly fabricate, but we also say or hint at drones."

"Perfect." I paused. "Or as perfect as I can think of. And I don't want to stress the boys, so..."

"I hear you. So, it's a good thing I've been writing the letter in question for D3AD_L1NX to send to everyone as we've been talking." Zie gave me a mischievous little grin and finally stilled the fingers that had presumably just been drafting said letter. "Though..." Zie clearly hated whatever zie was about to say. "We can't just have them go for it. Because the Peaceforgers need to have no time to react. Everyone needs to take their action at the same time."

"Dammit." Then I took a breath. "Okay. It's fine. We trusted them for the Demo Day stuff. We trust them enough to tell them things not to touch and timeframes. We can just tell them to get their plans into place. Do we just say in the next few days, letting them know it could be a while we're on hold, 'cause there's an issue we have to sort out for everyone's safety? Just tell them to have it be something that, with an hour's notice—if that sounds like enough—they should be ready to go?"

"This is fucking ridiculous," Rye noted.

I just nodded. It really was. But it wasn't our fault. This whole fucking ridiculous situation was on the Peaceforgers.

It took almost no time for everyone to reply. No details yet, just confirming they'd received and understood the message and would start making plans. Honestly, that was the easy part. I assumed that they were all now pacing their floors, trying to figure out just what the hell to do with this particular meat space predicament. Welcome to the fun, everyone.

I'd cleared everything but a table from a corner of the suite, then used sheets stolen from the swank hotel to block off the area. I'd made sure it had some good light in it, and I'd also covered the table, the carpet, and the walls with sheets. Unless I stupidly got my body in the shot (and Riles, zir eyes on a monitor, was in one ear to let me know if that happened), there should be nothing identifying picked up by the camera we'd tied to my forehead. I spread out the things from Zane's gift bag, made sure I'd forwarded any new bit of translated info that had come our way, and then pinged Engie to let her know I was ready if she was.

I'd opted not to use a voice modulator. It would have been easy enough for Engie to figure out who I was if she hadn't already guessed. Making my voice sound like a robot or a TV kidnapper wasn't going to do anything other than distract us.

"Hello?" I realized suddenly that we might both have to get used to each other's accents. I had no idea how clear we'd be.

Engie's voice was friendly and light, and had an accent my brain immediately understood. "Hello! It's lovely to have a voice to put with the text and, let's be honest, the company photo they kept putting on the news."

I winced. "Ugh. That photo!"

She laughed. "I assure you that we have all had to look Very Normal to pay bills."

I grinned. So we had. "As long as you know I'm actually painfully cool. You can't imagine how cool."

"Oh, of course you are," she assured me. "You even have one of those cool American accents like on TV. Almost."

"Almost. I hope close enough for you to keep working with us."

With exaggerated doubt, she said, "I don't know...Though, I suppose, as it's literally the fate of the world we're handling here, I can lower my standards a bit."

We shared a laugh, and then she said, "Right, let's see what we have and what we can make of it."

Like me, she'd read the user manual for the frequency detector. Unlike me, she had noticed *before* someone told her that it definitely could do some short-range transmitting and some signal converting as well.

We went through everything, even swiping through specs I accessed on the interface device. I took pictures or video as she requested it. I leaned in to get her close to things. I let her direct me in trying tools and settings.

In the end, we were held back by a lack of translated specs and a lack of signals to detect. The latter of which, so we're clear, was a good thing that just happened to have that one regrettable side effect.

She walked me through some things, took notes, and promised to get back to me ASAP if she had things to try. But, for now, there was nothing to be done.

Before we could say our goodbyes, Riles piped up in my earbud, "New message from Zane with steps for...looks like for setting up the frequency detector to deactivate Peacemakers and another few steps for seeing if you can even get the healing tool to turn on."

"Hey, do you have more time? We just got some new steps. Maybe even some stuff on the healing tool. Um...that should all be forwarding to you now..."

Riles confirmed, "Sending now."

"And maybe see if we can get the doctor on the call too, if that's okay? See if that at all helps with the magical miracle glove thingy?" The healing tool wasn't a full glove, but the one thing we could tell from its documentation was that it was centered on the palm of the person using it, with some loops that went around fingers and the wrist.

"I'll reach out to Doc," Riley said.

"Can you spare more time for us, Engie?"

She laughed, and I wasn't sure if it was at the nickname or the continued absurdity of our situation. "You're my full-time job, you know," Engie told me. "I don't know if you meant to be as generous as you've been, but I don't exactly have to take other work right now. Plus, again, literal fate of the world. So there's a very good chance I can spare more time."

Though we worked a while more and got Doc in the call to look at the healing glove with us, we didn't sort out much. It seemed like I'd programmed the frequency detector so I could push a button and deactivate a Peacemaker, but I'd have to go out and find someone to test it.

When I apologized for the waste of time, Engie tutted. "Please. This is all additional information, another look at how this works. Which also gives me insight into how *they* work, you know. You can tell things about people from how they build their stuff. I don't think this has been a waste."

With the healing glove, I *had* at least managed to turn it on. Not that that should have been hard; it had an activation switch. But I also seemed to have correctly followed steps to use specific finger movements to activate it. And, claimed Zane's message, I'd have to be able to move my fingers certain ways to heal with it, and turning it on with the finger movement method instead of the switch was a valid first test. So, gold star for me.

Mostly, I let Engie and Doc brainstorm. I looked at the specs on the interface device, or aimed the camera at it and moved things on it when they told me to, and made sure to keep my arm away from my body (because it would be just my luck the glove could also harm, and I didn't want to accidentally infect myself or something). We tried a few things, by which I mean they told me what to try and I did my best. Again, we were limited because we didn't exactly have flesh we felt we could safely experiment on to confirm any guesses.

Grudgingly, I said, "Um, what about our mutual friend, Doc? Beaten to hell and said he'd volunteer to let us try things out on him."

Doc made an offended sound. "What sort of hack do they think I am? The fuck I'm going to do medical experiments on *anyone*, much less someone I actually like."

"I'll remember that if you ever suggest I try using it on myself in one of these sessions." I laughed. But, also, I considered whether I could now try a thing or two out on myself. You know, 'cause it wasn't like making sure I had a cut on my arm that needed healing was exactly hard to do. I'd keep that idea in mind, just in case.

Everyone else in the suite had been very quiet as I'd had my conference call. As soon as the camera was switched off and the call was ended, the TV sound was turned back on and the low-volume patter of non-stop news anchor voices resumed.

"What did Doc say when you said you could try the healing thing on me?" Jonny asked.

"Mate, the fact he helps out people on the sly with issues doesn't mean he's bereft of ethics." I worked to take down the sheets as I talked, pausing to wink at Jonny. "Next time, make sure you're way less likeable. I feel like we could have talked him into it if he thought you were a complete bastard."

In mock disgust, Jonny shook his head and muttered, "Damn my charm."

"*Any* luck with that stuff?" asked Bryan.

"I don't feel like it, not really. But Engie says I gave her more useful data to work with." I shrugged. "Oh, though we now have a frequency detector that's programmed to both detect and—probably—*turn off* Peacemakers. Which is pretty cool."

"You just have to test it," Riles pointed out.

Testing it would mean going out, risking being caught in general. Risking being caught with Peaceforger tech in particular. And it kind of wasn't going to be good to get caught with that no matter which side got me. Which is probably why I suddenly had a stupid idea.

Without running it by my friends, I messaged Engalls. It was late, but I figured it wasn't too rude since it was a message, not a call.

You ever get your kid's head cleaned out?

Once I'd sent it, I said to Riley (quietly, because the boys were on rest, right?), "You know Engalls has a kid who had a Peacemaker in her head, right? A vI, so probably got that pulled out and it left a vII behind. Not sure he got that taken care of."

Zie immediately saw what I was up to, at least part of it. "Kot!" Riley looked like zie couldn't believe I was so foolish. In a lowered voice, zie asked, "What if you accidentally kill our one cop ally's kid?"

"I mean, my other option is to jump someone random in the street. Or to trust one of Lex's loud friends to let me try and then to keep their mouth shut." I shrugged. I just wanted results. "If you'll make sure there's a good place for us to meet? Probably not a swank place this time."

My phone pinged. It was Engalls.

No. Hospitals are slammed. Can you help?

And then I had another, slightly less stupid thought. And I messaged Dr. Scott.

Is there a price for which you'd meet me and a friend to take a bug out of a kid tonight?

I leaned over to Riles. "Okay, new plan. A little more complicated maybe. But also less likely to end up with a dead kid."

About 20 minutes later, I stepped from a shadow a few blocks from our suites and I got into a driverless taxi. I had as little on me as possible, and Riles was talking in my ear and watching via the camera attached to the hair clip peeking out from my stocking cap. As we neared the pickup point for Engalls and his kid, I checked in a mirror on the seatback in front of me to make sure that my cap and g/ap mask left only my eyes exposed. And even those I covered with sunglasses.

Engalls's kid was a young-looking 14. She was in all black as we'd requested, including a stocking cap, and looked pretty excited. Engalls had on matching all black and cap, and he looked far less excited. I'd asked them to pull down their own g/ap masks before they got in the car (we wanted to confirm identities easily), so her grin and his frown were pretty clear messages.

When the taxi pulled up in front of them, Engalls leaned down to look in and I pulled my glasses down, hoping he'd at least recognize my eyes. He nodded, opened the door, and ushered his kid in first.

As soon as they were in and the door was closed, I said, "You can and should pull your masks up now."

Even with masks, I could still very clearly hear Engalls's eyebrows tell me he was Not At All Sure about this.

Apologetically, I said, "I have to blindfold you. Can't have you seeing where we're going. Need to keep someone else's privacy."

The kid enthusiastically whispered, "Hell yeah! This is some cool-ass spy shit." She practically bounced in her seat.

More a pained plea than a scold, Engalls said, "Language. Come on." But he didn't bother to look over and watch her roll her eyes at him.

Riley laughed in my ear. "I love her."

I handed Engalls the blindfold to put on her, then reached across her carefully to put one on him.

"I don't love this," he grumbled.

"I totally get it. But literally everyone in this situation has things to lose. So..." I tried to sound more apologetic than I felt.

"Yeah, I totally get it too. Doesn't mean I have to like it." His grumble sounded even grumblier through the mask. "But if you can help..."

Before I could answer, the kid said, "I know I'm not supposed to ask questions, but I'm also not an idiot. Is this because there's probably still one of those shi—" She seemed to catch herself about to use something stronger than a minor Biblical swear word in front of her dad again. "One of those stupid bugs in my head still?" She snorted. "My stepdad would think that was an awesome thing."

I returned her snort. "Your stepdad is a jackass. And, yeah, this is about that."

"Cool." And then she nestled back into her seat and we were all quiet for the circuitous drive, with a few fake stops (though no car changes, 'cause the blindfolds sort of made that unwieldy) to Dr. Scott's back alley door.

As soon as we were out of the taxi and far enough away, Rye sent it on its way. And, once it was gone and we were in darkness, Dr. Scott's door opened and I helped her guide our blindfolded friends into an unlit room.

She closed and locked the door behind us (I heard the clicks), and then turned on a light. I took off my sunglasses and pulled my mask down whilst she pulled on her own cap and mask. Hers were clearly medical gear, not "cool-ass spy shit" like the rest of us were sporting. Then we guided Engalls and his kid to chairs. His was against the wall, where I'd sat watching Gran's surgery. (I ignored the wrecking ball to the guts when I had that thought.) His kid's was an exam chair with a backwards seat and a place to rest your face if the focus of the exam was the back of your body.

"Okay, so, nobody uses names. And people should probably speak as little as possible." I scanned the room. Even though I didn't see any identifying signs, I said, "Dad, I know you want to watch, but my doctor and I would be really, really grateful if you'd be willing to keep your blindfold on."

His sigh made it clear he couldn't hate the idea more, but he said, "Fine. I trust you. Don't ruin that." He left his blindfold where it was, but still sat like he was ready to spring into action.

I knew he couldn't see the smile, but I hoped he could hear it. "Thank you. Seriously." Then I turned to his kid. "Now, my soon-to-be-freed teen friend...We're going to have you lean forward, and we'll adjust things to get at the bug."

We helped her ease forward. Because there was a hole cut on the cushioned surface where she rested her head, which might let her see identifying things in the office, I couldn't have her take off her blindfold. I also didn't want to expose her identity, so she definitely had to leave it and the mask on. I trusted Dr. Scott, but it wasn't up to me to expose anyone's identity to anyone without, in this case, her own and her dad's permission. Unless the anyone I was exposing was a villain, but I didn't think this kid was that.

As Dr. Scott got her tools ready, I took a moment to pull out some tools of my own. First, I used our Peacemaker detector to confirm that, yep, there was an alien mind control bug in that young brain. Then, I used the frequency detector, trying to be quick enough that Dr. Scott might not notice, to confirm that it, too, saw the Peacemaker. It flashed exactly the notification I thought it should for an active Peacemaker.

Riley, knowing what was next, asked, "Are you sure? How much do you really trust Zane and Isa now?"

Fortunately, I couldn't actually answer aloud, so I didn't have to admit that it was one small part limited trust and a large part desperation. I just nodded, held my breath, and put the frequency detector a few feet back from her head. (Why didn't I get in close? Some completely illogical part of me thought that, if this was going to send out a Bad Signal, maybe it would do less harm if done from maximum distance. So I backed off as much as I thought I could. And, yes, I knew as I did it how ridiculous it was.)

"Fuck. Just do it!" Riles, in my ear, was clearly dying of the suspense.

Worst case, she's in a doctor's office. Dr. Scott can save her, I thought. I exhaled, nodding at my thoughts, working hard to forget that Gran had been in this office when her own Peacemaker did a Bad Thing, and Dr. Scott hadn't been able to save *her.* And then I held a new breath and pushed the button.

There was no way the kid knew what I was doing, so I'd like to give this year's award for *Worst Timed Yawn, You Know, the Kind Where You Squeak a Little* to the kid. For a split second, I was so sure that I'd hurt her that I wondered if I should just run. But then she squirmed, like she wished she could stretch, did a normal kind of yawn-sounding yawn…And I realized the squeak too had been part of a yawn, so I finally let myself exhale.

Zie must have either just known me well enough or have noticed I'd frozen, because Riley laughed and said, "I want to believe she did that on purpose. And I want us to adopt her."

I held up my middle finger where I was sure the camera would pick it up, then I used the finger to operate the frequency detector, to scan again with it. And it gave the "deactivated Peacemaker" notification. I did a victory fist pump before I noticed that Dr. Scott was watching all this.

She squinted at me curiously. I put my fingers to my lips, hoping that read not just as "quiet, please" but also as "secret; shh!" She rolled her eyes at me, but in a way that seemed more like "of course it's a secret, with you and your plots" and not too much "you are so annoying."

Whatever it meant, with no further ado, with the tiniest incision at the base of the kid's skull, and with a quickness that told me she'd done plenty of this lately, Dr. Scott took the offending Peacemaker from the kid's head.

Before she destroyed it herself, I suggested, "We should let the kid stomp it."

"Yesssssss!" The kid was very into this idea.

Dr. Scott shrugged and put it aside. We confirmed there were no more things in the kid's head, and Dr. Scott closed her up.

Engalls was still in a sort of "high alert" posture as he asked, "It's done?"

"It's done," I confirmed, and was glad to watch his shoulders release a little of the tension.

Once the kid was standing, Dr. Scott helpfully held up a generic, blue medical sheet so that the kid and I could stand in an empty-ish corner.

I pulled off the kid's blindfold, showed her the tiny Peacemaker vII, then put it on the floor. She howled like a triumphant barbarian as she jumped up and down, smashing it under her sturdy boots.

I didn't need to see her mouth to know she was grinning at me as she whispered, "Thank you."

I got her back into her blindfold, then cleaned up the fragments with a broom and dustpan Dr. Scott handed me. She typed some directions for making sure things healed right and they knew what to look for in the very unlikely event of post-operative complications, and I read them aloud to Engalls. There were no follow-up questions.

I whispered my own thanks to the doctor as we got everyone ushered back out to the alley.

She obviously didn't hate it too much, because I could hear her grin as she mimicked the kid and whispered in reply, "Yesssss!"

The taxi ride back to near where I'd picked up Engalls and his kid was quiet, but a more relaxed quiet. Though the kid was still practically vibrating with excitement over the events of the night. When we pulled to the curb, I reached over to take off their blindfolds.

Engalls regarded me seriously for a moment, then said, "I thought I was done feeling like I owed you something."

I laughed a little and quipped, "Don't worry. Still at least one big thing left that you'll be able to owe me for. I take gift cards." I gave him a wink.

He laughed a little, shook his head, then put a hand on the kid's shoulder. "Let's get home. And remember, not a word of this to anyone."

"Got it," she gave him a crisp nod. Then, before I could even think how to react, she threw herself at me and gave me a hug. "I hope I grow up to be as badass as you someday."

I returned the hug, but could only laugh. I saw how Engalls's eyes had gotten a little scared at that thought.

And then Engalls and the kid ducked out of the taxi and headed into shadows.

"We're *definitely* adopting her. Or at least pulling her into our questionable circle when she's old enough," Riley laughed. Then zie said, "Good job saving the kid. Gran would be proud, hero."

I didn't want to get emotional, so I just said, "I'm pretty sure we just gave her one of her top Weekends with Dad ever." Now, we just had to make sure there were plenty more weekends left for this species.

CHAPTER 16

I woke to Morgan on the news calmly explaining, "There's no need to worry. The shuttles you'll see crisscrossing your skies over the next two days are just doing some mapping."

Like she had a script, the news anchor (someone new; we hadn't seen Rachel since she'd called Morgan out in that interview, and Hillary was clearly still in need of some polish) asked, "Mapping?"

Morgan nodded seriously. "One of our scientists suggested that, rather than come in after disasters like the one in Bolivia, we might be able to at least help get a warning system in place. Our own planet has some volatile areas, so we've got plenty of solutions to suggest. But, first, we have to get as much information as possible. So, we're using our scanners to map your planet."

New Anchor smiled, a little too polished for my liking, as she looked at us. And just like she'd been chatting with some random city employee about a traffic jam, she said, "And there you have it, folks. Thanks to Morgan for keeping us informed about the situation. Don't worry. Maybe even give a little wave when you see the shuttles," she suggested chipperly.

I wanted to punch her in the face.

The boys were still sleeping, but Rye was up and working (hence, the TV on when I woke), so I relocated to the table. "What do you think they're really doing?"

"Probably actually fucking mapping the tectonics of the Earth, but just so they can more easily target and blow us apart," zie said, disgusted.

I sighed. "Probably not far from the truth."

"But, equally important, do we think this new anchor is one of their Peacemaker puppets and, if not, who do you think told her that she was good at fake smiles? Because, girl, no." And zie somehow sounded as disgusted by New Anchor as zie was by the Peaceforgers and their treachery. Which would have been funnier if zie didn't maybe have a point about Peacemaker puppets.

I wandered over to our kitchenette and poured some cereal, thinking about how surely the Peaceforgers were preparing to make a move, and soon. And I didn't think we were nearly prepared.

"Poppet, if we don't have to reprogram them for Peacemaker facilities, how long until we can probably deploy drones?" I poured my milk, considering the tiny carton size that was mandated by the little fridge in the suite. Whilst I was grateful to be somewhere with a fridge and good heating, I was eager to be back to living in a normal home with normal-sized appliances and normal daily troubles. Or at least to survive long enough to have the chance.

Zie made a thinking sort of hum, then said, "I'd estimate...mmm...I could be done by...Friday could be the day. I'm aiming for Thursday but being realistic about the likelihood." Zie failed to sound casual as zie asked, "And how about you? Where do you think we are on getting Kitty back?"

I considered being entirely encouraging, but I hated to even kind of lie to my people. "Honestly, I don't know. There are too many variables. But..." And the ideas tried to pull together in my mind, since I couldn't really count on more information coming my way. "I think I should build the absolute beefiest computer I can, maximum storage and processing power. Order the sort of parts that...aren't exactly on the open market. Not my gran's desktop, you know? Make sure it has every possible input type we can still get our hands on. And by 'we' I mean 'me.' Just build something that's bigger and badder than the reqs for a human-built AI. Which will mean we've done everything possible to have a space prepared for her and to make it possible for her to get into it."

"Connect it to the 'Net in case that helps give her more room or resources?"

I'd read the same books zie had, both fiction and reference, but I nodded in spite of images of rogue AI rampaging unrestrained through the world. "Absolutely. Plus, that way she won't feel like she's trapped with us. Because that's the plotline for a potentially fucked up story."

"Ugh. A story that's been told too many times. How many times do straight men need to tell it so they can feed their gross male gaze hunger?" (We'd also seen all the same "girl-shaped AI are exploited" films.)

"Exactly. And, then, I think we need to convince her to come back so we can see if we can...connect to her? Receive her? I don't know what the right verb is." I scrunched up my face as I considered, then shook my head and released the scrunch. "Anyway, I think I'm going to build it in the other suite. And I'll be ordering parts and building as soon as I can. Otherwise—"

Riles interrupted. "Actually, consider building it in here? So it's really easy for the rest of us to appreciate the badass piece of hardware you're building. And for the boys to feel included kind of."

I nodded. "Yeah. Okay. Probably. Anyway, otherwise, I'll be messing around with the frequency detector. Maybe seeing if I can figure out how to hack the interface device or make something else connect with it."

"We need cooler names for the tech...or at least shorter ones, so we can talk about them faster in an emergency," zie announced suddenly. Zie narrowed zir eyes a moment in thought (whilst I was still trying to figure out if zie was actually serious or just feigning it), then said, "We can just acronym the interface device. I.D. but like 'id' so it's just one syllable. Much faster to say than five."

I snorted a laugh. "Of course you went for 'id.' So now we just have to figure out which of the other two devices is the ego and which the superego." I laughed again.

"Mm. That's obvious, right? Superego is morality, so that's healing others. And Ego is reality, like the frequency detector senses the now. Or something like that." Zie laughed, finally sensing the absurdity of fussing over the names. "Good thing we're focusing on the important issues."

"So important," I agreed with exaggerated gravity. "Anyway, though not as indulgently fun as it sounds, I'm spending as much time with the ID today as I can." I yawned and stretched. "But first, time to order parts for the best computer build any of us has ever done."

I was pulling together my computer pieces as quickly as safety allowed. It was an odd assortment of parts at first, with those for interface seeming the easiest to get and quickest to arrive.

The boys hadn't been brought in on the Kitty plan yet, because I just knew they'd hate to miss out on making contributions to the hardware side of things. So, when I pulled some VR gear out, there was...a reaction.

"What the fuck kind of careless did you two become while we were out?" demanded Bryan, sounding more worried than mean.

Which was actually a fair question, given the history of VR gear. There was a reason that, right after virtual reality started to become accessible to everyone, once they'd worked out the costs and the interface issues that had always made it too unwieldy for normal people or regular use, nobody actually dared use it. There were so many confirmed stories of ways people had hacked the gear to do harm, and then just as many unconfirmed but no less possible stories. By the time it was abandoned by anyone who couldn't afford to have a specialist modify the gear and then inspect every program, there were too many people who'd had fingerprints and retinal scans stolen, and some who'd even been victim to intentional seizures, heart attacks, and brainwashing.

Not that everyone abandoned their gear right away, even once it became clear VR was being abused. Someone decided it was "just common sense" that, since augmented reality was less immersive, people would be safe as long as they only used the gear in AR mode. Kind of the reverse of "if you cover your eyes so you can't see them, the monsters can't get you." If you don't cover your eyes, if you can still see the real world (just with digital stuff overlaid), then the monsters can't get you. Which, yeah, way to be stupid, humans. Though, to be fair, marketing for some of the brands might have implied that reasoning in very persuasive and slick ways.

Gran had been almost as mad about the death of VR (and AR, though she didn't often mention it as a separate thing) as she'd been about how things had gone with flying cars. (Really, given how she was more quietly angry about this one, I suspected her disappointment and frustration here were more real.)

"Uh, well," I looked back at Rye, trying to guess how much to tell them. Then I suddenly realized I had zero energy for keeping them out if it took more than just leaning over and whispering to Riles. So I told them large parts of our incomplete plan.

I'd been right; they were really not happy that they couldn't help. And it was just going to make things worse if they didn't understand certain decisions, so I tried to throw them bones. I explained what the gear was maybe for (though I didn't tell them what we hoped Kitty might do for us) and that I was just trying to maximize chances to connect to Kitty. And then I let them decide how to divide it, but I gave them the VR gear and tools and let them set about making it safe. They had goggles, gloves, the VR computer add-on thing (though no programs beyond the basic operating system necessary to make it work and do set up), and the send/receive unit that let you go wireless piled between them on the bed.

Because letting them fix that was going to keep their blood pressures good, which was kind of like rest. Right?

I sat at the table with Riley, waiting for notifications that meant I needed to go pick up more parts that had been dropped off outside empty doors in the hotel. I watched the boys work, and I fiddled with the frequency detector (or would that be Ego?) and the ID. I was trying to see if I could get either to communicate with my computer at all. I was wary of anything that let the two devices communicate with each other, just in case the actions I'd take to do that would also make us detectable to the Peaceforgers.

As if we'd been mid-conversation, I said, "I mean, they look happy and relaxed, right? So they're resting even though they're working, right?" I was trying not to feel guilty about letting them do anything more than eat pudding and watch TV. (Honestly, I wished *I* were just eating pudding and watching TV...)

Zie patted my knee. "It's good. It's just enough challenge to make them happy without stressing them. Plus," and zie leaned back in zir seat, "I can't hate that the people who are better with hardware are the ones doing that."

"Yeah..." I sighed. "Well, at this rate, I'll be building tonight. So that should be fun, actually." I tried a new setting on Ego, the frequency detector, and it seemed to sense the existence of our computers suddenly.

I traded an excited look with Rye.

"Is that a breakthrough?" zie asked.

"I just...It's cool. It's something. But I have no idea." I sighed. "Isa has to have someone who knows more about their computers and maybe even ours. I'm going to ask."

Riles nodded, so I messaged Isa.

Thanks for the constant trickle of translations! Any word on a translation program I can load on the interface device? Any of your people maybe able to give us an overview of the concepts behind your computing, what programming looks like for you lot, or even just thoughts on how your computers and ours might interface? Thanks :-)

Right. Back to this new setting, even if I was working too slowly. I was feeling a particular emotion that you might think was laziness. In reality, it was this weird slowdown my brain can do when it's feeling overwhelmed by stress. When I'm pretty sure I can't actually do a huge task (or the many tasks) I need to do and I am just stalling before ruin hits. I tended to think of it as a dangerous state, but I somehow always made it through.

For now, I rode it. I worked through it, even if my pace was painfully slow. I pulled out our human frequency detectors. I tested to see if anything could see or be seen in a meaningful way by the Peaceforger one. I tried some of the basic transmit options, ones I didn't think would do harm.

The ID blinked. I paused and tapped the frequency detector screen again. The ID blinked.

It wasn't much, but it was something. I nudged Riley and showed zir. Fortunately, zie was as impressed as I was.

From the bed, Jonny called, "Hey, when are you going to show *us* the alien tech? Human hardware is great, but..."

Not one to miss a chance to sit by Jonny, I took the two gadgets over and tried to settle gently between the boys. It wasn't like I could just show it to Jonny and not Bryan. Especially not whilst they were sharing a bed.

"So, this one is the frequency detector." I held up the device in question. "Not only does it detect Peaceforger frequencies, like Peacemakers, but it can be made to transmit a little and to convert frequencies or things sent via them a little. Zane said it's quite basic, like our fobs for our cars, but more limited range. Anyway, they used theirs to deactivate your Peacemakers, and I used ours to deactivate one too once they sent us directions. And I'll give you guys the manual to read so you can learn it if you want."

"If we want," Bryan said mockingly, as if them wanting was at all a thing that was in question.

Ignoring him, I held up the ID. "This is the interface device they gave me, loaded with information but not connected to their network. Obviously. And I don't want to fuck with that, because I like us not caught. So, I've been trying to see what safe things—or things I think are safe—I can change or do with them, and see if that lets our Earth stuff interact with them. Which has mainly been a fail, but look!"

And then I showed them my trick. Which, admittedly, was not impressive to look at and most people might not see it as a big deal.

But Bryan grinned at me. "You found a thread to pull. A little something to start putting the puzzle together."

Because, sometimes, that's how a hack worked. You tried all the things, even the weird things, and then you found the one that got even a small reaction. And you teased that out and followed it...and suddenly you were controlling and exploring the evasive system like it was your own back yard.

"You should try other interfaces," Jonny suggested. "You're getting all these possible interfaces. More than you have on your own computer. Maybe you'll find one that's more compatible?" He started to type, creating a new spreadsheet on his computer to track test results, then he looked guilty. "Sorry. Instinct. I promise I'm relaxing."

I gave him a stern look and a bit of a weak go at a scolding. "I've already given you lads the VR stuff to play with."

Jonny shrugged. "But we're done already because we are badasses. So, unless you forgot how cool we are while we were away the last week, you can see how the contest of 'daytime TV versus methodically working through interfaces and options with you' might have an obvious winner."

I looked at Riles.

Zie said, "I think I stand by my earlier statement. If they're not stressing, if they're just lying there enjoying themselves," zie paused and we all snickered, our minds in the gutter, then went on, "without exertion," zie paused to sigh in a way that was both cheeky and mock sad, then finished, "then it's probably fine."

The boys confirmed, of course, that this seemed a very reasonable and wise stance, so they built a spreadsheet whilst I gathered our interfaces. I figured they could take naps in the inevitable breaks as I ran out to pick up more pieces of our supercomputer.

Working through input devices (and output devices, 'cause obviously the ability of the Peaceforger tech to interact with those might also tell us something), a pattern was starting to emerge. But I wasn't the hardware person, and neither of the boys were saying anything, so I thought I'd sit on my theory a bit. Until I got a message from Isa:

My person says they're not sure what all to say. But they think, if you want a thing to consider while they try to write a helpful summary, you should look into optical computing. Which, so you know, we derailed ASAP once humans started looking into it.

A short laugh escaped my mouth, and I said, "I was right!" I turned to grin at the boys. "I have a theory, but I thought it was too obvious to be good. But now..." I read them the message, then said, "We're getting best results with things that actively work with light."

"Oh, man, I thought that was too simple," Jonny groaned. "Especially because I was interested in optical computing for a while, so I knew all the reasons it wouldn't work."

Bryan patted his knee consolingly. "You aren't the first person to fall for the Peaceforger bullshit." Then he said, "I assume that optical computing is just, what, the signals are sent with light instead of electricity?"

Jonny nodded. "Yeah, it was supposed to speed up our computing, but there were a lot of weird failures and someone suggested there were quantum mechanics things we had to work out first. And then, before we did that, out of nowhere...which is something that we should now see as a red flag for Peaceforger meddling...Anyway, out of nowhere, someone made sure R&D on *quantum* chips was well-funded. And those chips were so much faster at the time. So..."

"So the fucking aliens made sure we didn't develop the tech that might let us interact with their tech or figure it out or get on their level or...whatever," I said.

We all nodded, looking at our spreadsheet.

Whilst Jonny edited and filtered the entries on the spreadsheet so that we could just focus on the stuff that involved light, I cleared away the rest of the gear.

Riles wandered over to help and reported, "I think the drones are programmed. Though we'll need to sort the satellite issue and the control machine on the ship."

Failing to sound as nonchalant as he probably meant to, Bry asked, "Anything I can help you with?"

"I think we actually have it, babe," said Riles. "I mean, seriously, sorting out this computing stuff is really helpful and as important as the drone stuff."

Bry gave me a look, trying to confirm whether this was bullshit. I nodded, confirming. He nodded back, accepting it.

"So, I'll also take over picking up deliveries," said Rye. "I could use a little movement." Zie asked me, "How much is left?"

I pulled up my checklist on my mobile. "Really, just another few. We should be able to start building in an hour..." I'd paid a premium price to make sure even the black-market things showed up quickly. "Except that I feel like sorting this out," I waved at the spreadsheet with interface device info, "might inform changes or at least how we proceed?"

"Oh, definitely," zie agreed. "Being able to build with their actual frequencies and tech in mind instead of guessing and hoping we bought a useful interface? Very helpful."

My phone pinged, and I forwarded the delivery notification to Riles. "It's all yours, poppet."

As soon as zie left, Bryan asked, "Okay, honestly, what chance do you think we have of saving Kitty?"

I sighed. "No idea. I'm building a computer that's so mindblowingly badass...Which means that the part of the plan where we give her a place to be is as covered as I can make it. And we're now maybe onto something to actually figure out how to connect with her. What with the optical computing clue and what we've been finding with how the gear interacts. But...Will our tech be compatible with what she is? Will it be big and/or bad enough? Will she want to be stuck there? Will we be able to manage the transfer of the data that is Kitty? Especially since I'm guessing she is a whole fucking lot of data, and that we'll need to have a steady connection for whatever length of time the transfer takes..." I shrugged. "I don't want to say it's a slim chance, but I can't reasonably say I have high confidence."

Bry nodded. "Riley knows."

"Of course zie does. But we have to do all we can and pretend, unless it becomes clear we definitely can't, that we're at least pretty sure we can do this. Don't we? Not just for Riles, but for Kitty. It's what we'd do for any of us, right?"

The boys nodded.

"Hey, not to change the topic kind of, but have we gotten footage of inside the ship?" Jonny asked. "I'm wondering if we can get clues about their computers from that."

"You guys didn't see any computer whilst you were there?"

They both shook their heads.

"Nothing more than that interface device," Bryan said.

"Though their door controls and other shit like that are probably connected to the ship's computer. Making those, arguably, computer interfaces," Jonny suggested.

"You guys see a lot of those?"

They looked uncertainly at each other, sighed almost in unison, then looked apologetically at me.

"Our room had a touchpad by the door. That was it. At least as far as I noticed," admitted Jonny.

"Yeah, and the adjacent torture room was really just a duplicate, but with a chair in it that made it easier to restrain and get at us," Bryan added. "They were pretty old school with their torture techniques. Nothing computerized about that."

Trying to keep my hero face on, even though we'd gotten the team's actual heroes back and should now be safe to resume our Team Run the Fuck Away mentality, I nodded thoughtfully, and turned to help myself to Jonny's computer. "Okay, well, what we do have—and all they seem to have let us see—is whatever is in the footage of their fake-y 'Hello, World' video." I pulled that up so we could watch it. Over and over.

Mostly, the row of Peaceforgers behind Morgan blocked our view. But not entirely. We paused and zoomed in on bits that seemed like they might offer hints (which was really just putting the image at full potential size and moving the player so that the part we wanted was what showed on Jonny's screen). There wasn't much to see. Though I got the sense (probably just my sci-fi-loving brain making shit up) that this was in the bridge of the ship, the walls and tables (consoles?) seemed pretty featureless, mostly just expanses of their usual light metal. There were a few sections that might be small screens or touchpads, but nothing that readily showed its purpose.

The one thing we did see when one Peaceforger changed which foot they were standing on or something like that was a couple of folks who might be working behind them. They seemed to be gesturing in the air, and two of the three who were turned to face the same direction had something on their faces. If it were on *my* face, I'd say it was an oblong with a missing section that outlined my eye, sitting on the edges of my optical cavity (so, running from the middle of my eyebrow, around the outside of my eye, and then to about halfway right under my eye). No surprise, it looked like it was made of their usual light metal.

"I've seen those," Bryan said.

Jonny nodded. "Yeah, the people who grilled us or whatever had one of those on most of the time."

"But not always, right? Same people, but without that. So I'm pretty sure they're removable." Bryan was leaned in as close as he could get to the screen, searching for more information.

"So, maybe it's part of how they see or connect with some of their tech." I chewed my cheek. I wondered if we could get one of those.

Bryan cleared his throat and visibly resisted the urge to sit up straighter. "We should get focused on digging into our narrowed list of human devices and what we can do with the Peaceforger tech."

Hardware boy, eager to do hardware things. Shocking.

It was a bit slow going, because that's the way being methodical tends to work, but we thought it was the VR gear that was giving us best results. We paused a moment to indulge in our new theory that this proved the demise of VR was also due to the damned aliens. Those bastards had ruined everything.

I channeled Gran and complained, "I bet they killed flying cars for normal people too. The assholes."

Everyone nodded in agreement, with Riles teasing, "Call 'em out, Gran!"

Then we returned to investigating, trying to refine, and trying to see how this setup would work with our supercomputer. Basically, we were getting the VR's computer add-on unit to talk to the Peaceforger tech (not smooth or eloquent talk, but talk nonetheless), though we were struggling to get it to connect to both Peaceforger devices at once. Still, it was a start.

And, when we were connected, we could put on the goggles and gloves and sort of pull the information out of the ID, so we could have multiple screens of info sitting in the air. We could scroll each screen, just like it was on the ID. So, for instance, I could pull up specs for multiple things at once and hang them side-by-side in the air. This worked in VR mode (where they floated in the blank VR starting space) and AR mode (where they seemed to float in the air of the room).

The same basic hardware setup, but swapping out the interface device for the frequency detector (which had somehow morphed from being called Ego to being called Igor, as we urged it to be a good servant and do our bidding), gave us less that was obviously cool. Such an Igor. Which wasn't surprising; there wasn't much here with Peaceforger frequency signatures. But I could see the radius of its transmission, allowing us to measure and confirm that it was about 4.35 feet. And, when we changed it to the setting that had seemed to let it see our computers, I could see what it saw. With my own eyes, thanks to the goggles, I could see the light energy that radiated from our machines. It was kind of cool. And, as we scrolled settings, I could see more mundane things (like heat signatures). Most exciting, when someone walked by in the hall, Igor could see through the walls and let me know an active Peacemaker was walking by.

Secretly, though, what I appreciated most was that, if I put Igor right by one of our human devices (like one of our phones), I was making progress getting it to display the screen in the air for me. It was especially easier if the human device was in 3D display mode. Hell yeah, Igor! When we got her to talk to us, I was excited to see what it would do with Holo-Kitty.

I felt my hope of getting Kitty back increase the slightest bit. We'd get her, use the drones to destroy the alien invaders, and get back to something like a normal life. Easy, right?

CHAPTER 17

Riley was out for the last delivery, and the boys were taking a well-earned nap. Or Jonny was. Bryan was stubbornly, with heavy eyelids, reading the manual for Igor with increased interest now that the little frequency detector was showing more visible results. I was trying to see if I could pull Igor's different control screens into the air, like I could pull documents into the air from the ID, so that I might be able to toggle settings without having to take off the VR gear. If not for the looming threat of human annihilation or subjugation, it might have been a perfectly pleasant Monday evening.

Pleasant even though Isa hadn't responded in the way I'd hoped to a message I'd sent to ask if it would be possible to get us, as I called them, "those little interface things your people wear on their temples for computer stuff" without being caught. Apparently, they were a "one per person" kind of thing. Losing one was a Bad Deal and would probably set Morgan and their fellow leadership cronies off.

Pleasant even though the chocolate cake was gone. (Look, it was really good cake and I was possibly PMSing, so its lack was felt.)

Yeah. Quite nice for a Monday. And then my phone made a ping that was specifically for Kitty sending messages. Perfect. I quickly took off the VR gear, ready to work things out with her.

Except that the message was:

HELP!!!!

Shit. Followed immediately by a message from poor Riles, out and trying to get home undetected:

Kot, can you???

I didn't want to stress Bryan, so I tried to keep my face casual as I gathered the VR gear, ID, and Igor; headed for the loo; and replied:

Yes. Kitty, 3D.

I flipped my screen to 3D, then put on the VR gear and turned everything on.

Kitty was large as life and twice as terrified, her eyes wide and her simulation of breath coming across as something near hyperventilation. Though she paused a moment at my unexpected appearance, confusion tinged with hysteria maybe. "What the hell?"

I shrugged. "I've got some new gear. I think it will help me help you. If nothing else, you're life-sized to my eyes." Then, I got serious. "What's wrong? Are you okay?"

She shook her head and took a long, steadying breath. Even so, she sounded like she didn't have enough air. (I was going to ask her about the breathing thing when it all calmed down.) "There's something else in here with me."

I put any of Igor's screens that I thought might be useful into the air and started looking for a setting that would let me see Kitty's signal. As I tried settings and toggled between VR and AR mode (just in case something looked more obvious in one view or the other), I asked, "What do you mean?"

"I was...I found the machine on the ship—"

"Oh!" I looked away from my holo-screens. "That's awesome, Kits!"

She ignored me, plowed ahead, like her words were running from the thing that she was afraid of. "And I was trying to fuck it up, so you would see I could handle this without your explode-y asses. And I...I must have tripped something up. Because, like, not right after but probably an hour or so after, I could hear something coming from the direction of the machine." She sounded about two seconds away from *Blair Witch* levels of hysteria.

I was narrowing down to the right settings; I had started to see a shimmering blue and silver thread that stretched from Kitty up to and through the ceiling. I flipped from AR mode to

VR mode; I didn't want to be distracted by my current surroundings. I was in the dark, with just the virtual things (Kitty and her thread), no longer seeing the real world, when I asked, "What did it sound like?"

"Like...angry, heavy breathing. And like footsteps clomping through the darkness. Like some big, scary, pissed off dude was looking for me." She whimpered quietly. "Holy shit. Katja, I don't know how to defend myself in a computer. But *you* do. I know you know this shit."

I did, in fact, know this shit. At least the human version of it. And I now thought I could see Kitty's thread become sturdy. I took all my video game experience (time to prove that that hadn't been time wasted!) and said, "I think I can follow you back in. Um...Can you take my hand?" I held out my VR-gloved hand.

And *I felt Kitty take it.* Hesitantly, because she wasn't sure this would work either. We both made little sounds of surprise and pleasure, exchanged a look of the same sort, when we felt each other. And it looked like that success had calmed Kitty a little. Fuck yeah, haptics!

Cursing the fact that I hadn't hunted down gear that would let me have more control and haptic capabilities, I said, "Ada, display a note. Content of note: Buy full haptic and control gear stat. End content."

Kitty asked, "Ready?"

"Aye. Let's do this."

And then it was like she let the thread reel her back in, pulling me along by the hand. I had just enough time to wonder if I'd experience it as going through the ceiling and the sky of the VR world. And then we were in darkness. Not complete darkness, but maybe more like a very dimly lit place once my eyes had a moment.

As soon as we had landed, Kitty let go of my hand. And I sort of popped back into the VR start space. Damn.

She quickly came to grab me again.

"Sorry. I guess you're stuck holding my hand for now," I sighed as we travelled. Dammit. I felt the same frustration that people handcuffed together in movies must feel. Out of curiosity, I asked, "What do I look like to you?" I felt a weird hint of vertigo when I tried to look at myself once we were done moving and back in the dark place.

"Well, now that we're here, you look like you're ready for a night out dancing."

I didn't hate that it wasn't just Kitty who got to look good in here. "Cool. We'll have to find a mirror," I joked.

And then it was like a mirror, one that looked just like the one in Kitty's meat space apartment, wavered into existence. And I could see for myself. Interesting.

"Kitty, did you make the mirror appear?" I was trying to figure out if I was somehow already impacting the computer—because that's where I had to assume I was—or if this was her doing.

"Yeah, I think it's me." She gestured to the dim contents of the space around us. "I miss being home, and this stuff keeps showing up depending on what I miss or want most."

It did look like some abstract community theater replica of her living room.

"But, look, that's not what matters," she tugged my hand to get my attention back on her. "You have to help me not get killed. Again."

I nodded, but I didn't know if she could see that. I thought so, since that would have moved my goggles, so should have been picked up by my gear...if my gear was at all important in this. "I will. I'm just trying to figure out the rules or how to work in this system." I looked around. "What's outside your home here?"

"I'll show you." She pulled me along towards the shadowy area where her door would be, and then out into someplace Seattle-ish. "I think I'm only kind of in control, because the *shapes* are right, but the facades of the buildings..."

The buildings, as if created by some movie effects person who wanted to give the audience something cool to look at during a hacking scene, were created of bright blue light. Light that appeared to be seriously densely packed with Peaceforger characters.

I was about to see if I could make something appear, when I heard a noise. The noise Kitty had heard. The mental image I got was that there was a raging minotaur loose in this digital labyrinth with us. Shit.

Without warning me, Kitty started running away from the source of the sound. I weighed nothing here—or she was very strong—because I floated along behind her. When I pictured getting my feet on the ground, I just managed to shift my angle of view a little; I didn't feel the ground. I was pretty sure that I was just some data piggybacked on Kitty. Which was going to make me much less useful than she hoped.

"We should try to see what it is," I said.

Panting, as if she was still someone who breathed, she asked, "How?"

I chewed the inside of my cheek as I thought, glad I wasn't actually running. "I think...There's no way the inside of the Peaceforger computer normally looks like Seattle. So *you* had to have made it look that way, at least to us. And we know you can make things appear..."

"If only I could make things disappear," she huffed. Then, "I don't mean you."

Did she feel when I squeezed her hand? "No worries," I said, just in case. "Plus, I have an idea, so maybe you'll even be glad I haven't been disappeared." (Did my tone come through? Did she hear that I was joking?) I pointed at a wall. "Let's pause here and I'll explain."

The noise had remained at the same volume; we weren't really outrunning her attacker.

"You sure?" she asked, not slowing.

"Hm. Okay, no, you run, and I'll tell you what you're going to do when we stop, okay?"

She let out a breathy little laugh. "I like that plan better. Delay the dying."

We were moving fast, no laws of physics here. I'd have to remember to get her to try flying. But, for now... "When we stop, you're going to do two things at once. Or you're going to believe that some things exist here that exist out in meat space."

Once I finished detailing what I wanted and convinced her she could do what I asked, she said, "Be quick," and then pulled us over to stop at a wall.

In my hand, I had something suddenly that looked like my mobile. And Kitty was very intently thinking about how the streets of Seattle had an army of cameras, and my mobile had a program to see through those cameras. Basically, I was (I hoped) having her get the system to report on itself and display the results in a way I could see.

As she focused on the cameras seeing the source of the noise, the mobile's screen changed. It had been black, but was now a blurry image.

"I know some of these buildings have hi-res cameras," I encouraged her.

She closed her eyes and screwed up her face and told the system to show her the thing. And then it did.

Maybe Kitty was making shit up, and that shit was displaying on my imagined mobile. Or maybe an enraged Quinn *was* storming through the streets towards us.

I felt a moment of joyous relief. It was Quinn! I could handle this. And we could build him his own supercomputer.

(My joy paused a moment to take in the unhappy irony that our one friend who totally avoided computers and thought they would steal our souls had ended up just that, a stolen soul in a computer. Damn.)

"It's Quinn," I reported.

"What's Quinn?" It was Riley's voice and the sound of the bathroom door opening and closing.

Unaware of Riley and zir question ('cause, in all the messing with settings, I'd managed to switch from using my phone as the Kitty receiver and mic to using the VR gear), Kitty asked, "You mean that lovely guy who let me hide at his place?"

Trying to answer both questions at once, I said, "Yeah, Quinn let us hide at his place. He got taken during an, uh, information retrieval mission. I guess you could call it that. We were ambushed by Peaceforgers when we left, and he ran right at them. We heard the Peaceforgers doing a lot of shooting and...So, we thought he was dead. Especially when they didn't try to use him to smoke us out like they did with poor 'Randa."

"Poor 'Randa," Kitty's voice was full of sadness for her lost friend.

Riley's voice, however, was full of impatience. "What the hell is going on with Quinn, Kot?"

"Riley's here," I told Kitty. "Riles, Kitty is being chased by what looks like a super pissed and murder-y Quinn. I'm guessing he was alive enough to download, like they did with Kitty."

"We saw they were working on people after me. We being Riley and me. When we were searching for info," Kitty said. "Maybe Quinn was one."

Not knowing what Kitty was saying, Riles said, "He must be part of their further experiments. We managed to do a search that told us there were more, but not who or what they were doing."

I laughed a little. "You guys are in stereo here. Right. Riles, I don't think I can influence things here. Not with this setup. But we should at least order more VR gear so that I can try new things, maybe not have to hold Kitty's hand to stay."

"You're holding Kitty's hand?" Zie sounded hungry.

"Yeah, poppet. I am. I don't know if we should switch..."

Reluctantly, zie said, "I want to say we should, but I don't want to somehow have a negative effect by doing that. What can I do?"

Kitty was tugging my hand. "What's zie saying? Does zie have ideas?"

"One sec, Kitty. Right. Riles, get a monitor hooked up so you can see and hear what I do in my goggles. And think whether there was any more info you noticed about their further experiments. Cos this looks like Quinn, but like angry Quinn, like he's hunting down someone who fucked up his people." I suggested, "Maybe he just needs to see us so he knows he's not hunting an enemy?"

"Hell no!" Their synchronized answer told me I'd have to come up with another idea. And quickly. The sound of him was getting louder, and Kitty was getting understandably antsy.

"Can we go back to running? *Please*," Kitty begged.

"Yeah. Okay." And I was flying behind her again, trying to come up with a solution as she ran.

Kitty ran on and on, and Riles and I tried to come up with a solution. Something that didn't involve putting Kitty anywhere near Quinn.

"If she's in the code, she should be able to query the other code, right?" asked Riley.

"I think so. Though it's more like they're...like when we insert some of our outside code in. It can influence the system it moves through—"

"No, but think about when we're in a system and some asshole tries to use their own code to come at us. Like we're all in the same streets. We can influence each other. We can use the things we see and sometimes things we can get from having system diagnostics tools look at the other person's code. So, can't Kitty have the ship's computer run a diagnostic on him?"

I nodded, knowing Riley *would* see that, what with meat space working that way, even when the digital didn't. I just had to think of a metaphor that would work for Kitty.

And then the wee lightbulb in my brain lit up "Got it!" I grinned. "Kitty, can you get us to City Hall, to the wing where the mayor has her office?"

"I can try. I can usually get into the buildings." She turned left, easily mapping meat space Seattle onto the glowing stacks we ran through.

"Kitty, I want you to start believing what I'm saying as we go, because I think you're just enough in charge of your experience that you can make things that you maybe didn't see with your own eyes in meat space, okay?"

She nodded and took a right.

"You remember when there were multiple attempts by that 'white separatist' group to off the mayor?"

Kitty snorted. "Fucking Nazis. Yeah, I think I remember that."

"They tried all that weird shit to get at her, which finally resulted in the city hall getting body scanners that were practically deep medical scanners. Remember?" I was hazy on details, because I hadn't had to pay much attention. I had never thought I'd be going to the mayor's office. Not bodily at least.

"Oh, I see where you're headed. Nice, Kot," Riles whispered.

Fortunately, Kitty knew what I meant. "Wasn't there the one dude who had an insulin pump that was actually rigged to help them set off some explosive compound they'd had inserted subcutaneously?"

"Totally! Yes. That group." Now, I needed to tell this like truth to make it easier for Kitty to believe enough to make it real where we were. "Okay, if we can get Quinn to run through those scanners, my mobile can hack their system and give us a lot of info about him. I'm hacking them right now with my spare hand." I tapped around with my digital hand on the screen of the mobile Kitty had imagined up for me earlier, which I knew I couldn't actually affect, just in case she looked back. "When Quinn runs through, the scanners are going to be able to show me everything he's made of. Every line of code."

"Makes sense," she said. And the screen on my mobile now looked like dancing characters, probably what she thought hacking looked like.

"To get him to go through, we'll probably have to go through. Fortunately, because of all the dangers, the mayor also has a back exit, so we won't have to go out the way Quinn's coming in." I was positive that was true, but I didn't know it. So now I had to make up what that was like, get Kitty imagining it. "When we go in the door, do you know the way to the mayor's office?"

"I do, actually. I helped deliver a petition to her once. We go in the front door, up the wide stairs, and to the left. The scanners are at the end of a short kind of corridor. It's...I think the end of the corridor with scanners is about 3 normal doorways wide. Then is the reception area. If you go off to the left of *that*, the mayor's office is three doors down a normal-width corridor."

"Great. Good memory!" I praised her. I hoped confidence would help her. Plus, now I wouldn't accidentally suggest an exit that couldn't be there. "Did you go past her office?"

"Nope. Just to it and back out. But I know there's an exit door at the end of that corridor. There's a sign." She had no reason to think I was bullshitting any of this.

"That's the door. We'll head for that. Once we're through, there are stairs you can take up or down. If you go down, it's just one flight to a door to the streets. If you go farther, it takes us to the garage. Got it?" I kind of wanted to suggest we imagine up some fast cars, but I didn't guess those would matter when Kitty was already running car-fast.

"Yep. Almost there. Do we have to wait for Quinn to go through before we can exit?"

Oh. A good, meat space kind of question. "Nope. Because my mobile is connecting wirelessly and my data plan is with a super reliable carrier, I can pick up the info from the diagnostic scanners even if we've run far away. Though stopping somewhere to read the results would be helpful."

"Feh," she spat out, unhappy about anything that stopped her flight.

Riles said, "Kot, keep your virtual mobile to your face so I get best possible view on the monitor. I'm recording so I can go through and analyze."

I had another thought. "Hey, Kitty, for a baseline, the monitors are also going to send me a scan on you when we go through, okay?"

"Okay."

We sped up the wide steps inside City Hall. Inside the buildings was just like outside. Any detail that Kitty remembered was merely outlined in glowing characters. Even the way the front doors swung as she opened them was traced by lights. Everything she wasn't picturing was vague shapes, built of or covered in glowing Peaceforger script.

"You guys are going to have to let Quinn get closer." Riley sounded as unhappy to note this as I felt to hear it.

"You know what? Why don't you lean close enough to the headset for the mic to pick you up, Riles? I'm sure Kitty would love to hear your voice. And I'm not telling her that." I'd been trying to keep the illusion of the real worldness of things somewhat intact, but I wasn't going to be the one who brought this news in.

"Not telling me what?" Kitty sounded preemptively unhappy.

In my ear, but also in the air around Kitty and I, Riles urgently said, "Kitty, stop running." I felt zir cheek all but touching mine as zie moved into the mic.

It was shocking enough that she did, just short of the scanners.

"Baby, I need you to walk slowly through the scanner and then stop. Kot, watch your mobile screen so you see all the results."

"I don't like this, Riles," Kitty complained, but she did as zie asked.

On my mobile, I was disappointed but not surprised to see that the diagnostic reading was delivered in Peaceforger characters. Of course. Dammit.

Once we were on the other side, Riles instructed, "I need you to walk a little ways down the corridor to your escape door. But if you run through it, out of the building, I bet Quinn doesn't bother going through this building. I bet he just goes around to the street. And I think we need the scanner info."

"You *think*?" Kitty sounded more angry than scared suddenly. "You might not need the info, but you're okay to risk my life *again* just in case you do?"

"Fair." Riles just sounded tired. "But...It's more than just that I think it. Bad word choice. I'm pretty damned sure we have to know what he is to take him out. And that means we have to get more info."

I bit my tongue about the fact that, at least for Kitty, the code hadn't been something we could use.

"Why can't we just go back to the library to search for answers like we did before?" She wasn't sold on zir reasoning, but she wasn't running. She was prowling and pacing just inside the corridor that had the door to the mayor's office and our planned escape. Or she was doing as close an approximation of that as she could whilst holding my hand.

Trying to help, because I also didn't want to have to get too close to Quinn yet, I got back to my bullshitting. "You know what happens when the scanners detect something wrong?"

Grudgingly and with a sigh, she engaged with my new attempt to tell a helpful story. "No idea. What happens?"

"Well, just in case someone has distracted or taken out the guards, there are some automated responses." I had to think quickly and make it realistic, hope it did something—anything—to Quinn. "Well, obviously, a thick plexiglass shield goes down to block the mayor's corridor. Plus one goes down on the other side of the scanners, so the person is trapped in the reception area."

"With the poor receptionist?" Kitty sounded sincerely worried about our imaginary receptionist.

"Well, it's not a delight, but a plexiglass shield also comes down around the desk. And the desk is made of blast-proof materials, so the smart receptionist just sits under their desk and has a drink of whatever they keep in their drawer."

She laughed a little. Good.

"If there aren't any other bodies, or at least ones with official ident chips, too near the one that set off the scanner, there's also one of those restraint foam systems in the walls. It encases the person from the shoulders down. Also, in case the person has infectious agents on them, the space is irradiated and some of those new aerosolized anti-virals are pumped in." Maybe we'd get lucky and the system would treat Quinn like a virus until we could save him?

"Wait, aerosolized anti-virals? That sounds like bullshit."

"I know it does. But they came out in the last couple weeks. There was a rash of stuff like that. We think it was the Peaceforgers. They've definitely had some of their people pretending to be pastors and doctors, trying to win trust. And they did some fixing up of the mayor's defenses just last week." I hoped the sound of my lies was keeping her from noticing that the sound of angry Quinn was definitely getting louder.

"Actually, I was just reading that the Peaceforgers were helping people do some improvements on stuff like that. I think Kot's right," Riles said, piling on the lies. "And since the ship is now over Seattle, they're treating the mayor like she's important. I think..." Zie trailed off like zie was looking something up. "Yeah, here's the article. They were in the mayor's office...and the rumor is that now there's Peaceforger tech, so way better than ours, installed and keeping the air clean of biological agents. Peaceforger anti-virals." Zie sounded very sure.

Almost like he'd teleported, I could suddenly hear the growl of Quinn echoing through the high-ceilinged City Hall entry. Shit. Guess we were about to learn how much Kitty had bought into our bullshit.

She whispered, "You better be right."

"Kitty, you have to believe us. Because you have to help make it so." I hated to put all the pressure on her, but...

"Are you talking shit, Riles?" she asked.

"I might stupidly not get around to telling you some things, but would I lie?" Zie easily wrapped the apology and the misdirection together.

"Okay. I believe you." And she shut her eyes tight, clearly trying to believe the hell out of us.

I kept my own fake eyes open, looking for any clues and ready to watch my pretend mobile's screen for info on Quinn.

Red-faced and savage, Quinn pounded up the stairs. He looked right, then left (where we were frozen), then right again. He wasn't following a path we'd left; he was sensing us out. So, yeah, Riles had been right; Quinn wouldn't have come through here just because we had.

He clenched and unclenched his fists, and his breathing was a growl. He stalked to the right, his head leaning and turning as he looked for signs of us there. Then he circled back and headed towards us, towards the scanners.

He saw us. And I hoped, holy shit I hoped, that he would see my face and remember I wasn't the enemy and suddenly calm down. Instead, he snarled.

"Quinn?" I ventured, kindly and not too loudly. Like I was trying to coax a scared animal.

And then he roared and raced towards the scanners. I badly needed to watch what was happening, but I really had to keep my eyes on my mobile. I had just peripheral vision to let me know he was still moving in our direction. I knew he'd hit the scanners when my mobile flashed with information.

And then it stopped. He was inside the scanners.

I looked up, praying to that deity I didn't believe in but had been pestering a lot the last 5 or so weeks, that Kitty had sufficiently bought our story. That she'd believed it enough to make it so.

I held my breath and braced for impact as he came towards us. I felt Kitty flinch, and she tried to put an arm around me.

And then a wall slammed down brutally and swiftly between us. It glowed like the rest, but I had to believe it was the equivalent of plexiglass. We could look away.

I whispered, "Run!"

Kitty fled, hitting the door to the exit with force that I felt vibrate up her free arm and down the other to shake me a little.

We had no idea what good any of Kitty's imagined building defenses had done beyond keeping Quinn from immediately following us. So, we were running again.

"I'm going to the library. You're going to help me find whatever info we need to finish this." Kitty wasn't asking our opinion of this move.

"Okay," I said. "And Riles and I will try to puzzle out what we can whilst you run. So, uh, I'll say your name when I'm talking to you before you get to the library, okay?"

"Yep." And she ran.

"Riles?" I needed zir to start and carry any part of the conversation zie didn't want Kitty to hear.

Zie leaned back, so my mic wouldn't pick up zir voice, and said, "It seems like all bad news. He doesn't seem to care that it's people he knows. Their code is, obviously, in Peaceforgerese or whatever we want to call their language. And I have no ideas." Zie sighed. "There's no way we'll have time to translate this code in time to deal with Quinn now. But...I'll get Ada analyzing this ASAP." Zie sighed again.

"What if we look at all this not as coding but from the perspective that this UI is what she makes it?" Fortunately, there was only one other "she" besides me, so I didn't accidentally say Kitty's name and pull her into the conversation prematurely.

"Maybe. But, Kot...Our options are to...let's call it debugging...Our options are to figure out how to debug Quinn. If that's possible. Which I hope we can find info on at the library..."

I interrupted, "But how would we be able to read that?"

"Oh, I think she just had no way to understand the language enough to translate what she sent to your mobile. Just like someone who speaks English can't read coding languages created by English speakers. But, remember, she's kind of uploaded a Peaceforger-to-English dictionary into herself. So, she'll be able to read words. And she'll read them out, like she did for me when we were working on searches, or maybe they'll look like English now that you can see what she sees. Sort of auto-translate what she reads before she displays where you can see it."

"Got it. And what are the other options? You said 'our *options* are,' so..."

"Unless you can think of more, we can try to cage him. But he's in a system where it's safe to assume he was released on purpose. Right?"

"Yeah, she says he showed up after she did what she could to mess up their machine."

"She messed up the machine? That's great!" Then zie tsked and asked, "Why didn't you mention that?"

"Because we were a little more worried about keeping her safe. Anyway, it's possible they became aware of her once she did that. So this is like...What's that rhyme? 'There was an old lady who swallowed a fly.' That's it."

Riles made an unhappy little grunting sound. "Right, so, Kits is the fly...And Quinn is the spider, swallowed on purpose..." Zir tone was glum. "I'm not confident we can get the system to let us actually cage him. I'd bet it didn't let Kitty's defense stuff at the mayor's hold for long."

"Right. So, debug?"

"Debug or...Fuck, Kot, debug or destroy."

"Destroy? You mean kill." My tongue suddenly felt heavy, and I couldn't imagine how I wasn't weighing down Kitty as we continued our digital run.

Rye didn't answer, but I did feel zir hand on my shoulder. And I wanted to protest, but I didn't think zie'd missed any options. Debug or destroy.

I could hear Quinn's growl again, faintly. Clearly no longer detained by imagined plexiglass or foam or anti-viruses.

In the library, the glowing and unreadable shelves of book-shaped light loomed. Kitty remembered the dimensions of the actual downtown library branch as much more expansive than I did. It felt much less solid than City Hall, like the rows went into infinity. Like the ceiling was higher and the shelves were taller.

"Kitty, did you not come here often?" I asked.

She laughed, and I swear the sound was nearly visible as it floated up to the grid of windows that formed the distant ceiling. "I came here all the time. Even when I was a kid. First place I ran away to." She smiled at me. "It just looks more like what it's always felt like to me. Like it was a space of endless promise and possibility."

"In case the sensors in the goggles aren't adequately mapping my face, I am smiling with delight," I told her, "because amen to that."

She grinned and headed towards the reference desk. There were two stools there, at just the right height that we didn't need to let go of each other's hands to get ourselves onto them. She turned on the desktop display, and it lit with details that told me she really had looked at its meat space counterpart regularly.

She held up our hands and noted, "I should have grabbed you with my left hand. I'm much better doing one-handed typing with my right."

Riley was giggling dirtily.

"Riles laughing at that?" She grinned, knowing the answer before I confirmed that zie was.

After a few taps, she had the screen ready for a search. "So, now I have to focus really carefully. This damned thing doesn't really care what I type and seems to pick up on any of my thoughts."

As if eager to confirm, it pulled up the file the Peaceforgers had on Riley. I heard zir make an "aw" sound as zie saw that on zir own monitor.

Kitty just gestured towards it, shaking her head. "And I can't tell what it will grab onto."

We both paused as it flickered, now displaying information on 1990s alternative fashions.

Kitty sighed. "Just...bear with me. And let me know when something you want to see hits the screen." She closed her eyes, thinking.

After a few more topics, I saw something I needed. "Hang on a sec." I tried to move my head in a way that would put all the parts in focus in the right order.

I knew it had worked when Riles said, "Well, fuck."

Kitty said, "I was thinking what you said about how they've used churches or something. Or that was one of the fleeting thoughts I was trying to push away." She looked at me. "You guys didn't know this already?"

The screen had a list of possible infiltration points for Divine Community to use for spreading the Peacemaker vII. "We knew about them being behind the beat down flu. And that they were using their status to gain trust that would let them do all this other stuff that it says they haven't yet. But..." I pointed at the one other item marked as being in progress. "We didn't know that they'd had vIIs in every inoculation they gave the last few years. That's...a shitload of vIIs out there. And in communities where people probably won't have the resources to take them out."

"Adding that shit to our to-do list," Riles reported.

"Okay, ready to move on," I told Kitty.

It only took a few more tries, and Kitty had info up on Quinn. We skimmed through it, and I read bits aloud to make sure Riles caught them.

As we'd suspected, they'd not killed him entirely that night at the plant. But they had done so once they'd uploaded him. Bastards. It looked like his designation was Attempt #10. Once they had him digitized and in a carefully constructed sort of digital holding pen, and "having learned our lesson when the data constituting the subject of Attempt #3 disappeared," they went to work.

"So, I got lucky escaping?" Kitty asked.

"Looks that way." I went back to skimming and reading particularly interesting bits aloud.

It sounded like their particular goal had been to see if they could maintain the "entity's" sense of self and data but change its manifestation. "If we can get a face we know MindKiller and their friends trust, one that retains enough basic personality and memories, we can draw them out. Maybe even have an advantage in a digital fight where they think they're facing a friend."

Riles was leaned in close for my mic again. "They fucked him up on purpose, to get us." Zie sounded sad. "His situation is entirely our fault." Ah, not sad. Guilty.

And I felt that same guilt. We'd dragged him into this whole mess. And, not only had the computer stolen his soul, it had also corrupted it.

We looked for details on how they'd done this to him. Unfortunately, since we didn't know how to rewrite the data they'd taken out to unleash his rage completely...It was looking more like debugging wasn't an option.

The last note was super recent. As I read it out, I felt my despair growing. "We've wondered if, instead of failing to cohere, Attempt #3 escaped into the system. In the event that the critical data destruction and corruption of the control machine just now was due to Attempt #3 taking actions, we're sending Attempt #10 in to hunt down potential saboteurs."

"And there's that confirmed," Kitty sighed. "I made this happen."

"Yeah, but you also did damage to the control machine. You slowed them down. Nice work!" I meant it. I could see we were going to need all the time we could get.

The screen flickered again.

"Sorry," Kitty cringed. "I didn't mean to."

"Don't change it!" I held my breath, hoping I could scan the display before she had another strong thought. "Riles, you see this?"

"Oh, shit. Confirmation that there are multiple control machines." Zie counted under zir breath, then reported, "A dozen. They aren't going to need satellites." Zie sounded like zie could cry.

Trying to pretend I was calm, I said, "Well, now we know they exist and know where they are. We'll just...make taking care of them the first step in Plan B. And get our remote comrades to help."

"Putting that on the list. Once we finish the Quinn thing, we have work to do." I could hear zir stealing zirself and felt zir move away from me so the mic didn't pick zir up anymore. "Kot, we have to talk about how to destroy him."

Now I was the one who could cry. I didn't know if I could do this. "We need to tell her."

Riles agreed at the same time Kitty demanded, "Tell me what?"

"That out there is Quinn. But he's been damaged in ways we don't believe we can fix. It is...We've found a computer thing we *can't* do. Not soon, at least. So, unless we can figure out how to help you rewrite him, and unless you're up for running for...maybe days whilst we do that figuring, we have to help you figure out how to...destroy him." I choked on the words. Ugh. I hated myself.

"You mean kill him?" Kitty sounded weary.

"Unfortunately. Fuck." I couldn't sulk. I had work to do. But I was really mad at the Universe right then. I thought about mentioning that the Peaceforgers had already technically killed him, but then what would that say about Kitty's state?

"How? I mean, how do I do anything to him?" She was listening, but her shoulders had a defeated set to them.

"I have a really stupid, risky idea," Riley's voice floated on the air in the library again, and zir cheek was brushing mine to get zir mouth back by the mic.

"Which means we have precisely one idea between us," I said. "So, you might as well suggest it."

We worked with Kitty to practice pieces of the plan, and then Kitty and I found the right intersection at which to be overtaken. And, once we stopped moving long enough, Quinn was quick to find us.

As he appeared on the horizon, Kitty said, "Promise you'll get me out of here."

"I promise that doing that is literally my top task right now. Has been for a while." I squeezed her hand fiercely. "I'll do anything short of letting the Earth get its arse kicked to make this happen."

She nodded, satisfied. And we waited as Quinn barreled down on us. Fortunately, he was still enough himself that, when we didn't run, he slowed down. Wary. Not just senselessly violent.

Finally, he stopped. He was still clearly intent on our destruction, but, if there was enough of him left, he must know that me not running from a fight meant I had a plan.

He took a step forward, looking around as if we might have snipers on the roofs somehow.

He took another step forward, head swiveling to see if we'd managed to get trucks to hurtle down the cross street at him.

He took the next step forward, and fixed his eyes on me. And took another step, searching my face for a clue to what I was up to.

One more step, and, moving my mouth as little as possible, I quietly said, "Now."

He was in the middle of an intersection where tracks for the electric trains crossed. Standing in the middle of the square of electrical wires that crossed the streets on poles at each corner.

In that moment, Kitty believed there was a sharp earthquake that downed the power lines, exposing live wires and triggering the electricity of the tracks somehow. (Fortunately, it only had to be possible in her imagination.) Any Peaceforger who saw this, from their perspective outside the computer, should be seeing a massive power spike.

We were seeing Quinn held in place by the electricity that surged through him.

And then we got to the extra-stupid part of our plan, because now Kitty believed that my arms were incredibly long, letting me get a hand near Quinn without losing contact with her and without making contact with him. We were stupid, but not "see if we can electrocute Katja" stupid.

And Kitty believed that I had on one of the Peaceforger glove-like healing tools, like the one we'd gotten from Isa. And she believed that the glove was now sending healing energy through to repair Quinn.

Any Peaceforger who saw this should see that some healing and repair programs had been deployed to the spot with the massive power spike. At least that was what we were trying to do. And we hoped, if they saw this, they'd read it as the computer trying to heal whatever was causing the power spike issue.

We hoped...

Quinn looked at me, his face suddenly pained instead of homicidal. He croaked, "Katja?"

I nodded. "They turned you into data and corrupted your code, but we're repairing it."

He shook his head. "I don't want to be in a computer." I saw his face fill with every belief from his childhood. He gritted his teeth against pain and emotion.

"We think we can get you out. You'll still be you," I assured him. "Just maybe in an artificial body." I wasn't sure how he felt about robots, so I didn't want to use that word.

"Or they corrupt me again and turn me against you." He let out a small sound, a wisp of a tortured wail that could have been ignited by the electricity or the fear. "Flesh is weak, but would never betray you. Not that way. But code..."

I knew what he was about to ask, and I was shaking my head before he asked.

"Finish this. Kill me. Save me from this hell." He sobbed, then choked out something like a laugh. "My fucking parents were right. If I make it to Heaven, my mom's going to be so smug." Then he was weeping, quietly, his pleading eyes fixed on me. I could see he was trying to lean away from my gloved hand.

Rye's voice came from the sky, edged with tears. "Please, Quinn. Please."

Through teeth still gritted, but now chattering as the electricity kept him jerking, he said, "Love me enough to let me go." Then, pitifully, "Please."

I nodded. My throat was almost too thick with grief to reply. I whispered, "Okay."

He looked immediately relieved. Somehow, in spite of the incredible pain, relieved.

I could hear Riles crying next to me, but fortunately moved just enough back from the mic that zir voice wasn't in this dark-skied world anymore. I cleared my throat as I pulled my arm in. "Kitty, pull me back. Keep up the electricity." I looked at Quinn. "Are you *sure*?"

He nodded. I could see that, whilst the healing that gave him back the constraints on his anger seemed to be holding, the repair it had done to the power surge damage was now being overwhelmed. He was in agony, but not changing his request.

"Love you, big guy," I managed, trying not to become useless with tears.

He tried a smile, but it turned into a grimace. The grimace turned into a wail, and his body now jerked like a puppet with someone different on every string. And then the jerking was a lightning-fast vibration, until he seemed to disintegrate in front of our eyes.

"You can stop the electricity now, Kitty," I said with a voice that sounded gentle to my ears. But I knew it wasn't gentleness; it was the exhaustion of one more loss.

We'd lost Quinn twice now. I was more determined than ever that we not have to say the same of Kitty.

Once I was sure she was safe, I let go of her hand, let myself be snapped back to the loo where my body had been the whole time. And then let Riles have a moment with the gear. I figured it was zir turn to hold Kitty's hand for a while.

After a few minutes, zie said, "I love you, baby, but we've got to save the world. And save you from this computer."

We were still red-eyed when we walked out to tell the boys what had happened.

CHAPTER 18

Even though we were beat, Riles and I both had things we wanted to finish before we called it a day. Zie needed to work on reprogramming the drones. I needed to organize pulling our remote people in. Plus, I hadn't even gotten to building my supercomputer, though I suspected I'd have happier results if I didn't do that whilst feeling quite so wrecked. Especially since it wasn't just an average computer build with standard parts.

Once the boys were updated and we'd at least put the supercomputer pieces out of the way (lest anyone trip on and/or damage them in the night), we dimmed the lights. I took a break to chat quietly with my Jonny and with Bryan who was stuck beside us. As hoped, it kept them off the computers long enough that their wounded bodies were able to pull them down into sleep.

I crept away to sit at the table with Riles and work. We paused a moment to lean against each other.

"I know this will be shocking coming from me," zie said, "but I've had enough drama for the rest of my fucking life. I will stay in every night forever if that's what it takes. Just...no more of this shit, you know?"

I snorted softly, something like a laugh. "I just might know, poppet. I just might..." Then I sighed, sat up, and said, "Though there will be few nights left for staying in if we don't stop the bastards from blowing up the planet."

"Yeah...Okay, back to my drones then." Zie shook zir head. "Not the kind of thing I had in mind for my nights of staying in." Zie laughed a little, sounding ragged, and turned back to zir screen.

I started drafting the message for our remote comrades, but I didn't get far before I got messages from both Zane and Isa. Neither of which answered the question I'd sent them earlier (had Peaceforgers killed VR?), but maybe the future needed a little more attention than the past at the moment.

Zane's was the least informative:

Something's up. No idea what. But don't get wet or drink tap water.

Isa's didn't explain much more, but did feel more useful:

We were told to avoid Earth's water. Don't go in the water, drink water that isn't already bottled, go in the rain, etc. They didn't tell us why, of course, but I'd guess this is something to do with the "mapping" shuttles all day today. Wish I had more info. Stay safe!

I showed Riley, who appropriately replied, "Are you fucking kidding me?"

"Not that we're surprised, right? We knew those shuttles were bullshit," I pointed out.

"Oh, girl, but we've all had tap water and showers today." Zie looked pale with worry. "Since the shuttles started."

My eyes went big. Oh shit. I took a deep, careful breath, trying to make good choices and not let fear rule me given fear is the mind-killer... "Right. Right. Okay. Um." I pulled my computer over. "We have to make orders *now*. Bottled water, wet wipes instead of showers, extra food in case this drags on...uh..."

"Dry shampoo. Face wipes and micellar water, that sort of thing, because I'm not going to die with a shitty face. And you want a *lot* of water, because we'll have to use it for food too. Unless we lean into stuff that doesn't take water...We can't order out because they'll be using tap water." Zie chewed a nail, thinking. "I know it's not very Seattle of me, but umbrellas. And waterproof gloves, coats, etc. Just in case we can't avoid going out."

"Getting disposable eating stuff too. We can't just wash dishes." I nodded decisively and got orders sent off, trying to figure out how to not look suspicious with even more running around to grab packages, most of them much bigger than the previous ones. And definitely all delivered to the building so nobody had to duck out for them.

"Dammit." Zie sulked dramatically. "Aliens ruin everything." Zie laughed at zirself and sat up, leaning towards me. Serious. "What do you think it is? I mean, what symptoms or whatever do you think we should look for?"

"Biological?" I suggested. "Using a stronger form of beat down flu to either drive everyone to healing centers, where they can get Peacemakered, or to kill us."

"Or maybe nanites?" Riles supposed. "I mean, since that's been their other angle, using those tiny bitches to sneak the vII into everything." Zie pondered a little. "They could just be flat out poisoning the water. Something that will kill us and leave everything else alone."

I chewed the inside of my cheek. "Any of that's possible with them. Any could make it easier for them to give us shots— though they wouldn't need it with nanites—or just kill us." I put my head on my arms, down on the table. "I want to go back to stressing about the security protocols in bank software and how to help you disgrace bigoted politicians."

Riles put a kind hand on my back, but kept exploring the issue. "We can bet that it will be something engineered to be undetectable by our equipment."

I turned my head, still rested on my arms but looking at zir. "Or engineered to work so fast that they aren't worried about someone finding it." I sat up. "We need to set up some news alerts so we have some warning when whatever it is starts."

"And make some ambiguous warnings to people online. I think I'm just going to do the sanest sounding version of a 'contrails are them poisoning us' post that I can," Riley turned to zir keyboard.

"Keep it ambiguous enough that it's not obvious, maybe even when you're messaging our remote comrades, that we have an inside source," I said. "I don't want to accidentally fuck Isa or Zane and lose our supply of info and tech."

So we paused in our discussion. Whilst Riles messaged folks, I set up alerts to go off for all the possible things we could think of that might show up on the news, depending on what was actually happening, when the effects of the "mapping" shuttles were felt.

With a little time spent at that oddly unstructured task, my brain woke up a bit. "Hey, we know they diverted their efforts to production of some kind. Zane thinks it's production of Peacemakers. If they aren't killing us, they're Peacemakering us, right?"

Riley nodded.

"Well," I went on, "that's a whole fucking lot of Peacemakers. Especially if your nanite theory is right. Even if not. Even if they just get that Peacemaker shit into anyone who isn't taken out by what's in the water. And that's in addition to the ones already out there. They're going for saturation, unless they're just trying to kill us. And, if they aren't trying to kill us, they must have high confidence in bugging us all."

"Buggering us all is more like it."

I snorted a laugh. "That too. So, what I'm driving at is that we're about to have so many Peacemakers in people that it's going to take years to get them all out. And that's assuming that everyone can find a doctor and the money to have it done. And who knows what damage would be done in that time?"

"Ah. Yeah, I see what you're driving at." Zie was squinting at the wall, thoughtful. "We have to find another way to get rid of the Peacemakers."

"Or at least to deactivate them until people can get them out. Plus, at least for certain bullshit countries without socialized medicine," I paused so we could both cough and mumble, "'Merica," before I went on, "we'll need to make sure we're easily set up to fund doctors and hospitals so that *everybody* can get their bug out."

Zie typed something quickly, then turned zir attention back to me. "We have to get them out of people and destroyed before any motherfucking human can reverse engineer and fuck us all over."

Zir computer pinged, and zie looked pleased at what zie read. "Engie says that it's possible, and she'll look into it, that we could use the same principles for deactivating—like we can program the frequency detectors to do—to send a slightly more substantial signal that might take out the nanites that make the vIIs. You know, at least the version that builds out from the nanites hidden in a vI. She says we only need to take out a few nanites in each to make the whole thing unusable."

"We have to get that woman so much tech and translations of specs. Really."

Zie agreed. "She deserves to drown in all the tasty tech."

It took maybe 30 minutes before I felt like our approach was arguably leaving our people in danger. So I wrote a more direct, but still hopefully careful enough, follow-up letter to our remote comrades, and sent an appropriately modified version to our other little group of trusted allies. I warned them that something had been seeded in the waters all over the planet by the shuttles. I told them that even inoculations from Divine Community were tainted, so we already had way more people with Peacemakers than we'd thought. And I asked the remote comrades to consider how to destroy control machines they could get at. Much as I hated to, I added:

At this point, given how likely it is everything needs to happen at once and that we could fuck things up by accidentally tripping on each other's plans, I need to ask you to do more than just wait for a signal to make shit blow up. I need to ask you to let me know enough about your plans that I can make sure you're not going to get in each other's way. I'll keep you all separate and won't tell anyone why, but I'll ask people to change or remove parts of their plans that I see conflict with someone else's if it seems more strategically on point. (Apologies in advance if you get asked to change. You've each been amazing up to now, but you've *all* been amazing. So at least your idea is being edged out by that of someone who is definitely your peer.)

Guiltily, I totally intended to let Bryan review strategies. After just these couple days back with us, though he wasn't going to be running marathons any time soon, his brain was in good shape and was hungry for work. Plus, the boys hadn't sucked as much at taking the naps they'd promised they would as I had thought they might.

After I sent the letter, I asked Riles, "So, at what point do we tell the lads our plan?"

"If they haven't already guessed?"

I shrugged, acknowledging that they might easily have guessed it all. Or most of it. The plan was simple. But I said, "I don't think they know you're going to coach Kitty to try to reprogram the ship's computer. Which, hey, Plan A is back on!"

Zie grinned. "Yeah. If I can finish drones tonight, I can get back to working with Kitty. And the VR stuff is going to make it so much easier." Zir eyes lit. "Oh, or maybe that holo-rig and display we got will make it even better…"

Ignoring the fun of Kitty in full-sized holo, I stayed with the main thread. "But we might also need to make sure they understand that, once we have Kitty off the ship, if she doesn't feel confident about her computer tweaks there…we're planning to blow it." I found myself feeling suddenly conflicted about that. Maybe it was the long day or that we had the boys back and my fury was tempered by that lovely change of circumstances. I added, "Though, seriously, I do strongly prefer Plan A."

"You two know this room is small, right?"

Riles and I swiveled our heads to find Bryan looking at us.

I winced. "Sorry. We'll be quieter."

"No, you won't. You'll come over here and tell me about Plan A and Plan B. Even if we aren't the architects or even allowed a real part in them, Jonny and I are part of this team. That means the actions of the team belong to us too." He was dead serious.

"Yeah, come fill in your battered boys," Jonny added from the shadows.

So we moved our discussion over. I sat carefully next to Jonny, and Riles settled on the edge of Bryan's side of the bed.

And, probably not wanting to be the one to bring up the "kill all Peaceforgers" part, Riles said, "I'll let Kot tell you the plan, but you should know that the Peaceforgers warned their people to avoid water—rain, tap water, etc.—so we're ordering in supplies to make sure we don't have to go out and don't have to turn on any taps. Because their shuttles were, like we all knew, up to no good."

Bryan nodded solemnly. "Got it. And at least we're living in a hotel while that's happening. Imagine how much worse if we'd had to go off tap water and stay indoors in some of the other hideouts we've had."

I couldn't argue with that. So, I didn't. "Right. As far as the plans go, Plan A and Plan B have two phases each. We already finished the first one, which is the same for both, where we get you guys back and figure out what the deal is with Kitty, whether she has a body or not." I paused, like I was waiting for feedback instead of stalling before getting to the killing part. "So, Plan A, which we *strongly* prefer, is that we work with Kitty to program the ship's computer. You know, first it sends a 'come to the ship' message to everyone, then it flies them all away and never comes back. And we download Kitty before the ship leaves."

I paused again. Bryan just nodded. Same with Jonny. It was really a very "us" plan. Hack a computer, fix the problem, return to life as usual. Yep. It was a plan geared at nobody getting hurt.

"And Plan B, which, again, is totally not the one we want but we...Look, we have to get the Peaceforgers off our planet. They're an invading force intent on killing or brainwashing us all. They're not going to be talked down." I didn't want to say it even so.

"Plan B is the drones," Bryan said. It wasn't a question. He knew we didn't have troops or even very good shooting skills of our own.

Riles and I exchanged a sad look, then nodded.

"Fuck." Jonny sounded weary. "I just want to be done being responsible for deaths. Even when it's people like the Peaceforgers, I just..." He trailed off into a sigh.

I squeezed his hand. "I'm totally with you. I am. But...I don't know what else to do with our resources."

"What about the satellites?" Bryan asked. "I know you said there were troubles before connecting to the satellites. Are we going to be able to totally control them during the drone attack? If we end up with Plan B, that is."

Riles shrugged. "I'd say we'll be able to, but the Peaceforgers could take them over again even if we think we've got them."

"Not that they really need them," I pointed out. "Kitty has, for now, put the machine on the ship out of commission. But their new control machines are spread out in a way that they shouldn't need satellites."

"Mm. Right. I'm more concerned about someone getting at the drones," Bryan said.

"Oh. Duh." I rolled my eyes at myself. "I feel like Rye and I shared that concern sometime in the millennia since this all started."

"And are the drones programmed for specific Peaceforgers or just for any Peaceforger not in a disguise?" Bry directed the question at Riley.

"Both. The specific ones are for Peaceforgers we know are in disguise or we consider highest pri, like Morgan." Zie hesitated, then said, "Though, if there's a way to exclude targets, I'd love to not accidentally shoot any of Isa's group."

"There should be. I can look into that tomorrow. Unless that's the day you plan to take action?" Bryan sounded like he really hoped that wasn't the case.

I shook my head. "Not tomorrow. Have to get Kitty's computer built tomorrow. But, uh, speaking of sparing particular Peaceforgers...Where are you with Zane? Not that we'd let the drones target them, of course. Just, you know, being nosy."

What I really meant was something more like, "Hey, are you still in love with them or am I allowed to keep being mad at them no matter what...and maybe accidentally let them get a little hurt when shit goes down?" But I'm far too sensitive and polite to ask that, obviously.

Bry considered the far wall for a moment before replying. "I'm not really sure. During our very slow escape from the ship, they told us why they tagged me and went along with their sister. And I get it. Plus, they put themselves at risk getting us off the ship, and they're now...they're stuck on Earth. And stuck in hiding until we solve things. So, I don't hate them. But...I'm a little tired and fucked up and...I miss the simplicity of 'Randa and of not fighting aliens, you know?"

We nodded. We knew.

He yawned and stretched as much as his wounds would allow. "Maybe don't kill them. And I'll see where I am After."

Ah, yes, the mythical After. A time we'd discussed, anticipated, and failed to get to for over a month now. I nodded my understanding.

"Okay, go away, you less-injured people. I need my beauty sleep." Bryan grinned and winked. He leaned back into his pillows and said, "I'm proud of you two. You're alright." And then he closed his eyes.

I kissed Jonny goodnight and quietly high-fived Rye (to celebrate that we'd been deemed "alright") as we headed over to finish our night so we could get to our own beauty sleep.

Due to a number of accidental, brains-on-autopilot close calls just in the little while between our high-fiving and bed, our last actual task of the day was to put big warning signs on every faucet. Silly with sleepiness, we used a marker to turn some toilet paper into warning tape and cordoned off the tub like it was a crime scene. Nobody needed to autopilot themselves to death or brain bugs.

CHAPTER 19

Tuesday was off to a bleary and grumpy start until we'd crept all over the hotel and picked up deliveries. It was amazing what clean faces and fresh coffee could do for even a badass world-saver's attitude. No wonder the bastards had gone for our water.

Once we felt human, we all got to work on our stuff. Riley was working with Kitty to try to program the ship's computer. They quickly found that the holo gear wasn't immersive enough, not as immersive as the VR. Cool as it had sounded to do the work in holo, we'd just have to save that gear for later. For vidgames or letting Kitty appear full-sized to us all after she was in the soon-to-be supercomputer.

I was putting together said supercomputer in a corner of the suite. One more benefit of not doing it in the adjacent suite was that, until we knew we were okay in spite of the rain and/or tap water we'd encountered the previous day, we could keep an eye on each other. Watch for...well, we didn't know what. But we were all clever; surely we'd know it if and when we saw it, right?

As for our supposedly resting boys...Bryan was analyzing the remote comrades' plans and writing up replies. Jonny was poking at the satellites.

Not a bad way to spend a day.

Of course, then Morgan and their other Peaceforger pals had to fuck it all up.

Suddenly, all of the broadcast channels we had open were Morgan, just like the day they'd pretended to arrive exactly a week earlier. In fact, the visual was just like that day from what we could tell. Except that Morgan looked disappointed this time, as did the row of Peaceforgers behind them.

"Hello, our dear friends of Earth. We apologize for taking over your airwaves again. However, we have spent the last week speaking to the few of you trusted to lead, hoping to offer you a great gift. Unfortunately, your leaders appear more concerned with their own power than with your welfare. We felt that, as you, the citizens, are by far a more numerous body than they, it wouldn't be fair to let your leaders make a choice for you. Especially not such an *important* choice."

They were kind of managing to pull off a Concerned Older Friend vibe. I hated them.

"We have studied you, tried to learn about who you are now and who your species have been. We've looked at the patterns of your civilizations, past and present. We have, on the one hand, seen that you do struggle to maintain peace. And, on the other but too similar hand, that you struggle because it does not come easily to you. In large and small ways, most of you engage in acts of un-peace daily. And yet many of you often say you wish for world peace. Enough of you that there are many situations in which expressing that wish has come to be considered a cliché. You say you hate war. Next month, many of you will even spend the whole month wishing for and singing about peace on earth. We sense that you are not dishonest, but that you have warring instincts. If you'll excuse the pun." They actually allowed themselves a moment for a rueful grin.

But they swiftly returned to Concerned Older Friend. And not just any Concerned Older Friend; this was Concerned Older Friend with a Solution. Which was kind of creepy to those of us who knew better. "And we are here to tell you that, as we have achieved true peace in our species, so too can we help Earth become a peaceful place." They leaned forward, intent on closing the gap between their species and ours in every way they could manage. "We too lived in constant conflict, and we have made a thorough study of peace. We know the paths to peace, and we know how to determine which will lead a particular species to its own best chances of lasting peace."

Tone and posture screaming their earnestness, they assured us, "We know how to help your species."

They paused and let that sink in. Though it looked like the only thing sinking in over in our suite was some serious dread and suspicion. This wasn't the long, slow, and secret advance anymore. This wasn't the careful cultivation of relationships to gently point humans in the right direction, an effort that they'd spent only a week on, so they must really be pissed at us. They must be done with the very long game they'd played up to this point.

No, this was just a step short of truth. This was the straightforward approach, masking only how far they'd go to make sure humans had peace forever. Unless, of course, they were about to openly suggest the peace of the grave or some unvarnished dystopian offer of serene euthanasia for any and all who were ready to be done.

Then they looked a little concerned, and they admitted, "Now, we first want to acknowledge that you might have some unpleasant history with what we're going to suggest. But we also want to assure you that *our* intentions, coupled with our advanced technological capacity, will ensure that this will go quite differently under our care than under that of those motivated by greed." Because they were looking straight at the camera, it seemed like they paused, watchfully, just long enough to see us nod or otherwise indicate that we understood and believed.

Then they gave us a small but very sincere smile, like they'd just known we'd understand and be reasonable about this. "In our time working to heal and tend to your sick and wounded, we've had non-stop opportunities to become well acquainted with your physiology. We've also been grateful for researchers and others who've freely shared their studies and information with us. Which is how we've come to know that the root of humanity's problem with un-peace is a combination of physiological factors, coupled with worries about the resources that keep you alive and add to your happiness."

As if anticipating the many philosophical and spiritual arguments that might arise, they raised a hand to stop us from saying anything, but spoke kindly. "I acknowledge that that is a simplification. That, if we were going to offer, say, a class on how to achieve peace without the physiological aid we're about to suggest, we might well be defeated by the nuance of the topic. Especially as we've promised that this solution is for the whole species, not just one group of you."

I had to admit that I was kind of in awe of how well they'd learned and taught themselves to use human body language. Unless they just happened to come from a society that, against huge odds, had the same ones we did. Because, as a member of the human species, someone raised entirely with humans, I had found that just a shift in nature like being Autistic made it so that typical human facial expressions and gestures weren't as natural to me as I'd have liked. So, grudgingly, I had a moment of respect for the assholes.

Then they held up something silver, something smaller than a grain of rice, on a thin sheet of some kind of matte, dark material, angled to be easily seen by the camera. The dark material contrasted so nicely with the silver something that we could even see the almost invisibly thin wires extending from it. The camera focused in on it and magnified it slightly. And I froze. It was pretty much what I'd feared it would be but had been sure they'd avoid talking about openly.

"They fucking are not," whispered Riles.

"Holy shit," Bryan agreed, just as stunned at the audacity of what was happening.

Morgan didn't pay any attention to us; they just went on in their reassuring Concerned Older Friend voice. "Some of you might recognize this as a Peacemaker. Though this version is so tiny that perhaps you haven't actually seen one."

This was, to be precise, the built-out form of the vII. This was what the little nanites in contaminated cures and inoculations, or hidden away in the more obvious vI until it was inserted into someone's head, pulled together to become. Unlike most people watching, I'd seen my share of the little fuckers, enough to last me a lifetime.

As they gave us a moment to work through our emotions, Morgan noted, with the edge of a chuckle, "This little thing sure has caused a lot of worry, hasn't it?" They clearly thought we might have reasons to feel foolish about that.

When the camera pulled back, they put the Peacemaker aside. They put their forearms on the counter in front of them, hands together, fingers laced, and leaned slightly towards us. It was such a human posture. And, even with those grey alien eyes, with no visible nose or ears, with poreless pale skin...They looked very clearly and humanly like the Kind Authority Figure, the Wise and Concerned Older Friend here to talk things out, that they wanted us to believe they were.

So very reasonably they said, "What we realized, as we explored options for helping you rise against the physiological factors holding you back from peace, was that someone else had already done all the work of fine-tuning the device we could use to deliver the aid. If only we could first help you see that the real danger wasn't in the hardware, in the little speck of metal itself, but in the way it was programmed."

Looking slightly ashamed, they sighed. "We don't want to cast aspersions on anyone or put ourselves in the middle of on-going human investigations any more than we already have. But we have to be frank: this speck of metal is a potentially powerful tool for good that was not being used correctly." They shook their head, quite disappointed in SWS.

(They probably *were* disappointed in SWS, but more disappointed that their scheme had been discovered and stopped. Those of us in the suite and others we'd brought in on things knew damned well they weren't disappointed about the original programming of the Peacemakers. This bastard had probably been in on the meetings to decide what the Peacemakers would do.)

They cleared their throat and resumed their Reasonable face. "We can program this so that all it does is resolve the physiological issues that incline you to un-peace. Frankly, they're vestigial things, left from a time when you had to fight for your lives to protect your small tribes from roaming predators. It's a sort of fear-induced reaction that, once under control, we are 98.5% sure will help you let go of certain other fear-based behaviors as well, ones that leave so many of you without basic needs in spite of living on an abundant planet."

Riles snorted. "Well, at least we know the rich won't go along with this."

"Obviously," Morgan noted, almost like it was an afterthought, "in order to make sure that nobody is at an unfair advantage or easily harmed by those who might choose to keep their drive for un-peace, everyone would need to accept this gift. And then we'll make sure you're set up to pass the gift down to all your future generations."

They gave us an "I believe in you" smile. "Alright, friends. That's what we needed you to know. We have an easy, painless, safe way for you to have lasting peace. To cut off even the *inclination* in yourselves for acts of un-peace. And all you need to do is accept it. We imagine you all truly want peace, and your leaders will let go of their greed when they see that it is the will of all their people to have this."

A URL appeared on the screen (voteforpeace.com), along with a QR code and two buttons (Yes and No). "For those of you with touch screens, tap Yes now to show your leaders that, yes, this is the peaceful future you want. We've also set up a web site, because we know some of you can't, in the current world, afford touch screens or the connectivity to watch a video on your phones. If you don't have touch screens but can scan it, the QR code will save you some typing. We look forward to delivering your overwhelming desires for peace to your leaders. We have an abundance of gifts to offer."

And then it was a black screen with the voting options for a full 5 minutes. During which we scrambled to look at the backend of the site whilst vocalizing how gobsmacked we were by this move.

The site was cheerful, slick white with a bright blue title (Vote for Peace!), a soft overlay of icons that were everything I'd ever seen used by humans as a symbol of peace and some I hadn't (that a quick search told me was just because I didn't live in the right cultures to have seen them), and just two buttons. But we didn't cheerfully click No over and over.

Poking into what was going on behind the clean façade, we saw that they were doing more than logging IP addresses. They were running some code that, we were pretty sure, was also collecting as much info as possible about anyone who clicked No. It looked like they could probably pin down, at least to an address or account holder (if someone clicked on their phone), who was against them. Yeah. No way we were clicking that.

Obviously, as we worked to take the site down, we made sure to drop info about the backend on every hacker forum, every contact we'd ever emailed, any public forum we could get to. Fortunately, in the event of something ruinous, Jonny had previously written a program to speed through the 'Net and post a message. So, it wasn't hours of us pounding at the keys.

Honestly, the only pounding I wanted to do right then was pounding drinks and/or pounding Peaceforger faces. Or faces of the powerful whom we'd warned and who'd ignored us. How's that for inclinations towards acts of un-peace?

It was good that Bryan was "resting," because he had time to keep an eye on the world once he sent out the responses to our remote comrades' plans. (Which, let's be honest, he finished during Morgan's little chat, because it wasn't nearly a little enough chat.) The rest of us worked on our things, and Bryan kept us updated on responses and reactions.

"Guys, things were going poorly for Morgan even before we warned people about the site code. Politicians started their denials as soon as they were called out, and plenty of people started freaking out when they pulled out the Peacemaker." Bryan was grinning. "They built their whole argument around freeing us from fear, but they totally failed to understand how fear was going to bite them in the ass."

He turned on the news so that the anchors could tell us some stuff whilst he dug up other stuff. Which meant we got to see belligerent or concerned faces, though mostly we just saw eyes as worried humans pulled up g/ap masks and scarves to protect their identities. We got to see angry crowds shouting at Peaceforgers in the clinics they were using as healing centers. We got to see them throw rocks, block entrances so that arriving Peaceforgers couldn't get into buildings, and all the other sorts of human behaviors that we only supported when aimed the right way. (So, for instance, I didn't support it when it was Divine Community Church members—humans, as far as I could tell—throwing punches and rocks back at the angry crowds. It wasn't hypocrisy; it was nuanced ideas about right and wrong.)

My favorite confrontation involved Shepherd Michaelson. Because his church's clinics were involved, and because he'd been chummy with Peaceforgers (I really needed to figure out how to expose to the world that he was chummy because *he* was a Peaceforger), the local syndicate of one of the international stations had gotten him on to share his insight. Maybe in the name of being balanced, or maybe in hopes of stirring shit because there were plenty of churches that criticized Divine Community and even more that were—according to Bryan— quickly posting their negative responses online, the news had also brought on a pastor from a local Protestant church.

It started like I'd have expected, with the reporter asking Michaelson his thoughts on the Peaceforger broadcast.

Now, I hadn't been paying loads of attention to his broadcast services in the last week, but I'd definitely noticed that his church was swelling with new members. And I wasn't actually judging. Not too much. We all want truth and some reliable source of answers. And, really, we do want hope and to believe in a better future. So, yeah, people went to where a guy was healing people and had predicted the aliens' arrival before it happened. This had all, I guessed, probably made Michaelson's confidence and/or ego swell right along with his congregation's size.

He flashed his perfect teeth, and excitedly replied, "I think this is amazing! How many millennia have we, as a species, wanted a way to lasting peace? And haven't we been told that peace is possible? As one who is devoted to the Divine, I have to point out that we call Jesus the Prince of Peace. That believers have a chance, an *obligation*, to give Him this whole planet as worthy travelers on a peaceful path."

He took a breath, clearly ready to enthuse for a while, but he was cut off by the pastor.

"Now, hold on a minute." The pastor was shorter and less slick looking, but he had a gravity and a respectability to him that seemed grounded in that lack of slickness. And he was clearly not going to let this bullshit keep flowing. "Setting aside the fact that so-called 'Shepherd' Michaelson here mainly talks about 'the Divine' and only brings up our Lord when it benefits him...I will absolutely agree that we call Jesus the Prince of Peace. But He never forced anyone to follow Him. He invited and blessed those who chose to work to be better and be His. But if He'd meant us to have the option for...What did they call it? For 'un-peace' removed, He could have laid hands and removed it. Instead, He put us on this earth with free will. We are here to use that free will to do good by our own choice. And this so-called solution the aliens suggest removes part of our free will. Especially if we're just going to implant it, what, in babies as soon as they're born? We should be our better selves by trusting God and working hard, not by trusting in a piece of metal that we *know* can be used for evil." He leaned forward and strongly repeated, "The Prince of Peace does. not. force. peace. Force isn't peace. That is out of line with God's way." He sat back, but his face made it clear he was ready for a doctrinal throwdown.

In the suite, we cheered for him. In the moment, I didn't care that there were some obvious flaws in the pastor's statement, even to someone like me who hadn't paid much attention to religion. I was delighted to see Michaelson hesitate a moment, to watch his smile get slightly less convincing. I ate that shit up.

And, as he opened his mouth to reply, the reporter asked, "Do the rest of you at all agree with the pastor here?"

And it got really clear what the producer running the news at the moment probably thought. As the reporter gestured towards the pastor, the screen filled with squares. With a variety of leaders from, it appeared, a variety of religions, who all basically said something affirmative, agreeing in general with the pastor, before dissolving into the noise of so many open mics and so many different points to explain why their religion also should be considered against the Peacemaker idea. I imagined the news people trying not to look obviously smug where Michaelson could see.

I didn't have to imagine Michaelson's reaction; after a few moments, they gave him his own slightly larger square on the screen. He was fighting a scowl and failing to get anyone to listen to him.

Even knowing the Peaceforgers were just going to be angrier, I couldn't help but laugh delightedly. "Nice job by your team," I mumbled to the air, just in case some deity I didn't believe in was out there to feel proud of anyone on the screen.

We all got in a couple more hours work before our day was interrupted again. This time by Jonny swearing.

"Fuck!" The quiet, steady tap of his typing stopped. He took an audible, careful breath, then mumbled, "Okay. Relaxing. Breathe. No stress allowed." And then he got back to typing.

I stopped, my hand over a CPU cooler I was attaching, and looked over at the boys' bed. But I didn't say anything. I wanted to see how things played out before I put on the "Dr. Scott said rest" broken record.

Bryan leaned a little towards him. "What's up, mate?"

Jonny shook his head, just once. "I want to make sure before I say anything."

We were all quiet, except Riley in zir VR gear, telling Kitty, "Okay, let's talk about what *you* think the inside of a computer would be like."

"Nope. Dammit." Jonny sighed, then looked up at the two of us watching him. "We're shut out of the drones. And we're not the only ones. Unless your sources say otherwise?" He looked at Bryan.

After a few moments of his own quick typing, Bryan growled, "Fuck." He sighed. "Yeah, the military has also lost access." He leaned back against his pile of pillows, looking properly worried. "I think the Peaceforgers just took away our Plan B." He looked at Jonny. "I thought you were on satellites, though?"

"I was. I am. And I was getting in. But then there was...like a rolling wave of satellites booting me out. So, that's also going on. Again, right?" he asked me.

"Aye," I confirmed. "The Peaceforgers seem to have shut us out of satellites for a few days whilst you lot were their guests."

I heard Riles say, "Hang on, babe. Ignore the next question." Then, more loudly, zie asked, "Are you guys saying the satellites are down, like when the Peaceforgers were getting off the planet?"

"Yeah, Riles, it looks that way," I confirmed. I looked over to where I assumed Jonny and Bryan were trying to prove us wrong about that.

They exchanged a look, then shook their heads at me.

"They definitely seem to be down," said Bryan.

"Hey, babe," Riles said, "any sign that the ship is moving again or doing something that would make them take down satellites? Can you try dipping into current communication streams?"

We all waited with zir for more info. I finished attaching the CPU cooler in spite of somehow feeling like it would make the waiting for info from Kitty take longer if I wasn't fully engaged in waiting with everyone else.

Finally, Rye nodded. "Okay, thanks. I'll let them know and be right back to work." Zie didn't take off the goggles, but swiveled zir head like zie was somehow regarding all of us (so, maybe in AR mode). "Well, we are maybe fucked. Kitty says there was an order to take out satellites and drone access and a few other things that sound like parts of the plans you guys read out loud from the remote comrades. And it cited...What did it say, baby?" Zie paused a moment, listening to Kitty. "Right. Thanks. It cited 'someone close to MindKiller.' So, uh, you guys might want to figure out who gets to hunt down the mole." Zir tone changed again. "Okay, I'm back. And now we *have* to nail this, or figure out how to release the satellites. Help us, Kitty Wan Kit-obi; you're our only hope."

"We got this, Kot. You keep building Kitty's new home," Bryan directed, and he and Jonny went to work. They had murder on their faces.

Before returning to my supercomputer build, I said, "You guys might want to check out a conversation on bugHunt...I think it was Friday. Thread started by kiss-the-sky, asking us to make sure opposing peace was the right call. Though," I noted, "there are really only four people it could be anyway. Since I'm going to go ahead and assume it wasn't one of us." I gave them all fake suspicious glares, but everybody was too busy working to notice and laugh. Which seemed appropriate.

"It's 5x5. They're the mole," Jonny announced.

"You sure? Show me," said Bryan, all business.

"And tell me what you're showing him, please," I asked. "I am so going to finish building this beast today. But not if I come look at whatever you have."

"Okay, I'll narrate as I show Bryan." Jonny clicked his way through things and explained, "Obviously, I dug into kiss-the-sky first, but they were busy messing with their own country's drones all day. No message history I could find, other than stuff I could see on the forum. And I just happened to choose 5x5 next." He cleared his throat and admitted, "Actually, it wasn't luck. I'm just a total nerd and decided to avoid the extra lag that would come from having to choose who to look at next by going through the three who weren't obviously suspect in alphabetical order."

With true fondness, and with an appreciation born of my own lifelong struggle with lag due to decision-making, I said, "Magical! Do go on, nerd."

"I noticed right off that 5x5 hadn't been on bugHunt at all during what would be today for them. I also couldn't see any sign they'd taken any of the steps they'd said were in their plan for attacking the Peaceforgers in their area. But, you know, maybe they were just waiting for Bry's feedback. Except that, as soon as they got Bry's feedback, during Morgan's broadcast, they started trying to figure out how to contact the Peaceforgers. You can see the stuff still in their computer memory from that. Then, from what I can tell, once we told everyone about the backend thing on the fucking 'vote for Peacemakers' site, they used that as a way to get the Peaceforgers' attention."

"Now I wish we'd at least used that to say shitty things to them," Bryan pouted. "I bet Riles would have thought of that."

"Huh? I what?" Zie had been distracted (summoned!) by zir name.

We all chorused, "Nothing, poppet."

There was a pause, then Jonny continued. "It looks like all they got in reply was GPS coordinates. Using Kot's camera program, you can watch as 5x5 leaves their house and meets a Peaceforger in an alley, handing them a piece of paper. Old school. Probably so they couldn't be caught sending a document. Which their printer log lets me know is this one. Because they didn't go far enough and handwrite it."

Bry whistled. "Which, so Kot knows, is a doc with the reply from me today and every theory they have about how we work or will attack. And the 'nyms of who they're sure is involved.

Fortunately, just MindKiller and D3AD_L1NX. Mentions that we are definitely also working with a doctor and engineer. And then a lot of theories and general tattling. Which, unfortunately, includes who's on bugHunt and has talked shit, so they've got the 'nyms of our three remaining folks in there too. Who, from what I can tell, aren't additional traitors. So, not all bad news?"

Based on the grumbling noises everyone made, we did not consider it not-all-bad-news enough. Dammit.

"So, I'm going to go ahead and out the fucker, okay?" Jonny confirmed.

"Sic 'em," Bryan agreed.

"Fuck 'em," I encouraged.

So much for me ever trusting anyone outside our group ever again. I wallowed in a small moment of "maybe we should let them destroy this stupid species after all," and then got back to my supercomputer. Hoping to download one member of the stupid species and maybe actually save the rest.

CHAPTER 20

We all paused for food when Riley took off the VR gear. Zir hair was plastered sweatily around the edges of zir face from hours in the goggles.

Zie stretched and rubbed tired eyes. "You guys. How long was I in there?"

"Well, it's dark out now, and the computer is almost built, so..." I replied.

"Holy shit. Way longer than I thought. Um..." Zie looked around. "Is there food?"

I stood up, did some stretching of my own. "There is if we make it." I surveyed the room. "Which of our fine 'just add boiling water' or freezer food options would you all like tonight?"

After taking orders, I boiled bottled water in the electric kettle and poured it into the requested meals, whilst Riley took care of the microwave components of the other meals.

As we walked over to the boys' bed with our food, I asked, "How's it going in there? You turned Kitty into a hacker yet?"

Riles confirmed that zir phone's mic was off, then said, "I don't know. She's trying, but...I think it's a combo of her not really being into computers and of the Peaceforgers' architecture not being like ours. We, uh..." Looking guilty, though it wasn't clear if it was because zie felt bad not being sure about zir girlfriend or because zie knew it was a really hard ask, zie said, "We might want to see if we can come up with a Plan C. Just in case."

Bryan poked at something that was almost the ramen meal it claimed to be. "I don't know if I'm just not smart because of...everything, or if there just aren't great options, but the only thought I have right now is that we figure out how to provoke the governments to deploy human forces. Though a lot of that involves gear with computers that could be hacked...or that has been taken away by the Peaceforgers already. Now that they have fucking 5x5 on their team."

We all ate in grim silence. I knew, either from having lived it or from the snooping we'd done when we first brought Jonny in, that we'd all been the sort of wildly idealistic teenagers who quoted the Smiths (but not Morrissey; fuck that bigot) and Comeuppance (that 2040s band, not the 2031 film) and even tried being vegetarian for a few years. And, whilst we were all omnivores these days, we still had a lot of idealistic inclinations. They'd always driven our hacking pursuits, and they included an aversion to physical violence. And if it had felt horrible to blow up one building with some entirely guilty people in it or even to program drones to hit specific people who were definitely invading baddies, the idea of causing actual war with human troops...It just felt so shitty. So, so shitty. But the Peaceforgers weren't going to bugger off just to spare me feeling shitty, were they?

We hadn't even finished our food before the next problem hit us.

My phone rang. It was Lex, so I didn't let it go to voicemail. "What's up?"

I could hear screaming in the background that sounded like Mina. Lex was terrified. "I think whatever was in the water must have gotten to Mina."

"What's going on? How can we help?" I made sure everyone was quiet, then said, "I'm putting you on speaker so we can both help." Once I hit speaker and mute, I whispered, "Don't forget that you two are still dead to everyone else right now, just in case."

Bryan nodded and pulled up a text doc so he could type anything he wanted to say. He did it to the muffled sound of Mina screaming threats.

"Okay, Lex. Tell us what's happening."

"I don't know. Just, suddenly, Mina got quiet...then she tried to stab our friend who's over. And then tried to stab me. And she just started screaming about killing us. Good news our friend is a big dude, so he got her in the bathroom and is holding the door shut. But it has to be something from the water, right?" Lex sounded frantic.

"How about you?" I asked. "She didn't stab you, but are *you* maybe feeling at all like you want to do any stabbing?"

I was keeping my eyes on the boys' screens, hoping they had answers.

Jonny: If this is about the water, there'd be a lot more of this, right?

I saw Riles opening zir laptop, probably searching for anything related. Which made sense, because we hadn't warned others, so the world should be full of people reacting to what was in the water.

"No, I don't think I'm going to stab anyone. At least nobody *human*." I could hear in her voice that her anger at the on-going Peaceforger shit in her life had pulled her a little out of her fear.

"I approve of your focus," I told her. "And have you guys been careful with water?"

"Dude. Your word is our command. So, I think so. We've been trying, yeah?" Lex sounded uncertain, but who wouldn't be second-guessing themselves, wondering what had water in it that they didn't think of?

Bryan: Does she have sedatives left from before? Put Mina under again?

I nodded. Great idea. "Hey, did you guys bring meds with you? I know, before, you were keeping her sedated..."

Lex laughed. "Like we ever leave drugs behind, yeah?" Then, "Good call. Uh...you wait here and me and the big guy try to handle this?"

"Do it," I said, then pressed mute. "Okay, tell me about waves of people going batshit."

"Yes and no," Riles said. "There was just a jump in people violently attacking those around them. And there was also an equal jump in people trying to stab themselves. But not as big as I'd expect if what's in the water was hitting people."

Bryan asked, "Have you got Ada cross-referencing for similarities between the people?"

"Huh." Riles looked at zir screen, confused. Then looked up at us.

There was some extra loud screaming from the phone, then sudden silence.

Riles hurried to fill the silence. "The first thing Ada has listed as she spits out possible traits to confirm or dismiss is that maybe they've all had Peacemakers removed...And they've all since visited a Peaceforger clinic." Zie paused a second. "Except Mina. We know she wouldn't."

Taking advantage of the muted phone, Jonny said, "Except we also know that they took her to their clinic against her will in the last few weeks, after her vI Peacemaker was out. Unless the Peacemaker that was removed in the theoretical scenario has to be a vII."

"And we also *don't* know if the water thing or whatever might have been done at the clinic would have...instant results or a timer or would need a minute to activate," Bryan noted.

"She's out." Lex sounded out of breath. "We'll keep her restrained and sedated, but...Any ideas?"

"Lex, Mina definitely hasn't been to any of the alien clinics since she got the last Peacemaker out, right?" I figured I should confirm.

Confused, Lex answered, "What? No. Never. When we've left this suite, it's always been at night for partying. So she couldn't even have, like, really stupidly slipped away to one."

"I figured. Just...we don't think it's the water thing, but we're seeing that a number of people went stabby tonight. We just don't know. So, we're trying to find common traits or experiences." I sighed. "I don't think we have more info for you. But we'll dig into this right away and let you know as soon as we have anything."

After I hung up, Riles said, "I think Kitty and I need to go searching again."

Whilst zie did that, the rest of us took a moment to watch the news. They'd found this story too. And they were reporting that Peaceforgers were showing up anywhere they heard of something like this happening. A quick swipe with one of their miracle hands, and all was suddenly well. People stopped stabbing. Cue footage of Peaceforgers doing super patronizing variations of "Good thing we were here to help, huh? This wouldn't have happened with Peacemakers in, you know."

His jaw clenched in anger, Bry said, "Confirmed Peaceforger ploy. Not that we're surprised." He sighed roughly. "How am I supposed to rest when those fuckers keep doing shit to elevate my pulse."

I sympathetically squeezed his shoulder. Then said, "I know Jonny volunteered to be our test, but I think Mina is our pressing need. We have to figure out the healing glove."

Before I could even message her, Isa messaged me.

Some new info just now. Confirming the violence tonight caused by our people. Gave me a chance to ask about the water, in case it was to blame. Thought maybe something to cause this. But this probably isn't it. Water is nanites. Kind that build PMs. We don't think PMs do this. My group are all so sorry but not sure what to do. How can we help?

"Bless. They're actually proactively offering to help instead of waiting for me to plead." I tried not to sound too shocked. "Also, Rye's guess was right. So...Go, Riles?"

"Get help with their ship computer," suggested Bryan. "That's our actual top pri. And I bet they're triggering whatever the stabby thing is from there, even if just sending the signal from there to their machines."

"Ugh." Jonny's lip curled a little in disgust. "Which might mean the machines we've been thinking of as Peacemaker control machines might do more."

I messaged Isa:

Any of your people have access to the ship's computer? Able to make it do some things for us?

Whilst I waited for her reply, I tried to make a mental list of other asks. I wished I knew more about her resources or her group, but I did know it was reasonable to keep it to just knowing about her and Zane. For all she knew, I'd get captured and not be as unbreakable under torture as Bry and Jonny had been.

She replied:

We wish. Positions with that are coveted. Been failing to get them for years. Anything else?

I hadn't thought of much, but I thought what I *had* thought of was important stuff.

Can you get us steps for if I wanted to use the healing tool to "cure" someone of what's going on tonight? Unless it needs to be whatever the magic hands are the news is showing. And can you get us specs on the nanites? Are they the exact same ones as in the PMs we've seen? Do they have weaknesses? Will deactivation work on them? Etc.

I read the boys her message and my reply. "Anything else I should ask?"

"Flat out ask if there are weaknesses her people have we can exploit. I'm so done with this shit," said Bryan.

"He's not wrong, but," cautioned Jonny, "maybe include that we're not going to use it against her group."

I added a little about that to the message before sending. Then the reality of what Isa had said hit me and I dropped onto the edge of the bed. "You guys, with the water thing, that's got to be...everyone on Earth. They aren't going to need our permission, are they?"

Jonny froze, then quietly growled, "Shit. You're right." He looked at me. "We're about to be like...well, choose your favorite zombie movie where there are almost no humans left."

Bryan looked up from his phone. "I've been messaging with Zane." He paused in case he needed to take some shit for it, but we were all a little too tired, so he went on without interruption. "This all felt out of character, right? Based on how Peaceforgers have worked up to now? They said that Morgan is kind of newly in power. That the old one of them, who'd been guiding all this for decades, passed away a few years ago. So, that's why there's a new feel to tactics. Zane says that Morgan talked a little, before they got assigned the leadership, about how we are clearly a species that's rotten to our core. And the only reason they didn't flat out just destroy us when Morgan took over was that people with plans in action, like SWS, and slightly less bloodthirsty people, like older people, convinced him to at least let this play out. But, basically...not to put the pressure on us or dial up the fear, but Morgan is even extreme for a Peaceforger. And trying to convince us to accept Peacemakers might have more to do with appeasing the older Peaceforgers until it's too late for them to object to what they're actually doing."

"So, we should make sure it's not just Isa who knows about the nanites," Jonny suggested.

I nodded. "Yeah, she seems like she's younger, maybe just older than Zane. I bet she's made sure she seems like she's on Morgan's side so she can get the goods. So..." I picked up my phone. "I guess I do have one more thing to ask of her."

One more request: Assuming you only know because you're young, can you try to leak the truth about the nanites to all your people? In case that somehow makes life harder for Morgan.

Because, right now, even just that would be a victory. Fuck that asshole.

As I was finishing up the supercomputer, about ready to try booting it, I finally heard back from Isa. No promises for other actions, but she sent some videos and some specs (and their translations!) that she thought might help. Plus, she cleared up the magic hands thing we'd seen with Michaelson and some other Peaceforgers:

"Magic hands" are just an implanted healing device. Really only done for people who are going to be full-time healers or who might need it to look like they're doing miracles. Lucky for you, our person wasn't due to get it implanted for a couple months.

I forwarded everything to Engie and sent Doc a copy of the stuff that was relevant to the healing tool. (We were going to call it Superego, right? SuperIgor? Ugh. No.) And then I sat down to watch and try to duplicate what the video was showing me to do with the glove.

A Peaceforger hidden behind a mask, a hat, and a voice modulator demonstrated the finger movements I'd been working on to turn things on. "One thing to remember is that activity in the brain involves energy. We don't want to say this is psychic, but one reason we're unsure about you using this tool is that it is designed so that part of using it is keeping your mind focused on the task. And it assumes the mind is a Peaceforger mind, obviously. But I'll try to tell you just what I'd think to fix the thing happening tonight. Try to give you a chance."

They had a dummy on a chair, and they stood behind it. In a slightly different tone, they asked, "Will you zoom on my hand, please?"

Someone else was behind the camera, because there was a slight pause, and then the requested zoom. I could clearly see their fingers. I'd never paid attention to the Peaceforgers' hands, but I was now relieved to see that they were super similar to ours, except for having only three fingers and a thumb.

I paused the video, and called over to Bryan, "Hey, Bry, does Zane just have three fingers?"

"Yeah, plus a thumb." He laughed. "Did you just now notice that?" Then he paused. "Huh. I guess the SWS execs and Michaelson all must have had surgery to make their hands look human. I wonder why I didn't notice that..." He pulled out his phone and started tapping like he was messaging someone. "We are definitely not the next Sherlocks."

I went back to the video, trying to mirror the small finger movements the person demonstrated.

Bryan soon reported, "Another prosthetic they can get. Mandatory for high profile, and about 80% of everyone else gets it too because humans are ableist bigots."

That checked out. I nodded and returned my attention to the video.

The person on the video said, "I would try to do these finger movements as quickly as I could. I guess that's true of anything I show you. Anyway, the whole time I do this, I think...Well, it's a mix. I'm thinking our word for 'on,' which sounds like this in case you can't make it work with 'on,'" and then they made a sound that I definitely couldn't say but could probably remember or at least keep a clip of to play in my ear right before I needed to think it, "and I'm seeing it turn on. So, watch closely to get that image in your mind."

I leaned in and watched as light built in the metallic circle in the center of their palm and then steadily spread out from there until the whole unit glowed white a moment. Then the parts other than the metallic circle changed to a slightly blue-toned glow. "And now it's on. You should master that before you move on."

I paused the video. Fortunately, I'd already been working on the finger movements for powering on. And it had almost seemed like I had it. But now, as I tried with a better understanding of how my brain was part of it and of what "on" looked like...I didn't have to use their word, and I had it turning on by my fifth try. And was steadily successful by the ninth. I did a little victory jig, then un-paused the video.

The Peaceforger said, "Now, if you can turn it on, it's time to talk about what you're going to do. I'm not going to tell you a lot of context, because I get the sense you need to use this right away. And because I don't want your mind to have extra things in it while you do this. I'll try to make more videos or maybe something like a dramatic reading of the technical manual later." They laughed a little. Then stopped suddenly. "I'm sorry. I don't want you to think I'm not taking this seriously."

They took a deep breath and went on. They showed the finger movements, showed how I should skim my hand over the person's head, and showed me what the lights would look like on the glove if it was working. "Which isn't a guarantee it's working, because it can mean other things. But, if this doesn't happen, you're definitely not doing it."

Standing behind the dummy, skimming their hand over the crown of its head, they instructed, "While you do this, try only to think about this one thing. What happened is that someone figured out that Peacemakers could be used to plant a sort of electrical seed. Not a piece of tech, but an actual manipulation of electrical energy in the brain. When the trigger word or image is heard or seen, the seed tries to ping the Peacemaker that should be in the brain. If the Peacemaker doesn't send the answering signal, the seed doesn't go dormant again. It sends out its burst of violence-inducing signals, and it keeps sending that until one of us takes that seed out." They shook their head. "Not a peaceful tactic. I'm sorry."

They took a deep breath and let it out, hand still demonstrating the right skimming motion. "So, what you're thinking as you do this is that you're drawing out a spark. You should picture it being the same blue as our tattoos. Uh..."

An anonymous arm was held in front of the camera, showing a tattoo that was partially covered by a hand. Trying to show me the color, in case I hadn't seen it before, without making it too easy for another Peaceforger to tell whose arm that was.

When the arm moved, the Peaceforger on camera said, "Thanks," to the person behind the camera, then turned their eyes back to the camera, to me. "And, in this case, as soon as you get it right, the behavior will stop. And the tiny bit of energy just, basically, dissipates. You don't need to do anything more. You'll just do this and think 'off' at the tool." They demonstrated the super basic finger movement for that.

I paused the video to give it a try...and turned the glove off on my first try. Super basic.

"So, just to put it all together..." They showed the whole sequence of actions. "You think 'on' and do this...Then you do this and picture the blue spark being drawn out...And then you turn it off." They looked around, probably at others in their room, as if making sure they hadn't missed anything. They nodded and looked at the camera. "I think that's it. Again, we're so sorry for our insane leader and we wish you every good favor from the Divine in healing your people."

I hoped the Divine was listening to them, because I had to put this to the test before I could call it a night.

I practiced the sequence a few times, with no way to know if I got the middle bit right. When it seemed like I had it as good as I could manage, I messaged Lex to find out when Mina might be awake again.

"Did you get it, babe?" Jonny asked.

I shrugged, unsure. "Maybe? I'll let you know after I see poor Mina."

"Not to be an asshole," said Bryan, "but I don't love you going there. There aren't a lot of us trying to save the world, and I don't see how we can spare you."

I nodded. "I know. It's not my favorite thing I'll do today, but we don't really have a better option for helping Mina. Or for figuring out if there's anything we can do about what's happening with people...other than calling in the Peaceforgers to help." I took a breath, pondering. "Um...We'll just have me switch driverless taxis in garages a few times. And...If anything happens, I guess somebody else gets to boot my supercomputer for the first time." I tried to think if there was anything else they'd need if I didn't make it back. "Don't forget to wipe my phone if I get grabbed. And...Oh, 'shower' thought I had, or a wet wipe thought, because water...We need to remember and do something with the idea about boosting a signal that will take out the Peacemakers. Like the one the frequency detector can send. I think Engie's already on that. I mean, if it's like the remotes for car key things, then it's radio waves. Near-field communications shit. And it has to be on the same spectrum as stuff we know, right? Even if it's past the edges of what we know? So...We figure out how to boost and then we radio wave the hell out of things. Um...Satellites just blasting it or take over radio? TV? Or...send to phones? I haven't looked closely at the new specs or info from tonight. So, that might be stupid. Also, do we know if magnets will fuck up nanites? Could we do something with that?" I shook my head, frustrated that I hadn't at least thought the ideas out a little more before I felt like I had to share. Just in case.

Before anyone could protest or tell me why my ideas sucked, my phone pinged and I held up a finger to pause them.

If it works on her like before, she'll be awake in about an hour. Get here by then please.

"Love to argue with you or tear apart my ideas," I lied, "but I need to put in my camera hair clip. And one of you needs to start getting my taxis lined up. We only have about an hour until Mina wakes up."

Because we didn't want any of us out in the rain, we had to have a driverless taxi pick me up at the hotel. So, we had multiple taxis pull in here and at other hotels, back to our shell games. And each was the first in a chain of taxis pulling into garages, me switching, and them pulling out to go to a new destination. We had enough taxis in play that I kind of felt guilty. It could already be rough grabbing a taxi in this city; we were definitely making it a rougher night for folks.

Mine wasn't even the first taxi to drive into the garage at the posh hotel. And the shell game was set up to keep taxis moving for as long as it took me to do my thing. *I'm so, so sorry, Seattle taxi takers,* I thought.

With my leet haxor skillz (aka the copy of the digital key Jonny sent to my mobile), I let myself into the private lift that would take me up to the nicer suites right from the garage in the posh hotel. Even with my software tracking and erasing my passage on cameras, even with my hat and g/ap mask on, we figured it would be kind of not bright for me to use the lobby and be seen by people, by eyes we couldn't access to erase. *Damned biological cameras!* I laughed quietly to myself.

When the lift stopped, Jonny said, "Don't freak. Holding the doors a sec until the corridor is clear." A second later, he said, "Go now. Straight ahead, last door on the right."

I hustled, knowing someone could walk out unexpectedly at any moment. At the door Jonny indicated, I knocked quickly, but then used the digital key to let myself in.

Lex was rushing to the door and stopped short, first confused by me entering unaided, and then relieved. I closed the door behind me, locked it, then let her hug me. I didn't take off my stocking cap or mask, and she didn't ask about that. She was savvy.

I tried to ignore the absolute comfort and luxury of the suite; being jealous wasn't going to help. I focused, instead, on the howling threats from the loo. "She's awake," I acknowledged.

Lex nodded and walked towards the noise. Her friend, the big guy who'd faced off with security at Gas Works and whom I was coming to think of as my favorite of her friends, just watched quietly.

"Would you maybe stand outside the door so you can come to our rescue faster if Mina somehow gets loose?"

He nodded and padded softly behind us, like he was anything but a big, shaggy mountain of a man. At the door, after we'd slipped in, he finally spoke. "You sure?"

Lex looked at me, and I nodded, pretending I was.

"Yeah. Thanks. Just listen for screams that sound different, yeah?" She grinned, and closed the door.

Knowing what was happening in her brain, I felt like I could see blue sparks in Mina's eyes. She thrashed and howled, no longer entirely coherent. "Kill you!" She gnashed her teeth. "Fuckin' come at me!" she roared. Her throat was starting to get rough and her eyes were rimmed in red.

"You actually got this?" Lex asked quietly.

"I'm as close to sure as I can be. But, uh, this is my first go at this. At even actually using this tech. So...I wish I were more sure. Sorry." I felt like an asshole suddenly. Especially when my options were to lie to someone I liked (never good) or tell an unwanted truth (rarely enjoyable).

I went to stand behind Mina. Or off to the side of her, rather, because they'd tied her to the toilet. I warily watched her arms and legs, as if they might suddenly gain inhuman strength and break the leather straps or handcuffs.

It occurred to me why they'd have that on hand, and I was pleased to hear Riles in my ear, also realizing.

"Tell her I love her taste in toys. Tell her!" zie pleaded.

"Inappropriate time," I said.

"Huh?" Lex gave me a confused look.

I rolled my eyes. "People in my ear."

She nodded like that was totally a normal thing.

And then I dug out the healing tool and put it on my hand, trying to push away my nerves. Trying not to let the raging woman tied to the toilet break my concentration.

It took me a couple tries to get the tool turned on. I closed my eyes, took slow breaths, and tried to get my mind into a state calmer than Mina...and even calmer than the rest of me. When I thought I was as calm as I could be, I tried to take out the spark.

The first pass was a fail.

The second pass was a fail.

I started to feel my brain getting distracted by failure and fear of continued failure.

I wondered if my hand was shaking where the camera on my hair clip could see, because Bryan was suddenly in my ear, calmly reciting the mantra against fear from my beloved *Dune* books. "I must not fear..."

He was on his third utterly steady recitation of it when I tried again. And the lights flickered briefly in the right direction. I thought I felt a brief vibration in the air, as if the glove were trying to talk back to my brain.

I did the next recitation of the mantra with Bryan, grateful that Lex didn't ask about what I was saying, then I said, "Okay. Now, describe this image I'm going to hold in my mind. A blue spark, the color of their blue tattoos, being drawn out of her brain by the glove."

I repeated it, and I heard my three in the suite and Lex quietly saying it along with me. Then they kept mumbling back that description as close to my words as they could remember.

I said, "Watch the lights. If the tops of the finger loops shift to that tattoo blue, then to as vibrant a pink...that's what I'll want to know when I ask. I'm going to close my eyes now."

I was managing to ignore the screaming Mina. I was letting the voices that were repeating the description of my goal be like background waves, and I turned on every bit of my capacity to picture things.

I rarely told anyone, but my mental images could get strong enough that they could practically blur my sight if I let them. I'd had to learn to hold back on imagining things intently when I got to an age that I realized not everybody worked like that. So I went there. I closed my eyes, cutting out the visual competition. And I pictured our exact scene, except that Mina's head was translucent. And inside her head, in a healthy pink brain, there was a flickering spark that, if I didn't know better, I would think was beautiful. And I imagined that my hand was like a soft vacuum for such sparks, gently but insistently pulling at it. Like a delicate black hole that called to the star of the spark.

I saw the spark floating towards me, saw how it lit Mina's black hair from beneath. Blue reflections that first preceded and then trailed the spark as it moved into and through and then out of her hair. Into the welcome blackness of my hand.

Three things happened at once.

One, Riles breathed out, "The lights!" almost ecstatically.

Two, Mina stopped screaming, started sobbing apologies.

Three, the air vibrated between my extended hand and my brain, and it sent a visual ripple across my mental image. It looked briefly like bright blue light expanding and dissipating on the ripples. I didn't dare open my eyes or breathe until I was sure I hadn't accidentally absorbed the spark and gone homicidal myself.

I felt...normal. For me. For the situation.

I inhaled and opened my eyes slowly. Lex was watching me, curious. I pulled my hand in to remove the glove.

"You okay, baby?" Jonny sounded more worried than I'd have liked.

I moved so we could all see me in the mirror. Or see my eyes. Which weren't bleeding or anything, so I nodded.

"She's safe to untie?" Lex asked.

She and Mina were looking at me, eagerly. I didn't know, but why let that stop me now?

"I think so. But maybe have your friend come in, just in case?"

Lex nodded, opening the door. She pushed me out, explaining, "Can't risk you. You have work to do still," and pulled him in.

Not long after, all three emerged.

"I think she's okay," Lex reported.

"You should get home," Bryan said. "I have a taxi that can grab you in a minute."

"And the corridor is clear," added Jonny.

I put a hand on one of Lex's shoulders and the other on one of Mina's. "Okay if I go? You guys good?"

Mina hugged me, still crying, then pushed away and said, "Get out of here, bitch," in faux fighting tones.

I winked at them, saluted their friend, and made my exit.

I didn't talk again until I was safely back in our suite. I'd had something like a mild panic attack in the back of one of the taxis, complete with sweating and a little heavy breathing. I was pretty sure that was my brain's way of saying we were just about at our quota for any sort of adventures ever.

Once I'd stripped off my hat, mask, and other outside sneaky gear, I kissed my people hello, then I messaged Isa.

Glove worked. Your video instructor is great. Would love more from them. Bullet wounds and deep cuts maybe? THANK YOU!!!

And then I sat to tell them what they couldn't see. I meant to turn on the supercomputer after that, but I was so exhausted I just fell asleep sitting on the edge of my bed instead. When I tried to fight it, tried to get up and move for the supercomputer, Riles tutted at me and pushed me under the covers. At least that meant I had something cool to wake up to.

CHAPTER 21

Wednesday was a work day. Riles was still beating zir head against the "making Kitty an alien computer hacker" wall. The rest of us were trying to figure out options for what we now knew was a *massive* Peacemaker problem. In all likelihood, we'd be lucky if there were even hundreds of people without nanites in them at this point.

We were also having to watch our asses, not sure what adding 5x5 to their allies might have gained the Peaceforgers. Well, not entirely sure. We saw that someone had taken down all our forums, the big anti-SWS and anti-Peacemaker site that had gone up right after Demo Day, and most of our information drop points. We could confirm that our other comrades had done data backups, so nothing had been lost. But the 'Net as a collaborative space was compromised.

They'd also clearly been working at hacking me, striking through the emails and messengers I'd used with the remote folks. I had to leave Bry and Jonny to confer with Engie for a while so that I could make sure I was safe...And then so that I could set up new messaging options for everybody who was left.

In a weird but not entirely surprising move, they also got 5x5 into a faux interview with Shepherd Michaelson. It was like some kind of hokey propaganda film, and it hit our notifications and the news quickly.

Sitting behind a backlit screen, with a serious voice modulator on to hide any hint of accent, 5x5 asked Michaelson to help them get forgiveness for the sins, the acts of un-peace, they'd committed under the command of MindKiller. And then they gave a not-quite-true, sensationalized version of the story (very "made for TV" and "based on real events," which meant close but totally not really) where they were the corrupted innocent and MindKiller (that's me!) was a homicidal, manipulative mastermind (that's not me).

"And MK might be dead, but they were working with someone called 'dead links' who took over when they died. And I think D3AD_L1NX is as dangerous and misguided as MK," 5x5 told the viewers.

Frankly, I was so tired of the bullshit (and I knew that this was really pointless anyway in the face of the Peacemaker nanites in the water), that I didn't even bother to pay attention to how the general public were responding. Besides, if I knew they were buying the 5x5 line of shit, it might make it harder for me to keep working to save them.

Once the 5x5 shit was sorted (because we woke up to it), I finally got to push the power button on my supercomputer for the first time. And it was glorious.

Even if you're experienced and building an average computer like you've built before, weird things can happen. You don't really know for sure that it's going to boot the first time you press the button. So sometimes you just push it like all is normal and you're resigned to whatever, because what else are you going to do? And sometimes, when it's your very first build or you've done something new or it's the biggest and baddest computer ever and your friend's life kind of counts on it, you literally hold your breath as you push the button.

It's not abnormal for there to be a small pause before the computer responds. But, if you're in the "hold your breath" group, it's just long enough to be sure you did it wrong and you are fucked and, dammit, you really hope you at least didn't do the kind of something wrong that ruins a part. Because, sure, you have money to replace it, but do you have *time*?

And then that beauty lit up, booted smoothly, purred at me like the kitten I'd never gotten to have. Like it knew it was destined to actually become a home for our Kitty.

I paused to exchange victory high fives and silent screams of delight with anyone not immersed in VR with their girlfriend. There might also have been some very undignified, very not-badass-hacker-cool dancing with joy. And then some shit talking at the Universe about how I *was* a cool badass hacker. And then, back to work.

We'd wisely ordered spare VR gear once we knew that was the magic. We didn't want to have a last-minute issue with our one set and be fucked by either having no backup available or by having to quickly order and use a new set without taking the time to make it safe. So, I could finish *all* the setup, no need to wait for Riles to take a break. No risk of interrupting zir and Kitty mid-progress to hook it up and find there were issues and lose work time for them. Nope.

I took my time, moving slowly through finishing set up, doing diagnostics, that sort of thing. Maybe lingering a bit on checking out bits that I'd had to order from less-legal sources.

There might secretly be governments or corporations with lovelier machines, but I was pretty sure this was the tastiest *personal* computer ever. Meow!

When the supercomputer was as done as I could figure out how to make it, I checked in on the boys. They were conferring over one of their machines, set on a tray that was pulled over as close to the middle of them as they could manage.

"Hey," I settled beside Jonny. "What're you lot working on?'

"No, first, how's the new baby? Now that you've moved beyond just booting it." Jonny grinned. "I didn't hear swearing."

I tried not to bounce, as jostling wounded people isn't polite. But I did grin widely enough that I was pretty sure it stretched to my ears. "It is a thing of unparalleled beauty. And we are making one for us when this is all over. I think I might be in looooove."

"Watch out, Jonny," laughed Bry.

Jonny made a dramatic angry face. "I will kick its quantum ass." He shook his fist in the direction of the offending supercomputer.

I laughed, then said, "But, hey, I'm happy to pretend you guys are doing something as interesting." I made sure my smile was super fake, and I lifted my eyebrows quickly as if to say, "Gimme your boring shit. Yay."

"Wanna hear about the app I created?" Bryan asked, sounding like every boring asshole who'd tried to impress people with their apps.

"Only if you also want to tell me all about your DJing career," I responded dryly. Because might as well invite all the unimpressive show-off shit.

We all laughed, then Bryan said, "But, seriously. Apps."

He turned the computer so I could more easily see the screen. "If everybody has a Peacemaker in, we need to be able to get to everybody with whatever we come up with. And since almost everybody has a phone, we started working with Engie's and your idea about transmitting to them."

They walked me through how they'd set up a program to create copies of the most popular apps and were staged to push their "updated version" and take over, temporarily, the app owners' accounts. They couldn't do it yet, though. Go too early and someone might manage to cry foul and cut them off, destroying their version and undoing the work.

They'd also been brainstorming apps that might fill the gaps, might get to the people who wouldn't have one of those popular ones. Once they built them, they'd have to implant them on the site without the usual review by that site, faking stats and download numbers, and they'd have to figure out how to get the attention of the intended audience.

They were also working to replace some of the bigger apps that were specific to a particular OS, phone company, or brand of phone. Ideally, they'd figure out how to hack the app that led to each OS's app store. Or even figure out how to push something, via brute hacking force, to literally every phone pretty much simultaneously. One phone at a time was a medium difficulty task, but all of them at once? If it hadn't seemed like such an important task, they might have been enjoying the challenge.

When Riles took a lunch break, zie looked less like someone who might be enjoying their challenge. I gave zir a questioning look, and zie just deflated.

I gave zir a side hug and said, "You're both smart; you'll get it."

Zie nodded, but it wasn't a convincing nod. And I got it. Hard to be hopeful when you know your success is what the whole species is relying on.

"I think we need to talk about what happens if I can't get Kitty programming alien tech soon." Riley sighed. "Any minute now, they could just, I don't know, turn on all the Peacemakers and turn off everybody's brains. And Zane told us before that, once they get a planet sorted, they take off. Which would also take Kitty. So..."

Hesitantly, Jonny suggested, "What if we just let them do that?"

Everyone kind of perked up, curious.

Not yet buying in, but clearly willing to consider it, Bryan urged, "Say more. But be sure to include what's changed in the idea now, since we rejected it a few weeks ago based on the fact they'll leave people and the means to wipe us out if need be."

Jonny squinted his eyes thoughtfully, obviously fleshing it in a little as he went. "So, we stay indoors and evade them figuring out we're here. They think they've won, and they leave. We don't have to do anything. They just...go. And, hopefully, the whole 'Peacemaker in every head' thing means the ones who stay behind don't have their guard up. And, once the ship is gone, we do our shit to reverse what they did. Plus, they probably re-enable the satellites 'cause they figure we're taken care of and they'll want to make sure the people they leave behind can reach them for at least a while." He shrugged. "So then we can use the drones to clean up whoever's left behind, which we hadn't thought of before. And we block the satellites so they can't call for help. And can probably get Isa's people to help then since the larger threat is gone. And...And I guess we can even just slowly and covertly turn off Peacemakers of people strategically, people who can help, as we take whatever time to make sure we own the drones and satellites. Maybe?"

I could see Bryan mulling it over. "Hmm. Maybe. Maybe we wrote off the general idea too quickly before. But they could come back, right?"

Reluctantly, Jonny conceded that they could. "But it seems like it's unlikely. And, when they got back, we'd have had a chance to get ready to just blow them out of the sky. Also, we'd have had access to the tech they leave with their people who stay."

Bry had moved on to cautiously nodding. "Not that Morgan is logical, but it does look like they'll basically just make sure the Peacemakers are all on and leave soon. Probably really soon. Call it a first victory early in their time as leader. If I were Morgan, I'd want to leave quickly enough that I could get a start on painting the whole experience rose-colored, right? They're seeming pretty damned frustrated, and they're alienating their older crew members."

"So, new Plan A?" I asked. "Any day now, they'll call us pacified—peace-ified?—and leave. So, we make sure we stay safe and we get Kitty off the ship. And then, once they go—"

Riley jumped in. "We make sure we have satellites, deactivate Peacemakers, and send in the drones." Zie gave me a grin. "And we retire like the secret but deserving heroes we are."

"We should also have a plan for securing any Peaceforger tech out there," Bryan said. "I don't want to sound like a paranoid asshole—or like someone who's had a steady behind-the-scenes view of powerful people the last many years—but I feel like…Even if not all of us want to work on it, I think I'd like to set up a secret effort to get their better tech, use it to improve our world, and have it ready to defend the Earth. But without letting the fuckers in power touch and corrupt it."

"And now I guess we know, if we were living normal lives, which of us would retire and which of us would become consultants." I laughed. "Not that I hate the idea. I might even enjoy some of that shit, once we're no longer on the run and all that."

We talked about timing, about how to best prioritize our own efforts and projects, and then we got back to our tasks at a much more relaxed pace. This plan sounded way more laid back than any that had occurred to us so far. Lower cost, no hard deadline.

Riles headed in to tell Kitty that we were now going to focus on pulling her out instead, and the rest of us got back to hacking app stores and keeping an eye out for new information.

My brain wouldn't stop turning over the fact that I had failed to notice that Peaceforgers had fewer fingers. I was trying to run over every time I'd seen Peaceforgers who weren't disguised, just in case my brain had blurred over something else. Which set off a string of things, my brain skipping thought to thought, until it landed on the video from the fueling station.

My brain noted that sometimes I adapted too quickly to some things. For instance, that Zane had that long Peaceforger tongue and could use it as a weapon. By the time they'd used it on Bryan at the fueling station, it hadn't seemed weird. I hadn't even thought to make sure we'd edited the tongue out of the video before we sent it to law and media contacts, because my brain had just categorized that as typical for Peaceforgers. And typical things often just became unremarkable to me. And, voila, I adapted without even realizing it.

I wondered if Zane's hands were visible in that video. I wondered if anyone else had noticed. I wondered why nobody had noticed the tongue in that video at least. I realized it might be helpful if they did, so I sent off some notes...and then I plotted what I might send out to the 'Net and to emails of the world in general if nobody took action on my latest note as quickly as I'd like.

Knowing the Peacemakers were actually already in play must have been lifting the workload from most Peaceforgers. Or maybe Isa's people were just feeling how soon their time to help would be gone. Either way, I felt like a (very happy) conduit for their translations of specs and instruction manuals all day. And Engie was pretty much as happy as she could be, short of the pasty invaders just leaving.

Of course, with the angry mobs at the clinics, things were rockier for any Peaceforgers who did healing. I hoped it didn't sound like I was nagging when I finally realized that probably included the one who'd done my video and I messaged Isa to check in.

Your friend who made the healing video ok? I see how rough the crowds around clinics are right now.

I reined in my enthusiasm for human-on-alien violence a little as I thought about how we probably only had access to one Peaceforger who could help with training me on the healing tech, and as I thought about how we knew not all of them were actually bad. I watched the news, looking for anything in the Peaceforgers who got attacked that might tell me that they were one of ours. I mumbled, "Come on, humans. Just don't kill anyone we need."

Isa responded after just enough of a delay to let me start stewing in my worry.

Thanks for asking. All of ours are okay so far!

I reported to the suite at large, "In good news, our enthusiastic fellow humans haven't managed to damage our heretical healer yet. There's still hope we'll get to spare you boys from having to heal the natural way."

Before I could return to scrutinizing footage of healers under attack (Healers Under Attack! The latest overblown, pearl-clutching documentary!), the news switched footage. But it wasn't new footage. And it wasn't being voiced over by dodgy New Anchor.

Our old friend Rachel was back, perhaps further proof of sentiments shifting the way we wanted. "Most of you are familiar with this footage." She paused a beat as the video of our boys being shot started. "We all watched, stunned, as one of the leadership of Divine Community Church directed the gunning down of these two men."

Was she about to act on the note I'd sent earlier? I perked up hopefully.

I heard Riles mumble, "Hang on, baby," then zie must have toggled the settings so zie could see the room behind whatever city-styled computer location zie and Kitty were in.

At the same time, I heard Bry say, "Shit, mate. It's us."

I didn't take my eyes off the screen, but was pretty sure they were breaking relaxation rules and leaning forward. I made the news window expand to push all other windows into a tiny column on the side of the screen.

Rachel's dramatic pause ended, and she pushed on to what I desperately hoped would *not* be revealing who "these two men" were. The footage paused right before Zane showed up, and Rachel said, "But we've noticed something that most of us seem to have missed the first time around."

The footage advanced very slowly, and she narrated. "Slowed down, watch the space between the hoodie-wearing person whose back we now see and the wounded man nearest that person."

I gasped, shocked and delighted at what I now knew was coming.

They played it once, Zane's tongue clearly visible at that speed. And Rachel asked, "Did you see that? Let's play it a few more times, a little more slowly so everyone sees it."

As they replayed, I said, "We didn't tell them about that when we passed off the video because we didn't want to accidentally set off human panic and make the Peaceforgers just nuke us from orbit."

"But you didn't clean the tongue out," Bryan said, somewhat pointedly.

I didn't even feel guilty. "Yeah, we were kind of speeding away from the scene of your murder and trying to cover all the angles on our own, without our best meat space guy, so…" I shrugged. "Oops."

Rachel directed, "Now, let's move forward to where we get something of a peek at the person in the hood."

They let the footage play at normal speed, then slowed as Rachel pointed out items of interest.

"If you look carefully, the person's hands are pale and have one less finger than the 4 you might expect. And, if we freeze right there…" The footage froze and zoomed in a little. "It's grainy, but you can see that the person's face is also the same pale tone. A pale tone that we are now used to seeing on the people visiting our planet. The ones who seemed to have arrived on November 8th. But this video is from the 5th."

In the dramatic pause that followed, Riles whistled. "Oh shit. Morgan is going to be *mad*." Zie sounded pretty delighted by the fact.

"So, what have we just shown you? It is our belief, and the belief of experts in video analysis and in anatomy, that the hooded person is one of the alien visitors, and that they have long and apparently dangerous tongues. Pretty 'un-peaceful' tongues." Rachel's tone was just barely on the professional side of sarcasm.

They replayed the moment that Zane's tongue hit Bryan, and Bryan obviously stopped moving as a result. The image changed, showed Rachel—restored to her rightful anchor chair—looking calm, slightly smug. She smiled almost sweetly—almost—and concluded, "We look forward to hearing from our visiting 'friends' about what it is we're seeing in the video."

I was torn between being way too amused and being afraid of Morgan's reaction. This was such a human provocation, and it couldn't be going over well.

And the video pretty immediately spread like wildfire without me having to execute my own contingent plans. It was on the news channel's site within seconds, as quickly as they could grab the clip from their own stream and post it. And plenty of people hadn't waited for that. There were clips posted that started a little way in, as soon as the person watching realized this was going to be something worth seeing. It was showing up on other news channels' sites and broadcasts immediately after, producers no doubt scrambling to get on this before their viewers switched to the other channel.

By the time, maybe 30 minutes later, that Morgan sent a video reply (knowing better than to engage anyone live, it seemed), anyone on the planet who was awake had to have seen it.

And Rachel was back to introduce Morgan's vid. How was she managing to sound both "peak news anchor chipper" and dry? "While they couldn't make time to talk to us, the following was sent to our channel—and to other channels that picked up the story we reported earlier about the aliens' secretive early arrival on our planet—as a response. We'll play it and let you come to your own conclusions."

It was just Morgan and their two partners, Jayden and Emery, this time. Morgan sounded wounded, but had clearly worked out their story before anyone pushed Record on this. "We're disappointed that we weren't approached for comment until after the video from the fueling station was broadcast and dissected. And we accept that some of the blame is ours. We withheld some information from you, and now that video has broken the trust that exists between our peoples." They took a moment, as if preparing to tell a truth they felt ashamed of. "Sometimes, in our mission to spread peace, the bad influence of a culture we're saving impacts one of our people. It's very rare, but this young person you see in the video is one of those rare consequences. The people we saved before we came to Earth had a parasite that eroded their reason and led to un-peaceful behaviors. This young person was undergoing treatment, but snuck out and took a shuttle to Earth at maximum speed. They did, indeed, beat us here by a few days. And, clearly, fell in with a questionable element. While we did find and retrieve them within our first day here, unfortunately, the parasite consumed their brain. We were never able to get details about their involvement or interactions with Shay Brice. We apologize for not telling you and for the harm they did. But we assure you that there are no others infected and that they died a death worse than any penalty you could have inflicted." They paused a moment to look pained, then offered us a weak smile, like they had to fight through sadness to manage it. "We look forward to continuing to improve your lives and help you find your way to peace."

In the studio, Rachel was, arguably, just smiling politely. But it sure looked to me like she was also somehow calling bullshit. Sweetly, she said, "And there you have it. Let's hope they're right and there's nothing out there that shows a different timeline or more damage done."

I didn't know if she was hinting that they had just that coming or hoping someone had more to send them, but I almost sent her what we'd sent the leaders who'd gotten our "Aliens!" email. Almost. I didn't want to further poke the hornets nest that was Morgan. I'd sent her enough for the day.

The rest of Wednesday passed uneventfully. I didn't get to try to get Kitty into the supercomputer, because she hated not winning at the ship computer thing and insisted on staying to keep trying as long as possible. And I didn't get to try to heal the boys, because (we were told) the Peaceforger who could do that video hadn't gotten in until late (but they hoped to have something for us in the morning). And I didn't really get to do anything other than pass more info to Engie and prep more Trojan apps to deliver whatever we came up with for deactivation.

Of course, what wasn't uneventful was that Engie thought she was on to something that might do more than deactivate the nanites. She thought she could make them disintegrate or move themselves to places from which the body could expel them.

You know, like miniaturized guys exiting through tear ducts! Though, once I build it, I still need to figure out how to test. Don't want to leave the whole species more brain dead than they already are. LOL.

We started looking into getting her brains. Not animals, because fuck animal testing. But we figured she might be able to try on cadaver brains, brains grown in vats, or something. We didn't know what "or something" was, so we started by having a place that specialized in that sort of thing (because I guess plenty of scientists needed brains?) deliver a few each of cadaver brains and vat-grown ones to her. Of course, to cover our tracks, we also had to throw in some other organs (we made sure they were vat-grown ones and that a courier would show up right after she got them to deliver them to transplant patients). And, of course, we also sent similar packages to other places in an organ-y version of our shell game. All intercepted by couriers who'd get them to hospitals, because don't even get me started on the sad state of the transplant list.

Once the deliveries were on their way, we did some poking to make sure that patients who were too poor to get to healing centers or to buy their way up the transplant list suddenly found themselves at the top of the list, in possession of transportation, and on their way to get those organs.

Hey, we're hacker assholes, but we have our soft spots. And we also hated waste. So, you get a transplant! And you get a transplant! And...Yeah, sorry, old meme. But I was excited and put this on my list of things to do regularly After.

I was crawling into bed, feeling plenty spent, and almost ignored the ping of my phone. But I was glad I didn't. I grinned as I read, then reported, "Here's a nice bedtime story for everyone. I just got directions for letting the ID be online and probably not get caught by the Peaceforgers. So, some of us—sorry, boys—get a little extra fun tomorrow."

I yawned and nestled into the blankets. An easier Plan A, some more damage to Morgan's reputation, and now a massive tech boost? Not bad for a Wednesday.

Of course, I didn't bother to read them the next message that hit, just before I closed my eyes. Also from Isa.

Just FYI: risking that interface device stuff because, between news RE our early arrival today and some of our older people now rumbling a bit less quietly about Morgan's leadership, Morgan is looking desperate to get a solid ending, whether it's peace or otherwise. If they go off the deep end, want you to have any possible tools.

Leave it to that bastard Morgan to dial down my happy glow. Fortunately, they'd soon be headed out to somewhere else and I could stop waiting for the other shoe to drop.

CHAPTER 22

I didn't feel great Thursday morning. I felt kind of disconnected and prickly. I did a sort of high-level assessment of myself as I ate breakfast. This wasn't a totally weird way to feel. One of the things about how my Autistic brain works is that, when I'm overwhelmed, I might feel, well, disconnected and prickly. And we were now...I had to think about it. My building had been blown up on 6 October, and it was now 17 November. So that was getting close to a month and a half of things being Not Right.

Basically, if my brain just couldn't handle all this without some reactions that might not be ideal...That was probably neither surprising nor anything I was going to beat myself up about. Unfortunately, I also couldn't give myself a break. Not yet.

Plus, if I looked at a calendar, there were probably hormones doing their usual bullshit dance. Even on the Extend shot, I still dealt with menstrual cycle fun every 6 weeks. Ah, Extend...It wasn't as handy or as convincingly marketed as Eliminate—you know: *Extend pleasure by preventing pregnancy without stopping for birth control!* (Not that it prevents STIs, but why mention that?) *Extend your cycle to have more days without the hassle, but without losing the clearest indicator that the birth control part is working!* (I guess that sold some people?)—but I didn't tolerate the hormones in Eliminate at all well...Which was even more of a shame now that I was a fugitive. Anyway. Hormones and brain fuzz and stress, oh my.

So, yeah, not in top shape. But at least this was all hitting me whilst in our most comfortable hideout. And with a more laid-back Plan A than we'd had.

Even so, there was work to do, a world to save, so I wasn't going to sit the day out.

I started by forwarding new info from Isa to Engie, skimming things briefly to see what we had. It was a random assortment, probably just compiled as people were able. There were some things that should also go to Doc, so I routed those to him as well.

Before I got to the ID, and with my brain feeling even slipperier and less connected, I checked in with Engie.

How are trials going? And you're working with Doc, right?

I noticed I had a new vid to watch for the healing device. Excellent. Maybe I'd heal the boys first. Then mess with the ID modifications. Then...

I yawned, closing my eyes for a second. My brain fired, blipped, and the dark space behind my eyes was lit by white. A clear image of a white room (*a pure white room*, said my brain) with shining figures at the far end that might be Peaceforgers (*or angels*, suggested my brain). I opened my eyes, and froze. What the fuck?

My phone pinged. It was Engie.

4 decreasingly damaged brains later and I think we're there? Think I've managed a sort of data-filled tone that does as hoped. Maybe now even without ruining the brain. I don't want to say for sure until we do a few more tests. And...I don't know what it will do to a living brain. Or what it will do to the Peacemaker kill switch. Can you find me someone horrible with a nanite Peacemaker to test on? LOL. But, seriously.

I laughed but messaged that we'd try. I said aloud, "We need to find someone alive that we feel okay letting Engie test on, but she thinks she may have the tone sorted out."

Plenty of options for test subjects, really, I thought. *Not sure why I'm being so precious about human life when the whole species is rotten and deserves what it gets.* Which seemed and felt a bit too vehemently anti-human, more than my usual human-focused crankiness. But also seemed reasonable and like maybe I should do something about the whole shitty lot of humanity.

...Yeah, fuck humans.

...

I gripped the edge of the table. "Uh, I think we have a problem." I could barely get the words out. It was like some controlling snake was weaving into my brain, coils tightening, tongue flicking, and it didn't want me to talk.

It kind of wanted me to shout. Or maybe murder the fuck out of all the bastards standing between humans and peace.

I felt it uncoiling then, expanding. Rolling out in scaled waves to crush who I was. My ears were full of its hiss. I could taste its hunger dripping down my throat. Oh shit oh shit oh shit.

I felt smudged plexiglass come down between me and myself, like I was stuck in the back of a taxi that someone else was driving. (Yeah, metaphors all mixed up. Why couldn't shitty things at least make me feel metaphorically consistent ways?)

I willed and I pushed, thinking of how I'd told Kitty to program the computer she was in by just believing things were a way, sure that what I was doing now was trying to push electrical signals of my own back against an invader. I had a (ridiculous) flicker of imagined self, badass hacker in shiny black clothes shooting electric code strings from my palms at the villain.

I thought I managed to say, "Nanites. In me. Stop me. Fucking. Test. On. Me." But my teeth were gritted. And all I could tell for sure was that my body was about to grab the gun from my bag and shoot my three friends.

With a ghost of relief, I suddenly felt something around me physically. And I could hear around the hissing, like the machine that had taken over had just needed to rev up when it booted and was now at a quiet hum for its regular operation.

"Riles, do you need help?" Bryan was probably already climbing out of bed.

"Don't think so. Got this belt around her fast enough. Should still have zip ties in one of the bags." It sounded like zir teeth were gritted with the effort of strapping me in.

I knew which bag, but my mouth had stayed all clenched jaw and grinding teeth. Only more so, like the nanites had amped up what I'd been doing when they got control. I tried to joke about it to turn down my fear. *Guess those bastard Peaceforgers owe you a nightguard and some dental work now too.* Yeah, I didn't laugh at me either. But at least some portion of my thoughts seemed to be my own again.

Still, it felt like my brain was two parts, with the civilized part held back and the animal part being whipped up to murderous rage and fear by some third actor. By a fucking Peacemaker. (Which, for those of us keeping score, meant Riles was the only one of us who'd kept a clean brain through this whole shitstorm so far.)

I couldn't control my arms, but I could feel Riley zip tying them to a chair, and then my legs. Just like we'd done with Jonny only a month or so ago. I wasn't sure if I'd been cut off from audio input or if everyone was just being quiet, until I heard one of the boys cough.

So, I could sense everything and I could think. But I couldn't reach all my brain or use my body. Cool...just...fuck.

"You know how to do the deactivation?" Jonny asked.

Right. I'd shown him and Bry how to use the ID to deactivate Peacemakers. Hope surged and helped me calm down. They'd deactivate the bug in my brain, which didn't seem to be working like I'd heard Peacemakers worked, but maybe this was the expanded capabilities. Like when they'd made that girl kill those kids.

They'd deactivate and I'd insist, in case I hadn't been coherent, that they test Engie's data tone on me. And we'd get back to Plan A.

It sounded like Jonny was telling Rye how to deactivate. Good.

How had this happened? Had to have been nanites in water, right? I had hoped, since we'd seen nothing going wrong in us, that what water we'd used before we were warned had already been in the hotel's pipes. Which suddenly sounded really stupid.

"Okay, Kot." Bryan sounded calm, in control. "We checked. The rest of us are all clear. No nanites. At least none the frequency detector is picking up. So, once we take care of you, we're good." Quieter, but I could still hear, he said, "Don't turn her around. In case they're also sending info from her brain."

I tried to at least close my eyes, now desperate to not somehow give us away. No go; my eyes stayed open. What could I see? Not much (I'd looked down at the table when I'd gripped it) but still too much (a hotel-branded pen). Enough to come for us if someone was looking through my eyes at the moment.

How had this happened? At first my brain scrambled through the days, wildly grabbing moments to examine. But then I calmed. Okay, had to be Monday before we knew or Tuesday when I went to help Mina. And I didn't know if it was real, but suddenly my brain offered up a crisp memory. The taxi had been wet from driving through the rain. It picked me up in a garage, but drops still spilled from its door when I opened it. I'd written it off then, entirely focused on getting to Mina and healing her, as sweat from fear and the hat that seemed too warm given I didn't actually go outside during the many-taxis trip. But, in retrospect...Dammit.

Riles put a blindfold on my eyes, probably one I'd used with Engalls and his kid. Good call.

Zie explained, "It's almost over, but just in case they hadn't started looking through your eyes..." There was a pause. "Okay, I'm going to click deactivate. Can you nod?"

My head nodded. I didn't do it.

"Can you tell me my birthday?"

My mouth opened, and I tried to shout, "It's not me yet!" but still couldn't. Instead, my mouth growled, "I will fuck your eyeballs with a knife if you don't let me up."

"Yeah, so I love you, bitch, but we're going to try again." I heard zir pad over to the bed, zir multiple fashionable belts gently tapping against each other as zie walked, and have a mumbled conversation with the boys. Then zie came back, and said, "Okay. Once more. If you can hear us, we'll get you back, baby."

Pause.

"What's my favorite ice cream."

Another growl from my mouth. "I will tear you into pieces too small to bury."

"Girl, stop! What if my bae hears?" Oh, cheeky Riles. Then, serious. "Please hold. Again."

Tapping of belts. Quiet talk. Grunting in pain from the boys, like when they'd get up to piss. Definitely out of bed and walking towards me. The idiots were going to damage themselves over me.

I felt wildly guilty, but I didn't wallow in it. Wallowing wouldn't help anyone, so I worked to talk myself down. I reminded myself that the guilt belonged to the Peaceforgers and that freaking out did none of us any good. I didn't know if I could help, but I definitely wouldn't do any good by letting my brain go to pieces. Or go to more pieces.

"Are you..."

"Yeah, I'm trying..."

"Like this, right?"

"Dammit."

The boys were also having no luck pushing the button from the sound of things.

Riles demanded, "Okay, back to bed. I'm calling Engie."

Boys, breathing heavily, got back to bed. Riles, using my phone probably, started a phone call.

"Hi. The one of us you usually talk to seems to have been gotten by the nanites." Pause. "Yeah, we tried. It's not working." Pause. "That would be great." Pause. "Uh-huh." Pause. "Okay, I'll try again." Tap of the belts, and I knew Riles was right behind me. I could feel zir practically touching my neck, making sure zie was definitely in transmission range. "No. Nothing." Pause. "Okay. Let me know."

I couldn't hear the conversation as zie reported to the boys, just the mumbling sound of them having it. Then sounds in the bathroom. The sounds of Riles going through our bags of gear. And then my chair was dragged, with grunts and swears that told me it was Riles solo (so the boys weren't being totally stupid about their health), into the bathroom. It was a slow struggle, though at least the hotel was cheap enough to have that industrial carpet with pretty much no pile height to it that made it *less* of a struggle. But my head sweeping around and flailing back to try to hit or bite zir didn't help. The sound of...fabric? behind me.

And then Rye took off the blindfold and said, "Just in case you're trapped in there, and because we aren't set up to do another 'hostage in the living room' situation. We'll figure out food when we can."

I was facing the far wall of the bathroom, with sheets from the posh hotel—best impulse theft ever, apparently—tacked to the ceiling to form my other three walls. Letting me see nothing, and just enough out of reach that my head failed to get near and jostle or grab-with-teeth to take them down. But, kindly, Riles had put a monitor on the wall so I'd have something to stare at. Its volume was loud enough that I couldn't hear whatever might be happening in the other room, but not loud enough to get complaints from the neighbors.

And...that was it. I spent Thursday trapped there, whilst my body thrashed every chance it got, every time it had energy. When it started screaming, Riles put a gag in its (my) mouth, assuring me that zie had made sure it was clean.

As if zie knew what I—the me that was currently just a voice trapped in her own head—was thinking, how I was laughing, zie clarified, "I just bought it new. I did *not* spend any of my limited bag space on toys."

Mostly, the monitor played movies I liked. Bless. When it didn't play that, it played the news. So I at least knew that the world was still full of protests and attacks on the Peaceforgers. By evening, the rumor was that the healing centers would be closed indefinitely now, seeing as we nasty humans weren't being civil.

I was sorry for those who'd missed out on healing, but I also knew that that was the least of humanity's problems at the moment. Lucky for them, even without me, the Peaceforgers would surely leave soon. And, hopefully...

But then my hope faded. Because my hope had been Plan A. But if Peacemakers were causing people to act like I was now...And if we couldn't use the signal boost idea or even every frequency detector we could get to stop them (to stop people acting like I was acting) right away...And if Peacemakers were probably in almost everyone now because of the water thing...

Instead of just waiting with pacified fellow humans for the Peaceforgers to leave, deactivating or having Peacemakers surgically removed as possible whilst we waited for Engie to perfect the tone...

Instead, we'd probably lose a lot of our potential doctors to Peacemakers in their own brains. (Physician, brain surgery thyself?) We'd probably watch a lot of our fellow humans destroy each other. Hell, Morgan was surely secretly thrilled that, instead of peace, they'd turned up our kill instincts and inclined us to take out even our best friends.

So...I was going a bit dotty from being alone and freaking out in my own head. But it sure seemed like sitting back and being cool was off the table. Like humanity was fucked until either Kitty used the Peaceforgers' ship computer to deactivate all our Peacemakers (was that even a possibility?) or until Engie perfected her data tone.

Shit.

I stewed in my disappointment and worry (and frustrating inability to even just share my realization with my people in the other room) for hours...Even after they'd turned off the monitor my eyes had been aimed at all day, I stewed...whilst the damned thing—my meatsack, piloted by the nanites—just stared at the darkness, straining at the zip ties. Both my body and I worthless to our jarringly different causes.

I did something like falling asleep when my body finally ran out of energy. Behind its closed eyes, I was trapped in a darkness that reminded me of the stress dreams where, at the most dangerous moments, my dream self couldn't open her eyes.

CHAPTER 23

My eyes had been open a while, still not under my control. I knew my friends were up when my screen came on. News to start the day. One plus of that was that the Peacemaker really liked watching things with Peaceforgers. So, it kind of just went to neutral and soaked up what, to me, was the news channel's way of trying to summarize what had happened the last 12 or so hours when people in our time zone might have switched off screens or slept or otherwise not been sufficiently slavish to the offerings of dedicated, 24-hour news channels.

It was more of the same, though it was starting to look like scary numbers if you compared the anti-Peaceforgers crowds to the rapidly growing pro-Peaceforger ones. I felt the Peacemaker-controlled part of my brain both get happy at this and also get thirsty to join those crowds and bash in some anti-Peaceforger brains. So, yeah, more of the same.

I tried to see if there was anything I could suss out about the Peacemaker in my head, anything I had missed. I couldn't close my eyes, but I tried to force myself to visualize it like I'd visualized the spark in Mina's brain. I didn't have the glove (*oh, how I wish you were here to draw this out, SuperIgor*), but maybe the glove wasn't the only Peaceforger tech that could be impacted by my thoughts? I hoped I could at least sense, I don't know, maybe something that would let me know if I was transmitting. I was worried as hell about that.

But I learned nothing new. So, again, more of the same.

Around 09:00, we had another airwave takeover by Morgan. Lucky, lucky us. (Well, my Peacemaker brain thought so. But it had poor taste, so.)

This time, they had as many people behind them as they could fit on the screen. I got the feeling they'd packed the ship's bridge. They'd definitely done the whole "taller people in the back" thing to make sure viewers got a truer sense of how many of them were there. And none of them looked happy or friendly.

At best, some looked tired of all the shit. But some looked openly, assertively mad at us. There were crossed arms and glares.

Ever inappropriate, my brain joked, *Oh, no! I think they're dumping us.* Cool, brain. Haha. (Shut up, okay?)

Morgan gave us a moment to absorb their glare, and they were now doing the thing where someone talks really evenly and kind of quietly and you know that you are in deep shit. "Like all of us, you have certainly noticed how fear has driven so many of you to be your worst, most un-peaceful selves since last I spoke to you. You are so afraid of letting go of your un-peace that you now fill your own streets with violence."

They actually cut to a montage, minus the music that's the true magic of any montage, of that violence. They did a good job of showing the wide range of locations and types of people involved. It would be hard to watch and think bigoted thoughts about how it was just whatever group you were biased against doing this.

When the shot returned to Morgan, we were getting the look most of us had seen right before parents punished us harshly in our worst-behaved teen days. And their face was tight with the anger, disappointment, and spent patience on which that look was founded. "We have offered you the invaluable gift of peace, at no real price. We have healed you without asking anything in return. And we have seen your worst natures. Those worst natures that we've now shown you just a brief glimpse of."

Their voice went on, but now it was over a montage of past wars and human cruelties, rubbing more of those brief glimpses in our faces. "Your history is full, shamefully full, of your acts of un-peace. Of lives made worse or ended by you. And we have offered you, you who claim you want peace, an easy path to it. You need never see such images as these again outside the confines of a history that becomes increasingly ancient. And you have greeted that offer with more of the same."

If I'd been in charge of my body, even knowing what the bastard was up to, I'd have been crying with heartache and shame for my species. The Peaceforgers had done a masterful job of choosing images. Battlefields. The dying on those fields and in the hospitals that cared for the casualties who struggled to hang on to life. Those who starved or lived in abject poverty as their lands were ravaged. Bodies beheaded. Weeping women and children. Loyal horses and dogs slain in the fighting. On and on. All the things that had always made me wonder if we were worth saving. So, yeah, well played.

"We could leave you to your slow, gross destructions. We could remove your species and its threat from the universe."

Oh shit. If I were in charge of my heart, it would have gotten a little chilled just then.

"Or we could just take control. We could force you to accept our gift as easily as we control these people."

As the scene changed, in that blip of time, I wondered if they could possibly be about to do what I thought they might. (Spoiler: Yes.)

The new view was a man and a young girl sitting quietly beside each other on a couch in a room that was set up like a living room but that seemed more like an empty office space. The man sat passively as the child stood, picked up a bat leaned against the couch, and then smacked him in the head with it. The child put the bat where it had been, and then sat by the man again. He was collapsed into the corner of the couch. I couldn't tell if he was alive.

"If you will not act for yourselves, your world, and your children, we can act for you. We can save your children from your heritage of un-peace."

The screen showed Morgan again. "It is a wound on our souls when we must resort to so assertively assisting any species in making the correct choice." They almost actually did sound wounded for just a moment. But then their voice got crisply dominant again. "We suggest you take a couple of days to think about the choices you've made and the choice you *should* make. And, just in case some of your leaders want to make unwise choices in the interim, please know that any airplanes will be seized in the air. And those currently in the air should proceed to their nearest airport or expect our involvement. We'll get some more instructions directly to your leaders, but we know you pilots in the air now can hear us. We're also watching missile silos and other sources of un-peace. You who are in power, don't choose destruction before your people have a chance to choose peace."

I rolled my mental eyes. Still trying to play it like the leaders were the "problem" here. And maybe they were? Because why else would the Peaceforgers not just sit back and let the nanites work? Why would Morgan make a move that would surely make older Peaceforgers unhappy? Maybe they were too close to done to care. And...maybe we weren't the only ones who were being paranoid about water. Or maybe they hadn't reached full nanite saturation in the water yet. Yay?

"Choose wisely so that we may all feel joy at your future. A future that will be decided by the time the last of you falls asleep Sunday night."

And then the screen went black. And it stayed that way a while. One more show of power.

In the black, I wondered which machine they'd used to make that happen. I wondered what adjustments Riley and the boys were making to their plan. (*Their* plan, because nothing was mine anymore. Nothing but the portion of thoughts that I could control.)

In the quiet that came with the black, I heard Bryan report, "Definitely no access to satellites, and any country that had somehow missed that they had no access is discovering now."

"Yeah," Jonny confirmed. "No satellite action, but a lot of scrambling by everyone in power who's not already taken over by their Peacemaker and down in the riots."

"Speaking of," said Bry.

And he must have reminded them I no longer had TV noise in my ears to block out their sounds, because that was the last I heard until the news came back. And the news was chaos. I couldn't tell how much was caused by Peacemakers controlling people, because riots and online posts and calls from freaked out people and terrified-looking politicians (backdropped by additional, scurrying, terrified-looking politicians and their staffs) seemed like pretty reasonable reactions to what we'd all just seen.

By the clock on the news channel's ticker, it was about two hours later when I heard people come into the room behind me. There was some pained groaning near me, maybe someone settling onto the side of the tub beside me?

A hand pulled back the sheet on that side. Not enough for me to see the person, but I could tell it was Jonny's hand. It tried to hold my hand, but my body twisted and squirmed violently just in case it could hurt him. He moved his hand up to my forearm and gently rested it there.

From the other side, Bryan's hand found its way to my upper arm, just out of reach of my snapping mouth as my body tried to get my teeth on that hand. Like Jonny, he just rested it there.

The sheet behind me made the slightest sound as it was carefully lifted. Must have been Riles. My head twisted around but didn't manage to see any faces. And then, from behind, Riley (I guessed) put the blindfold on me.

Rye said, "I'm going to just duck under so I can see what I'm doing." There was some shifting and I had the sense that zie was, indeed, right behind me now.

My body jerked my head back. It didn't connect with anyone.

Riles whispered, "Nope," then said, "Okay, I'm the one doing the talking in case the nanites are transmitting. And, just in case you can actually hear us, Kot, we wanted to tell you what was up. But we didn't want to give them a new voice, which is why you're not being told this by other voices. But I'm supposed to tell you that he loves you. And we, the rest of us, love you too."

Zie sighed. "So, it seems like we don't have time to fuck around. And we're failing to find a way to get Engie the live test subject we were hoping. Um...I heard you tell us to test on you, and I hope...Fuck...You guys, are we sure?"

There was a pause as...I'm guessing the boys both nodded.

"Okay, so, if you're in there, I don't have a way to see if you still mean it." Zie didn't love where this was going.

I *did*. Because I did still mean it. I was no good to anyone this way. And it was pretty clear that time was short if we were going to somehow solve this.

"And we got a note that, well...Yeah, I don't want to say too much. But Morgan's weekend deadline is definitely, at best, ours.

And you're good at things I'm not and…We're going to test the data tone on you." Zie made a desperate sound in the back of zir throat. Then, not to me, zie whispered, "I don't think I can push this button."

I felt enough motion from Bryan's hand that, though that one stayed on my arm, I was sure he was taking over the actual button pushing with his other hand. As usual, he was the one of us most capable of doing the brutal, necessary things.

Riles whispered, "Are you sure?" then, "Thank you." At a normal volume, zie said, "So, we love you and we're sorry—and Engie is already preemptively so sorry you don't even know—if this wrecks your brain or trips the kill switch. Okay."

Just in case, I thought my love and goodbyes as loudly as I could. And, as much as a body-less thought can do such a thing, I braced for whatever it was that was coming.

There was a harsh tone, a grating and modulating sound that kind of reminded me of when Gran had played a clip of what it used to sound like when people had to dial in through modems to connect to the 'Net. Which made sense, because that was the sound of data.

The sound consumed everything; I barely existed as even a particle of thought. My body bucked as much as it could, zip tied to a chair. It screamed around the gag. It/we/I was screaming, gravelly waves of pixilated grayscale. We/I was being scrubbed raw. I was ground to dust. Blown by a breeze of cold code.

And then I was fading into blackhole-ness, the white fleeing to leave nothing but abrasive darkness. And then nothing.

…

…///

//////

I was still in the bathroom. The blindfold was gone. The monitor was off. The sheet was there.

I was still in the bathroom.

I was still alive.

The kill switch hadn't triggered and...

And I had at least an enough not-damaged brain to notice this.

And...I had to confirm, but, yes, I had just looked around. I had moved my head. Moved it as intended, so probably me and not nanites doing that. And it definitely seemed like I was the one who had moved it.

Of course, the gag was also still there. Dammit. But, okay, fair. They didn't know who or what would be waking up.

I tried to take stock so that *I* would know. And, not that I could feel the Peacemaker in me before, but I thought I was me. The smudged plexiglass or the snake or whatever other metaphorical things I'd thought of previously *seemed* to be gone. And I thought my brain was working as expected. I quickly told myself the lines of code I'd written to break the encryption that all the banks had been using in '48. So, yeah, I seemed to be there.

I did what movements with my body I could, trying to make sure I was in charge. I tried to do unexpected things, in case someone or something particularly clever was playing some guessing game and just making me *think* I was the one moving things.

Sure that I was myself and unharmed, though really fucking sore and tired, I had to figure out how to get their attention without making them think they'd failed. Which had to not be anything that was random or thrashing.

I bounce-scooted myself over enough that my left foot touched the side of the tub. I wriggled my foot carefully and determined that I was just loose enough to tap a pattern on the side of the tub. Good thing this wasn't a posh hotel; the side of the tub was likely to be hollow and echo-inclined. Not like some kind of noise absorbing marble that would have turned my efforts into dull thumps. It was just a shame I had forgotten all the Morse code I'd learned for fun one summer as a kid. I kind of recalled thinking that, at the very least, SOS had a nice pattern that I'd never forget. Except that I *had* forgotten. So much for "never."

I settled for tapping out the first 5 raps of "shave and a haircut." I paused, then did it again. I could pretend I chose it because it's how I knocked on doors (it was), but really it was because I literally couldn't think of any other pattern to tap. At all. After the third time, someone did the last two raps on the door to the loo.

When they didn't come in, I did the first 5 alone, then they joined me for the "two bits" part. The door opened quickly enough to make the sheet blow a little in the breeze. I kind of worried that a common knock would be all it took to get Riley (because the person was moving too fast to be one of the boys) to forget caution.

Fortunately, zir brain, like zir body, wasn't wrecked. Zie ducked in under the sheet behind me, as zie had the last time. "I'm going to take the gag out. If you scream, I'm going to bludgeon you. Okay?"

I nodded.

As zie undid the strap, zie mumbled, "I swear to fuck, if this is just a smarter Peacemaker setting…"

As soon as I felt the strap undone, I pushed my tongue against the gag, as if I could help push it out. At least it wasn't a big ball gag; I'd have been so much sorer.

I didn't even talk at first, just moved my jaw and mouth, taking in what soreness I did feel. Then, with a throat ripped up by a day of screaming, I whispered, "I don't think I'm brain damaged, but I'm definitely dehydrated."

Still cautious, zie asked, "And when is my birthday?"

I had the ridiculous urge to fake rant about stabbing zir eyes, and I laughed a little before I caught myself. Quickly, I said, "Yours is 6 February, 2026."

"And you were totally going to make a joke about something violent, weren't you?" I couldn't read zir tone.

I started giggling and nodding. "I am the worst."

Zie laughed. "That might actually be *more* convincing proof that it's you, you idiot." Then zie sobered. "Okay, I'm supposed to ask you three questions before I let you go though. So, two, what was your cat named."

"Ouch." I dramatically winced. "I'm tied up and hungry and you have the nerve to remind me that I *never fucking got a cat*." Sulkily I added, "Because a stuffed one does. not. count. And it's not funny."

"Yeah," Riles patted my shoulder, "I almost let you go with just two after that reply. But Bryan will *know*."

"He *will*," I agree. "He's like you are about sexy things happening, but for us fucking with his plans."

"Last one then. Um..." Zie hadn't come prepared. "Oh! I know. What nostalgia thing of Gran's did you hate most and why?"

"Nothing. Not now," I sadly replied. Then sighed, "But, before, when I could afford to dislike anything of hers, I really hated her old computer. The one from when she was younger. Because she wouldn't let me touch it. And I really, really wanted to."

"She's back!" zie called, and ducked around quickly to cut me free.

With a cheeky grin, I noted, "I want you to know that, because you have a knife, I am resisting the urge to pretend I'm not actually back and tackle you and make you scream." I laughed.

Rye laughed too, mumbling, "You're an asshole."

Zie was not wrong.

As I cleaned the body that was now mine again and ate, they caught me up.

We had no satellites or drone contact. So, we had to get Kitty in charge of the Peaceforger computers or hope that Morgan would take his crew and just leave our Peacemakered brains behind.

Except that Isa was sure, because Morgan had mentioned it to a group of them, that we were all completely fucked after this weekend. One way or another. Riles handed me my phone and I read the message myself, lying drowsily between the boys, my head in Jonny's lap and his fingers petting and gently twisting my hair:

Weekend is all you have. SERIOUSLY. Morgan told all of us that they've heard that humans are so polarized in their views about us and so violence-inclined that there are groups planning actual war-like attacks. But then told smaller (younger) group that, given how you're all acting, they're going to have the PMs make you extinct each other if you don't fall in line. Make everyone else think they're now proven right about how un-peaceful you are, and show the rest of us see how zealous they are for peace. They're working hard to make sure they'll be in charge without protest on the next planet, and you're seen as ruining that for them. I can't apologize enough. Tell us how we can help. Really.

"Whoa. That is one super-not-sane Peaceforger. And that was what I started to fear the situation was whilst I was in the loo," I said. Then I sighed. "So, never mind just waiting for them to leave."

"Kitty and I are working hard, because that's what we have left." Riles looked stressed as hell.

"We're back to the original Plan A then?" I felt like there was more I should be taking into account, but I was tired as hell. And that was after I'd been out cold a few hours. Apparently, being knocked out by having your Peacemaker disintegrated didn't count as resting.

"But now we've also got the apps," Bryan reminded us. "So, we can clean up the Peacemakers easily...once the Peaceforgers are gone, of course."

Jonny's fingers paused. "Can you even imagine the mess if we accidentally made the whole planet defenseless for a few hours before they were all back on their ship?"

Before we could imagine, Riles suggested gleefully, "Maybe we should be strategically positioned when we set it off. We'll have a few hours to do some meat space crimes unimpeded!"

"And here I thought you two were fine without us. Now that you appreciate our apps, maybe you'll appreciate our DJing," Bryan teased.

I yawned, stretching carefully and loving the feeling of being free—from the Peacemaker and the chair—and that I could stretch at all. "Okay. So...Oh, wait. Not that I want it, but our other option was the military?"

Bryan sighed, unhappy to remind us of the situation. "Militaries will all have Peacemakers too. Peaceforgers can just turn them into puppets, have them do all the extra damage they can do with tanks and fighter planes."

"Because I bet they've done it before," Jonny had had a thought. "Like when some trained thug fired a warning shot outside Kot's. Rookie move, like some excited, supposedly peaceful alien playing with a new toy and getting as close as they'd ever gotten to shooting a gun."

"Yeah, that's actually the best explanation for that...interesting choice," Bryan agreed. "And maybe why another trained group of thugs didn't stop, and I mean no disrespect to our kick-ass dead comrade, a sedentary hacker dude from swallowing cyanide and triggering a computer wipe when they raided his place. Because it's not like they can't afford gear and training or even just seriously experienced thugs."

I rubbed my eyes. "So, true Plan A with none of our backup plans or our alternate 'pretend the original Plan A never existed' Plan A." I let my eyes stay closed. "Go, Team Lost Cause," I muttered. I had lost track of all the plans and their parts.

And that was my grand contribution to Friday. I was too wrecked, even though I'd basically lost two days of work to being possessed by the Peacemaker and doing nothing. I'd have to definitely not fuck up at all, because it sounded like another two days was literally all the species had left.

CHAPTER 24

I was terribly grateful to discover that I was waking up feeling refreshed and not too much worse for the "fun" of my previous two days. I tried to remember what I was supposed to be working on, what had been on my to-do list before the Peacemaker flipped on. And did we have a timeline yet? I didn't think I'd heard one. But I knew we had a deadline, so I knew the timeline wasn't long.

Riley and I sat with the boys as we ate the instant oatmeal I'd made. I was trying to eat at a steady pace, afraid of going too fast and fucking something up or overwhelming a body that hadn't been up for eating or willing to be fed. We were trying to figure out loose ends or possible opportunities not taken.

Jonny was messaging EP, trying to see what was up with his family. He wasn't getting an answer. "I'm glad I had them get rid of their phones, because not calling them is..." He shook his head. "I was okay to let them think I was gone for good, but now that maybe everyone is going to die."

I squeezed his hand. There just weren't good words for that.

Riles had mostly been poking at zir oatmeal. Zie said, "I think we have to move ASAP. Like, it has to be today if we can. Tomorrow is...well, it's obviously definitely got to be by tomorrow."

Bryan nodded. "And we actually wasted time with most of those apps. Even if we get things onto the stores right now..." He waved at the news, a non-stop report of fights and riots over the Peaceforgers. "Those aren't people who are going to download apps."

"I bet," theorized Riles, "the only reason we still have news is the Peaceforgers have left enough of the assorted stations' Peacemakers off or not flipped to murder mode so that they can report this. If they stoke the fear...They don't even have to turn on all the Peacemakers. I'd bet there are people in those riots who are only driven by fear, not by bugs in the brain."

We shared a moment of silent nodding. Yeah, that sounded probable.

"Right." I took a deep breath. "We have a million things to do, and I'm two days behind. So...Riles, I should have some new things going on with ID and Igor, and then I can try to help. Yeah?"

Zie nodded, and we all got to our things.

Not that we didn't already feel the flames at our feet, but Isa messaged and the imminent direness of it all was really, extra, undeniably clear.

Morgan has told us all to be ready to leave. Everyone who can now is supposed to return to the ship immediately. People who can't or who have things slowing them down--eg if you're an artist and you don't want to leave that behind so need to pack and buy supplies to last until you can synthesize more--are supposed to be ready to leave by Sunday night. We're all finding excuses to hang back. Let us know if you can use us.

I wanted to weep. I didn't, but I really, really wanted to. Instead, I messaged her back with nothing left to lose:

First, thanks for the continued docs. I see them still hitting my inbox. I know you're working under serious danger and stress too. We will let you know if there's something more you can do. Please let us know before you go. And, is Z's temple computer interface thing still working? Did they have one? Just realized that might be an available spare. Be safe!

I turned back to my short list of actions. After I sent a quick note to check in with remote comrades, confirming that their plans were also ruined and unworkable but at least they were avoiding water and keeping their brains, I got back to my Peaceforger tech stuff.

I knew I should focus entirely on the instructions for letting our ID connect to other things, but...it made sense to me to make sure as many of our people were as capable as possible for the final fight, maybe the Final Fight. So, I busted out the glove video instead, the one that I hoped told me how to use SuperIgor (haha…fuck it; I was going to just go with that because names take time and we didn't have time and I was starting to be mildly amused by the dumb names) to heal wounds like Jonny and Bryan had.

My favorite video instructor was back. "This will be a little harder, because you'd usually also have a diagnostic tool on your other hand to help you know exactly what you were doing. I don't think you'll do harm if you only kind of know, but consider me disclaiming, okay?" They considered their dummy, this time lying on a table. "It's the same principle for both, and similar to what you did before, but you're not drawing something out, so the hand action is a bit different." They glanced at the person behind the camera. "If you would."

When the camera zoomed on their hand, they showed me the motion, describing it as they did so. Then showed it a couple more times from two different angles.

"See that light change?" They did it once more, making sure I saw the pattern. This one went straight to pink, then bright white, then back to the barely-there-blue.

"Now, let's go through the hand stuff. I'll be doing the mental images too as I do the hand movements, so my lights will change for the healing bit, but yours might not." And they slowly went through turning on, healing a wound, and turning off. They repeated the process.

I paused the vid to do it a few times, to make sure I memorized it. Just for the sake of my memory and to prepare myself if there were any interruptions—so my brain wouldn't freeze up if things didn't go exactly on plan—I went through the sequence for healing wounds. I practiced until I was as sure as I could be that I had the moves down.

"Now, the thoughts aspect. If you just think something like 'heal' as you move your hand over the wound, it might try to stitch together, but that's not going to get you best results. Especially not if there are deeper injuries than what you see. Certainly much slower. Not dangerous, I don't think. But you're probably not someone who does things half-assed. So, even if you're not a doctor, I want you to have as accurate an image as you can. Maybe you ask the person what the human doctor told them or just have them describe all they know in detail. Uh, just guessing, but maybe you can get into the doctor's computer to get records? Not that I'm supposing anything about you." They chuckled.

"It's not going to let you make the body do a wrong thing, because this is really just speeding up the natural process in this case. By a lot. So, as specifically as possible, you're going to concentrate on...nerves or blood vessels coming together, on flesh regenerating to close gaps, that sort of thing. I guess now is a good time to admit that, aside from hand gestures, the mental stuff is always that straight-forward. So, if you get to learn more, hand gestures are what you want. And what I'll try to find time to record for you. Okay. That's it. Good luck!"

In helpful news, I kind of remembered what I'd seen and been told as we helped Dr. Scott tend to the boys. In unhelpful news, I was about to go face the two people most likely to pull hero attitudes on me. So I just went "doctor in charge" on them.

"Right, boys, one of you needs to take off their shirt now. Let's have a look at your worst wounds." I was lucky that my approach was just unexpected enough to keep them from immediately protesting.

They did pause, but then Jonny said, "When my partner tells me to take off clothing..." and winked at me.

I grinned. "Correct response." I got close, trying to recall which injury specifics belonged to which people. I decided, given the protests were likely to start as soon as they realized what was up, that the bullet wounds looked like the ugliest and most impeding wounds. I took my hand from behind my back, already gloved, and said, "Lie back and let SuperIgor work." I made a little wave with my hand like SuperIgor was flying. Very mature doctor in charge here.

Jonny started to protest. As predicted.

I held up my other hand and lovingly said, "Shut the fuck up. Remember, you volunteered as tribute. If anyone on our side gets hurt, me knowing how to use this might help. Plus, tell me you won't work better if I can even slightly fix this up." I raised an eyebrow, daring either of them to make that false claim.

They shut their mouths. Excellent.

"Right, now, quiet as mice. Because I need to concentrate."

Turning the glove on was no problem. Good start.

I situated my hand over the main grouping of bullet wounds on Jonny's torso. "This one...or, I guess, these...They feel the worst?"

"Yeah. Horrible fucking gang of pain," Jonny confirmed.

I nodded, closed my eyes, and tried to mingle thinking "heal," just in case I had wrong images, and really visualizing (in my overwhelming way) the wounds healing. I did the hand motion and thought really hard. After a few seconds, I looked. It didn't look better.

I shook off the failure, took a breath, and reminded myself that this was harder than taking out sparks, and Mina had taken multiple tries. I tried to leave my eyes cracked so I could see if the lights cycled as expected when I made the hand motion. Not quite. Maybe...I tried again, keeping my ring finger and pinky together to pretend I had only three fingers. And that did it.

I closed my eyes and visualized...And I felt waves of red drifting slowly up from Jonny. Under my hand, I felt a healing white light start to form in him. I kept thinking hard until I realized I was swaying.

We all looked at the wounds. They looked only half as bad. Hell yes!

"How do they feel?" I asked, trying to quietly assess whether it was the healing that made me go unsteady or whether I'd failed to breathe whilst I concentrated. (Failed to breathe, I suspected.)

Jonny took a moment to consider, then gently sat up. He grinned. "Still painful, but I'd no longer consider whether I'd rather die than sit up and move."

I nodded, a satisfied doctor. "I think I'll do Bry, then back to you. Keep you both equal?"

Bryan got back on his protest thing as I walked around the bed. "Not that I wouldn't mind not hurting, but...If Jonny feels like he can pretend to be at normal levels of function—in an emergency—as he is, then maybe you just do that for me too and then get back to work? You've been working on the solution to, uh, the Kitty conundrum. You can finish healing us after that."

Grudgingly, I agreed. "Fair point. Now, shirt off, lie back, and think of England," I commanded.

When the boys reported their apps were ready to be pushed, by brute digital force, onto every phone because they were fucking geniuses, I made sure to claim credit. "Good thing I healed you. Notice how you weren't done, then I fixed you a little, and now you *are* done? Hmmm..."

Appropriately, they flipped me off and suggested places I could go that didn't at all sound like nice holidays for a doctor as accomplished as I was.

"And if we don't get every phone?" Riles had paused zir Kitty coaching for a quick meal.

"It's not really about the phones or even proximity," Bryan replied. "If I understand Engie correctly, this is literally about a sound we play around the world. Volume, not proximity. Sound waves that reach the nanites. Hell, since it doesn't fuck up people without Peacemakers, and since the water supply is contaminated, maybe we just need this played over the whole planet on a regular basis until we're sure we're all safe."

"Adding that to the to-do list," said Jonny. "But also adding earplugs to our shopping list, because that sound is worse than being stuck listening to your first boyfriend try to play folk songs on a guitar he just is not good on."

"That's...specific," I laughed. Oh, the thrilling stories we had yet to share about our lives...

Whoever had written the directions for me to get ID online was lucky I'm a hacker. Though, to be fair, they were far from the worst technical writer whose work I'd seen. Which I guess meant I was lucky as well.

They'd been very thorough and careful in describing what things I'd do. Even better, they had tried to translate the things I'd be interacting with. Not just "key in these characters," but also "which basically means '10 PRINT "Hello, World!"'." And, sure, they could have been lying... (I did what little I could to try to map any characters they listed to our wee glossary of Peaceforger language pieces.) And, sure, I was damned uneasy programming any computer using code that I didn't understand. (More than one too-trusting person had used code they found on the 'Net but didn't understand—code that the surrounding text swore did a particular thing that they wanted done—and opened the door to malicious behavior.) But I took it super slow and careful, and I did it anyway. Because I knew there were risks. And I also knew we didn't have a lot of options. Fun times...

At that pace, it took me most of the day to get some connections made. Igor (our trusty friend the frequency detector...good thing I'd gotten greedy and asked for a spare) kind of connected to the supercomputer (like they were using tin cans and thread and whispering to each other). ID was able to connect to networks in a way that probably wasn't going to end up with us being raided by Peaceforger thugs (we all held our breaths, held our guns, and watched footage from hotel cameras to see if any masked meatsacks came for us; they did not). And then...Nobody had written directions for it, because I hadn't wanted to mention we were doing it, but I had been picking up every clue I could from specs and instructions and my own fucking around...And then I got ID in the loop with Igor and the supercomputer.

It felt rough, slow transfer speeds, lag-plagued...but I put on our second set of VR gear, the set connected to the supercomputer, and I used that to control ID and Igor in AR mode. And something about being able to see the pieces in the strange reality-overlay had me thinking I could see small tweaks to make, like working with fussy knobs instead of code. I thought I could see the signals that were ID reaching out to drink in info, as well as a persistent signal that I assumed was the Peaceforger network trying to follow the action back to ID.

I don't know if it was delusion, my subconscious putting together all the pieces it had picked up as I'd worked with Peaceforger things, some kind of Autistic focus, or what, but I suddenly felt I kind of got the tech. Like, at least on some level, it had clicked. At least ID and Igor. I couldn't have clearly explained it, but seeing the colors and the way they chose to visually manifest things...I stayed away from what I thought would let the Peaceforger network find us, but I tested it. I followed my gut. I experimented. I even got just enough of a shimmer from my supercomputer that I did a little (old school, with keyboard) parameters tweaking there. And it *seemed* like I'd stabilized the connection between the two Peaceforger tools and the human one. It *felt* like I had. And, fuck, I wished I knew more than one or two Peaceforger symbols, 'cause I thought ID wanted to help and was probably talking to me.

I took the VR gear off long enough to forward (to Engie and/or Doc, as appropriate) the now-heavier flow of specs from Isa (which had gotten even heavier after the evacuation order), plus specs that had been on ID that I hadn't been able to get at until I connected it to the supercomputer. And then I sent Isa a message to check in on the Peaceforger-to-English translator they'd been working on. Though my backup plan was to see if Kitty could do it and also be my connection to the ship. Sorry, Kits; I didn't have another way to spread the work out.

Whilst I waited for Isa's reply, I checked in on the boys. They were antsy, itching to go, creating an unnecessary cover story about a coalition of countries building a sonic weapon and planting evidence of it a variety of places...some of it for Peaceforgers to find "just in case," and some for snooping humans to find After.

I also had a look at the healing glove (I kicked my brain; please, find a better name than SuperIgor) with the new setup on.

With the joint triumvirate of tech powered up and the VR goggles on, it was a much more interesting view. I could watch the glove go from having the faintest signal (like it was in constant standby mode), to having sparks of signal when I moved my fingers, to having a complex signal ecosystem when it was on. I could see that it was sending nearly transparent waves (only visible because they rippled my view) towards me. It seemed like it was following the body it was attached to so that it could determine which brain to take directions from. But it was also reaching out. Not too far, maybe half a dozen feet. It felt like a reach that was passive, not quite preparatory, waiting to be directed. But—and I really hated that this tech made me turn to instinct and gut...but—it sure felt like those passive signals were tasting the environment around it. And maybe they were? I didn't know enough about how it really worked. Maybe it used, I don't know, free-floating particles of matter or some shit like that to do some things? It just *felt* like it was reading the surroundings. If I saw transmission signals, that would have worried me. But I didn't, so I was intrigued instead. (And, no, I don't know how I would have known a transmission signal. I just felt like I would have.)

"Hey, which one of you wants to be my next experiment?" I turned my goggled head towards the boys. "I'm wireless, so I'm coming to you." I also quickly pushed the view from my goggles to the TV so they could watch.

The polite fuckers quietly conferred, and Bryan said, "It sounds like, maybe because it was injury on top of injury, Jonny is feeling a little worse than I am. And, frankly, I don't like the look of that cut on his right arm." He pointed at the angriest of the visible wounds on Jonny, the one that, if I recalled correctly, had been the deepest.

It didn't look *horrible*, but it was the least not-horrible and the most-stitches-having of the wounds I could see on them still. So, I ignored Jonny trying to protest and argue for why Bryan should be healed, and I put my hand above the wound.

And, let me tell you...The glove was definitely sensing that there was a wound near it. In fact, as I'd approached, it had seemed to aim its passive signals at the boys. But it was more than seeming now. And, as I made the hand movements that should turn it to wound healing mode, it wasn't just the lights on the glove that changed. There was a shifting of the signals, manifesting as light in my AR view. It looked like there were pale, reddish exhaust waves off the back of my hand, and the front emitted the whitest light I've ever seen. It welled from my hand to encompass Jonny's arm. But it was also shot through by cold, blue lines that targeted the wound. To me, they seemed like arms on a loom, like they weren't just telling the flesh to knit but were actually doing the knitting. I knew that wasn't what was happening (it was probably more like fast needles of energy pummeling the area with "hurry up and heal" signals), but my brain interpreted it how it interpreted it. And, once it looked like we could probably just take out the stitches, once I stopped thinking healing thoughts, it all subsided.

I'd forgotten they could see, but then Jonny said, "I think that was my favorite TV show *ever*. Fucking awesome!"

I grinned, then walked around the bed. "Bryan, you stubborn bastard, your organs took a kicking. I want to see if the glove can at least sense there's hurt if it's just internal. Submit to my ministrations!"

Bryan complied, shifting clothing, and mumbling, "*Just internal...like that's nothing...*"

I thought it kind of saw the bruised kidney I'd been thinking of, and Jonny agreed.

"I think it's got something, Kot."

I nodded, then tried to heal it before Bryan could protest. Though I didn't quite know what it would look like, so I couldn't be sure it was as dramatic a result as with Jonny's cut. But the white light and blue lines of energy appeared, aided by a few thicker columns of yellow. I had no idea how long I should go, so I just stood there a while, picturing what I thought a healthy kidney looked like, imagining a bruise—as I knew bruises on the outside—slowly fading out of that imaginary kidney.

"Oh. Huh." Bryan sounded confused. "I think there's an ache that's gone."

"Good." I stopped, and watched the glove as I turned it off. "I guess I'm not against all human experimentation." I pushed the goggles up and grinned at them. "Okay, now to see if Kitty is a different story through this rig."

As I linked zir VR gear to the supercomputer, I explained to Riles and Kitty how, to me, the whole setup seemed to work. I felt pretty damned grateful that the supercomputer was, indeed, super; it should easily be able to handle running both of us on gear. Maybe this would let us team up and get things sorted? I wasn't even sure.

My phone pinged. "Hang on. It's the Isa ping."

If you can get it from here to the interface device, we've got it ready for the device. Or will have in about 5 minutes. My person has been at it all day since they got freed up from other things so they could prep to evacuate. We'll send it over ASAP, with instructions for installing on the interface device. It's our big translator, but changed to make it easier for you to just put it on in the background and appear to run the device in English.

It took me a second to remember what I'd asked her about. Then, "Brilliant! You guys, they've just finished their translator. I'm about to be able to use ID with an English-language display." I grinned. "Kitty just dodged a bullet, 'cause she was my Plan B for this."

We killed 5 minutes on some food, because this was about to absorb all our attention until...well, until it was done. So, we also made sure the boys weren't going to have to do any bending or heavy lifting if we were distracted. I ate as I got the translator transferred, moved from the online space we used for receiving files over to the supercomputer, and then through to ID. It installed so easily...and I could now read it all.

"Bryan, Jonny, if you two can think about our best way to get this running for Engie and Doc, who don't have IDs, that would be super great." I pulled my goggles on. "Now, let's go see about that bloody ship."

I set my goggles to show only virtual elements, VR mode, so I was in an endless dark space that only held me and a generic humanoid body that had Riley's head. I looked down and saw that I had the same generic body. I asked, "Do you see my face too?"

"I do. And, no disrespect, but it's high-res enough that I can tell I'm not the only one who desperately needs this over so we can sit on our asses for a year." Riles didn't laugh. And zir face looked shadowy with exhaustion.

I hadn't really paid attention, but we were all looking ready for some couch time. "Well, give it a day or two, and we'll either be on the way to a better work/life balance, or we'll be dead and that balance will be permanently irrelevant."

"Ready for Kitty?" zie asked, ignoring my grim summary of reality.

"Aye. Let's see what we've added to the equation here. Let's see if it helps."

I saw zir hand make a motion that looked like pushing a button, and we suddenly had Kitty.

She greeted us with, "You guys look better when I'm in control," then laughed. "Okay, so, now what?"

Riles gestured to me. "Kot's the one who has a special relationship with the gear, so..."

I looked around. The only change to our surroundings with Kitty's arrival was that she brought her connective thread, the one that tied her to the computer. "Because we now have the ID, and in English, so I should now be able to tweak it..." I pulled some of its virtual displays in front of me, looking for connectivity information.

I tried to move quickly, but not so quickly I accidently hit a wrong thing and somehow fucked us. I changed parameters, allowing as much outgoing data as we wanted, and only allowing incoming data that travelled back in packets sent by the outgoing data. Which sounded kind of weird to me, but was an option they had and also kind of made sense if I did the mental version of squinting, so...

I made sure that the supercomputer was showing everything it got, plus the view from Riley's and my goggles, on the TV. I didn't want the boys to have to wonder what we were up to. Didn't want to have to slow down to update them.

"Right. Here's what I think is going to happen," I told anyone within earshot. "I think that we're now going to be able to follow Kitty's signal from here and use it as a back door. Um...I think our best bet is if we go ahead and Kitty waits a moment to follow? I don't know how the timing works."

"Is this happy thoughts and pixie dust or some other kind of flying?" asked Riles.

"I think the VR gear is our controls, which means we probably need to let Kitty drag us around once we're in...Unless you fancy some bruised shins from stumbling around in the meat?"

Riles grabbed Kitty's hand, giving me an unsurprising answer to that question, but suggested, "So, this is like games? We aim ourselves at her data stream and...go?"

I nodded. "Just so you can copy me if I don't fail...I'm going to grab her thread with my gloves, and I'm going to climb it like I could never do with that fucking rope in gym class." I took a deep breath, hoping this went nothing like gym class, and I reached out to put my hands around Kitty's thread.

I could feel it! I might have squeaked a little excitedly. And then I started pulling myself up, hand over hand, hoping this would speed up since we were in the crunch. Fortunately, it was all digital, so it didn't require actual muscle strength beyond what it took to make the gesture. I tried not to think about the boys watching us, like we always knew we'd do if we were in the room with someone looking foolish and doing the VR thing.

"Right behind you," Riley said. Then, after a few seconds, "I'm going to try a thing." And suddenly zie was zipping past me, laughing victoriously. Though zir avatar disappeared, zir voice beside me in meat space said, "Just imagine you can grab and pull and throw yourself up the data rope. Like...Like when you put your finger on your screen and swipe hard to have it scroll itself a while. If that makes sense."

It did, though it took me a couple tries. But, soon enough, I was zipping up into blackness...And then I was standing in Kitty's digital living room. Though it looked like she'd built it out to be even more of her flat. I saw doors to her bedroom and her sewing room at least.

"Guys, can I come to you now?" Kitty, via Rye's phone, was also in the meat space near us, though her voice simply floated in the air of her flat as far as our ears were concerned.

"Baby, I always want you to come where I am," said Riley, waggling zir digital eyebrows.

Kitty popped into view, and looked around. "Okay, what next?" Now, the gear perceived her as near, and her voice also came in through the VR headphones.

I nodded, one crisp movement, trying to hurry us along without coming off like an asshole. "Right. Now, quickly as you can, you take us to where you think, in your city UI, the control center is. I think we still want to send an 'everybody come in *now*' message to hurry along anyone who's lagging, then make the ship leave, and make it never able to come back."

"Anyone know how we steer Seattle?" Kitty laughed. Then said, "I honestly don't know. Can you do anything to this place now?"

I tried to will the UI to change, not really sure how that would work. And it didn't. Work, that is. Then I started trying to see if I could see the code somehow, hoping I could will it into revealing itself to me. I could not.

"Let's go into the city, see what occurs to us as we go. And we can show you things we've tried," said Riles. "Probably head towards downtown, Kitty. That's where the action would be in meat space."

It turned out that we *could* kind of change things in the Peaceforger computer, but we weren't nearly as capable of doing so as Kitty. She was part of the code in a way; we were on its surface still. And we spent hours in a very boring "methodically try everything we can think of and that the boys shout at us" montage. I was really going to need to figure out how to get life to stop making me live the hours of montages in real time. Dammit.

We ate protein bars without coming out from our gear and the world it was letting us access. We politely ignored it as we each took bio breaks without daring to unhook from the interface. We sat in chairs, exhausted, and laughed as we watched Kitty pull us, sitting on invisible chairs in the virtual world, through the air to the next thing we wanted to try. (We were able to stay there without touching her with the new setup, but she was still the only one who could really move well. So, handholding remained the norm.)

Finally, I admitted, "I am wrecked. And I have literally one idea left, and I'm not sure it's wise."

Wearily, Riles shook zir head. "It can't be worse than my 'maybe if I fall asleep plugged in, I can dream it into obeying' idea. So..."

It was, according to the time display I pulled up, Sunday in the wee hours. And we had basically failed. Right. Time for the possibly foolish moves.

"Kitty, take us to City Hall, please," I requested.

When we were in the large foyer of City Hall, I looked around, pondering the best way to do this. "So, the mayor is in charge, right?"

They nodded.

"Which means that the computer with highest access to things is, arguably, the one at her desk." I didn't believe this for a minute, because corporations were the true power and there were some federal offices, but I just needed Kitty to believe. Or believe enough. At least for as long as she had more power in this space than me or Riley. "Kitty, if you'll take us up?"

It was kind of eerie, even though I knew it shouldn't be, to go up those steps again, pulled by Kitty just like the day Quinn chased us. She must have been feeling it too, because she hesitated before passing through the scanners. And I noticed we all looked around for signs of the plexiglass walls or the entrapping foam or anything from Quinn's struggle. But it was clean, like the code had swept itself up in our absence.

Down the hallway to the left. To the third door, which was actually double doors with a plaque to the right of them. I suspected, in meat space, that the plaque had the mayor's name or something, but it was blank here, Kitty unconcerned about that detail.

The doors opened easily, which was good, because I hadn't figured out yet how I'd use brute force or hack through defenses in here. Could I just *think* code at it like what I'd use if I were doing this via a keyboard?

The office was larger than it should have been, and so was the computer on the mayor's desk. It looked like the sort of impressive and not-quite-real computer you'd see in a movie where computers took over the world. Kitty might be believing the right things to let me do what I wanted.

She pulled us over to the computer, and it was on, its screen glowing with a home screen in the latest OS, as if someone had turned the brightness up to maximum.

I pointed at the chair. "Anyone mind if I sit down and do a little work?"

Kitty didn't even wait for Riles to reply, just floated my virtual ass into the virtual chair.

"Okay, here's what I need you guys to do whilst I work. Kitty, I just need you to keep knowing that this computer is the main command center computer in Seattle. The mayor sits here, and she can see or change anything. If she wanted, she could fuck with traffic lights, change the parking rates in the meters, close the reservoir covers, make the displays on signs change. Anything. You, the citizen, don't have to understand it. This is a conduit to the heart of the city, to what's *behind* the city. Yeah?"

Kitty nodded. It's not that she wasn't smart enough to know better, but she understood that this was a fictional Seattle she lived in. Which meant it could have some different rules. More a video game of Seattle written by someone who didn't know how to write games than a replica by some digital maestro capturing its truth faithfully.

"Riles, I'm probably going to need help with translation. Can you grab a couple ID screens and help make sure I understand what I see here? 'Cause I think it's going to be...a trip."

Zie pulled the ID screens together, and Kitty stood to the side of the desk.

"I'm not going to look, in case I think things and get in the way," Kitty told us. "I'm just going to sit against the desk, knowing this is the conduit you said." And she closed her eyes and sat. In reaction, the computer seemed to glow a little more, even its plastic parts leaked the light.

I grabbed the keyboard, but neither it nor the mouse seemed to change the screen. I typed blind, because I could get to a command line in my sleep. Nothing.

But I knew it was there, I could see a light that just felt (there I went with the feeling again) like it was a glimpse of the unfiltered core of the Peaceforger system. I just needed to get through the screen to what was behind it. Instinctively, I punched the screen.

It made a soft crunching sound. A spiderweb of cracks spread across the unchanging image on the screen, and the light was shooting through in dust mote-sized beams. And I was tired enough that the logic of dream took over, but I also understood that I was wiping away the UI Kitty had imposed. I reached with both hands, wriggling my fingers into the cracks, forcing them to widen. I pulled the hands in opposite directions...

And the façade of a human machine parted and crumbled. In front of me was a display more like the one I could see from ID when I looked at it with the VR goggles.

"Kitty, can you just sit that way and believe for a long while? We are totally mayoring the shit out of Seattle right now. We are in the city's insides." I didn't want to say more, to cause her to change it, but I needed to know if I had time.

Confidence seemed to let the image in front of me get sharper edges, better resolution. And Kitty grinned without opening her eyes. "Silly mortal. I can literally do this forever."

"Fuck, I love you," Riles said. Then zie pulled the ID screens over by the city controls.

And we got to work.

Learning a new programming language on the fly, created by an alien mind, whilst the death of the species loomed over us and we were tired was not exactly ideal for success. Things got a bit easier when we figured out how to get an ID screen to mirror the ship display we were working on (so English could happen). We managed to get it to display things in a directory style that way. We just had to figure out the Peaceforger approach to organization enough to figure out where the command types we wanted might be. (I didn't want to start trying to guess at things in a faux command line scenario. That was way too open-ended a situation.)

We scrolled listings, wishing the boys had been able to stay awake so we could have more eyes on the screen. It wasn't until I'd scrolled past it that Riles saw a communications listing.

I opened that and scrolled for something that sounded like it would be an "everybody in the company directory" sort of message. We argued about what time to set it to send our "everybody back to the ship *now*" message, then hoped we'd gotten it right. And we moved on, exhausted but no longer complete failures.

We stumbled through some directories that we thought might help with our other goals or with some of the things blocking us. We found that turning off the control machines or even unlinking the ship from them required an additional access permission. Damn. So, the machines stayed up.

On the other hand, we found that turning off the satellite block was in our power. I wasn't sure how much that would help now, but they were our fucking satellites, and we weren't just going to let some alien bastards take them away. (Though we didn't find or stumble across a way to take back our drones. Selfish assholes taking away our toys...)

We found the ship navigation directory more easily. And then beat our heads against it for an hour. It was creeping into Sunday morning in a way that could not be considered night any longer. We kept getting either no response or a fucking useless error message, something just a bit too vague for users, but just clear enough that the person who wrote it would probably think the user was stupid for not understanding it. Of all the shitty things for their culture to have in common with ours...

Finally, desperate, and low on wisdom because I'd now been up all night...and without the boys to stop me...I messaged Isa, quietly dictating to my phone, worried my hands moving or taking off gloves might fuck something up.

If you were trying to do something on your network and you got an error that said "Remote verification not enabled," what would you think that meant?

Whether she was an early riser or just worrying, I didn't know. But she replied so quickly that I was definitely going to have a crush on her for a little while.

Depends on what you're doing. Usually means you're trying to do a thing from the planet that you need to do on the ship. Dare I ask what you're doing?

"Fuck," I whispered. Then, "You're doing great, Kitty. That wasn't about you." I sighed. "Riles, switch to AR mode for a second and look at my phone screen."

Zie paused a moment, then said, "Well that's...not the right answer. Okay. Let's try part three?"

I nodded. "Yeah. I think that's also a nav thing?"

"Like, a blocked contacts list, but for coordinates?"

"Or even a list of dangerous places to avoid," I suggested.

We found neither. Nor did we find anything else that looked even vaguely like that. And we tried until the boys woke up again.

"What did we miss?" Bryan asked.

Riles just shook zir head. "Ask Kot. I think I need a nap. If that's okay?"

"Yeah, poppet. Get a little sleep," I agreed. "Probably something we should all do."

"Should I open my eyes? Are you guys done for now?" Kitty asked.

"Next time you connect to us, do you think you can do it starting from here? With the computer as it is now?" I wanted an idea of how much time things might take.

She opened her eyes, made a little surprised face at the glowing display, then said, "This is what the mayor's computer is like," as if writing that rule into the simulation. Then she looked at me. "I think I can do that."

I smiled. "Cool. And thanks for hanging out during this. I know it wasn't fun."

Her returned smile was droll. "Only slightly less fun than watching you guys play vidgames."

After zie made a wounded face at the suggestion that we were anything but a non-stop party, Riles asked, "Do we just take off the gear to exit?"

"Yes?" I grimaced at my own lack of clue.

Zie nodded, leaned over to kiss Kitty's cheek, probably wishing zie had some kind of full face-and-mouth mask for it. Then zie lifted zir hands and blipped out of the virtual space.

Kitty gave me a little wave, and I returned it before removing my own visor.

We'd updated the boys and I was almost asleep when I got my really fucking stupid idea for a Plan B. I mumbled it to the boys, figuring I'd just deny it as sleepy nonsense when I woke from my nap.

Because we had no more days. It was Sunday. And, even more so than usual, nobody was going to have time for my foolishness.

CHAPTER 25

And, too soon, my alarm went off. I couldn't spare the time for even the three hours of nap I'd taken though, so I didn't complain, just sat up. Staring at the screen of my silenced phone. Thinking horrific, swear-filled insults at my phone didn't count as complaining, right?

It was Sunday. Morgan was surely poised to flip a switch and let us (make us) wipe each other out. Fuck.

My brain pulled together slowly, aided by a coffee Riles put in my hand, and by everyone being quiet. I could have cried at the politeness of people not trying to talk to me right off.

"Oh." My brain and eyes finally aligned. Isa had messaged whilst I slept. I tapped to read it.

Have Z's temple device for you. And the hand net that works with it. Anything else? We are all at your disposal today.

"We have a temple interface thing. You know, in case we're somewhere without our VR goggles. Like..." and then I remembered my half-asleep plan. "Hey, Bryan, did I actually say my plan out loud last night?"

He nodded. "You did."

"And? I mean, was it so bad we shouldn't waste time on it when we could spend that time thinking of another? Or...Maybe you thought of one?" That last question had actually been a plea. I needed him to have thought of one. Because my plan was...not fun.

He pondered a little. "I wish I had another plan, but I'm still slightly brain-fogged most the time and...Jonny and I grudgingly agree that this might be what we have now." Looking truly mournful—maybe due to being disappointed in himself or not liking what my plan involved—he said, "I think that's the new plan. And, based on the timing of things, I think you better hurry with your coffee."

In the month and a half since Jonny had blown up my office, I had done a lot of questionable things. And the most questionable of them had been things that I had had a part in conceiving or at least had had a voice in. Which included the exceedingly questionable thing I was about to find myself in the middle of.

I tried not to dwell on the fact that, if Kitty had been a hacker or if Isa's heretics had included a navigator (or even someone confident enough to fake it and just capable of hacking their own computers), this might not have felt necessary.

I pulled my cap down lower, trying not to smear my pale makeup, and wondered why I hated myself so much.

Next to me, Riles leaned over and whispered, "What the fuck is wrong with your brain?"

I shrugged and whispered, "I'm not the one who agreed to go along with my stupid plan, you sad bitch. So, see to your own brain." But, because I was in an ill-advised situation, I didn't stick out my tongue. I did, however, grab zir hand and cling to it a moment.

We were tucked under the glass awning of a building downtown, just feet from the entry to Isa's condo. If I looked to my left, I could see that the door was slightly cracked, and Isa was keeping an eye on us. Watching for my nod.

In my ear, Bryan asked, "You sure?" He'd asked about a million times in the last few hours.

I looked at Rye, who looked as terrified as I felt. Part of our paleness was probably not the makeup. Zie nodded.

"Unless you have a new plan now," I whispered. "But the sun is setting, so..."

"Okay. One sec." Then Bryan said, "Jonny, you have the satellite signal ready?"

"Just say 'go'," he replied.

"Go."

And as soon as Bryan said that, we heard the phones and the computers and radios in the cars all around us make the U.N. emergency tone and play a message. It was also playing through TVs and other devices that could receive signals. There weren't pedestrians around, and the car windows were closed, but we knew the message was telling drivers to pull over and turn off their vehicles immediately. Telling everyone to get to a safe and stable place where they could brace for an impact. We'd turned the speakers off on our phones, just in case we were in hiding or something when this hit. And we hoped not too many Peaceforgers still had human phones. And that every country (or at least most; that was a more reasonable hope) had implemented this particular alert system as planned. I mean, who wouldn't want to know about a global threat so they could kiss their arse goodbye?

Around us, not everybody obeyed it immediately, but a few people did, and then the others followed. I hoped the signal was at least that successful everywhere.

Once it was looking good around us, I whispered, "I can't speak for the world, but we're good here. And yay for paranoid airplane bans guaranteeing all the planes are pulled over already." Might as well appreciate when the Peaceforgers' bullshit worked to our advantage.

"Jonny, keep that going a while," Riles said. "Just in case. It might help sell this as a human-on-human thing."

We waited a few minutes. The streets I could see had ground to a halt.

I put in earplugs. "Send the rest now."

And then the air exploded with the grinding scream of the data tone, pushed through the apps we'd forced onto everyone's phones before Rye and I headed out. Blasting through radios, TVs, and the same computers that had just delivered the emergency tone. And, at least from our perspective, all of humanity collapsed. (Without crashing cars!) At the very least, they would now no longer be infested with Peacemakers, no longer be puppets for Morgan's faux human civil war. Which was probably going to have gone down that very night otherwise.

When the sound stopped, I took out the earplugs, put my earbud back in, and nodded to Isa. She nodded to someone behind her.

After a pause, I heard someone urgently reporting (into a Peaceforger version of a walkie talkie, one that would make sure the news got to Morgan fast), "Everyone here has collapsed after a horrible sound. Tell Morgan I think this is something to do with that sonic weapon I alerted them to earlier today."

And then we heard all the Peaceforgers ping. Or, rather, their modified phones pinged, getting the message we'd programmed earlier. The one thing we'd managed in our hours with Kitty. Even as we were programming it, we'd considered letting Morgan make the call, but then we thought we should be sure. Riles and I didn't want them adding some extra "and burn all humans on your way out" clause to their message. Plus, we hoped all humans collapsing would be enough of a freak out that people would just assume one of their own had panicked and called them all home. After all, who wouldn't?

And then my heart was in my throat, because it knew what was coming. I suspected it was hoping to escape my body and get far, far away from another infamous "Katja does something really fucking stupid" moment.

A crowd of Peaceforgers flooded out of Isa's building. A sea of pale faces enveloped us. Carried us with it to the nearest shuttle. Into the shuttle.

Even with Isa and Zane right by us. Even knowing that everyone on the shuttle was one of Isa's people. Holy shit. We were going into the belly of the beast. We were trusting people we didn't actually know. Trusting them not to betray us, not to fuck up and accidentally let us get killed. Trusting. Not a strength (or weakness, frankly) of mine.

The takeoff was smooth, like a lift in one of those buildings downtown that was so high there were specific lifts for the higher floors. But I still found that Riles and I were gripping hands.

Some part of my brain, programmed by my decades of dreams and maybe too tired to realize this wasn't a dream and this was dangerous, was screaming in joy. So fucking excited to be In An Alien Shuttle. Headed to An Alien Space Ship. *Can you belieeeeeve it?* it shrieked. And I thought-shouted back at it very loudly, *Not now! Shhhhhhhh.*

Yeah, Riles had been right to question my brain.

But then zie was leaned in, and whispering so quietly we were lucky it wasn't the ear with the earbud, "Holy shit, space ship!"

Nerves of various flavors filled my stomach with a writhing mass of something big and clattery. Maybe huge, shiny beetles, with pincers of dread that occasionally caught stomach lining.

For a moment, I wasn't sure my knees would hold.

Zane and Isa turned to put their own little temple device things on our temples, and then slipped the net gloves on us that would also help with computer control. Like dressing scared children. And I could see their tense faces. And then I could practically smell it. And I could hear that many of the Peaceforgers were making that humming noise Zane made when they were nervous, the one that made me think of a calming "om" during a yoga session. Everyone on this shuttle was petrified.

I swallowed my fear. I whispered the mantra against fear from *Dune*, hoping it might help others. "I must not fear..." And I slipped the healing glove on my non-netted hand, hoping SuperIgor wouldn't have to come to the rescue. Hoping I wasn't going to have any more things to put on my hands, 'cause I was out of hands now.

I lifted my hand a little so I could see the lights of SuperIgor, and I concentrated. I wanted it on so I could be helpful immediately if needed. I saw others noticing, nodding. A couple more pulled them out. A tall person looked at me until I looked back, and I thought I recognized their eyes.

"Nice technique," they whispered, grinning. "You must have had an incredible teacher." They winked.

I'd have bet money it was my video instructor. I don't know why, but that made my eyes try to tear up. Shit. I smiled and mouthed, "Thank you."

But then I could feel we had leveled off, slowed down.

Isa said, "Everyone remember the plan. If you just can't, that's okay, but make sure not to leave gaps as you walk away, please." Then she said something in their tongue.

Zane whispered, "She just wished us all the Light of the Divine and true peace."

I nodded my thanks, hoping their Divine was something real enough to hear and react.

Almost immediately after touchdown, which was gentler than a lift getting to its target floor, the shuttle door opened. And the landing bay was a wide, bright expanse filled with panicked Peaceforgers. I didn't get to see much detail as the group in our shuttle moved, keeping us in the middle. And I didn't dare do much gawking, both for fear of getting discovered and for fear of bringing on some serious sensory overwhelm.

I looked then, confirming there were others in hats, so we didn't stand out for that. I tried to keep track of our progress, in case I had to get us back to the shuttle without help, but we moved too quickly and I had too few visual markers (rounded places where walls met ceilings were, distressingly, all the same, and I had no real grasp of the Peaceforger symbols on the walls and doors) and we were moving too deep into the ship.

I noticed we lost a few people, all of whom whispered apologies as they ducked away, but most stuck with us. My head spun as I tried to keep track and tried not to feel too overwhelmed by all the newness and the sensory input.

Isa whispered, "Nearly there. Get ready."

Our group compressed a little as we entered a room. It didn't look like the bridge, at least not what I'd seen in the Morgan videos, but it looked like a control center of some kind. And we headed towards a back wall.

Isa hurriedly told us, "This is a redundancy room. In case, over the centuries or due to an accident, the bridge loses any functionality. Which means there are cameras here, but it's the only way we can guarantee you'll have enough access."

And then our group reached the target wall, and the people in front of us moved aside, hemming us in by a keypad and small screen. A person in a cap, a shirt with a joke about binary (so, a nerd like us), and jeans, their human eye contact lenses in and making them look like a scared tech support friend, pushed over to be by us.

"Okay. I'm going to help you get up and in." They used one hand to tap the keypad, and another to tap first Riley's and then my temple tech. "Sorry that hacking is considered un-peace. I swear I'm going to learn how to do it when this is over."

I could now see the screens hung in the air from when Tech Support had touched the keypad. I didn't mention to them that part of our secret was a rogue AI; never admit you aren't as badass a hacker as everyone thinks. Or that we were fucked if the tech didn't work as we'd hoped, if we didn't manage to get those screens displaying in English for us.

"You seeing that?" When we nodded, they said, "Now use your netted hand to copy what I do so we can make sure they work for you."

We tried to ignore the crowd around us and the sound of people in the corridor shouting. And we managed to swipe and flip the thing Tech Support had.

"Good. You are as in as I can get you. I'm going to just shut up and let you work now." And they stepped a little bit aside, giving us room to move our hands.

Riles pulled out zir phone, tapped the screen, and whispered, "Kitty, we're here. Can you find us?"

She showed up on zir screen. "Yes, but I'm still working on the computer part of finding you."

"Remember, you're everywhere. So...if you're in the mayor's office, go next door, to the deputy mayor's office and see us turning a diamond kind of symbol around in the air," Riles suggested. Then zie said to me, "I can feel this temple tech. It's not just projecting over my eye; I think it's also listening to my thoughts like the healing glove. I'm going to try to use that. Keep spinning that diamond thingy."

I nodded. I felt it too. And I kept flipping the glyph Kitty would be looking for to find us. I tried to imagine Kitty and being inside the computer with her, not just on this side. I pushed and forced my way into the data conduit I could feel that was connecting my brain to the temple tech. I didn't really get in, but I felt almost there.

"I see you guys! Kind of. Like ghosts." Kitty's voice now seemed like it was also echoing from the temple tech.

Next to me, Riles tucked zir phone into a pocket, trading it for a frequency detector briefly. Then reached over to my backpack to pull out ID. Zie held it and I used my spare hand to get things linked up like we'd had them in our suite. Minus the supercomputer, of course. We could see it all as if we had on our

VR goggles. That boded well. We pulled up a translation screen, the same we'd used to work with the mayor's computer in Kitty's UI. We didn't know if any of this would help, but it at least felt useful just by virtue of its familiarity.

Riles said, "I'm closing my eyes. I think I can get in. Kitty, pull me."

I heard a shout in the corridor.

"They know you're here. Hurry," Isa urged.

I tried to ignore the sound and movement of grappling behind me. I tried to see if I could track Kitty and Riles, but I felt like the ghost she saw me as. Or maybe their digital selves were that, like a whisper being delivered to my brain by the temple tech. The output of ID told me they were at a computer where they could access the directory we needed. Fortunately, Riles seemed to be zooming right to the nav stuff.

Bodies were bumping into us, and I heard someone who I thought was on our side shout a direction in their language. There was a push, and our people managed to drive the incoming bodies to and through the door, closing it behind them. Leaving just a handful of us. Isa, Zane, Tech Support, and a couple others I didn't have any connection with beyond the last...had it even been half an hour? It had probably been closer to 15 minutes, but it felt forever longer.

I heard Riley whispering, an argument. "Look, we don't know coordinates."

I asked, "Does anyone here know enough to tell us coordinates of somewhere far away from here?"

The few heads left in the room shook.

"Nope," I reported.

I heard Kitty as a whisper, "Then I'm going to say we just point them at the damned sun. Fuck them all."

Riles calmly whispered, "That's not you. Don't be the stereotypical murderous AI, baby. Remember, you're a creator. You make beautiful clothes and you believe that everyone is equal and...and you're less an asshole than us. Come on."

I whispered, scrambling for useful encouragement or metaphors or something, "Kitty, if you can hear me...Look, you're the boss. The...badass seamstress, right?" I could feel my tiredness making me talk rubbish, but it was just coming out.

Because I couldn't handle a murder that big, it turned out. "So, I don't know, maybe change where you are from a city to...something clothing related. Something you know you can run. Fuck. I'm too tired. But...you can control the damned computer like a...like a sewing machine or pattern design or...some other clothing tool. And we're just here to make sure it gets a proximity approval or some shit it needs for nav commands. But...Wear this bitch like a jacket. Like some avant garde shiny jacket. Like..." I was losing the plot. "Like, maybe it's not even a tool. Because, the way computers integrate with all the ship's parts, maybe it's more like you're wearing it? And then, I don't know, hurl it deep into space. Fuck. I don't know. I'm tired. But toss it somewhere out there instead. Like, when you move to the supercomputer, you're taking this off and throwing it across the room the same way you would clothing. Or something." I shut my mouth. I was fuzzy-brained and might as well have been wasted. Definitely rambling. At the very least I'd been talking too damned fast. "I'm sorry. I'm incoherent. Riles, where are we?"

"Okay. Deep breath, Kot. Um...Good news is I just need some kind of coordinates, 'cause I'm now in and can make it go. Bad news is I don't see a way to stop them coming back. So...I don't know what to do." Zie sounded about to cry.

Fuck.

"But I'll keep trying. I'll find a star chart or something. And I'll erase our coordinates."

I breathed carefully. "Cool. Good plan. Just...quickly, please." I wondered how much time my verbal vomit had cost us.

The door wasn't going to hold. My brain scrambled.

"Isa, or any of you, can you broadcast a message to get people into their pods or whatever you sleep in during the long travel? Maybe everyone needs to be checked for adverse effects from the data tone? And then," I turned to Tech Support, "can you block any ship-wide announcements after."

They nodded. "Yeah. I think I can do the computer part. Isa?"

Tech Support and Isa moved to a nearby patch of wall. They made quick work of the tasks, then pulled up a screen.

"It looks like a lot of people are already obeying," Tech Support reported. "I don't think most know about you being here." They counted. "I think we've only got a dozen still out and moving. So, once there's a chance, we just need to put the not-moving ones into stasis."

The door was easing aside. I was spectacularly grateful they weren't a gun kind of species.

"Riles, hurry. I'm going to be distracted by getting beat up soon." And I stood, facing the door. Having watched too many movies, but not closely enough, I had my hands up in something that probably wasn't a real defensive or offensive posture. In my tired-as-hell brain though, I was sure this was some martial arts starting pose. Feet wide, elbows bent, palms forward-ish. I could have laughed at my ridiculousness if we were anywhere other than being rushed by aliens who'd probably like us dead at this point. I wished I'd brought a gun, even if I didn't trust my aim and wasn't sure I wouldn't fuck things up with a misplaced bullet or by getting caught by some unknown scanners on the ship.

I realized I hadn't heard the boys. Urgently, as one of our allies threw themselves at the Peaceforger squeezing through the gap where the door was opening, I whispered, "Jonny? Bry? Can you hear me?"

I might have gotten a crackle. Shit.

"Hey, Tech Support. Uh, I mean, computer demonstrating friend?"

They looked up at me. "Tech support?"

I winced. "Yes. Sorry. My brain is a mess. Uh, can you boost signals to and from the earbuds we have in?"

They nodded, "I can try. And I'm Sean." Small smile and wink, so I knew they weren't mad.

I realized my arms were actually trying to move into position like the 1984 *Dune* movie, like my glove was a weirding device. We were in trouble if my brain was supposed to be part of our solution.

And then the ally on the door was down. And there was tussling as they tried to trip up the Peaceforger who was pushing through. My heart leapt into my mouth and I just let my body do whatever "form" it thought was useful. So, sure, hold yourself that ridiculous way, body. You're the One. You know kung fu. Whatever movie reference gets you through this. I snorted at myself. And I started trying to talk myself into a fighting mindset. A quiet, aggressive mumble. Part encouragement, part stoking the anger.

"Okay. You're going to be like a wild animal. You're going to eat their eyes. You're going to suck their blood. These assholes who killed Gran and tried to enslave your planet. The fuckers who killed your friends," I growled. "You're going to suck them dry. You're going to drain them and leave them like dry leaves. Fuck them!"

And then I was wild with fear and sleep dep and anger and looking at the hand pointed at the door, the palm with the healing device, and I just...I did the gestures to heal in reverse order and I thought wounding. I threw in the gestures for drawing the spark out of Mina and I thought draining. And I used every bit of my rage to fuel my will. Fuck this piece of tech being the superego; I'd turn it into the manifestation of my id.

And I watched in awe and hunger as the waves around my hand, made visible by the temple tech or maybe our frequency detector, roiled and surged and shot redly forward. Like I was some kind of fucking wizard, casting fireballs or some shit. And I advanced to make sure it hit. I let its own passive search turn into an aggressive hunt. And I pushed the wound and drew the energy.

I felt the edges of my mental images encroach upon and frame reality. I felt my emotion, heightened by sleep dep and hormones and all the meltdowns I dared not have, fuel and direct it.

And the Peaceforger they hit stumbled. I saw bright blue bruises blossom on their face. They grabbed their sides. I thought separating and rending and here, have the wounds back that you gave to my boys. And they made a strangled sound and fell.

And I heard someone gasp near me, but I kept going, because there were more bodies in the door. Bodies aimed at me and at my Riley. And they were going to hurt before they had a chance to get to me, much less to my Riles.

I put another one down, blood trickling from their mouth. And I was now starting to be a little freaked out by myself, but I was also disconnecting. So, fuck it.

I started to bludgeon the next one. That should leave nine, right? And I could hear that I now had the same growl Quinn had. Another we'd lost. And I was now growling a litany of names in no specific order. Gran and Quinn and Kitty and Huw and 'Randa. Fuck. Fuck. Fuck.

And then Kitty's voice. "Kot, you can stop."

I didn't.

"Kot, I did what you said. I'm wearing the ship. You can stop."

I didn't. And a fourth Peaceforger went down.

Then, with the same tone she'd used to deliver the lecture a month ago in her flat, about how I'd been a sexist asshole, she demanded, "Katja, what the hell legacy are you creating? Is this the person your grandmother raised you to be? Is this what victory looks like? Knock it off."

And then there were arms around me, holding me and pressing my hands down. And Riles was saying, "She has maintenance robots grabbing them. It's okay, Kot. You can stop." And the arms felt more like a hug then. And zie was whispering, "It's okay, Kot."

And I watched a sleek and shiny bot roll in, firmly wrap arms around a Peaceforger (like arms were wrapped around me, but not like that...like they were an errant beam), and pull them away. And then another. And then I had boys in my ears.

"Kot? Riles?"

Riles replied, "We're here. We're finishing up. We just have to stop Kot from killing anyone."

Gently, Jonny said, "Kot, it's over. They're off planet and their bugs are dead and you can stop. We can go home. Please, baby..."

"Come on, Kot," Bryan piled on. "Kitty is showing us the scene. Turn the glove off." He tried a joke, "Put SuperIgor up, up, and away, yeah?"

It wasn't any one thing. It was all of it. Sinking in. It was the tiredness hitting me. It was my healing glove video instructor slipping in the door, battered but alive, coming behind me to carefully try to push my hand through the motion for turning it off. It was the people I'd lost. It was the people I still had, talking me down. It was a month and a half of fear and running. It was finally being at our long-desired After.

I don't know. It was everything. And suddenly, I was still. Maybe too still. Maybe scary still. But I turned off the glove, slowly took it off and pocketed it. Turned to ask Riles, "We did it?"

Kitty answered from some speaker I couldn't see. "I put the ship on like a jacket. Like some bizarre wearable art that I'm going to alter and then send away. Or at least one with robots in the pocket I could get going as I moved us up into space. We'll have to see what I can do with the rest."

I looked at the bodies, suddenly overwhelmed with shame. "How many dead?"

Video Instructor shook their head. "None. You didn't manage that. And I've got my glove too." They looked around. "We'll just get them to stasis, okay? They'll heal there."

I nodded, then pressed my hands to my face, the netting on the one hand cold still. "I'm so sorry."

They put a hand on my shoulder. "To be fair, we started it."

I wanted to see the ship, before we left. And Kitty wanted to make sure there was nothing left she could help with before we got her into the supercomputer. And then we'd go and let Isa's people figure out getting the ship far away.

As we walked, Isa told me her plan. "We'll make sure anyone not already vetted as being on our side is in stasis. We'll reprogram the...I guess you could call them sleep learning machines? Anyway, we'll change them so that the version of the doctrine they teach is ours. We'll do shifts. Maybe in a century, we'll pull people out one at a time and see where they stand."

She paused so I could be obnoxious and take a selfie in front of a window that showed I was definitely not on Earth anymore.

"We'll mark Earth as dead, dangerously full of radiation, that sort of thing. And we'll try to erase its coordinates entirely." She nodded decisively. "Basically, make this ship a sane one."

"Guys, I hate to intrude," Kitty said from a nearby wall, "but there's something happening on the bridge. The cameras are covered, which is why I checked the sensors that show life signs. I don't know when it happened, but those aren't on in there. And I'm having to work to block...I don't know what. But someone is at the computer there."

"Dammit," complained Riley. "So close to out of here."

"You don't have to," Isa said. "This is our problem now."

I sighed. I really wanted to go, but even without boys in my ear telling me what to do, I already knew I wasn't going to leave yet. "We should help make sure you're safe and ready to go. Don't want you having nasty surprises once you no longer have murderous humans to help." I winked, like it was a joke. In spite of my actions just minutes earlier. So, a joke to cover my shame. Good times.

We rushed to the bridge. Fortunately, Kitty had a maintenance bot crew meet us there. And, super-fortunately, these bots could handle more than just sweeping. Like they'd shown in the redundancy room, they could hold and lift heavy things. And, it turned out, they could cut through doors that were jammed.

As soon as the door was down, the bots rolled in, each of the five grabbing a Peaceforger to carry (kicking and protesting) to stasis. Which left a group I recognized. Of fucking course. Morgan, Jayden, and Emery weren't a surprise; this was their bridge. But there was Michaelson and a couple people who I kind of recognized from Divine Community stuff but who I hadn't recognized as important enough to remember names. Probably the other two in Michaelson's three. Shay was there, so clearly moving up in the world. Her other two must have been among those dragged off, meaning fewer people to stop me punching her. And two faces that had me quietly putting the healing glove on in my pocket: SWS CEO Mary Johnson and her ever-present COO James Smith. They were missing their third, of course, CFO Jennifer Williams, because our efforts on Demo Day hadn't been fruitless.

I vaguely wondered what conspiracy of control had been run by the spare three Peaceforgers in the group the bots had cleared out. But I also vaguely wondered if maybe the Divine—or some other deity—was real and had brought together this ruling body of murderous fucks so I could kill them all in one place. Though, obviously, it was more likely they'd used rank as an excuse to hide out in the control center.

Johnson looked up from the computer she seemed to be fighting with and sneered at me, "Oh, look. It's *MindKiller*." It wasn't clear who she was talking to as she asserted, "I told you we should have planted bombs in her apartment instead of bugs." She and Smith exchanged a savage look.

Smith's mouth lifted a little into something like a snarl. "We'll get revenge for Jen after all."

Johnson stood up and closed ranks with Smith. Shay fell in behind them. Morgan took a step forward, beside the SWS assholes but not in a way that at all suggested anyone but Morgan was at the top of the leadership hierarchy. Emery and Jayden stood just barely behind them. So, basically, the enemy line was right there. And, fortunately, focused on us instead of on whatever they'd been doing at their computers. For a moment, we all just stared each other down.

Riley, behind me, was quietly mumbling an update to the boys and Kitty. Then said, "Going to loop Kitty into our earbuds, so she can speak for herself, tell us the stuff only she can see."

As soon as Kitty was joined, she said, "I think they were trying to do something with the control machines. They think there are still Peacemakers in play. Going to try to take out the machines now."

Careful not to react to the voices in my ear, as if the scene on the bridge was the only thing happening, I gestured at the ranks that faced me. Anyone could surely hear the scorn and hatred that clung to my words as I asked, "I take it these are the assholes who were in charge?"

"Yes. And still are." Morgan's posture got even better. "Time for you to get off my ship." Without looking, and in a tone that was more command than question, they said, "Shay?"

Shay had been behind others, so I hadn't noticed her hands. But they were hard to miss now, full of an automatic weapon she'd clearly gotten a taste for whilst trying to kill my boys. I was somehow surprised that I didn't literally start vomiting my loathing and rage.

I could hear bots coming behind me, but Shay was going to get off enough shots to kill me, Riles, and Isa before the bots got there. And those other assholes were going to smugly watch.

I had the closest thing to a weapon, if I could make it work again. I did the "on" finger motions with my hand still in my pocket, then worked through the "draw it out" and "wound" motions as I pulled my hand out. For a moment, I thought time had slowed in that useful way it seems to during some crises...But then realized I wasn't going to manage to pull the glove out quickly enough. It wasn't that time had slowed, but that I was too tired to move at speed. And Shay was savoring our impending death and the fear that must surely be on our faces.

I knew the waves were working up, I felt them rise up as an image of her and her thugs shooting the boys locked in my head. I was going to replace that image with one of me inflicting parallel damage on the Peaceforgers in front of me. I whipped my hand out of my pocket, hoping against hope...My own fear replaced by satisfaction as I swore I saw the confidence on the faces I hated, the faces that were behind all the misery and death of the last 6 weeks, waver. They must have seen my own confidence coming in, my own weapon coming out.

That was probably why Shay stopped savoring and pulled the trigger.

And then, simultaneously, there was the loud shout of gunfire and a blur. My eyes, treacherous in their sleepiness took a moment to parse out what was happening, to see it. To see Shay's gun on the floor. To see Zane with a blue spot spreading on their back as they struggled to keep Shay from getting the gun again. Blue...It took a moment, but then I realized, from the color they turned when they blushed, that it must be blood.

I pointed my palm at the others instead of Shay. When Emery inched towards the gun, I asked, "Do you know what I did with this earlier?"

They froze and I saw on their face that they did. As they closed ranks with the others, I could see they all did. And I took a step forward.

"Give me an excuse," I growled, hoping bravado stolen from movie heroes would work. I realized I was too tired for rage, and I didn't know if I could actually do it. Though I planned to try. I could feel the energy building. I felt the litany of names of those we'd lost crawling up my throat.

I heard voices, my people, who could see me in person or through cameras. They were hazy as my rage started to push back the tiredness. I didn't so much take in their words, but I knew they saw what was coming and they were trying to talk me down. I noticed Isa and Zane weren't trying to do that.

But then the bots came in, blocking my shot as they moved to secure my intended targets, and took the deposed leadership to stasis. I didn't even get a chance to follow through. And a very small part of me was relieved. No more death or damage to be added to the list of my misdeeds.

When one of Isa's people who'd come running with Zane moved to follow the bots, Isa directed, "Make sure to put them away from everyone else, somewhere we can secure." She turned to me. "I'll let everyone think they died and...I guess I'll learn how to do punishment." She didn't look entirely comfortable, but she sounded fierce enough that I believed her.

I redirected. I crouched over Zane, trying to change the energy of the healing glove. Trying to heal them, but there was so much blood.

Riles was holding their head in zir lap.

They coughed, and blood trickled from their mouth. Barely managing a whisper, they asked, "Bryan okay? And the other?"

"They are," Riles assured them. "Just relax. Katja can do this."

Except that I was still making the motions to switch to healing mode when Video Instructor rushed up and took over. Which was probably the only reason Zane didn't die. But, hey, as long as there's a reason, right?

Somehow, it looked like we were going to make it out of this one. Like we just had to get Kitty out and then...Then it was done. The gang—what was left of us—all back together. World saved. Humanity no more enslaved than it had been before.

It was all I could do on the shuttle back not to weep with relief.

CHAPTER 26

Isa had her people drop us off right outside the garage of our hotel. She'd made sure to load us up with anything portable that might be of interest, and she'd promised to send me all the info possible before they left Earth orbit, as long as I promised that we were going to safeguard it. "I don't want you to be vulnerable if someone else comes along, but I also don't want to hear that our tech is what you used to destroy yourselves."

It was a fair concern. So we'd be like the Librarians (blame Gran for my dated references), but for alien knowledge and tech. Nice.

We loaded luggage carts with our treasures. As we were turning to head in, Video Instructor (who was called Rhys) stopped me.

Guiltily, I said, "I know. I'm sorry. I promise not to use the glove as a weapon again."

Rhys nodded. "Yeah, I know. I could see it in your eyes earlier. Which is why I also want you to have a diagnostics tool. And I'm going to make you a full instruction video—to go with the written documentation you got—before we go." They handed me a small bag with the tool in it. Then said, "But I'm also supposed to give you the keys to Isa's place and to Zane's place. They know you were pushed out of your homes and thought you might like options for where to live while you rebuild your lives."

I took the keys, feeling the weight of concern behind the gesture. "Thank you. Tell them we're grateful."

Rhys shook my hand warmly and walked slowly back to the shuttle.

Upstairs, when we arrived with the luggage carts of treasure, Bryan asked, "Just gear? No Peaceforgers?" Clearly hoping to see Zane.

"They'll live," Riles said, "but not without some help. I'm sure they'll be upset to have missed a chance to at least say goodbye."

"We could ask Isa to stay a while?" I offered.

Bryan sighed. "No. Them going is for the best. I don't think Earth is safe for any Peaceforger now."

I didn't think so either. Humanity was not going to wake up happy.

"Well, then I better get Kitty home so she doesn't leave with them," I said. I booted the supercomputer and set up the gear. I couldn't wait for all my work to pay off, for one last life saved.

Riley got Kitty on zir phone in glorious Holo-Kitty 3D. "Baby, you ready for a new coat?"

She pretended to consider it. "I don't know. The one you're offering is way less eye candy, you know?" Then she grinned and took a deep breath. "Okay, talk me through this."

I put on some VR goggles, just in case she'd need some kind of help I could give better that way. "I'm going to remove the setting that's blocking ID here from the Peaceforger network. You should be able to go from the network to ID, and then use the connection I've sorted to slip into the supercomputer. Um..."

"Follow threads," Riles suggested. "Like ID is the needle's eye, and the thread of where you are, you're going to pass through ID and into the supercomputer?"

Kitty nodded. "Remove the block and let's see what I can see."

I flipped ID to be seen by and accept data from the Peaceforger network.

"Oh! I see that tiny dot...I'm going to go see if I can move to it. Watch your screens." And then Kitty was off the phone.

With the VR goggles on, I could see a stream of incoming data from Out There somewhere flowing into and through ID to the supercomputer. And the supercomputer was purring. I handed the goggles to Riles and sat to watch how the supercomputer was doing.

After a couple hours, Riley said, "Something changed. What's up?"

I squinted, "It was quick, but I thought the transfer must be done because the computer's not working hard anymore."

Rye's phone pinged, and zie put it straight to 3D.

Holo-Kitty looked...resigned? Too calm? She said, "Baby, put on the goggles and let's chat."

From my perspective, she stayed tiny, but for Riles she'd have become life-sized. She reached out, probably taking zir hand.

"Baby, I can't come over."

Without hesitation, Riley said, "We can get more. More storage or memory. You tell us what size you wear, and we'll tailor this dress to you," zie weakly joked.

"I've had time to think, while I've been transferring. And to talk to Isa." She seemed to take a breath, consider her words. "If I want to make sure the Peaceforgers don't come back to Earth again, I have two choices. I can tell the ship to fly into the sun, then download ASAP...and kill thousands of people, not all of whom are evil or beyond saving. Or I can stay here for as long as it takes to figure out how to use their sleep teaching thing to clear up their crazy or to come up with some other useful plan where I don't go full cliché killer AI."

"But I already lost you once..."

She reached out again, maybe putting the hand on zir cheek. "I know, baby. But, this time, I'm not dead. Your girlfriend is being an AI astronaut. Isa says I'm very welcome to help reform her people. And that sounds pretty cool, doesn't it?"

"If I say it doesn't, will you know I'm just being a selfish bitch?" Riles was trying not to cry.

"Absolutely. And I know it's because you love me. Which is also why you want me to stay...And *I* love *you*, which is why I *would* stay if there were another way to make sure the Earth is safe...from Peaceforgers, at least," she assured zir. "But, now, I should go. They're finishing up all the information they promised you, and they really just want to get moving. I think they want to leave this shame behind."

Fuck. I felt that. I was eager to do the same with my own life.

"Will you come back?" Riley asked, sounding more hopeful than pleading.

Kitty paused, then shook her head. "The ship won't dare for a very long while, if ever. Um...I don't know if I can fit all of me in a shuttle's computer and come back on my own, but I'll check if it's not too many years before I feel like it's safe to leave them. And also, I love you, so I'm breaking up with you. Because pining for your intergalactic AI girlfriend is not as fun as it sounds."

I quietly walked away then, wanting to give them some space. Grateful that Kitty had made it clear that this wasn't our failure (my failure), but a choice that would be her saving humanity. Again.

Still...I climbed carefully onto the bed between the boys, feeling glum over Kitty's choice. "I didn't accomplish my task. Kitty isn't coming back." I sighed. "We are going to need to keep Riles loved and distracted."

And there were plenty of distractions.

We had to keep an eye out and make sure nobody woke up from their Peacemaker purge nap and did anything stupid.

We had to make sure the data tone got sounded across the world to kill any nanites left, and do it a few times over the next few years, just in case.

We had to check on families, who mostly weren't worth the time to check. Except Jonny's, who I'd meet sooner rather than later now that he wasn't a fugitive.

We had to have a proper memorial for Gran, once Kitty and Isa had checked through the ship's computer and confirmed she hadn't been uploaded. I finally got to meet Sarah then, and the stories she told only confirmed that, at least since her 20s, my gran had always been too cool.

We had to help Kitty surprise Riles when she got a little more control and figured out how to keep communicating with zir from a distance. (And we had to get ready for the day when the ship got too far away and the messages stopped.)

We had to clean up data to make sure our names were clear out in the wide world.

We had to catalog the tech and specs from the Peaceforgers and set up a team that would work, probably the rest of our lives, to protect and develop what we could. The name for the team, and the debate about whether it even needed one, seemed likely to go on for quite a fraction of those lives.

We had to see that traitors (like 5x5) got what they had coming, and that the rest of the team got some kind of benefits from what they'd done. Even if we couldn't tell the world.

We had to de-Narnia the rooms we'd lived in during the last phase of the whole mess. (Though we'd been tempted just to let people stumble into that and see what rumors started.)

We had to move into homes, not just hideouts. And had to see if Jonny and I could share one of those homes without murdering each other when the world wasn't at stake. (We figured we could, if we were mindful. And if we remembered that we had the option of hanging out in Isa's old place—which Riles had quickly called dibs on—or Zane's old place—which Bryan had gotten a little sentimental about having—when we wanted space or wanted to give each other space.)

Though first we had to spend a week in separate suites of a posh hotel to make up for weeks of living in some questionable places, all packed together.

We had to snoop into the interesting things we'd stumbled over and set aside during the 45 or so days our lives were anything but normal. (This included the intriguing mystery of my grandfather's disappearance 51 years earlier, which refused to be solved easily. I asked Kitty to look in the Peaceforgers' computer to see if maybe they'd been behind the light in the sky, but she didn't find anything by searching for his name. And all they had reported for the date he disappeared was that some rockstar that was one of theirs had had a successful show and that they'd retrieved a missing temple device thing.)

We had to spend some time seeing what would have happened if we'd tried to be a band. (Nothing good, it turned out. Though Bryan and Jonny, the two with any experience, did not suck and seemed likely to maybe try more in the future.)

We had to see what it was like to be social-ish again. Dancing, meeting up with or travelling to see some of those who'd worked with us, campaigning to make Fire in November a local holiday. You know, all very normal social pursuits.

We had to spend a solid month doing nothing of consequence and all the things we'd said would come After. Because After was finally here.

We had to make sure each of us had a supercomputer of our own so that there were no custody battles over the one I'd built.

I had to finally get the cat I'd wanted my whole life.

And, really, we just had to figure out how to live normal (for us) lives again, how to heal from what we'd lost, and how to build futures even though we now *knew* the universe was full of possible dangers.

But, if we didn't build futures, what else would we do? Let the people who *hadn't* saved the world build the futures? Let them keep the world on the ugly trajectory of greed, fear, and bigotry that had made the Peaceforgers' aims look not-all-bad? We might as well have left the Peacemakers in people's heads if we were going to do that.

And, if there's one thing I was never going to do, it was let somebody's bug—literal or metaphorical—live in my brain. My brain still had too much to do.

END

ACKNOWLEDGEMENTS

Thanks go to Clarissa C.S. Ryan and Sarah Keliher, yet again. Ever wise and reliable and willing to tell me the truth.

A weird slice of thanks to Ernest Cline, who unintentionally caused a trilogy instead of two individual books in a shared world. And that after finally giving me the push to finish writing a book at all.

Thanks to Tom Furness for many things, but relevant to this: Thanks for being the first person who made me feel like I had a personal tie to VR. During the writing of the Peaceforger books, that led first to shame that I was giving VR a bad name...and then to a solution.

Thanks to Wade Racine for making sure that the St Crispin's Day speech was extra memorable for me. And for being a solid gamemaster who demanded enough from me as a player that it helped me learn to come up with plans and solutions. It also probably did more to help me learn to work with a group—instead of as a lone wolf—than any so-called group project ever has.

Thanks to Jana Wright for *The Librarians*. It might have seemed small, but it was my last hurdle to getting done. Once again, saved by her clever brain.

Boundless love and thanks to my Simon, who didn't live to see this to publication but was there for every draft of every word in this trilogy except the very last one of this book. Who sat by me as I wrote, made sure I took breaks, and purred away my anxieties over getting it right. I can't imagine how I'll write future books without you, Simon HandsomePants.

Thanks to the others, family and friends and creative strangers, who have been my comrades and who have fed my soul and kept me moving through my own battles. Sometimes you gave obviously big things or added some painstakingly made creation to the world, and other times it was as simple as just the right meme posted on your social media to give me a moment. (And, seriously, this is why you—all of you—should do whatever kindnesses or creative work you can. You can't always know what war you're helping fight.)

And, as ever, sincere thanks to you, the readers, who have followed this story through three books to its end. Your kind notes, your creations inspired by the books, your reviews, and all the other ways you showed some love were the fuel that kept me going with this writing thing when the going was tough.

Looks like this is now my After. Time to find my next challenge to overcome. See you there?

Photo by Jesse Means

Amber Bird is...A writer, a rockstar, and a sci-fi simulacrum...The author of the Peaceforger books, a published poet, the front of post-punk/post-glam band Varnish, half of transatlantic Autistic musical duo The Companions, and an unabashed geek...An Autistic introvert who was saved in many ways over the years by music, books, and gaming...An idealist and dreamer who now writes (books, poems, lyrics, blogs) and makes music in hopes of adding to someone else's escape or rescue...And, yes, the model for that Magic card.

Learn more about Amber-related things at amberbird.com.